TEARDROP

Denis Gray

iUniverse, Inc.
Bloomington

Teardrop

iUniverse books may be ordered through booksellers or by contacting:

iUniverse
1663 Liberty Drive
Bloomington, IN 47403
www.iuniverse.com
1-800-Authors (1-800-288-4677)

ISBN: 978-1-4759-6582-7 (sc)
ISBN: 978-1-4759-6581-0 (hc)
ISBN: 978-1-4759-6580-3 (e)

Library of Congress Control Number: 2012922822

Printed in the United States of America

iUniverse rev. date: 3/1/2013

A LOVE SUPREME
John Coltrane

CHAPTER 1

"Uh, you gonna play your hand? What you got—or what, Teardrop?"

Maurice "Teardrop" Williams's ears might as well have been tone deaf to what Shorty Boy Logan had just said.

"So you got what? A seven and a three showing? Hid up beneath them top cards, then I'm in trouble—if you sporting you twenty-one, man."

Maurice "Teardrop" Williams's face was handsome, was probably too handsome for any fifty-two-year-old bluesman. Sharp features. Soft skin. Brown eyes. Brown skin. A great face it seemed for bluffing at blackjack late at night in Bunky's Better Bunks, a roadside motel, after playing a blues gig at Freddie's Freeloader in Atlanta, Georgia.

Kenneth "Shorty Boy" Logan was the one dealing the playing cards. Shorty Boy Logan looked like his nickname—a bluesman as short as the mostly dealt-out deck of cards on the rickety card table in the yellow-lit room. Shorty Boy was holding the cards in his hands as if they were strangling them. Shorty Boy wasn't a young man, but with his nickname, it tended to keep him just that—young (only, not as young as springtime— not even close). Oftentimes Shorty Boy Logan felt like his nickname had just been handed down to him by Uncle Cirrus (the older brother of his father, Clover Logan) just yesterday, down in Justice Alabama, at the age of four. "Gonna hold, huh, Teardrop? That what you … Wanna hit? … I'll take that for … You ain't got a ace hid up beneath them cards, do you? Hell, man, you bluffing. Bluffing big as a hosed-down hog at a county fair! Probably got you no more than … what, fifteen, sixteen … m-most …

Well, you know I got me a eight and a two showing—ten too. Could have an ace, right? Twenty-one," Shorty Boy said, tugging his plaid, brown pub cap that fit his head snug as a rug even if sweat poured from it like Niagara Falls.

Maurice "Teardrop" Williams was a world-famous blues player, a great singer/guitarist/ songwriter. Kenneth "Shorty Boy" Logan played second guitar and tom-toms. There was a third band member of the Teardrop Williams's Tearmakers band, Johnny "Twelve-Fingers" Eakins who played piano. At the moment, Twelve Fingers Eakins was in his room next to Teardrop's, sleeping. Said he was "tired as hell" before turning in for the night.

"T-Teardrop … ," Shorty Boy said suddenly, seeing that something seemed wrong with him since his body was shaking—only, shaking like it was trying to fight off a two-day old fever that seemed to be gripping him, obviously shaking him from inside out.

"Teardrop, you're shaking. Your body's shaking like crazy, man!"

Teardrop's hands held tightly to the card table, so the rickety little table began shaking like crazy too, its legs and flat-surfaced top.

Shorty Boy shot up from the card table and got over to Teardrop, but it's when Teardrop stood and his body shook even more, like it was going to shake all the room's stagnant air out.

"I can't do this anymore. Continue like this. Not without my wife, Shorty Boy. Maureen!"

"It's been seven months, Teardrop. Seven—Maureen's been dead. She's been bur—"

"Seven months too long, Shorty Boy. Maureen, I need her, Shorty Boy. I don't need this, want this kind of life anymore. Living it out of a suitcase. Out of hotel rooms, at my age. Making music with no purpose. Not understanding why anymore. Knowing, always knowing I have to go home anyway once I'm through. Home, home—carrying it around in me like another piece of luggage out on road trips."

"Shouldn't feel like that, thataway," Shorty Boy said. "A-ain't what nobody wants to happen to you, man."

"But it's what I'm feeling. All the time."

"Don't know that. Or hear it in your playing."

"Arlene. I must call her. It's what I'll do. Tell her I'm coming home."

Both looked over at the bright-red telephone on the short-legged nightstand.

"Arlene will understand … She'll—"

"Gonna step out the room. Now k-knock on the wall if you need me for any reason, Teardrop. Y-you hear?"

"Thanks, Shorty Boy."

"Ain't gonna wake Twelve Fingers. Solid as that man sleeps. How the man ties it on for the night. Leave that alone."

Knock.

Teardrop had knocked on the paper-thin wall. And within seconds, there was a corresponding knock on Teardrop's door. Teardrop laughed. "You know you can come in, Shorty Boy, without—"

"Ain't just Shorty Boy, Teardrop. It's me too. Me and Shorty Boy."

"Oh ... oh, sorry about the knock, Twelve—"

"No, was awoke when Shorty Boy come in the room. Tiptoe in. Why your knock don't disturb me none."

Twelve Fingers Eakins was heavyset, tall, and with a wide wall of a back. His face was black like a burnt-out sky. His clothes were rumpled. Stylewise, he had a penchant for suspenders (dark blue today). His was an old soul.

"Twelve Fingers got the news, Teardrop. Told the man."

Teardrop sat down on the narrow bed. "I apologize for this sudden decision, Twelve Fingers. Whew." Twelve Fingers and Shorty Boy sat in the chairs at the card table. "It probably was building up in me. All along. Far before today—"

"And hell, gotta explode. Way it done tonight, Teardrop," Twelve Fingers said.

"I've been swimming, I suppose, in dark, murky waters these past few months without actually having any real sense that I was."

Twelve Fingers Eakins eased his heavy back in his chair. "Don't worry, you know," he said, snapping the suspenders and then looking deeper into Teardrop's eyes.

"Think so?"

"Do. Just don't bring it to the music any. What you going through. Don't mix it in between them notes you playing. Why, don't hear it, at least."

"What I tell Teardrop, Twelve Fingers, exactly so," Shorty Boy said.

"I think so too, Twelve Fingers. In our lives, we've all had personal losses. There're moments though when I wish I was the one who died and not Maur—"

"No, man, don't do that. Ain't good wishing on something like that. Seen a man's fortune change from wishing that. Putting that kind of bad vibe out there—ain't healthy for nobody," Twelve Fingers said with great respect toward Teardrop.

"Everything can go bad, downhill quick on you. Just good 'nough that you love somebody like Maureen. And she love you back."

"The memories of her are still too strong for me. It feels as if I'm back to where I was when she died," Teardrop said, looking at Shorty Boy and then at Twelve Fingers. "I guess I just want to be to myself. I'm still looking for answers I still can't seem to—"

"More like find yourself, don't you think, Teardrop?" Twelve Fingers said.

Teardrop laughed. "Whoever that is. Wherever Teardrop Williams is hiding."

"All of us gotta go there one time or another to find it."

"I know. But I thought I'd done it—the hard work. I went deep enough after Maureen's death. But it's clear now that I haven't."

"Still better answers to come then."

"You gotta believe that, Teardrop. Where Twelve Fingers's taking you."

"So Arlene, what she say? When you hit her up with the news that you was coming home, back to Walker City?" Twelve Fingers said.

"Surprised. But pleasantly so. We had a good … an excellent talk."

"Good," Shorty Boy said, removing his pub cap while wiping his head clean with a crimson-red handkerchief he bought in Memphis, Tennessee.

"And don't worry about the rest of the circuit—"

"B-but we have two gigs left, Twelve Fingers, on tour."

"I know you the boss, Teardrop"—Twelve Fingers laughed—"but I'll take care of everything. You sick, man. Down with the flu or something as bad." Twelve Fingers paused. "I'll pull a bunny out the hat, don't you worry. Yeah, you know me, how I do."

"And as far as a guitar picker, don't worry any, Teardrop. Red Ball Dupree owes me a favor. Perfect time now to collect on the boy. Red Ball's getting somewhere in the blues business. Making a name for hisself," Shorty Boy said, sticking the handkerchief back in his striped shirt pocket. "Hop on the phone with the boy tomorrow. Arrange for him to meet us. Hook up with us in Memphis."

"You guys are great. Have really been t-terrific about this."

"Should be no trouble with Mac, Teardrop," Shorty Boy said. "He's heard of Red Ball Dupree too. Just ain't picking a grape off a vine. Ain't chancing that."

"Mac … Mac, he's been a wonderful manager. Between you two and Mac. Over the years, truly, I've been blessed."

Twelve Fingers and Shorty Boy smiled.

"You get you some rest now, Teardrop. Put yourself at ease," Twelve Fingers said.

"I am tired," Teardrop admitted.

"By the way, Teardrop, uh," Shorty Boy said, "uh, what was you holding? Them cards of yours on the table. Am curious as hell."

"Take a look for yourself, Shorty Boy."

Shorty Boy shuffled off to the table. He looked down at the card that was beneath the seven and the three, the two exposed cards, Twelve Fingers's staring at them too.

"Man's bluffing, I know it, Shorty, big as day!"

Slowly Shorty Boy lifted the turned-down card up.

"Damn! Damn! Beat you, Teardrop! Beat you! Beat you blind as a bat, man! Pay me, Teardrop! Pay me my money. A dollar, Teardrop! One dollar!"

"Sixteen. Sixteen. Trying to get over, bluff with sixteen. What, what you got Shorty Boy?"

"Hell. Ain't much better," Shorty Boy said, flipping his bottom card over. "But better 'nough to beat Teardrop. Seventeen, man!"

"Blackjack." Twelve Fingers grimaced. "Why I don't play you and Teardrop blackjack. Don't play scared. Can't. Don't try to bluff my way through nothing. Ain't good for nobody's nerves. Least not mine."

Shorty Boy stood staring down at the three cards as if his pockets had been picked clean.

⌁

Next morning.

"Woke Red Ball up. Oooo-we, Teardrop, boy used him every cuss word under the sun—and then some. Never know a boy to curse like that. Uh, but says he's gonna meet me and Twelve Fingers in Memphis tomorrow. First thing the sun sets."

"Are you sure, Shorty Boy?"

"Red Ball's word's solid. Boy's got that kind of reputation going already in the business. So me and Twelve Fingers ain't gonna have to worry when we get to Memphis. Ears still ringing though. Tend to forget how a Alabama boy can cuss if somebody step on his sleep early in the morning."

Teardrop had his leather suitcase and small vinyl bag and, of course, his smooth black guitar case with Miss Lillian inside. Miss Lillian was the name of Teardrop's light-blue guitar, a guitar that was as faithful and true to Teardrop as the sun and the moon to the sky.

Teardrop, Shorty Boy, and Twelve Fingers were in Bunky's Better Bunks' tiny, plaster-peeling, pink-painted lobby. A cab was on its way to take Teardrop back to Atlanta's Hartsfield-Jackson Airport.

"This here is temporary, this situation now, ain't it, Teardrop?"

After breakfast, they took a short walk around Bunky's, saying they needed a breath of fresh air and then wound back, trying not to think too much but thinking all the time anyway.

"It's not what it feels like now, Twelve Fingers," Teardrop said with caution.

"What you mean … p-permanent, Teardrop?" Twelve Fingers's face looked like it was about to crack open with pain.

"Since I'm talking about time, Twelve Fingers, I don't know how much time. It just feels like something that'll take some time for me to work out. To, I—"

"It just that we been playing together for thirteen years. That's a long time for any band—especially so a blues band," Shorty Boy said. "Long time, man. Playing together."

"Sounds unlucky now though?" Twelve Fingers said, his chin down on his chest. "Unlucky as hell." Twelve Fingers took a go at snapping his dark-blue suspenders.

The three sat on a stitch-torn, worn-down couch facing the window out to the early day Atlanta sky and battered dirt road so they could see the taxicab arrive to Bunky's.

"Don't think for a second I don't know what this means, Shorty Boy. What I'm asking of you and Twelve Fingers. Breaking us up like this. With such short notice. Last night, I, well, I didn't sleep well. I don't know when I will."

"Don't think none of us do, Teardrop," Twelve Fingers said. "We breaking up something special. Good as it ever been for me. With a blues band. Hell … good as hell."

"Been like a party for thirteen years. One big blowout after the other. Who the hell in they right mind gonna wanna party to end?" Tears had pooled in Shorty Boy's eyes.

Teardrop hunched forward and began rubbing his knuckles. "Blackjack...," he said.

"Blackjack!" Shorty Boy and Twelve Fingers said jointly, apparently jarred by what Teardrop just said in a voice they didn't understand but knew was reliable.

"You said a very interesting thing about blackjack last night, Twelve Fingers."

"Which was, Teardrop?" Twelve Fingers said, his thumbs fiddling with the suspenders.

"Bluffing, Twelve Fingers. About the act of bluffing."

"But, Twelve Fingers, the cat was talking about blackjack. Cards. Not no--our band, man. Teardrop Williams's Tearmakers. Thirteen years of playing music together."

"Bluffing, I should state, for the purpose of clarity, and what you said about a person playing 'scared,' Twelve Fingers."

"Right, do say it."

"What it means. What it causes you to—its cause and effect. Of course, if you bluff with cards you lose, and it's only money. Something of monetary value you no longer have. But when you bluff with your feelings, become deathly afraid of them—begin to pretend they're not there—"

"It gonna swallow you whole. Big as day one day. You playing with life then. Don't wanna be scared of that. Short of killing you."

"Probably somewhere, at some time, Twelve Fingers. At some point." Pause.

"I've taken my first step, and already, it feels as if it's a big, really big, important one. That I'm getting one step or ... or two steps closer to what I must be after."

"Just don't sink in it," Twelve Fingers said. "Just don't let your body sink down in it, Teardrop. To w-where it begins to feel comfortable. Till it sinks you down so low you can't—don't wanna move no more. Don't get to that."

"That won't happen, that I can assure you. I'm smart enough not—"

"Ain't nothing to do with smart. So let me set that straight. 'Cause smart ain't smarter than everything. It's when you careful—it when you being smart about something. How I find myself beating most things down that get on top me."

"You're right, Twelve Fingers. I won't argue with that," Teardrop said.

"Careful ... like common sense," Twelve Fingers said, his chubby finger tapping his head.

"Look, hell, look what's here," Shorty Boy said as his voice downgraded to a whisper.

"Said shortly," Twelve Fingers said. "Mean it. Don't mess around with a man's time or money."

The sight of the lime-green taxi dimmed them far more than what was anticipated.

"So ... we gonna talk ... ," Twelve Fingers said.

"Yes," Teardrop said.

"Keep things going."

"Yes, Twelve Fingers."

"End of a beautiful thing. Beautiful thing ... all I can say, Teardrop. End of a beautiful thing."

"But ... but not our friendship, Shorty Boy," Teardrop said. "N-not that."

"Uh, no, no not that—but the band. T-the Tearmakers, Teardrop. Org-organization."

The taxi's horn honked loudly outside Bunky's. The taxi driver was looking through Bunky's front window not angrily but with greater seriousness.

"This was like a bolt outta the blue. Hit like lightning striking a bottle. Shattering it all to hell. Smithereens."

"I ... I know, Twelve Fingers."

"Man, if I don't hug you again, then ..."

"Me too ..."

They hugged each other.

The taxi's horn honked again.

"Arlene, she's a good daughter, Teardrop," Twelve Fingers said. "Ain't she though ... But just don't let her become a helpmate for you. Seen that happen too. More than once. That ain't no good neither. That scene."

Teardrop was in the backseat of the lime-green taxi. It was 10:18 a.m. His flight for Walker City, Iowa, was scheduled for 11:22 a.m.

Sitting in the taxi's cream-colored backseat, all Teardrop could think of was getting back home. Certainly not on the road with the Tearmakers traveling up and down highways where he knew he no longer belonged. That time spoke to yesterdays in his life, he thought, when Maureen let him live that life, be a bluesman. She had to be strong during the tough, daunting, lean years when finances were hard on the Williams family. Maureen never wavered. She stood by him.

But it was always Maureen's willingness (she was a grade-school teacher) to let him be who he was that he most loved and cherished about her. She let him make his dream come alive in the rough and tumble blues world, where the string is thin and pieces so fragile you're at constant risk of losing so much so fast without ever really getting yourself into the game.

Maureen made me, Teardrop thought. *Just by her quiet confidence. Maybe I pushed myself so hard careerwise because I didn't want to fail her. If I failed ... then she too would have failed—come up short. It wouldn't be just me then but Maureen too.*

And now it didn't matter. Not any of it. It took me four months before I went back out with the group. Back on tour. Four months. I guess it was too soon. Too early. Asking too much of myself too soon. I was forcing this thing to some unnatural conclusion. Writing songs to make sense out of my grief. Singing them. But disguising them with different feelings, meanings. Not to the point where ... What is the point? What is the point of all of this? This is why I can't get anywhere with this. It all becomes pointless—nothing at all binding it together. I'm out there, somewhere alone, desperate to find something. And even if I do, I don't know if I'll value it or, for that matter, recognize or establish its value.

Because all I'll do is compare it to Maureen—and then render it valueless.

How could you, Maureen? How could you die before me? Leave me this way? I was supposed to die first, Maureen. Not you. Before you. Me. Me. Me.

CHAPTER 2

"No, don't meet me at the airport as planned, Arlene. It won't be necessary. I'll come in by taxi."

There was a change in plan, and Arlene didn't like it. It just didn't sit well with her. Jamal was in his room; and this medium-height, brown-skinned, striking-looking woman, Arlene Wilkerson, in flats and blue slacks and white starched shirt, was standing at the front door of the house. It was Saturday, and the door was open and the air cozy to a fault in Walker City, Iowa.

The next question was, "Where, Dad? To where? Should Jamal and I, should we meet you at your house or—"

"Your house, honey. I'll come directly to your house. How's that?"

"Not to want to meet me at the airport. I took it to mean you wanted to be alone for an even longer stretch of time. That time alone on the plane wouldn't be enough. That … just how is it, Dad? How has it become for you since Mother's death?"

And now he wanted to come to her house and not go to his, the house she was raised in.

"Granddad …"

"Not yet, Jamal. But soon."

Jamal'd entered the vestibule. He was seven. He was a boy tall for his age (the tallest second grader in his class), spindly. He'd used the back stairway, just off the kitchen, to reach downstairs. He loved to wear horizontal pinstriped T-shirts that Arlene ironed and starched, but by noon, it was all but gone, the T-shirt a mess of wrinkles. He was wearing a red-and-white striped one today and sneakers, PRO-Keds.

"I can't wait to see Granddad. I know he bought me something nice, Mom. He always does when he goes away to play with Mr. Eakins and Mr. Logan."

Mildly perturbed, Arlene said, "Just don't make it the object of your attention, Jamal, all right?"

Jamal was confused. "What ... what exactly do you mean by that, Mom?" He laughed. "Sometimes I think you forget I'm only seven years old, ma'am. Not fifty."

First Arlene laughed, and then when it died, her agenda rebounded. "Your grandfather's coming home shouldn't be confused with him bringing you a gift every time he does, Jamal. It shouldn't be your sole object of attention."

"No, no, Mom. I wasn't saying that, ma'am. Uh, not at all. Uh ..." Jamal and Arlene walked into the living room. Jamal sat on the comfortable couch. "Granddad ... well, it is something to look forward to when he comes back from playing with his band, ma'am. It's like, it's just that he always buys me nice stuff all the time."

"Yes, uh, yes, he does."

"Mom, are you worried about something?"

"Jamal—"she looked sharply at him—"no nothing. Nothing, honey."

"Because if you are, you know you can talk to me about it. Like always. Right?"

Arlene smiled, brushing back a strand of hair loose on her forehead.

"I know Granddad's back early."

"Yes."

"From his trip, ma'am. And why is he coming here? To our house? I thought—"

"Jamal, let's try not to think too much. Your grandfather must have his own reasons. O-okay?" Arlene said in a whisper. "Now, have you done your homework? All of it yet?"

"Why, uh, most. But Ms. Powell really piled it on this weekend. School'll be out in a few weeks—I guess she hasn't forgotten. Really wants to leave a real good impression on us!"

"Don't you have big problems. At your age to—"

"Mom, I'm here to listen to you when you have a problem and stuff. So why can't you do the same for me when I—"

"Especially when it comes to homework and … Ms. Powell?"

"Right. Right." Pause. "You don't do that with your students, do you? Pile the home—"

"Some—"

"Until it hurts!"

"Times."

"Yes, ma'am. They're college kids …"

"So they've had plenty of experience with mean, grouchy old teachers like me by now, during their educational lifetime."

"Yes."

Temporarily Arlene had forgotten why she was at the front door but then refocused her attention to what she'd been doing.

"Okay … let me get back to my homework. Uh, call me … call me, Mom, when, as soon as Granddad gets here—please." Jamal was off the three-cushioned couch.

Arlene laughed to herself, for all Jamal had to do to access the second-floor landing was go to the house's front staircase, but he chose, mostly, to go to the kitchen's back staircase as if he were a secret agent accessing a secret passageway in the house he alone knew of in this clandestine world he traveled in.

Jamal was walking toward the kitchen when, suddenly, he stopped dead in his tracks. "Mom, I really miss Grandma. E-especially at times like this."

Arlene could feel her eyes burst into tears; only, she restrained herself.

"Yes, we all do, Jamal. All of us."

"Darn … darn …"

Jamal left the room.

"It's not the same. It'll never be the same without Mom. Not for you or me, Dad."

Arlene sat on one of the two armless living room chairs but now was back standing in the front door's tall archway. She hadn't been back at the door for too long. She was expecting her father at any minute.

"Any minute now, Dad. Any minute now you should be here."

She'd thought about going out onto the porch but didn't wish to appear overly anxious. No, she'd thought, standing there at the door was more than enough. For she must not put a rush on things she had no control over. But she was sensing something different was happening to her life, some sea change but, for the life of her, couldn't put her finger on it, address it, feel what exactly its pulse was. But this sudden shortening of her father's tour forebode something was on the horizon and, at least, attracting her attention.

Over the phone, she and her dad had a "good" talk, as he'd said. But they hadn't really gotten to the heart of anything. He'd simply said he was homesick, his reason for cutting the tour short. And she didn't care to pressure him by pushing what was at the heart of him out into the open, his reason for coming home. She played the dutiful daughter, Arlene thought, by lending him a sympathetic, needed ear.

"They'll all come out in time. He'll share them with me. I've never felt closer to him since Mother's death."

And as if her feet had hit an oil slick on the hallway's wooden floor, Arlene was out the house dashing at top speed to get to her father.

"Dad!"

The taxicab was pulling up to the house.

"Arlene!"

Exiting the taxi, Arlene hugged Teardrop like every bone in his body was being strength tested. Then she grabbed hold of his brown leather suitcase with great vigor.

"Thanks, Arlene."

"Old habit, I guess, Dad."

"That it is, honey."

Teardrop reached back into the taxi, getting hold of his guitar case, and then shut the door.

"Hi, Bert!"

"Oh, hi there, Arlene!" Bert the taxicab driver hollered back. "Got him home from Des Moines International safe and sound, Arlene," Bert said, tipping his short-brimmed plaid hat with gusto at her.

"Thanks again, Bert."

"My pleasure, Teardrop. Ain't a fare I'd rather make, especially from International! See you good folk now. Back to local business, I guess. Teardrop don't arrange every day for me to pick him up from the airport. Get a call in from Atlanta, Georgia."

And then the blue-flame taxicab, with Bert in it, took off quite slowly, lazily—like its gas tank either was registering low or sprung a leak.

Arlene sidled up to Teardrop.

"I know better not to touch Miss Lillian though, Dad. I have that much good sense."

"No, Arlene, not on your life or mine."

There was plenty of front yard to the house. Oftentimes Jamal would complain by saying there was too much since he, not voluntarily, helped, along with Arlene, keep the front yard in tip-top shape. The mowing part really turned him off. When he mowed the lawn, it seemed it stretched for miles and miles across Iowa's wide-open plains. But it was old farmland converted into suburban landscape with the nearest neighbors distanced well apart within this black enclave of Walker City called Trinity—there being no historical record of its name, Trinity.

"Granddad!"

"Jamal! Hi there, Jamal!" Teardrop stopped dead in his tracks to gain a better look at him. "Jamal, looks like you've grown a few inches on me since I left on tour. Like your head's ducking clouds. My gosh!"

"Two inches, Granddad. Ms. Powell, my teacher, measured me!"

"The infamous Ms. Powell."

"Well … whatever you want to call her. I just know she gives out a whole lot of homework every day, sir!"

"And who likes homework, Jamal. Tell me!"

"Dad, please don't make it any worse."

Dinner was served. There'd been corn and beef to be sure, an Iowan staple. It was just her and Teardrop (Jamal was back in his room doing his homework on a Saturday evening). Jamal's parting words were, "I'm almost done." So both Arlene and Teardrop felt relieved, almost as if Ms. Powell had assigned *them* a mountain of homework or remembered second-grade teachers from their distant past who had.

"Thank you, Arlene. I needed a good meal. It did hit the spot."

Arlene, earlier, had cleared the kitchen table.

The kitchen was big and spacious. Aptly, it would be considered an old-fashioned kitchen if the house had age. The kitchen size big families gather in and enjoy in ease and comfort. And off to the side were the backstairs Jamal so frequently used for his personal travel.

"I'm sorry about Jamal, Arlene. His gift or, should I say, the lack of one during my road trip."

"Dad, Jamal'll get over it," Arlene said dismissively. "Trust me."

"It's just that up until that phase of the tour, I hadn't found anything for him I liked. B-but I'll definitely make it up to him at a future date."

"Dad, Jamal won't lose any sleep over it. Not the way he—"

"It's just that it's become tradition between us—and it's been broken."

"Sometimes there comes a time …"

"Yes, I suppose so. You're right. I could've looked for something in the airport, but—"

"At the time you had other things on your mind."

"Well, I did. Most certainly did."

"Far more important things. W-was it why you didn't want me to pick you up from International?"

"Arlene, yes. I've made a decision about my music and my life: I'm not going back out on the road. I'm giving up my music. My career. Q-quitting the music business as of today. It's final."

Arlene couldn't believe what she'd heard, never mind how rapidly her heart beat. This was totally unexpected: for her father to give up something he loved and had given his life to with such dedication and passion.

"There's no more joy in my playing, Arlene. I … I can't, simply can't find the joy in the music anymore. I've lost it—"

"Mother, Dad?"

"Your mother. Yes. Yes … It's enough that … that I can get up each morning, out of bed. Yes, your mother, I'm back to—it feels like I've regressed. Been knocked back in time. Or even, at times, worse."

"Worse than before? How could it be any—"

"Worse … yes … worse. This time it really feels it's permanent. That life has really stopped me cold, dead cold in my tracks. That there's no way out of this thing. Not through prayer, not through some miraculous event. It's the continual pain I'm living with daily since your mother's death.

"I just couldn't get rid of it out on the road with the Tearmakers. Playing for my fans. Thoughts of your mother only made things worse. The pain of coming home to an empty house scared me. Wiped me out."

"Dad …"

"So I wanted to get home to get it over with. The pain of not coming home to your mother, over with. It's all I've been thinking. The thought of it in six days, six more days—I no longer could bear it. All of it overwhelmed me. I shouldn't've left Walker City in the first place. My life, as I once knew it, over, Arlene. My career as a blues player."

"This is such an incredibly sudden decision … I, you've been a blues player, a musician all your life, Dad."

"No, that won't change, I won't let it. I'll play Miss Lillian. I'll continue to write music. It's just my career. Active as a musician, blues player—there won't be any more of that. It's finished. Playing club dates—local or otherwise—is done with. Is final."

"I'm shocked, Dad. Truly shocked by this. This revelation."

"So was I, Arlene."

"It's the only way I can summarize my feelings. Truly, I thought the road would do you good. Getting away from Walker City. Not produce the opposite result."

"I know financially there'll be no problem."

"None."

"It's good to know I have some financial freedom. That it's possible for me to walk away with no financial burdens."

"Dad," Arlene said, now taking Teardrop's hand, "you ... you have thought this through, haven't you? Every detail, aspect of it?"

"I had to. This is life altering. Everything I've worked for, stood for over thirty years has suddenly ..."

"It's why I'm asking that maybe you have to give this more time. Pause. Distance. Mother wouldn't want this. It would break her heart. You forsaking your music like this."

"I—"

"Not at any price. For any reason."

"So what am I supposed to do, Arlene? Go through the motions?" Teardrop took Arlene's hand, folding his over hers. "A musician can't do that. I know I can't. Fake it. Ruin the, what's the very essence and integrity of the music I've created?

"And if I sing with the pain in me, with that gut-wrenching honesty, then each night—I might as well die. Because the songs I sing, the blues I play—what I am—will surely kill me. I know that now."

Arlene could believe this, in her mind and heart, what her father just said, loving him as she did, how she'd always, since little, feel emotionally attached to his music, how so often it rushed at her like an ocean's roar.

Teardrop stood. He walked away from the kitchen table and then returned to Arlene.

"Now do you understand, Arlene? The seriousness of this? The depth of my pain? This confession I've made to you?"

Arlene shook her head. Teardrop sat back down. "So ... I feel it's better to avoid it. Any notion of it."

"Dad, be right back."

Teardrop was standing at the living room window. "Oh ... yes, Arlene. Of ... of course."

The evening was winding down. It was 7:48 p.m. Teardrop peeked at his watch. *It is getting late*, he thought. *It ... it is.*

Arlene reentered the kitchen.

"Arlene, I didn't realize it'd gotten so late. I lost track of the time."

"What—"

"It's seven forty-eight," Teardrop said before Arlene could check her watch, but she checked it anyway.

"So it is, Dad. As they say, time flies when you're having fun. With a special person, time flies."

"Come on, young lady. I think that tribute to your father deserves something irresponsibly special." Teardrop took hold of Arlene and was hugging her Frankenstein-like, stiffly rocking her from side to side— playfully, much to both their delight.

"Dad, Dad, Dad," Arlene laughed.

"Well, you deserve it. After that masterly prose."

"Dad, want me to drive you home now? Dumb question, I guess, suppose. Of course I will. Who else would but me?" Arlene giggled. "Let me get Jamal."

"Ar-Arlene …"

"Yes?"

"Have I gotten in your way this evening? N-now don't look at me as if you're going to crown me with a rolling pin, be—"

"Because I am! You get in my way? Dad, are you—"

"I mean, honey, after all, you are a professor. Have your college life, responsibilities. I know how valuable your time is with—"

"And I can't find time for my father? My own—"

"Now, now," Teardrop laughed nervously, "I have taken up a lot—"

"Dad, the hole is getting deeper!"

"No, I don't want that—especially when I was going to ask you …"

Arlene waited.

"Oh never—"

"Dad, what's wrong?" Arlene was standing back in front of Teardrop, looking up at this tall, elegant man.

"I don't want to go home tonight. Back to the house. I … I don't want to, if … if I don't have to, Arlene."

Arlene looked more troubled.

"I was wondering if I could spend the night. Here. Here with you and Jamal. J-just for tonight."

"Oh, Dad. You know you're welcome. More than welcome here. We have more than enough room for you, you know that."

"I was thinking about it, Arlene. I mean, when you stepped out the room, it's when this strange, odd feeling swept over me. Just … I have no idea as to what it was, but I don't want to go back to the house. Not tonight."

"Do you know how excited your grandson's going to be about this?"

"Well … I'm excited by the prospect too. So count me in."

Teardrop's guitar, Miss Lillian, just happened to be on the bed next to Teardrop as he began unlacing his shoes gradually.

"Everything feels so comfortable, Arlene," Teardrop said, looking around at the room, its neatness prevailing.

"Some days I wish I had a house cleaner like Mrs. Porter. It'd come in handy."

"It's good to have her. Since I'm not much of a housecleaner. The Pine-Sol smells so delicious on the floors when I come in off the road."

"Lucky you," Arlene sighed. "Yes, there are days when this house feels too big for me."

"But your college work is so demanding on you, honey."

"Mrs. Porter may be getting a new client, and soon. Very soon!"

"Jamal …"

"Just came in to say good night to Granddad, Mom. And let you know how great it is that you're spending the night with us, sir."

"Why … why thank you, Jamal."

"So welcome aboard."

Jamal kissed Arlene and then turned to Teardrop. "By the way, Granddad," he said, looking at Miss Lillian, "I h-haven't heard you play Miss Lillian in a long time. A *real* long time, s-sir."

"So what're you suggesting, Jamal? Is that a hint of some kind you're—"

"Yes. Boy oh boy, I'd love to hear you play Miss Lillian, Granddad!"

Arlene stood behind Jamal, draping her arms over his shoulders and part of his narrow-framed chest.

"And the feeling's mutual," Teardrop said, leaning partly to his left. His hand touched Miss Lillian. Then out the black guitar case she came, this smooth-wood, blue-painted queen of a guitar, making her stage entrance—if not in a blues joint, than what was close enough in this intimate, personal setting.

Jamal sat on the bed, about three feet from Teardrop. "Miss Lillian," Jamal said in a hushed whisper. "She looks the same, Granddad. Doesn't she, sir?"

"She sure does. Miss Lillian's wearing the same makeup. The same set of clothes. Dress and shoes and earrings of her liking."

Arlene smiled, for it's the same thing Teardrop said to her when she was nine, ten, after Miss Lillian entered her life and occupied the Williams's household a few years, and then for good.

"Now, Jamal, let's see how she's going to talk tonight. Her opinion on today's events."

"Dad!"

"Well, Arlene, you know how Miss Lillian gets—she has an opinion on everything. If anybody should know, you should."

"Yes, Dad. Miss Lillian's not one to bite her tongue!"

Jamal laughed as if tickled.

With shoulders hunched, Teardrop's body was more comfortable; even his feet looked more relaxed in his shoes. "So how was your trip, flight into Walker City, Miss Lillian? You know you can always tell me chapter and verse."

And so, beautiful notes drifted out Miss Lillian, exquisite in sound and execution, the kind of notes Teardrop Williams was legend for playing on the blues circuit.

"Oh, so that's the way you feel about it, huh?"

And Arlene's body, unknowingly it seemed, slipped over to a chair and sat. And then Miss Lillian's sound became rapturous, befitting of any audience, a court—king, queen, a blues crowd at the Gut Bucket Blues or the Blues Pot or a family on a late Saturday night, sitting at 12 Randolph Road in Walker City, Iowa, or any audience gathered anywhere.

Had a good trip … don't say?
Airline hostess served you on a silver tray?
Nothing second-rate for you.
Like overcooked meat or warmed-over stew.

First class, all the way,
Teardrop Williams is such a gentleman,
Said … he'd pay!

"Miss Lillian!" Arlene shrieked as if Miss Lillian were a person. "How could you say such a thing about my dad!"

"Some nerve, huh, Arlene? Taking advantage of me like that. When we go out on the road. Guess Miss Lillian knows a free meal ticket when she sees one."

"Dad, why should she change?"

"No—why should she. Oh, she knows how to wile her way ... seduce me, all right. But we did have a good flight home. And the food, the airline food, was quite good."

"I've never had airline food," Jamal said.

Teardrop yawned.

"Granddad."

"And it's time for bed for—"

"For everybody but you, Mom."

Teardrop put Miss Lillian back inside the guitar case. "How come, honey?"

"I have a book to read ... oh, about this thick." Arlene's fingers spread about three inches apart.

"You're going to read a book as thick as that in—"

"Say, about three quarters of it."

"And I had the nerve, was naïve enough to ask. I should know my daughter better."

"Just like you know Miss Lillian."

"Even though I don't know half the time what Miss Lillian's going to say."

"Y-you don't, G—"

"Jamal, that's a subject for another day. Let's say we hold off on that. Your grandfather, plus Miss Lillian, have had a long, grueling day."

Teardrop raised his right hand. "I second that!"

"All right. Okay, Granddad. But I will get to the bottom of this. I will. Promise I will."

"Oh, I know you will, Jamal," Teardrop said, leaving no doubt he would. "And if you should forget, I'll be there to remind you. To talk about who really makes Miss Lillian talk."

"Right, Granddad."

"Me—"

"Or some invisible, magiclike, mysterious figure," Arlene said with a seven-year-old's talent for the theater of the imagination.

"Yes, Mom. Yes."

Teardrop grabbed Jamal, tickling him beneath his rib cage.

"Ha! Stop, Granddad! Stop! Ha! Y-you know I'm ticklish there!"

After Teardrop finished tickling Jamal, he stood to hug him around his shoulders. "See you in the morning, Granddad."

"Sure thing, Jamal."

"And thanks for staying over, you and Miss Lillian." Pause. "Good night, Mom."

"Good night, Jamal."

Jamal exited the room. Teardrop walked up to Arlene and held her. "Sleep as late as you like, Dad. I'll drive Jamal off to church, but then I'm coming back. I'll ask Elizabeth Downing to bring him home. I'm going to skip—"

"N-not because, on my—"

"No, Dad. My work. That book of mine. It has to be read. Monday, I'm giving a lecture on it."

"My brilliant daughter—"

"Who's no more brilliant than her brilliant father."

"No less!"

"Isn't it nice to know we belong to the same admiration society. Haven't missed a payment."

"Always have been. Always will be, Arlene."

Teardrop walked Arlene to the door.

"I think I'll sleep well tonight, honey. Comfortably, knowing my family's around me."

CHAPTER 3

It was eleven o'clock.

Arlene was buried in her study. It was as if she'd locked herself inside a lost cave. The room was set up for convenience with most of her materials at her fingertips. Reference materials were contained in a big wooden cabinet with five well-oiled drawers properly marked. Then her reading materials, a gaggle of books, were lined up on an eight-shelf built-in wall bookcase with color-coded labels identifying subject matter. As for the her students' graded papers, they lay in a wide-mouthed, wire-meshed basket she'd devised. She took pride in its simplicity and practicality.

As for Jamal, he'd been driven to Sunday school. In fact, he was expected back at any minute now with Elizabeth Dowling. But when he got into the house, he would see the study door was shut and know just what to say (after all these years)—hi and good-bye—through the door and nothing more. If he didn't, she just might throw the book she was reading at him.

The book she was reading under a goose-neck lamp at her oak desk was titled *Climate Change—The New Economics of the 21st Century*. In another hour or so, the book would be read, and then she'd begin preparing her lecture notes (step no. 1), which were always economical and to the point once edited down (step no. 2).

As quick as a mouse, Arlene's eyes darted off the page.

After she'd driven Jamal off to Sunday school, at about 8:20 a.m., she got back to the house at about 9:45 a.m. By then, Teardrop was cooking breakfast. Something she expected. He said last night he'd slept like a baby, and that was good news to her ears.

"I didn't want to have to worry about you, Dad. I know you can handle yourself all right—emotionally well. I miss Mom. Every day. Jamal, there's not a day that goes by that there's not some mention of her. Something Jamal fondly recalls. But mine go much deeper—Dad's too. She was our life. Every day she was alive."

Looking directly into the goose-neck lamp's light, she now wondered how today was going to work itself out, knowing yesterday, for her father, was but a postponement for what he'd ultimately have to face today.

"Was last night good enough? Surrounded by family. Not on the road with the Tearmakers. Shorty Boy and Twelve Fingers. Not sleeping in a hotel room but at home with Jamal and me. Will you be ready today? To face whatever it is you must? Mom not being in the house, Dad, waiting for you to come home?"

Teardrop stuck his head into Jamal's bedroom.

"Up for lunch, Jamal?"

Jamal sprang off the bed.

"How about it?"

"You bet, Granddad! Uh, Granddad, looks like Mom's never going to come out her study this morning. Been in there for so long already."

"Hard work. Your mother's nose is to the proverbial grindstone, as the saying goes."

"Ham and cheese sandwiches?"

"It's what I was thinking, ham and cheese sandwiches. Great minds, they seem to think alike."

"There's plenty of ham in the—"

"Yes, I saw it this morning when I made breakfast."

Teardrop and Jamal had taken the back stairs. They were down in the kitchen.

"Mom's going to teach me how to cook one day. When, whenever she gets around to it. Finds the time—whenever that is."

Teardrop opened the refrigerator door and pulled out what was needed for ham and cheese sandwiches, putting them on the broad butcher block countertop.

"Uh ... just ham and cheese for—"

"Don't worry, the lettuce and tomatoes are for me. And the carrot, well … Jamal," Teardrop said with a twinkle in both eyes, "is for my eyes."

"Oh …" Jamal laughed back. "I don't have to worry about that, Granddad."

"Only when you reach my age, Jamal. You still have forty-five years and counting."

Jamal sat down at the kitchen table. "As long as there's no rush." Jamal had changed out his Sunday attire and was wearing a striped T-shirt, one that was blue-and-white-striped today.

They'd finished eating for a while now and so were chatting up a storm.

"Once I had a teacher like Ms. Powell. The spitting image of her. But we didn't meet until the fourth grade. Was when we became acquainted— engaged in the pursuit of excel—"

"Finished! At last!" Arlene said triumphantly while entering the kitchen. "Everything's finished. Now all I have to do is be brave enough to stand before fifty or sixty eager-eyed college students and convince them I know what I'm talking about in Mary Bethune Lecture Hall at ten o'clock Monday morning!"

"Don't worry, Mom, you'll knock them dead!"

"Or bore them to death. So … I see my two favorite men have dined."

"Uh … Granddad made ham and cheese sandwiches for us, Mom. Wasn't that great of him?"

"Hungry, Arlene?"

"Am I!"

"Then sit, honey. Join the party. One ham sandwich coming up!" Teardrop was at the refrigerator. "Uh … will that be ham and cheese—"

"Or lettuce and tomatoes like Granddad's sandwich, Mom? And a carrot on the side, ma'am. Carrots, you know, are good for the eyes." Jamal had said it with such a big belief.

Teardrop stepped out the house and onto the roomy yard. Why he went out into the yard, he didn't know, but he suspected it was to clear his mind. *Yes*, he thought, *to clear my mind*. He looked back at the white front-porch steps and, within seconds, climbed them.

"Arlene," he said, inside the house. "I'm ready for the drive to the house."

And it's what Arlene told Teardrop at the kitchen table before Jamal washed the dishes and Teardrop dried them, the dirty dishes the Williams/Wilkerson family were responsible for—that she'd drive him to the house when ready.

Teardrop laid Miss Lillian's guitar case atop the car's backseat. Jamal sat in the front seat of a red Chevrolet Impala Arlene would often declare you could see a mile down the road even on the foggiest day in Walker City, Iowa.

"Granddad," Jamal said as the car moved out the driveway, "how about a blues song?"

"Oh … you're pushing your luck with your grandfather. Last night was free. But today you might have to pay for his services."

"Handsomely, Jamal. It doesn't come cheap. Your mother is an economics professor, so she knows all about our capitalist system: supply and demand in the open market."

"Whew … ," Jamal said, relieved. "I'm just glad Mom's not a physics teacher—those words are really hard to understand. I've heard them, sir." Jamal's forehead broke out in a sweat.

"Well, your granddad did major in … his degree is in—"

"Now you really want to bore the boy, don't you, Arlene? Unnecessarily."

The red Impala had backed out the driveway, turned sharply to the left, and then righted itself.

"It's another beautiful day in Walker City, it appears. So peaceful. Serene."

"If not play Miss Lillian, then sing, Granddad? Would that be okay, I mean?"

"Jamal, you mustn't be so persistent, honey."

Jamal, seemingly, totally disregarded Arlene.

"Come on, Granddad. F-for me …"

"The first lesson you must learn about the blues, Jamal, is this: that it doesn't wake, really wake up until eight o'clock at night on most days. And never on Sunday. Sunday's God's day."

"The first thing? Then what's the second?"

Teardrop looked at Arlene and both laughed.

"The second is, uh, the second thing is … is, it can wait until tomorrow. Monday. Right, Arlene? The blues, that is."

There staring at them on Dawkin's Road was another sprawling lawn with large shade trees dotting the gorgeous grounds. There was all this green lawn in the back of the square-sitting, white-painted, aristocratic-looking house that calmly focused the eye. The car made its way up the winding road, the tires kicking up the loose gravel as it moved effortlessly toward the eleven-room beauty of a house that sustained the graceful, classical lines of other houses of note in the small populated section of Trinity in Walker City.

Arlene felt some kind of a live drama in the house, a biting tension, so she looked back at Teardrop in the car's backseat, whose eyes only made direct contact with the house. She felt she was a part of those eyes, the staring into the wide windows and the house's wood-planked front porch and amply spaced front door. Even if her childhood was long ago, right now, at this instant, it was revisiting her, the happiness the family shared, the memories it cherished, the family member who'd left them, her thoughts as aligned to her father's as powerfully as they'd ever been before.

"Mr. Kelly really makes the lawn look good, doesn't he, Mom? M-maybe we should have him mow our lawn, ma'am. Hire him," Jamal laughed wickedly.

Arlene only half smiled at Jamal's apparent teasing—the ultimate elimination of at least one of his weekly chores.

"Dad, everything d-does look terrific."

Teardrop and Arlene lived about two miles from each other in Trinity. There was a garage off to the right side of the house. The silver-toned Oldsmobile was parked inside, Maureen Williams's car—for all intents and purposes.

"Yes, it does," Teardrop said, having delayed in replying. "Yes, the old place does."

The red Impala pulled up to the white-painted house. For some reason the three just sat there and relaxed. Whether it had to do with the pleasantness of the day or the short ride over or habit, it was pretty much hard to tell.

"Sometimes I forget you and Jamal are so near, Arlene. I could walk home if ever worse came to worse."

"A stone's throw, Dad. No more."

"When I'm old enough, I'll be able to ride my bike from our house over to yours, Granddad."

"Which will be soon, Jamal. In the blink of an eye."

Jamal's face bubbled. "Right, Granddad. Boy ..."

"Well ..."

"Your suitcase?"

Teardrop removed Miss Lillian from the backseat. Arlene stepped out the car, and so did Jamal. Both beat Teardrop out the car, much to Teardrop's amusement. "I didn't know you two were so eager to get rid of me. Had no idea!"

"Dad," Arlene said, lifting the trunk, "don't blame Jamal and me for your slow reflexes."

"Must be my tired blood. Or—"

"Granddad, do you pay Mr. Kelly much money to mow the grass? Do the yard work?"

"E—"

"Won't give up, huh, Jamal?" Arlene said, closing the car's trunk, having pulled Teardrop's case out. "Know when the odds are stacked against you."

"Never, Mom. There has to be another solution to this—"

"Jamal, I think, personally, you were a lawyer in diapers—at least it's what your grandmother thought. When you cried in your crib. The racket you made. Am I right, Arlene?"

"Absolutely."

"Well, you can't blame me for trying, sir," Jamal said, red-faced.

"No, Jamal. That we'd never accuse you of."

Jamal and Arlene turned toward the house; only Teardrop didn't.

"No, there's no need to do that," Teardrop said walking back to the car's trunk to Arlene. "For you to come in with me. That'd be silly. What you've done is e-enough."

"D-Dad," Arlene said, visibly upset.

"N-no, it's all right, Arlene. It's all right," Teardrop said, taking the suitcase from Arlene. "I can assure you, honey."

"We can't go in with you, Granddad?"

"Not today, Jamal. It's too lovely out," Teardrop said, looking up into the bright, crisp sky and passing clouds, "to spend time inside a house. That I wouldn't ask either of you to do."

Arlene glanced at Jamal, and for his sake, she suppressed her feelings. "Yes, Dad ... just look at the sun in the sky ..."

And it's when Jamal looked up at the sky too.

"My kind of day. My kind of day," Teardrop said exuberantly. "In Walker City."

"M-mine too, Granddad. Mine too," Jamal said as if he didn't want to be left out.

"Rain tomorrow though. It's what they said over the radio this morning. So better that you take advantage of the good weather today," Teardrop said, kissing Arlene's forehead and then reaching for Jamal, who held his waist. "There's always someone who wants to put a damper on the county parade."

Teardrop was on the broad-sweeping porch. The car was about to take back to the winding gravel driveway that emptied out onto Dawkin's Road.

"Talk to you soon," Teardrop said, waving at Arlene and Jamal.

"Yes, Dad."

"Yes, Granddad."

And as the car started moving away from the house, Teardrop started moving toward it, pulling the house keys out his pant pocket. Having taken Miss Lillian out her case, Miss Lillian strung, by a leather strap, across the middle of his back and with tiny movement.

Teardrop walked through the house, what was the measure of it. At least twice he'd touched everything in the house. Touching things as if to find Maureen through them, as if she'd left something of herself behind, traces of her for him to find.

Teardrop was out the house as if he'd been chased from it by what his mind could no longer bear.

"I don't know what I was looking for … hoping to find. I'm still badly confused by it."

He'd been home for about an hour, trying to relax, find comfort, but now contemplating the very condition of his mind and what it would take to find peace and comfort in staying in his own house. To be able to do it tonight, fixated by the very thought of it.

"It's what I just came off the road for—to find this balance, t-to work all of this pain out my system. Out … in some real, realistic way."

And he'd been standing out in the front yard for well over fifteen minutes, out in the hot sun, not in the shade that was more than accessible if it were his choice.

"What can I do? What?"

He looked back at the house, for his back had been to it, and felt an uprising in him, a smell of new, raw, bitter pain. Just the thought of that house and him, again. Again! Again!

"Like before!"

But last night I slept well, Teardrop thought. At Arlene's. It was a good night for me. Arlene and Jamal were in the house. My daughter and grandson. Family. Family. "I slept better than I've slept …"

He hadn't slept well, easily, not since Maureen's death. A time frame could be attached to it—sure it could, Teardrop thought. There'd been no restful nights, not since Maureen's death. There was always some interruption, something to jar the night or crack it open, something sharp and in control—and then out of control. It's all he could count on the night for, these bouts, these battles; it seemed nothing could stop them, that they were endless, faceless.

"But last night I was able to sleep. My night went well for me." Teardrop took a few steps forward but then, as if challenged to do so, swung his body with full authority, awareness, to look at the house.

But it took only a matter of seconds for his body to recoil and shake as it did in the motel room in Atlanta, Georgia, Bunky's Better Bunks, two nights back in front of Shorty Boy Logan as if he were looking at something grotesque, opaque—beyond his ability to cope with or conquer on any night or by any means or on any one's terms, something that would sustain its power over him forever.

But instead of running away from the house, Teardrop ran toward it. And when he got into the house, the living room, this huge room Mrs. Porter had cleaned so winningly, the smell of Pine-Sol and all, Teardrop picked up the phone and waited for the voice on the other end to respond.

"Come for me, Arlene. I'm in the house. I can't spend another minute in this house. Not another minute more!"

Sunday night, and tomorrow school was in the offing for Arlene and Jamal with it being Monday. Jamal had gone to bed announcing to everyone that he was prepared for Ms. Powell's class tomorrow morning.

Arlene was coming out the bathroom, having showered. Her robe was white, terry cloth, and ankle length. It was 10:12 p.m.

"Dad," Arlene said, entering Teardrop's room.

"Still love those showers of yours?"

"They're quick and efficient."

"Thanks, Arlene. Thanks."

"Dad, this is your home as well as mine and Jamal's. There's been no reason for you to think differently."

"Why would you think that, Arlene, when you and Jamal were by the house pretty much 90 percent of the time."

"True. Jamal and I were always by there. And it was 95 percent of the time, not 90. And Mom made up for the other 5 percent—not you."

"No, not me. I was spoiled rotten. It's why, I suppose, I'm surprised this house feels so comfortable to me. Like home. When I really didn't drop by here that much."

Arlene liked hearing that, his feelings toward the house.

"And this bed ... I slept well last night. Un-uninterrupted."

"Then ..."

"Yes, Arlene?"

"Not every night?"

"No."

"Since Mom's been—"

"Yes, yes. Of course."

"All ... all this time, Dad?" Arlene asked, astonished.

"The nights haven't been good to me. But last night, in the house, I went the night w-without—it was remarkable. Even though the customary happened, thinking of your mother before falling to sleep. That, I don't think, will ever change. Nor would I want it to."

"It's what I do too—school, work, Jamal, any associative problems during the day, no matter how big or small, never supersede Mom. She's always the first thought I have, and the last."

"What do you say to her?"

"I always say, just say good night. Good night, nothing more."

"Simple, to the point," Teardrop said. "Thanks for sharing that with me."

"There's so much we've shared, Dad, and yet—"

"So much that hasn't been shared—since your mother's death. I suppose we have a sanctuary. A private place that we both maintain."

"Yes."

"We do need that."

"For our resourcefulness?"

"Resourcefulness, yes, you're right. But there're things, daily, that try us. The slightest thing can conjure up memory of your mother. Unexpectedly. So you must absorb the feelings they produce. Or there'd be nothing, at the end of the day, that'd be left of you. You'd be too emotionally drained if you didn't."

"There's so much emotionally that you have to carry around with you when a loved one dies."

"Often, it seems unending." Pause. "It's why I wanted to die first, not your mother. Wished it. "

"Oh, oh, Dad, please don't—"

"That I die first. You might as well know another dark secret of mine. I knew what it would do to me. I envisioned it—that it would snuff my insides out like a flame. It's how I always felt about such a tragedy."

Arlene removed her terry-cloth robe. It was hung in the closet; she was naked. She replaced the robe with pajamas, blue ones. She'd brushed out her hair, and now it was set in rollers, something she did seven days a week. It was 10:52 p.m. Every night she tried getting to bed by no later than twelve o'clock—and here she was, beating herself by at least an hour and some minutes. The short, stubby lamp on the night table was on. She was over at the bedroom window and, as suddenly, looked over at her bed with the quilted red diamond-patterned bedspread pulled back and the pink sheets in the white light, all too welcoming.

"How much sleep have I lost in that bed thinking of you, Mom?" Her head shook. She continued staring at the bed. "It hasn't been easy. It's the hardest thing I've known, losing you. I love you beyond belief. Beyond the thinking of it. But Dad's pain is greater than mine, Mom—and why shouldn't it? The life you two had together. The love you two shared. It was nothing short of miraculous. A model, a template for others."

Arlene walked toward the bed and then got in and then turned off the light. "Thank God I'm here for him. Not just me, but Jamal too. Family. We're such a strong family."

Arlene curled up in the bed. In a matter of seconds her mind felt calm, deliberate. But then she almost felt out of control, like she did practically seven months ago when she knew her father was in the house and what he must be going through nightly without her mother—it mirrored her feelings now: cold and shivery and elusive.

"There is such a desperate despair in you, Dad. Such an awful, desperate despair. I'm so worried for you—but don't worry, Jamal and I will be here for you. Do all that we can to try to make up for Mom for you. I know it's nearly impossible, but we'll try. Make every effort to.

"You just mean so much to us. I don't want to lose you too. N-no one was to die first—in any particular order, neither you nor Mom."

CHAPTER 4

Two months later.

"Dad, we're ready," Arlene said from the house's high deck of deep-lasting grain material painted gray. The deck was newly built.

"Don't worry, Arlene, I checked my watch. I didn't lose track of the time, even though I think Miss Lillian was hoping I would. I did say three o'clock."

Teardrop was drawing nearer the house.

"And how is Miss Lillian today?"

"Garrulous. Talking up a storm. Had a lot to get off her mind today."

"Dad, sometimes I wish you'd taught me how to play the guitar. A twelve-string guitar."

"No, your mother objected. Wanted you to learn the piano. And she won out, thumbs down."

"You didn't put up a fight for me?"

"Who me? With your mother? When her mind was made up?"

"A lot of good it did me, the piano," Arlene grumbled. "My piano lessons."

Teardrop was on the deck with her. There was deck furniture as well as yard furniture. But also, there was a thickly wooded area in the back of the house that Teardrop and Miss Lillian would enter into—and then wend their way back to the house after each stay.

"You got the short end of the stick," Teardrop said, putting his arm around Arlene's waist, "when it came to musical talent, I'm afraid. It's always a fifty-fifty proposition anyway, when two families are involved. Which side wins out in the end. Will tilt the scales of justice."

"Mother's side of the family. The Akins side."

"I'm afraid so. The Atkins, a sad lot when it came to music. Not brains, intellectually though—just music.

"And so, where's Jamal?" Teardrop said, looking around the backyard. "My itchy grandson?"

"Where else but—"

Honk!

"In the car. He's been looking forward to this, I think, as well as me."

"The big move. Me moving into the house. Who would've thought this? Not me. Not by a long shot."

"But now, on face value, Dad, it seems inevitable."

They stepped onto the kitchen floor.

"One day blending into the next, until … You've been a lifesaver for me, Arlene. You and Jamal pulling me out the doldrums. Depths of despair, honey. My life's back on track, the right track. They're fulfilling now. It-it's all I can say…"

"We've both benefited. Both gotten something very special out of you living here—and it's only going to get better down the road."

"It's what I think too. My moving in with you. One hundred percent."

Honk!

"Ha. Our second warning from Jamal."

"One more and we're dead!" And then something Teardrop had been thinking about for a while came to mind.

"Arlene"—Arlene was getting her pocketbook—"hearing the horn, the car horn. The car, your mother's car, the Oldsmobile …"

"Right?"

"Let's sell it. Put it up for sale, honey. I have no real use for it. No need for it sitting in the garage all day. Idle."

"M-Mom's car?"

"Yes. I see no reason why it shouldn't be sold. It seems the only practical thing to do with it."

"Of course, Dad," Arlene said as if she'd just felt her father remove yet another burden from himself and their family.

Honk!

"Oh, oh …"

"We're dead! Dead! I think you'll have to fix your grandson's favorite meal when we get back to the house!"

"What? Pork and beans?"

"Jamal, we're coming, honey. Your grandfather and I. B-be right there!" Arlene shouted, sticking her head out the front door, sure to get an immediate response from Jamal.

Jamal was in front of the house, on the sprawling green lawn. He was being a typical seven-year-old.

"So everything's done with, Arlene."

"Yes."

They were standing on the house's grand old white-painted porch.

The house's furniture, from top to bottom, had been covered in white sheets. It was classical furniture, something that was in Maureen Williams's bloodlines, the search for the elegant without bowing to snobbery.

"I think we've done the right thing. Handled things as best, well as could be expected. Your mother would be awful proud of us. Her house is in order. Just like she left it when she died."

"Yes."

"Every two weeks now, Mrs. Porter will clean the house. I don't see why there should be any more attention given to it. The grounds, uh, Mr. Kelly will continue to maintain," Teardrop laughed. "I hope the inside of the house doesn't resemble a haunted house. For any reason, appear in any way deserted by us."

"You know, to be perfectly honest, Dad, at the time that thought did cross my mind."

"Mine too."

"But from a practical sense, to protect the furniture, by putting sheets over it—who cares what it looks like. Anyone else thinks."

"Right, honey." Pause. "It's good that we can trust people in Trinity. That they're neighbors of ours who we've known for years."

"And it doesn't hurt"—Arlene smiled—"that you are the great Maurice 'Teardrop' Williams of Walker City, Iowa."

"Arlene, come on, don't make me blush any more than what I already am."

Arlene pinched Teardrop's cheek. "On you, Dad, it looks good. Very debonair."

"You think so, huh?" Teardrop hesitated. "And so now, as of today, the house, we don't have to worry about. Because I wasn't going to sell it or rent it out to anyone. Not on your life!"

"Perish the thought!"

"Yes, perish the thought. This house will never be sold, not while I'm alive. Nor rented out just as a source of income either. But for the car, as far as it's concerned, Arlene ... ," Teardrop said, still holding on to Arlene's hand, walking to the right of the house where the garage stood as a freestanding entity, "that I'll begin working on tomorrow. I know the car's in mint condition."

"It should be easy to sell. Even though ..."

"I know, honey, I know, but ..."

It's when Jamal attracted their attention, for his seven-year-old spirit seemed to want to move onto things a far cry different than that of starchy adults.

"Mom, Granddad, look at this!"

Jamal executed a smoothly controlled cartwheel on the grass. Now he was wiping his hands clean. "Not bad, huh?"

"Excellent, Jamal. Excellent."

"As long as you don't ask your grandfather or me to do a cartwheel."

It's when Jamal executed another cartwheel just as smoothly controlled as the first one.

Again, he wiped his hands. "Ready?"

"Ready. I guess he has things to do back at the house."

"Always, Dad. I think ... it's the cross he bears."

"Indefatigable."

The three piled into the red Impala. Before starting the car, Arlene thought it best to give her father a moment to himself; Jamal seemed acutely aware of this too.

"T-thank you, Arlene."

Then the red Impala made its run over the gravel driveway. Only Jamal was looking back at the house from the car's front seat, waving at it, the seat belt rubbing against his narrow chest.

"Good-bye, old house," Jamal said. "See you, okay?"

Teardrop's head didn't turn back to look at the house. Not today.

"Honey, I'm turning in."

"Oh yes, Dad."

"Still at it, huh?"

Arlene stretched out her arms and then grinned. Her hair was set in rollers. "Summer school's not as labor intensive as the regular college year, but there're nights when it seems it."

"Like tonight."

"Dad, what can I say?"

"As long as it's the exception, not the rule."

"Exactly."

"I locked up, so you don't have to, honey. Arlene, this'll be my first official night here, in the house."

"Yes, I know," Arlene replied with spunk; her pretty eyes were clearly excited.

"I do need this house. This life. The energy it contains. I am glad I can admit it. That I didn't try to put up imaginary walls around my feelings."

"It would've had such a negative effect on you, I think, if you had."

"Tomorrow I'm going to fix Jamal's toast now that the old toaster's here in the house. Moved in with me today. Missed it the past two months."

"Dad, don't dare leave me out," Arlene said.

"Oh no, no, not you."

"The magic of the old toaster."

"It's like no other."

"How old was I when Mom bought it?"

"Uh … let …"

"It had to be around—"

"Ten at the time. Yes, it was ten. Three years older than Jamal."

"Seventeen years you've had it."

"And it's still the best toaster in town. Walker City. The king of toasters. Bar none!"

"I know Jamal can't wait for the toaster to perform its magic—never mind me."

"I'm just going to have to get peach jelly for myself."

"We have grape."

"I know. I checked. But only peach jelly for me." Pause. "Well … let me let my brilliant daughter get back—"

"Dad …" There was a plain, placid look on Arlene's face.

"I'm happy, Arlene. It's the happiest I've been—"

"Since Mother's death?"

Teardrop nodded his head.

"Good night, Dad."

"Night, honey."

Teardrop was making his way down the hallway to this room, when he heard Arlene say, "Peach jelly, I don't know why I've been eating grape jelly all these years, Dad. When I've always loved peach jelly."

CHAPTER 5

Three years later.

Ursula Jenkins's skin was as smooth and black as a newly polished pearl. Her father, Harry, was short and her mother, Iris, tall. Ursula Jeanette Jenkins got her genes from her mother. She wore a close-cropped Afro, something that, for 1997, was out of style; but on Ursula Jenkins, it looked quite the "thing," extraordinary. But Ursula Jenkins wasn't about what was in style or out since she set her own edgy, dynamic style. She was bullishly independent, a trait she exhibited even as a child. A trait that, on occasion, got her into a world of trouble, debate, and, oftentimes, controversy.

Byron Jeffries was holding court, something he had a habit of doing. Byron Jeffries was twenty-three, black, and a stockbroker in New York City. He was in downtown Manhattan, in the Renaissance Bar, a black and Latino hangout, on a Friday evening, after work, socializing, unwinding with friends, basically— shooting the breeze.

"I'm telling you, man, this song I heard, 'River of Pain,' is the greatest, uh, excuse me, the baddest blues tune ever recorded by man or beast. And as y'all know, I ain't even into the blues scene—trip that much."

"Yeah, we know," J. C. Day said flippantly.

"Yeah, yeah," Byron Jeffries said forcibly.

"So how'd you come by it, Byron? May I ask? It get dropped on your doorstep?"

Teardrop

"One of those freak things situations, J. C. Let's just call it that. Uh, uh, excuse me, Ursula," Byron said, his voice changing from high pitch to low, "but me and the sister were making love, knockin' boots, you know the deal, doin' the nasty-nasty, when—"

"When the CD dropped?"

"Yeah, right, right. Dropped. Dropped. Precisely. After all, it was her place. The girl's digs. We were hitting it up. On all four cylinders of four. Uh, I didn't know her taste in music, man, just that she had some fine legs and a big booty to boot. Big and round as a melon, man!"

"And don't ever let it be said Byron Randolph Jefferies ever passed him up a sister with fine legs and a big booty to match, right, Byron!"

"Shit, and so what you think, J. C.?"

Byron Jeffries, J. C. Day, and Ursula Jenkins were sitting at a square table with two bottles of Heineken, a scotch and soda, and a Diet Coke. Music was ripping through the Renaissance, a lively Latin number that could make you shake like crazy or like Tito Puente in your seat.

Byron took a swig of Heineken; his eyes bugged. "Yeah, we were doin' the nasty-nasty all right, when this tune—"

"'River of Pain'—"

"Yeah, 'River of Pain' came on. And, man, I mean right then and there, in … in the bed w-with this outrageous specimen of a female …"

"What, Byron?" Ursula said, purring softly.

"Yeah, what … Byron?"

"Tears, a flood of tears shot into my eyes. You believe that shit? Hers too. Killer tears while we were making love, man. W-while the girl and I were gettin' off, we began crying like crazy. If you can believe that shit.

"Tears flowing out our eyes … down our cheeks. The two of us, man—for real."

Ursula Jenkins and J.C. found the words they'd just heard hard to believe, and they looked at each other with total skepticism.

"Man, it blew my mind. Cork. Totally."

J. C. lifted his glass, taking a sip of his scotch and soda calmly. "Must've, Byron. Must've," he said like he was still the Doubting Thomas.

"I mean it. Mean it, J. C., Ursula. Sweetie. It was like being connected to something long ago. I-I know Marvin and Smokey do that to me. I mean, since I'm up into the hip-hop scene, serious with that—but with Marvin and Smokey, there are some moments. Really special moments for me. That old R & B tip.

"But this song put an ache, a real one, in me. Made me feel old. Creaky. Like I've lived ... know what I mean? You know, like I'd traveled through that blues dude's life or something freaky like that. L-let me through, in through the door with him. To witness the pain with him. Put me right there, smack in the middle of it."

"Some sad shit, huh?"

"No, not so much that, J. C. Not so much that, but it was like hey, man, like something that could happen to anybody. Any one of us. Say, that kind of pain."

"A commonality then," Ursula said.

"Yeah, Ursula—that. That." Byron scratched his head with a fever. "And then when he played that guitar of his, man, me and the sister flipped, bodies began rocking like nobody's business. I mean it. I ... I mean the blues dude's playing was so delicate, sweet—it was tripping me out. Just tripping me and the sister the hell out."

Ursula took a sip of Diet Coke. She drank white wine but loved Diet Coke.

"See, uh, see it was like each note meant something. Came from something, somewhere—was saying something to you. Slow. Slow. Nothing was in a rush. Like the music was saying, 'Hey, stop, man, take a listen. Let me tell you something I know is true. Weren't hip to before. B-but I am. Got the secret. In my hands. My guitar. The blues, man.'"

"Man, this is getting heavy, downright ... real heavy, Byron," J. C. said.

Byron's brown skin burned red in the Renaissance Bar's low-sitting lights. "Yeah, it ... it was like an epiphany, man," Byron said earnestly.

Ursula and J. C. laughed.

"And so did you tell Ursula and me this little story because you got another notch on your belt, another female conquest of yours, or—"

"The dude's name is Maurice 'Teardrop' Williams."

"Oh ... oh no," J. C. said, cracking up. "No wonder you and the sister were tearing it up. Balling mightily, Byron. Listen to the name. I would too if somebody like a Maurice, ha, 'Teardrop' Williams was crying in my soup while I was doing it."

"Ursula, have you heard of the dude?"

"Yes, Byron. I have."

"Who hasn't Ursula heard of, right, Ursula?"

"He dropped out the music scene ... uh, oh, let me see ..."

"Come on. Come on. I know you know, Ursula. Got my money riding on you. Big time. Banking my whole week's pay on you, sister—the little I make. Sees my bank account."

"Three, uh, three years ago. Right, ri—"

"See"—J. C. smiled—"knew you'd come through!"

"Nineteen ninety-four."

Byron's right hand dashed down inside his tan suit jacket, and out flashed a CD.

"This is it. This is the little number. I copped it today at J & R Music Store, man. Before I shot over here to the Renaissance."

"I'm not familiar with his music though," Ursula said. "I've just heard of him. This Teardrop Williams, mind you. That he retired from the music business. That I know."

"So that means touring—"

"Yes. Essentially, it's how they make their living. The small amount of money a blues musician can make from it," Ursula said.

"Except for B. B. King and John Lee Hooker," J. C. said.

"Of course they're the exceptions to the rule." Ursula laughed. "But I'm sure Teardrop Williams was doing okay. Was making a decent income before retiring."

"And no more recordings, Ursula?" Byron asked with a sad look on his usually bright, cute, boylike face. "For, for three years now?"

"No. It's all-inclusive regarding retirement. Pretty much standard, Byron."

"Too bad. Too bad. It's the CD I bought you, Ursula. *River of*—"

"You, you bought me, Byron?"

"Yes." Byron smiled. "Bought you, Ursula. For you, sweetie. Hey, with you being a writer, journalist and all. And someone who loves music—"

"But jazz is Ursula's thing, Byron," J. C. said. "Ain't into the 'get-down, lock-it-tight shit,' not unless she wants to get funky—into the mix."

"Ha. Definitely. Yeah, man. Ursula goes highbrow on us now and then," Byron said, laughing with J. C., "but the sister can git down when it counts. Crazy wit' it."

"Know I can!" Ursula said.

"Ain't got to twist the girl's arm on a dance floor, we know that!" Byron said.

"Sister can bang with it. Bang it all night!" J. C. said.

"But hey, I know enough about the blues to know jazz is a ... a—"

"Derivative. Derivative form."

"Yeah, it's what I was trying to say, before my brain locked on me. So … here you are, my dear," Byron said, handing Ursula the CD.

J. C. angled his head to the right. "Hey, he's a cool-looking dude if I must say so myself."

Ursula looked at the picture on the CD too. "V-very handsome. Q-quite."

"For someone his age," J. C. quipped.

"He's not that old, J. C.," Ursula said.

"All blues men are old," J. C. said. "All of them are old to the bone. Old as dirt."

"Just want you, for you to hear that track, Ursula. Don't know about the rest of the CD's tracks. She programmed the box, but the title cut is worth every cent I shelled out for it."

"So, uh … you and the sister cried you a river of pain, huh, Byron? A river of pain, huh, man? Was flowing … huh, Byron? Flowing out, huh—"

"What I said. Ain't ashamed of it. Not for a minute of the day, man."

Ursula was studying the CD with a lot more intensity.

"Thanks, Byron."

"Figured if any of my *real* friends"—Byron glanced at J. C.—"would appreciate it, it'd be you, sweetie."

"Byron, you didn't answer my question, man. Any of it, m—"

"Ursula," Byron said, looking up at the Renaissance's ceiling, "did you hear someone say something? Something of significance, that is?"

And the music in the Renaissance played on, but it was a reggae number rendered by Bob Marley battering the walls with his propulsive reggae beats to no end.

Ursula Jenkins lived in Jamaica, Queens, New York, close to a subway stop. In fact, she was a block from the E and F train lines. She lived in an affordable four-room apartment, was single, and loved dogs, cats, and kids (and not particularly in that order).

Ursula came out the bathroom. The apartment's temperature was conducive for her attire: a skimpy nightgown. She'd washed her face and done her normal nightly grooming. It was Wednesday night. Byron had called for the little get-together at the Renaissance Bar tonight. It was three years ago she met Byron Jeffries through a mutual friend. Immediately, they hit it off. There was no romantic thing between them, it was strictly platonic, but Byron, being a man, tried, initially, to hit on her. But Ursula put him down easy, like a helicopter landing on a heliport's super soft padding.

She was three years his senior but didn't throw it up in his face—not once. But at the same time, she liked someone else anyway; only, it didn't work out. Don Richardson, being a professional man, found greener pastures in Atlanta, Georgia. Ursula didn't follow him down there even if he'd asked her to. It's just that she didn't like him enough to upend her life on the East Coast for the South, or him.

She'd met J. C. Day through Byron. He was dating, had a girlfriend, something serious, so she never had to worry about J. C. exerting his "man thing," putting the moves on her until she put him in his place too.

The bedroom lights were off in the small, comfortable bedroom that Ursula decorated with plenty of style and panache; the local flea market on Jamaica Avenue playing a big part in her shopping habits. Ursula used the faint light still in the room to depress the CD button on the boom box and then slowly adjust the headset to her head.

"Now for the moment of truth," she said. The boom box was on the floor, next to the bed. Maurice "Teardrop" Williams' CD was on top the bed. Such a handsome-looking man, she thought again. Really striking, his pose, his eyes—really everything about him. Such observation induced this natural enthusiasm from her.

Ursula wanted to listen to the CD this way, in her bed with her headset on—the time, ll:21 p.m., the prospect of tomorrow, another hectic day. The music flowed through the headphones. Ursula knew she wouldn't hear "River of Pain" for a while since it was the CD's final track.

"Beautiful … ," she said right off as the music began snaking through her ears.

Ursula didn't expect to say that about blues music; she'd expected to hear something rough cut, raw, like fabric being torn by teeth and sweat, not this. For there was such patience in Maurice "Teardrop" Williams's playing and thought and storytelling and truth and beauty and passion—and a will for exploring and exposing all of them at once, in one complete package, Ursula thought.

"And this is only the CD's first track. I guess I'll be in for something real special soon."

And so the first track led to the second track and then the third track, and Ursula had been counting them, the CD's tracks, for she knew "River of Pain" would be the CD's fifth tune.

"Mmm ... how can it get any better than this, I wonder?"

And the music, the fourteen minutes or so she'd been listening to it, was mesmerizing, was some kind of balanced joy, ideal—where her heart wished to leap for joy but stayed still, silent, like the guitar's soft twang would settle, spin out a peaceful space in time, unify the cosmic vibrations uniformly and then with some kind of temperate grace and will.

Ursula's eyes stayed shut, the near-summer nights still cool enough, refreshing enough for her to push back the light-textured bedsheet, no closed, shut apartment windows or air-condition humming during New York nights, only the air releasing natural breezes in making Ursula's bedroom feel exquisitely restful.

"This is it. This is it!" Ursula said, knowing the CD was up to track no. 5, its final entry.

And so Ursula did not want to be disappointed; she did not want to say Byron Jeffries was wrong, that he'd gotten all of this stuff wrong, that "River of Pain" was a not a failure, not the greatest tune he'd ever heard, not when she knew jazz music and classical music and rhythm and blues music and all the great masters who'd composed all the magnificent music, and Maurice "Teardrop" Williams had not grabbed those stars—had come up, in fact, far short.

And then, yes, the music had reached Ursula's ears and she waited for more and more ... and more of Maurice Teardrop's music whirl from out his CD *River of Pain* from her big boom box on the bedroom floor, breathing music out its speakers like mad and miraculous.

Ursula Jenkins was a young New York City freelance writer who was in great demand. She'd made her mark as a magazine journalist, remarkably so, over a two-year stretch. She'd worked for *Sources*, a national magazine, but left them last year. Now some of the national, big-name magazines were chasing after her. But for the past few months, Ursula Jenkins was enjoying her freelance status, the freedom it afforded her (and her rent was getting paid on time!).

In the literary field, Ursula was known as a thorough researcher, one who, once she'd gleaned the information, put an original, a one-of-a-kind spin on the article. She'd just completed a provocative piece on America's welfare system: "The Untold Facts." Prior to that, she'd written an article on the black novelist Ralph Ellison, "The Man Behind the Invisible Man," for another literary publication, one that won her a ton of plaudits. Currently, she'd been bandying around several of her own ideas, plus editors from numerous competing magazines had approached her with ideas she was giving serious consideration to. Needless to say, not all of them excited her, but some did suggest interesting possibility.

But this morning Ursula was in her bedroom at her personal computer coasting on Maurice "Teardrop" Williams's every note. The music she'd heard last night drifted her into a solid sleep and now made her feel especially awake, exhilarated, ready to take on the world as it were.

The first thing she said this morning when she woke was "I have to find out more about Teardrop Williams. I have to." And it was what she was doing at her computer: hoping to find out more information on Teardrop Williams from the Internet's Yahoo! search engine.

She had washed and brushed her teeth, was in a sweatshirt and jeans and sneakers with the funky shoelaces. She hadn't eaten breakfast, something that, in her daily regimen, was always optional; but at 8:21 a.m., there was still plenty of time for her to change her mind. She'd been up since 6:50 a.m.

But last night for Ursula, it's as if a new world had opened for her, a world Teardrop Williams lived in, knew about, and she didn't. But he was, in his music and lyrics, so intimate and personal regarding it, in sharing it, articulating it, that it meant she had to explore more. And it seemed, for now, the more she'd explore, scratch the surface, the more she'd want to know, investigate, discover—as if it were some ennobled quest of time and place and spirit begging for her attention.

And today was the beginning for Ursula, the start of it. Right now, she thought, sitting comfortably in front of the computer, it feeling like a mission. But a mission tickling her imagination, her curiosity, like nothing had since her Ralph Ellison article—something which had shined a light in her too, sparking her journalistic appetite.

"No computer slipups today, okay?" Ursula said to her computer, it having crashed a few days back. "No downtime, off-line, I'm not in the mood. No more tricks up your sleeve, please … Not now. Not today."

Three weeks later.

Ursula had her phonograph out in the living room. There was a stack of at least fifteen albums.

"Muddy Waters, you're up next, after Memphis Slim. So I hope you're ready, Muddy."

Ursula, already, had listened to Lightning Hopkins's *The Legacy of the Blues* album. Before that, it was Son House and then "Champion" Jack Dupree and then "Mighty" Joe Young. It was a week and a half ago that Ursula went on her little shopping binge buying a batch of blues albums. She'd begun with Howlin' Wolf, Albert King, and then Muddy Waters … And then found out about Sunnyland Slim and Robert Pete Williams and Juke Boy Bonner, and a rash of other bluesmen. It's like she was in this blues world, this place where she felt most black, like a Negro spiritual. Like it was birthing the blues in her belly.

"Oh … I can't get enough of this stuff. Never!" Ursula gushed. "I can't. I just can't!"

But up to now, after the week and a half immersion of herself, she hadn't heard anything from any bluesman as powerful or evocative as "River of Pain." It still ranked, as Byron said, as the truly greatest song ever written. And she knew Maurice "Teardrop" Williams lived in Walker City, Iowa, and that he was still alive, fifty-five-years old, and that was all, the end of the Maurice "Teardrop" Williams's trail—something that had turned cold like tuna on ice.

And habitually with Ursula, the less she knew, the more she needed to know. Once her appetite was whetted, her curiosity pricked, it's when she was at her best, at her finest and most dangerous, became this supernova that could move both heaven and earth, if needed.

She walked over to the record player.

"Sorry, Memphis Slim, but I'm gonna have to stop you right there," Ursula said in her best blues dialect. For suddenly, Ursula had a phone call to make—and she knew who to. While listening to Memphis Slim's "Only Fools Have Fun," she was hearing *River of Pain* play out in her head, a CD she played every day.

"Dan, this is Ursula Jenkins. Fine … fine. How are you? Dan, I have an idea I want to pitch to you. One that might interest you. When? Tomorrow? At ten o'clock? That—yes, that'd be fine. Dan. W-wonderful."

CHAPTER 6

Dan Gottlieb's office looked like a chess board with chess pieces: orderly and pristine. It's like dust never got past his office door, the room healthy and germ free and Gottlieb successfully surviving yet another day.

Dan Gottlieb was as neat in dress, a Fifth Avenue tailor's dream. It was ten o'clock, and Dan Gottlieb and Ursula Jenkins were just beginning their tête-à-tête at *Currents* magazine. Gottlieb wasn't completely uptight about his attire though; some days he wore loafers, adding a "cool" look to his tasteful wardrobe.

"You look lovely, Ursula."

"Thanks, Dan."

And Ursula did look lovely in her sky-blue, simple, pitch-perfect dress. She wore little makeup. There, seemingly, being no need to—not with the native glow of her dark, smooth-colored skin and alluring to-kill-for eyes.

"Dan, thanks for the time. I appreciate it," Ursula said with sincerity.

"Anytime. Anytime for you, Ursula."

Dan Gottlieb was young like Ursula but in his early thirties, a bachelor living on the Upper West Side of Manhattan's island of young ambitious entrepreneurs who not only made money but minted it.

"I mean, the series you did for the magazine a while back produced a sensation around here. Magazine sales went through the roof."

Gottlieb was the editor-in-chief of *Currents* magazine, a family owned and operated magazine, one of many owned by the Gottlieb family. He was warm, sincere, bright, decisive, a real do-gooder (mensch) with a big heart—someone perennially upbeat and charismatic simply because of his rare intelligence and raw, snappy energy.

"And why you used the word 'pitch' over the phone yesterday, confounds me. If you're hot about something, an idea, then I know it's something great, out-of-this-world fantastic."

Ursula crossed her leg, looked down at her black nylons, and then up at Dan who was sitting at his desk, Ursula sitting at the side of it, frowning.

"Uh … yes, Ursula …"

"I don't know, Dan, this one might be hard—a tough sell. I might be throwing you a knuckleball, not a curve, with this one. So I'm not ruling it out."

"So what's that to mean?"

"Well …"

"Ursula, come on … out with it."

"I know you like, the magazine likes offbeat stories, Dan. Not your usual fare, ordinary run-of-the-mill stuff."

"Sure, of course. *Currents* magazine maintains that niche, prides itself for having established that kind of cutting-edge reputation in the print media." Pause.

"I'm enamored. Completely enamored. The blues," Ursula said breathlessly. "Have you ever heard the blues, Dan?"

Gottlieb laughed. "Lookit, I might be a Jewish boy from Woodmere, Long Island, Ursula, who goes to synagogue, uh, temple every Saturday and who listens to his cantor, but I have heard the blues once or twice in my lifetime, I might add, and find it downright enjoyable."

"So, uh, is there any blues player you can name? Off the top of your head?"

"Hmm … let me see." Dan swiveled in his high back leather chair. "That's a good, uh, darn good question, Ursula … Hmm … how about B. B. King? B. B. King. Yeah, Ursula, how about him?"

Ursula laughed. "Why'd I know you'd say that? B. B. King would be the first bluesman to come to mind?"

"He is a blues guy, isn't he, uh … ?"

"Of course. Yes, and it's what I would've said, probably a few weeks back too: B. B. King."

"Well, because he's popular. Is a commercial success. He's made a lot of hit records. His music's gotten lots of airplay. And has a following."

"His music became mainstream. Marketable. One of the rare, few blues players, B. B. King and John Lee Hooker, to enjoy such success."

"John Lee Hooker, now I've never heard of—"

"But I was introduced to a blues player," Ursula said, getting to the point of the meeting, "by the name of Maurice 'Teardrop' Williams. A good friend of mine told me about him."

"A … a catchy name. Can give the guy that much credit. So … ?"

"Yes, I know. My friend, his name's Byron, told me he'd heard the greatest song ever written or sung by any black artist dead or alive."

"Wow … then that *is* saying something."

"And to prove it, Dan, he bought a copy of Teardrop Williams's CD *River of Pain* for me to listen to."

Dan grinned. "Why that sounds provocative, all right. Very …"

"Teardrop Williams, Dan, has left the music business behind."

"Then he's still alive."

"Yes."

"Retired then?"

"At age fifty-two."

"Fifty-two?"

"In 1994. Maurice 'Teardrop' Williams—"

"Well … I guess a blues guy, musician can retire at the age of—"

"But why? Why did he retire? Return to Walker City, Iowa? For what reason?"

"But why is, should that be so compelling a question for anyone, uh, to ask? Since so many musicians re—"

"At the peak of their form, Dan. Their talent? At the top of their game?"

"And so, what, you want to know. Know why—"

"Someone as great as Teardrop Williams would want to drop out the music scene when his music's reached such an extraordinary evolution. High peak of artistry. Yes, Dan. I want to know why, and badly."

"But, Ursula, Ursula, here you are, someone who's black, sophisticated, erudite, and who loves, not just loves music, but knows the historical relevance of it, and if it wasn't for your friend, uh …"

"Byron."

"You wouldn't know who this Teardrop Williams person is either."

"But I did know, Dan."

"Okay. Okay, granted … then, then his music then. What it sounded like, then."

"Yes, yes, that's true. I only knew who he was. By name. That Teardrop Williams was a blues player, not his music."

"So why, tell me, Ursula, should anyone else, my readership care to know who he is? Since no one really knows him, the average Joe in the street, or his music. And I don't mean that in a mean or nasty, derogatory way. Just in an honest, perceptive way. Being as honest and straightforward as I can with you."

"It's why I brought this along with me." Ursula's hand was down inside her pocketbook.

"A compact disc? Ursula …" Dan laughed. "What, the convincer, huh?"

"Yes, Dan, *the convincer.*"

Ursula knew full well Dan Gottlieb had an office with electronic equipment—she'd seen it before, the sexy setup.

"Ursula, uh, really, let's not take this too far, okay? Uh, go overboard with this sort of thing, thing of yours. I—"

"Am—"

"I don't want to pooh-pooh this idea of yours, because already I can see you're passionate, fired up about it, but CD or no CD, I don't think this idea of yours will work. And I would want to back you 100 percent, if I were to give you the green light.

"For it to work. Y-you know that, Ursula. How I am with my writers. The total support and respect I lend them."

"Dan, do you want to put the disc in the machine, or would you like for me to do it for you?"

"A little cocky, huh?"

"No, Dan. Very cocky. You don't want to mess with this black sister this morning!"

"So I see. So I see," Dan said, coming to his feet, someone who was of average height and build. "Okay," Dan said, taking the CD from Ursula. "I'll do the honors since you insist—but under protest. Under strong, passionate protest," Dan laughed, shaking his fist in the air and then laughing more.

Ursula laughed. "It doesn't matter. But I promise you, It'll be an experience you soon won't forget, or regret."

"This *is* passion, Ursula."

"You'd better believe it is."

"Well … this'll be the first time I've listened to a blues song, what"— Dan looked at his Rolex—"at ten eight in the morning?"

"Honestly, I don't know of too many people who do, Dan. Black or Jewish."

"Thanks, Ursula. I do appreciate that."

"This will work, Ursula! This, this will work!"

"I'll make sure it does."

"Oh … oh, what an idea, concept this is. And it's my profit, my gain to be a part of this. T-to bear witness to it—and then, in some token way, bring it to life … to bear fruition." Dan Gottlieb's white skin was a beautiful picture of pink.

"It's more than 'token,' Dan. You are the vehicle, the source."

"But you'll be the engine."

"Look, look, Dan, we're already tossing these metaphors around at each other."

Dan was standing, not sitting. It was as if he couldn't sit.

"I was crying, Ursula. You saw me. I couldn't contain myself. Throughout the whole thing. I mean my cantor, my rabbi … it was just—"

"Every time I hear that song, Dan. Every time I hear it …"

"How often do you actually play it?"

"Every day. Every day since Byron gave it to me."

"Couldn't do that. Not a daily dose of it. It'd be too much for me to handle."

"It's like a magnet. The way I'm drawn to it. And don't ask me why, because I don't know why. I just don't."

"No, sometimes a person doesn't know why. They just have no earthly clue. But Maurice 'Teardrop' Williams has to come to the consciousness, attention of the world!"

"Dan, my … my goal is modest."

"Mine isn't. Not after that experience. Teardrop Williams, if we get him to interview with you, will be splashed right on the front of our magazine cover. Proudly, I might add. *Currents* magazine."

"Wow. That, now that would be exciting."

"He's like a hidden treasure. One of this country's, America's hidden treasures. Everyone should hear his music, know who he is. Everyone. And it's a shame, a crime if people don't get a chance to. A true injustice."

Ursula slipped the CD back into her pocketbook.

"I mean a Jewish kid like me, I probably would've never heard or ... or even been exposed to something like this. Not in my culture."

"Don't worry, there's plenty of Jewish music I have no idea exists."

"Pain, suffering—we can't dislodge it from the human psyche. The human experience. It's what binds all of us, Ursula, all races, cultures—whether we're willing to admit it or not."

"Dan, I'd like to get started on this project right—"

"And you'd better say 'right away.' Get cracking on it right away." Pause. Uh ... not unless you're on assignment with another—"

"Story? No, no, you can rule that out. Not on your life!"

"Then you're mine. All mine."

"This is something I've been looking for since my Ralph Ellison profile."

"And that was a gem, even though it was for another magazine—one I'd rather not mention. Give free advertising to. Not one bit. Ha."

"It's funny, Dan ..."

"What is ...?"

Ursula's beautiful black skin seemed to have what was a special aura. "When you least expect something—"

"It's when it happens. Drops in your lap like a ticking bomb. It's amazing sometimes, isn't it?"

"It truly is. Before and after Ralph Ellison, I had some wonderful articles to write, but ..."

"It's so great being writer—is that what you're saying, Ursula? To find stories and bring the human drama in them to life."

"Yes. To find the life within the life, break it down, analyze it, see how it works—the whole spectrum entails."

"Teardrop Williams could become something like a cult icon. Figure. Given the exposure, chance."

"But like I said before, Dan, my aims are modest."

"But this could be a match made in heaven—I mean with your writing talent and, and Teardrop Williams's music. Dignity, both of you have such dignity. True, true dignity and grit, Ursula."

"Hats off to Mom and Dad."

"By the way, how are they doing these days over in Jersey City?"

"Oh, fine."

"Tell them I said hello, would you?"

"Shall do."

"And so your budget for this assignment, project, is how you wish to set it. Just send in the expense sheet. As far as everything else goes, we'll work it out with Judy." Pause. "Free around this time tomorrow?"

"Ten o'clock? It'll be fine, just fine, Dan."

"Ten o'clock it is. Let me see … let me circle that on my calendar. Done deal. And how about Audrey, Audrey Teitlebaum, your editor on this one?"

"Fine. I really respect Audrey's work, her editorial style. We really work well together as a team."

Dan rubbed his hands together, and his smile could be plastered on a Forty-Second Street billboard. "This is exciting stuff, Ursula, don't you think? Maurice 'Teardrop' Williams, a cult hero. He won't know what hit him."

"The blues legend from Walker City, Iowa."

"Hey, I like that. Sounds great. Great copy."

Ursula was armed with more information than a Boy Scout. Soon she wanted enough information to stuff a bear with. But she had McKinley Scofield's name, Teardrop Williams's manager for some twenty-odd years and his telephone number (business number).

Ursula was back home from Dan Gottlieb's office, *Currents* magazine, on the phone, in the process of setting things in fast motion. She'd called Teardrop Williams's record company, Torch City Records, spoke to the head honcho, Mark Wainwright Jr., identified herself, and asked for Teardrop Williams's home phone but was told that was verboten under the noblest, best-intentioned circumstances but that she could contact Teardrop Williams's manager, McKinley Scofield—"Mac, who still handles all of Mr. Williams's professional affairs."

"Hello, may I speak to Mr. McKinley Scofield, please."

"Yes, ma'am, speaking. And whom may I ask is calling?"

"G-good afternoon, Mr. Scofield."

"Good afternoon," McKinley Scofield said in a long, syrupy drawl of a voice.

"Uh, yes, good afternoon, Mr. Scofield. Why, uh … my name's Ursula Jenkins."

"Why, sounds like the advantage is yours then, all yours, my dear, since you know where I hail from but I don't know your whereabouts."

Ursula laughed. She was amused by what Scofield said. "Uh, I suppose that it is to my advantage, Mr. Scofield. I'm sorry. Then let me start over.

My name's Ursula Jenkins, and I'm calling from New York City, to a Mr. McKinley Scofield, in Gains Port, Florida."

"Now we're on equal footing, Ms. Jenkins."

"Yes, yes we are, Mr. ... Mr. Scofield. By all means."

"I would say call me Mac since you sound so young, sweet, and tender—but this old man's been tricked before by such mistake and indiscretion."

Right off Ursula sensed McKinley Scofield was a real "card," that she was in for a long, bumpy ride with him no matter the seriousness of her pursuit.

"I'm twenty-five."

"I'm sixty-nine. So call me Mac."

"No, Mr. Scofield ha—I'd rather keep my distance, even if I'm calling long distance."

"Smart girl. Smart girl."

"Thank you."

"Now ... how may I help you, be of service to you, Ms. Ursula Jenkins?"

"It's Teardrop Williams. Mr. Williams."

"T-Teardrop? Teardrop Williams?"

"Yes—"

"Your inquiry to me is ... is about ... regarding Teardrop Williams?"

"Yes, I'm a writer, a journalist, Mr. Scofield. A-a freelance writer."

"And what's your desire, your intention, Ms. Jenkins?"

"To, I'd like to write, uh, do an article on Mr. Williams for a New York–based magazine, *Currents* mag—"

"And in so doing, you'd like to interview him. Mr. Williams? Is that it?"

"Yes, by all means. Pre-precisely, Mr. Scofield. Pre—"

"What would be necessary, imperative to write this magazine article of yours."

"Yes."

"And so don't you—of course you don't know. Teardrop Williams does not, I repeat, Ms. Jenkins, does not grant personal interviews."

"No, I didn't know that, Mr. Scofield."

"Not to anyone."

"I—"

"Anyone."

"I—"

"Mr. Williams is off-limits. Out of the music business he retired from in—"

"Nineteen ninety-four."

"You know then …"

"Yes, I know, Mr. Scofield. B-but I heard 'River of Pain' and—"

"Indeed, indeed. The greatest blues song written by any bluesman living or dead. Possibly the greatest song ever written, period. It's remarkable what it does to people when they hear it. Emotionally. Strikingly remarkable."

"Yes."

"I suppose you aren't a blues connoisseur, Ms. Jenkins. Knew nothing of Teardrop Williams at the—"

"Not until I heard 'River of Pain.'"

"Yes, it's converted many a wayward sheep. Ha. Soul." Pause. "We were lucky that day—it's all I can say. Two months before Mr. Williams retired, the band went into the studio to record. It's when Teardrop surprised us with 'River of Pain.' Out of nowhere. When we first heard it, all we could feel at the time was grateful, blessed. Praise our good fortune."

"I'm sure, Mr. Scofield, that you must have. That—"

"And it's still selling, you know. Making m—"

"Uh … yes, I—"

"Well … I know you're calling from New York, Ms. Jenkins, long distance, and it has been a pleasure talking, to talk—"

"But … but, Mr. Scofield …"

"But, Ms. Jenkins, I believe our conversation regarding Teardrop Williams has been honorably terminated, my dear young lady. So the word is 'no'—I made no bones about it. Mr. Williams wishes to protect his privacy now that his music career is over. He's retired from it.

"I'd like to say, go on record as saying, Mr. Williams is happy as a lark with his new life."

Ursula looked into the light slicing through her bedroom window. "But how can he be, Mr. Scofield?"

"Ms. Jenkins … now you're showing a reporter's true colors. Attempting to interpret something you know absolutely nothing about. As I said, this is a private matter. So no more will be discussed, pursuant its regard. It will not be opened like a Pandora's box."

"I-is it, Mr. Scofield?"

"This conversation's over, Ms. Jenkins. And I will bid you a good day, something customary for Gains Port, Florida, since I don't know the local habit in New York. I do hope you will bid me the same courtesy."

"Well …"

"I …"

"Well …"

"Yes, good day, Mr. Scofield. G—"

"Good day, Ms. Jenkins."

And that was that as Ursula heard the loudest click she'd heard from a telephone's receiver in her ear in her life. Ursula's hands shot up to her face as if her lungs had emitted a sudden shriek to the skies. There was a cold, numbing shock in her. Slowly, she put the phone down in its cradle and then was hit by a sudden revelation.

"This does mean a lot to me, doesn't it? I didn't know it did, not until now. I am gravitated to this whole thing as if, as If I'm being pulled to it by something or someone. It never—this has never happened to me before regarding a story. Never as strong or persistent as this."

Ursula fell back on the bed. She was in the same attire she had been this morning at *Currents* magazine, her visit with Dan Gottlieb. She looked up at the overhead ceiling, and the more she lay on her back, the madder, more angry, she became. She was fuming, venting.

"The harder the problem, the harder you hit. That's the way I've trained myself. It's always been my philosophy. And I'm not changing now. Backing down now. Not for anyone! McKinley Scofield, Maurice 'Teardrop' Williams—no one!"

Ursula sprang off her back. Within seconds, she was back on the phone.

"Mr. Scofield, this is—"

"Ms. Jenkins? Ms. Jenkins! I spoke to you before, Ms. Jenkins!"

"I will not give up on this, Mr. Scofield. I will not."

"You won't, will you? So tell me, Ms. Jenkins, what's in it for you?"

"I heard the genius of Teardrop Williams. I heard it on one recording, and it should not die, Mr. Scofield. Not a genius like that."

And then there was this crackling silence between Ursula and McKinley Scofield that could, seemingly, catch on fire with a single whiff of wind.

"And you say you're twenty-five?"

"Yes, twenty-five."

"And are so full of wisdom, astuteness. Are so refreshingly endowed with it."

Ursula did not reply.

"I'll call him, that's what I'll do, Ms. Jenkins. Call Teardrop."

"Thank you, Mr. Scofield."

"I see you are a special young lady. You must be a heckuva good writer. Now, uh, your phone number up there in New York City ..."

It seemed Ursula had been on top her bed by the phone waiting for Mr. Scofield's call for an eternity, but it was only ten minutes. This story, the Teardrop Williams story, did mean a lot to her. Suddenly she was feeling obsessed by it, that in just two weeks' time, by some strange circumstance, had taken over her life. And now looking at the phone, she felt the possible pain of rejection once again loom, coming from McKinley Scofield. But it didn't matter, she thought—she'd found a direct path to Teardrop Williams.

The phone rang. Ursula jumped (literally). It rang again. She picked it up.

"No, Ms. Jenkins. No. The answer is no. Mr. Williams said no."

"No?" Ursula said, her chest burning like a torch.

"I told him the situation, how this whole idea of interviewing him for an article, writing about him came about."

"No ..."

"Mr. Williams' life is a simple life. A complete life. No hotel rooms. Life out on the road. He has a daughter Arlene. And grandson Jamal."

"He, Mr. Williams has a daughter and a grandson?"

"Yes, it's all he needs, apparently. After all, it has been three years, Ms. Jenkins, and this kind of life has grown on him. He is as comfortable—"

"But don't you feel that music's been robbed of—"

"His genius? Yes. I was shocked by his decision to leave the music business when he did, how he did, my dear. As well as Shorty Boy Logan and Twelve Fingers Eakins. They were shocked too by the turn of events.

"But it has been three years, my dear, and we're all getting along just fine with our lives. The condition of our lives. I must admit."

"And it is a shut and closed case then, Mr. Scofield? That's it? A shut and—"

"As I said, Ms. Jenkins," Scofield said edgily, "what do you know about any of this?"

"I meant no disrespect to you nor—"

"What do you want me to have, Ms. Jenkins? Guilt feelings? I wasn't the one who woke up one day and, and ... Ms. Jenkins, I do admire your grit, tenacity, but Mr. Williams has advised me to tell you no. And it's what I've done. And so—"

"It's no then?" Ursula said challengingly.

"Look, young lady, you've taken up a great deal of my time and patience today. And—"

"Would you call Mr. Williams back and tell him I love his music, Mr. Scofield. Could you do that? That I love his music like so many of his fans do. It's all we'd like for him to know from the bottom of our hearts, Mr. Scofield."

Three days later.

"Thank you, Byron. I owe you a lot."

"Uh … yeah … uh …"

"Man, Ursula, you've got the dude turning red," J. C. said.

"Might as well have my face match my socks!"

"Red!"

Ursula, Byron, and J. C. were back at the Renaissance Bar. It was Ursula's treat—to include J. C. There were two bottles of Heineken for Byron, one glass of scotch and soda for J. C., and a bottle of Diet Coke for Ursula. They had barbecued ribs (with the sweetest of sauce), fries, and corn on the cob for dinner; so they were well fortified for the evening.

"So you're in the sky?"

"Saturday, Byron."

Byron took a swig of beer. "Walker City, Iowa. Seems a long way away from New York City."

"Out there with them 'Hawkeyes'—that's what they call them, isn't it?"

"I don't know, J. C.," Byron said. "Just hope you bought you a cowboy hat and a pair of boots, Ursula. Pard-ner. And a six-shooter to shoot a few stray possums out on the dusty trail."

By now J. C. had heard *River of Pain.*

"Thank you, Byron," Ursula said, grabbing Byron's hand, "for making this project possible."

"Wow, Ursula, your hand's warm. Hot as hell!"

"Hey, let me feel it, let me see for myself if …" J. C. took hold of Ursula's hand. "W-what's going on with you, Ursula? What's the—"

"I … I don't know," Ursula said in a stifled voice. "When … when Mr. Scofield told me yes, Mr. Williams had granted the interview, I guess I've yet to recover completely."

"You're a hot sister, I'll tell you that though!" J. C. said.

"I know it's not going to shake the music industry up, Ursula, but you really are doing something of real value—merit."

"Second, I second that, Byron," J. C. said.

"Mr. Scofield was excited by it too."

"Did you show him your, that stubborn streak of yours. The stubborn side of your personality. Never say die. The whole nine yards. Willing to fight to the bitter end."

"What do you think, Byron?"

"You roll over like a dog? Did Scofield give you a read on Mr. Williams's feelings?"

"No."

"Wonder what kind of dude he is, away from his music, I mean."

"Warm. Loving," Ursula said quickly.

"Hey, I know you're talking about his music, but the music doesn't always reflect the man behind it. Translate to that. The man and the artist could be as opposite as night and day," J. C. said.

"Could be, J. C. But Teardrop Williams lives with his daughter and grandson. So, uh …"

"In a loving setting," Byron said. "Surrounded by love. I … I suppose, all the time."

"Probably takes the kid fishing twice a day in those Iowa creeks. Country life. Dip your big toe in the water. Catch you a couple of porgies ha, then call it a day," J. C. joked. "A good country boy having a good ol' country day in Walker City, Iowa. "

"Down by the ol' creek, the water-hole with a fishing pole, huh, J. C., and a jug of home-brewed lemonade?"

"All the fish you can fry. Then eat. Free. Hee-haw!"

"I'll remind myself to tell the natives, the locals of how you two feel about them when I—"

"Us northerners."

"Get there." Ursula chuckled.

"I guess you've got the laundry list, your list of questions?" Byron asked. "That you're going to body slam the poor guy with?"

"Do I ever!"

"Sounds like you're loaded for bear," J. C. said over the din of music in the Renaissance.

"Batteries in the old tape recorder?"

"I really don't need one—"

"What? You've got—"

"Total recall, J. C."

"Shit, what, you, you remember all our conversations? Every single one? The ones when Byron and I—"

"Yes, every one of them, J. C. They're all sitting snugly in my memory bank."

"Sitting snugly in your—"

J. C. shuddered like he'd just caught a cold. "Girl, now, Ursula, now don't start nothing. Don't try blackmailing me, shit. 'Cause you ain't getting no money. Maybe Byron, but not me. Byron's the one making the big loot. Living large. Is a stockbroker. I'm just a poor guy trying to pass the New York State bar exam, man. Before they catch on to my black ass. My—"

"So tell me, Ursula, why do you carry a tape recorder then when you don't need it? How come, sweetie?"

"Oh … because it makes the person—"

"The interviewee—"

"Yes, J. C., the interviewee—"

"Like saying that."

"Feel more at ease, relaxed, when they see the tape recorder. For they won't feel they'll be misquoted by the interviewer. Uh, anything like that."

"Can't blame them," Byron said.

"Not at all," Ursula said.

"This whole situation, thing, Ursula, somehow feels like fate at work, doesn't it? Really. Byron buying the CD, you going ape, flipping over it. The story idea. Running the idea by Gottlieb at *Currents*, getting some serious flak initially, then the dude lightening up, seeing the light, calling Scofield the same day, no from him, then no from Teardrop Williams, then the *big* yes—the one to clinch the deal, whole deal, deal maker for you."

"J. C., are you sure you're not after my job? Seriously?"

"Yeah, J. C., great job, man. You just passed the New York bar exam in my book."

Ursula looked away from both Byron and J. C. and, after thinking for those four or five frozen seconds, said. "Don't think I haven't given it considerable thought—how all of this came about. How lucky I feel. How fate must've had some hand in it. Lucky ... indeed I'm lucky."

"So, sa-lute!" Byron said, hoisting his bottle of Heineken high in the air in the Renaissance.

Then Ursula hoisted the bottle of Diet Coke and J. C. his glass of scotch and soda. And together they said, "*Sa-lute!*"

Two days later.

This was nervous time. Panic time. Even though it was only to be for three days— Saturday, Sunday, and Monday—in Walker City, Iowa, this was panic time for Ursula (straight out of a scene from a Woody Allen movie. The movie? Take your pick.).

But for Ursula, it was clothes, always wearing the right clothes for her interview. In one-on-one situations, what you wore always said a lot about you. Mostly Ursula wore dark-colored clothes—black, dark blues, and browns, anything to be the one to blend into the backdrop, take the club out her hand. Never did she want her interview subject to feel dominated, put upon, intimidated. She'd take the backseat, the secondary role—always focus the spotlight on the subject/interview, make sure that they felt in full control, were the interview's centerpiece (of which, no doubt, they were).

Her voice usually gave her enough authority, heft: strong, confident, passionate, interested. This was not only Ursula's interview technique, style, but Ursula's personality. She never went far afield of who she, as a person, basically was. She gave what she hoped to receive back: a clear, linear projection of meaning and substance, the full flesh and bones of it and its effect, consequence. And she never went for the jugular.

Ursula entered the interview with this hope. It's why she was this nervous. She knew great artists, actors, writers, musicians, dancers reveal themselves as clear as crystal, put themselves up against the mirror of life, and reflect it back in all of its strangeness, power, darkness, light, stripping it down, dismantling it to some place where the heart and soul are—humanity having a chance, voice during the process. But by listening to Teardrop Williams's CD *River of Pain* for so long, this daily ritual consuming her like some wildfire, her thoughts, a simpatico was now strong inside her. She could feel Teardrop Williams's privacy, this privacy issue in him—as if his music were squarely enough.

Last night she imagined how the interview would go, this middle-aged man, handsome beyond belief, any spoken or written words. She knew, intellectually, that he was a gentleman, this Maurice "Teardrop" Williams. That he was loyal to people and they, in turn, loyal to him. Mr. McKinley Scofield had been his manager for over twenty years, and in the music business, cutthroat, ruthless, shifty, profane, perverse as it is, Ursula knew that, in and of itself, was self-revealing. How now living with his daughter Arlene and grandson Jamal, it was family at the center of Teardrop Williams's life. He was sitting down in something like a warm tub of water he obviously liked.

And now Ursula's nervousness grew more profound—the clothes, what to pack for the trip to Walker City, Iowa—but more because she was about to invade this world of Teardrop Williams, fly into it with a tape recorder that would tape everything he would say or not say. Who would bring that other world back to him, to remind him of what he was to the world, how he once felt about it, why *River of Pain* had touched her soul and Byron's soul and J. C.'s soul and Dan Gottlieb's soul and so many more fans of his along the way who thought of Teardrop Williams as more of a blues hero than a blues recluse in Walker City, Iowa, doing whatever he was doing to steer clear of his genius, hanging it on a back fence like a dirtied shirt waiting for the wind, the air to clean it or freshen it, but knowing it was not to be worn again, handed back to the world as something special, a prize to see—not against Teardrop Williams's skin, it wasn't.

CHAPTER 7

Saturday. The next day.

Ursula decided to wear a wheat-and-black three-button jewel-neck tweed jacket with a knee-length skirt. She'd gotten into Walker City, Iowa, an hour ago. Her itinerary included Ms. Ruby Ingram's boarding house, where she was to stay for two nights. It wasn't Walker City proper but on the outskirts, only a few miles from where Teardrop Williams lived, making it quite convenient and comfortable for her.

It was 11:46 a.m. Ursula's interview was for two o'clock, so she had plenty of time to kill. Ruby Ingram was an elderly woman, one Ursula found pleasant and accommodating in her five-room boarding house just off a dirt road, Marble Place, with a clean, fresh-smelling area of woods and grass ringing it as was the case for most Walker City residents.

The Midwest region of the country was nothing new to her; she'd traveled this route before—Kansas, Iowa—so the Midwest offered her few new surprises. Of course it was a far cry from New York, but what wasn't? But on the plane ride in, she thought much of Iowa, that it was dubbed the "middle state," bordered by North Dakota, Nebraska, Wisconsin, Illinois. That Iowa, historically, got its state name from the American tribe the Ioway and that the bones of their history were buried in Iowa's rich, prosperous soil that produced so much foodstuff for the nation's food supply.

She was in her room (one room, to be exact). There was a bathroom with a bathtub and a toilet, but a common kitchen was set up for boarders to eat their meals. Ursula took a quick glance at her first set of questions, all memorized, tightly strung in her mind. But she would discard the question if the subject/interview opened up better areas of thought and inquiry—tastier meat to chew. She showed her flexibility like any good interviewer who was agile-minded, nimble, who relished the unexpected, earnestly appreciated spontaneity.

And she had to give Teardrop Williams his due. She had to get to the heart and soul of the man as if mandated by her own heart and soul, her own spirit, to do so. She had not, for a second, taken her mind off her responsibility; and it felt huge in her stomach—not like butterflies, but more like bats, something as rancid for her indigestion.

Ursula, then, pulled Teardrop Williams's CD out her pocketbook and looked at it. "If he's more handsome than this in person, I'll just die!"

It was 1:45 p.m. The taxi was called for, and now it was told to go to Ms. Arlene Wilkerson's place at 12 Randolph Road. Ms. Ruby Ingram had said before Ursula had left the boarding house, "We all love Teardrop Williams in Walker City, Ms. Jenkins." And this helped produce another sharp shiver in her spine.

And now the taxi stopped, and Ursula saw it was the house, felt it, and that Maurice "Teardrop" Williams was inside, somewhere waiting for her. And so Ursula felt this connection so strange and true and accurate that her body actually shook. And then for that brief second, before she paid the taxicab driver, she wondered how Teardrop Williams felt about all of this.

Out the taxi, Ursula took in a deep breath, and then another, and then felt her confidence return—that she could do what she'd set out to Walker City for, this idea she'd concocted.

Ursula was on the house's front porch. Her finger pressed the doorbell. When the door, with little delay, began to open, Ursula wished, suddenly, she was on the first flight back to New York City.

"Ms. Jenkins?"

"Y-yes, Ursula Jenkins."

"Please, would you please come in, Ms. Jenkins. I'm Arlene Wilkerson. I'm Teardrop Williams's daughter."

"T-thank you."

Arlene's hand was extended to Ursula. They shook hands.

"It's quite a long trip from New York to Walker City, Iowa, Ms. Jenkins."

"Yes, it is."

"The plane ride alone."

Ursula, when she stepped into the house, thought the Williams/Wilkerson home was as attractive as was Arlene Wilkerson, how the furniture was arranged and its fine quality.

"And then the car ride from the airport."

"Yes."

Ursula entered the living room along with Arlene as Arlene led her.

"I'm Jamal Wilkerson."

Ursula's head turned, for Jamal was to the back of her.

"I'm Teardrop Williams's grandson, ma'am," Jamal said with tremendous pride.

"I'm Ursula Jenkins." Ursula and Jamal shook hands. Jamal's eyes were shiny bright while looking at Ursula.

Ursula didn't know Jamal's age, but he certainly was tall and gangly and cute-looking, to say the least, she thought.

"But it was a pleasant flight down, I hope, Ms. Jenkins?" Arlene said.

"Yes, very."

Both Arlene and Ursula were seated on a floral three-cushioned couch as Jamal continued to stand and observe attentively. He was wearing his PRO-Keds, blue jeans, and a striped T-shirt (of course).

"New York, right, Ms. Jenkins, ma'am?"

"Yes."

"Wow!"

"Jamal, honey … it's all right," Arlene laughed. "Jamal's at that age … age you see."

"Oh, yes …" Ursula giggled.

"What age, Mom?"

"You'll know, Jamal, one day when your children are your age."

"Gee … Mom."

"Are you thirsty, Ms. Jenkins?"

"No, no, not at the moment, for now, Mrs. Wilkerson."

"W-what do they do in New York, Ms. Jenkins?" Jamal asked, blurting it out.

"Oh …"

"It is just about one o'clock," Arlene said, glancing at her watch. "I'll get Dad, my father for you, Ms. Jenkins. He's off in the back."

"T-thank you." For Ursula'd been wondering all this time just where Maurice "Teardrop" Williams was, why his daughter met her at the front door and not him.

"I'll be right back."

Ursula smiled. Arlene left the living room.

"You are … are very pretty, Ms. Jenkins. C-certainly are pretty, Ms., uh, Ms. Jenkins. Ma'am."

Perfectly taken aback by Jamal's sincere remark, Ursula openly blushed. "W-why thank you, Jamal. For the compliment."

"Very, very pretty, ma'am." Pause. "But, uh, now … now back to what was my original question," Jamal said. "What do they do in New York, Ms. Jenkins. Uh, up there, uh, ma'am?"

Ursula thought she was being drilled by a younger version of Ursula Jenkins. Her male counterpart living in Walker City, Iowa.

"Why, what they do in Walker City, Iowa, Jamal?"

"It's not what I've heard, with all due respect, Ms. Jenkins, ma'am."

Ursula wanted to laugh out loud but didn't but would try to outduel this young duelist. "No?"

"No, ma'am."

Ursula looked at this cute-looking (soon to be handsome-looking) young inquisitor and knew she wasn't going to be able to square dance around him no matter his age; his heels were dug in, what seemed, solidly into Walker City soil.

"Well … to, uh, answer your question, honestly, sincerely, Jamal …"

Arlene was out on the back porch. She wasn't for this. She was opposed to it, her father's interview with this New York City writer, Ursula Jenkins. Why did this woman think it necessary to fly all the way across country, out here, to meddle in her father's life?

"Tell me why. I had to be gracious toward her. Civil."

When her father told her McKinley Scofield had passed this information on to him, it'd angered her. Knowing that Scofield had been pressed by this woman angered her more. She was angry at Scofield for not presenting a stronger front, argument for the Williams family, and at Ursula Jenkins for being so *damned* persistent about the interview in making it possible.

"Why didn't she just stay in New York City, where she belongs?"

The past three years of her father's retirement from the music world had been ideal. She and Jamal had taken care of him, given him a beautiful life. What they had was special. Each, daily, had their own special routines, of how their days were filled.

It was two minutes to one, and it's when Teardrop emerged from the woods in back of the house as Arlene knew he would, since he said he'd be on time for his interview with Ms. Jenkins.

"Dad," Arlene yelled from the back porch, "Ms. Jenkins is here."

"She's here, Arlene?"

"Yes."

"Good, good," Teardrop anxiously replied from a good distance away.

Teardrop was carrying Miss Lillian, not playing her—having done enough of that inside the thick-set woods. He looked healthy, his loose-jointed stride and long legs gobbling up plenty of ground. He was in tan slacks and a brown zippered Windbreaker with a white open-collared shirt and brown rugged leather boots he enjoyed wearing. He really looked relaxed, almost, it seemed, to the point of masked boredom.

Teardrop was maybe twenty yards from Arlene. "So what's Miss Lillian up to today, Dad? Has to say?"

"A lot. Her usual talkative, garrulous self."

"Well ..."

"What's she look like, Arlene? All ... all night I was wondering to myself, honey."

"A-attractive, Dad. Very attractive. Ms. Jenkins is—"

"Tall? Short?"

"Tall. Q-quite tall for a woman."

"Young. She's twenty-five, it's what Mac mentioned to me over the phone."

"Yes, Mr. Scofield," Arlene said, trying to hide her disdain, hoping she had.

"Arlene, would you have Ms. Jenkins come out here. To the backyard, I'd, would ... would you do that for me, honey?"

"Of course, Dad. Of—but, Dad, you are—"

"I'm fine, Arlene. This attention. Am ... am looking forward to it, the interview with Ms. Jenkins, in fact."

Arlene went to get Ursula.

Teardrop looked up at the house and then down to the ground. And now he wished he hadn't agreed to this thing he'd consented to with McKinley Scofield. This young lady from New York City flying out to interview him about what? *Who am I?* Teardrop thought. *River of Pain, so what, so what—that was so long ago, so tucked away in the past for me, remote. It's not who I am now, today.* Those things are never who you are now—it's what you were then. At the time. Not definitive but, rather, relative. Standing on that cliff about to be pushed off, hoping it will kill the pain or shatter it into so many pieces. It could be used by a thousand different people so it could be carried in them, their souls, so that it could free his.

"Mine. Mine. How selfish of me. Alarming."

Last night he wondered so much about Ursula Jenkins. The night was long. It seemed practically sleepless for him, impenetrable. He couldn't make heads or tails of it. He wondered what Ms. Jenkins looked like. Yes, he wondered how tall Ms. Jenkins was, yes; but what he wondered most was why she was after his soul, for as sure as there was a God, and he knew there was, he knew Ursula Jenkins would be after his soul, the one piece of himself he wanted to hold on to more than anything else of value he had.

"Just settle down now, Teardrop. This can't be as bad as you're making it out. I won't let it."

And yet here he was, ready to do this—and why now in his life when he had Arlene and Jamal and friends, people who gave him what he needed … so much support and love. *What can my life say to anybody? Do for anybody? Ursula Jenkins,* Currents *magazine interested in me?*

Why me, Maureen?

The house's back door opened, Teardrop looked up, and the first gleam from the sun caught the cornea of Ursula's right eye.

"This is Ms. Jenkins, Dad. Ursula Jenkins."

"Hello, Mr. Williams."

"Hello, Ms. Jenkins."

"Dad …"

"Yes, honey. Yes, honey, I'll see you later."

The door closed. Ursula and Teardrop had not stopped looking intensely at each other.

There was a wooden table and wooden benches on the back deck. An umbrella stuck out the wide table. It was a very relaxed, inviting setting to say the least. This tall structure standing on four solid stilt legs to be exact, dug far down into the ground.

"Uh, Ms. Jenkins, if you don't mind, would you come, come down here. This would be fine. Just fine for us, I would think, to conduct the interview."

Teardrop was standing in this broad area where there was another wooden outdoor table with an umbrella and chairs, another perfect setting.

The five white Adirondack chairs with corn-yellow seat cushions mixed in with the natural setting with spectacular results.

"Gladly, Mr. Williams. Coming right down."

Teardrop smiled and then walked to the bottom of the wooden stairs, taking Ursula's hand in helping her down the two remaining steps.

"Thank you, Mr. Williams."

Teardrop chuckled. "You're quite welcome, Ms. Jenkins."

"Just follow me."

"Yes. Shall do, Mr. Williams."

Then they walked over to the table, and Teardrop assisted Ursula once again as he pulled the white wood-planked chair out for her. She sat. Then Teardrop followed suit.

"Arlene, my daughter, offered you something to drink?"

"Yes, she did, but I'm not thirsty, at least not for now."

"But later, I'm sure. I prepared a nice punch for us."

"Oh, you did, Mr. Williams?" Ursula replied, surprised.

"Just don't ask me what's in it. It's my secret recipe."

"Oh … why it's safe with me."

"You're sure?"

"Yes, quite, Mr. Williams." Ursula wanted to wink but thought better.

There was a pause, and Ursula used it as an opportunity to look at this handsome man, she thought, with the sexy mole just below his right cheekbone—this Maurice "Teardrop" Williams who looked more handsome in person than on his CD cover. Maybe it was his personality, she thought. The smile that sat like a sunset on both cheeks and seemed it could resist change.

Teardrop was still smiling. "I know my throat'll be parched later, Ms. Jenkins. I must admit, must admit I am nervous about this, all of this … this interview with you today."

Ursula leaned forward. "Oh … thank you, thank you so much for sharing that with me, Mr. Williams. Your feelings."

"I've been interviewed before but not so extensively. It is to be three days, isn't it?"

"Y-yes, it is, Mr. Williams. Three days."

Teardrop laughed, wondering, *What can I possibly say in three days that could be of interest to anyone? That could hold a reporter's attention? Fill up a reporter's tape recorder?*

"So that's Miss Lillian!"

"Yes, Miss Lillian, Ms. Jenkins. Fully exposed. Out her case. Without any makeup on or shoes to wear. Or jewelry, for that matter."

Teardrop sat Miss Lillian upright in the chair beside him.

"She's so beautiful."

"If you were to ask her for her opinion of herself, she'd say elegant. Nothing short of elegant. Conceit runs in Miss Lillian's family."

"Oh it does?"

"It's in her family genes. DNA."

Ursula laughed with delight.

"Did you meet Jamal, my grandson?" Teardrop said, extending his long legs.

"Indeed, I did, Mr. Williams."

"I hope—"

"Yes, I was thoroughly drilled."

"A lawyer or who knows, maybe a writer, a writer like you, in his future."

"It was what I was thinking, Mr. Williams. It's not out of the realm of possibility." Pause.

"You are a good writer, aren't you, Ms. Jenkins?"

"Yes, I am, Mr. Williams. An excellent writer."

"And why's that?"

"Because I believe in what I'm writing about. My subject."

"Hmm ... do you? Belief goes a long way, doesn't it? A belief in something."

"A long way, Mr. Williams."

"Then shall we begin the interview? Suddenly I'm eager—and know you're loaded with questions for me."

"Y-yes, I am."

"And a tape recorder?"

"Got it!" Ursula said, reaching down inside her pocketbook, pulling the tape recorder out and putting it atop the table.

"Fresh batteries?"

"Fresh batteries. Bought them yesterday."

"Where? In New York, Ms. Jenkins?"

"Jamaica, Queens."

"I guess they keep things freshly stocked on the shelves in Jamaica, Queens."

"At least where I shop, they do."

"The advantage of a big city, Ms. Jenkins: choices."

"Where I live, there certainly are enough."

"Needless to say, but Walker City does have its advantages."

Ursula nodded her head.

"Even though sometimes I wonder if we're exaggerating our status, our importance by calling ourselves a city, if you know what I mean, am getting at."

All Ursula could do was laugh loudly and broadly.

Arlene was back in the house. Jamal said he was going up the road to play with his best friend, Armon Brewer. Arlene had gotten to the study. She knew she shouldn't be doing this but was just the same. She'd taken the chair by the desk and put it at the window. There were white lace curtains in the window for her to peek through, down onto the backyard. The chair was square with the window. Arlene sat.

This is my right. I've earned this right. I'm afraid for Dad. This woman, Ursula Jenkins, does not belong here, in Walker City, interviewing him. I don't like any of this. Not any of it.

It was two and a half hours later.

"Is the tape recorder tired of listening to me yet, do you think, Ms. Jenkins? My stories?"

"No, Mr. Williams, it's still humming along."

"Those machines—if they could talk!"

"Some do, actually do."

Teardrop smiled more generously. "I know. Don't I. My grandson's told me all about them."

Then Ursula settled back in her chair, expecting more conversation from Teardrop, only, Teardrop clasped his large hands together, and his eyes looked like lazy clouds on a summer day. It's when Ursula took the initiative, or the tiger by its tail.

"Mr. Williams, it's important I interview someone other than you for the article."

"Who? Someone like my grandson, Jamal?"

"Yes, yes, ha. I'm sure he would have a lot to say—add to the article."

"A lot. Uh, to make it more rounded—it's what you're saying, Ms. Jenkins?"

"That and ..."

"What?"

"But who I really mean are people like Mr. McKinley Scofield."

"Mac."

"Yes, and Shorty Boy Logan and Twelve Fingers—"

"Eakins."

"Yes."

"They're all good friends, Ms. Jenkins. Associates. People I deeply trust and respect."

"So then you approve my potential access to them?"

"Yes," Teardrop said, adding nothing more.

"It's important to know."

"Yes, it is."

Teardrop looked down at his boots, and then at Ursula. "And there will be no lying or fudging—not from any of them. They're all straight shooters. After all, we were all in the music business together. Were after the same things. Built our lives around the same dreams ... ambitions. Threw ourselves at the same possibilities with the same caution and, at times, the same reckless abandon.

"They'll have a lot to say. I'm sure, Ms. Jenkins. Knowing them. Of tremendous value to the article. So of course you have my personal approval."

Teardrop, momentarily, again, looked away from Ursula; and it's when Ursula stole another peek at him, private, unguarded—the kind to make you shimmer, as had Ursula.

"Ms. Jenkins, I know you must be hungry. I know I am. This has given me an appetite. A hardy one, I might add."

Then Ursula became conscious of just how she was looking at Teardrop Williams. "Uh ... yes, yes, I am."

"Then you'll stay for dinner? Eat, have dinner with Arlene, Jamal, and me?"

"No, Mr. Williams, I ..."

"Now come on, Ms. Jenkins, go back to Ruby Ingram's place? Have your dinner there?"

"Yes. All ... all right, Mr. Williams. Yes. I-I'd be glad to. Happy to. Thank you."

"You certainly won't regret it. Be disappointed. Both Arlene and I can cook up a storm. We're teaching Jamal, but I'm sure you know what a chore that is."

"I can well imagine, Mr. Williams."

"Only, it's even worse than you might imagine. But I remember when I was a boy, when my parents ..." Teardrop's eyes suddenly became teary eyed. "Oh ... uh ... well ..."

"They're deceased, Mr. Williams, both your parents?"

"Yes, both ... both, Ms. Jenkins. Mom, then Dad. Not unlike ..."

And there Teardrop stopped, and Ursula looked at him and told herself she wouldn't pursue, pry, go after this target; as an interviewer, she could so clearly see. *But tomorrow I will,* Ursula thought. *Tomorrow. Not now. I'll find a way to get at it, crack it open. But not now, today. I'll just make a mental note of it so not to forget.*

Teardrop seemed clearly upset but momentarily recovered.

"No questions while we eat though, at the table, okay? They're the only ground rules I'll issue."

"Just observation."

"Observation?"

"Between bites of food."

"Why of course observation. Plenty of that. Be my guest." Teardrop looked around the vast yard. "We'll eat out here, if you don't mind. It's something, as a family, we most enjoy doing whenever we can." Long pause.

"The bugs certainly seem to enjoy it. Our company, that is, Ms. Jenkins."

"Not—"

"Yes, you heard me correctly, Ms. Jenkins. Bugs. Hungry ones at that."

"The taxi will be here any minute. Bert's in the area, Ms. Jenkins. And when Bert's in the area—but my daughter, uh ... Arlene can drive you—"

"No, it's all right. Mrs. Wilkerson's busy enough from what I observed today."

They were in the living room. Ursula looked to her left, into the house's vestibule, at a grandfather's clock with an antique umbrella stand of artistic interest to its right.

"An heirloom passed down to me by my father. I thought Arlene might like it. Arlene likes antiques. Besides economics, she's a history buff. But then again, economics is history, in my opinion, Ms. Jenkins: the economic trends of the time that directly reflect history is history."

"Your daughter's very bright. It just shines through her."

"I agree," Teardrop said.

A car honked.

"Well, there's Bert, Ms. Jenkins. Has gotten here in what feels like record time."

Ursula got up from the couch. Then without warning, Jamal dashed into the living room.

"Jamal, where'd you just—"

"That's for you, Ms. Jenkins?"

"Yes, I'm afraid so."

"Darnit!"

Ursula laughed.

"You didn't expect Ms. Jenkins to spend the night, did you, Jamal?"

Jamal stood in front of Ursula. "I wouldn't've minded, Granddad. Uh, n-not at all!"

"Well, at least my grandson's honest, Ms. Jenkins. You can say that much for him."

"Thank you for the compliment, Jamal," Ursula said extending her right hand to him.

"You can learn a lot from a magazine writer, a lot," Jamal said.

Ursula and Teardrop practically giggled aloud.

"You can, Granddad. I know you can."

"So tomorrow, Ms. Jenkins? Same time? Same place?"

Ursula agreed.

"Mustn't keep Bert any longer than necessary. He's not a New York cab driver, I know, but he still has a meter in his cab that clicks upon response and a family to feed."

Teardrop and Jamal were seeing Ursula to the front door.

"Ms. Jenkins will be right there, Bert." Teardrop looked down at Jamal. "Your mother, let me call her, I'm sure she'd like to—"

"Mom's in the bathroom, Granddad. I heard the shower running. A few minutes ago."

"A ... a shower this early, Jamal? That's unlike your—"

"It's all right, Mr. Williams. Would you say good night to Mrs. Wilkerson for me. And thank her for everything. The dinner. E-especially the dinner. I'm sure I'll see Mrs. Wilkerson tomorrow. And I don't want to hold Mr.—"

"Ha. Just call him Bert. Everyone in Walker City does. I'd be surprised if Bert could tell you his last name these days. In fact, I'm pretty sure he couldn't."

When Ursula got to the taxi, Bert (whatever his last name was) opened the door and Ursula got in. The window was rolled down, and Ursula waited until the taxi pulled off, and it's when she waved back at Teardrop and Jamal standing out on the wide front porch.

Arlene stepped out the tub, wiped her body off with the towel, and then took her bathrobe off the curved bronze hook on the back of the door. She turned, looking into the misted mirror.

"Ursula Jenkins must be gone by now. Finally."

Her hairbrush was positioned at the sink's edge. She picked it up and began brushing angrily though her hair. The hairbrush was put back to its previous spot.

It's when Arlene heard footsteps; they were unmistakable. The bathroom door opened. Teardrop was in the second-floor hallway.

"Arlene, a shower at seven o'clock, honey? That's not like you. Unusu—"

"Has Ms. Jenkins left, Dad?"

"Yes, she wanted to thank you—"

"But of course she'll be back tomorrow so that she can."

"One o'clock, like I told her—same time, same place. Jamal seems to like her a lot, in fact, thought she was going to stay over. Spend the night with us. In the house."

"What-whatever would make him think that? Sometimes your grandson, as smart as he is, doesn't act ten, Dad. But more like five or six."

"Jamal's just excited by the attention I'm getting. Let's just attribute his overzealousness to that. A journalist from New York City. A magazine writer. This is all new for Jamal. If I were ten, Arlene, I'd act like I was five or six too."

"I don't know, Dad. I don't know … ," Arlene said, fighting such conjecture.

"She is pretty though. Very pretty," Teardrop said, now walking past Arlene for his room. "And Ms. Jenkins is an excellent listener."

"It's her job. Her job to listen," Arlene replied tersely. "To be a good listener. It's what she does for a living. She's basically a professional listener."

"Granted, Arlene. But she's an exceptional one."

Arlene closed the bathroom door.

Teardrop had entered his room when she did.

Ursula held the tape recorder. She pressed the erase button.

"I don't need anything on this tape. I remember everything. Everything. Everything Maurice 'Teardrop' Williams said today."

She felt like a schoolgirl, weak at the knees, the ankles—at whatever point a crush on your high school teacher, a college professor, makes you weakest when it happens.

"The things he said. The things he said—and how he said them!"

He had the wisdom of the ages, Ursula thought. He used all the right words, created all the right impressions—a writer's dream. For already, Teardrop Williams's life was beginning to unfold like a good book—chapter one, two …

"How many chapters are left? H-how many, I wonder."

Already, this magazine assignment felt too short. Just two days left with Teardrop Williams? Just two days to mine gold, strike an ore. It just felt, suddenly, shriveled, stunted.

The tape recorder returned to her pocketbook. Then she put the pocketbook down on the bed as she looked down at the dress she'd laid out for tomorrow. Either she was going to wear that or a pair of brown dress jeans, shirt, sports jacket, and sneakers. And Teardrop Williams made her feel so downright at home.

"Oh well … I'll have to decide what to wear tonight, won't I? Before I turn off the lights."

It's when Ursula began contemplating everything that'd happened today, looking at the one outfit on the bed and thinking of the other one. And it's when her reportorial instincts kicked in.

"Mrs. Wilkerson doesn't like me very much, does she?" Pause. "Maybe when I first arrived, got to the house, she was able to suppress her feelings—that, that brief interlude with me in the living room. But not out in the yard, at the table. When we ate, I became persona non grata suddenly for the entire meal.

"All her attention was devoted to Mr. Williams. Exclusively. Not even Jamal got in the way of them."

And then, abruptly, Ursula was struck by the adjective she chose to describe what she saw: "devoted."

"Why'd I choose that word in that way? Why, I've never used that word like that before. Not in that kind of odd context."

Ursula looked at the dress laid out on the bed as if it'd turned from a dark brown to a bright red.

⟨flourish⟩

Sunday.

The tape recorder was on the backyard's table. Up to this stage, conversation was animated, Ursula asking the questions, Teardrop answering them—elaborating on them.

"It … it amazes me though, Mr. Williams …"

"What's that, Ms. Jenkins?"

"That you have a chemistry degree. Majored in chemistry—a bluesman. I do find that extraordinary."

"Well, like I said," Teardrop laughed, "with my background it was quite natural. My father, a math teacher. My mother, a science teacher. I had an early advantage and curiosity in science. And my father made sure my math was, at an early age, up to snuff. Very early on in my training."

"Which it was."

"Yes, which it was."

"Something I dreaded in school, Mr. Williams, math."

"I knew one plus one equals two when I was in diapers, Ms. Jenkins."

"And your parents encouraged your music?"

"Yes, always. But made sure I was pointed in the right direction academically. And I never fought them. I had far too much respect for them, Ms. Jenkins. But I knew what I was going to do with my life when I first picked up the guitar. That was never at issue with me.

"I pretty much knew how things would turn out. The world would revolve on its axis."

"Well, I, along with a whole lot of other people, am glad the blues took precedence over chemistry."

"A white coat," Teardrop laughed, "and lab work. No, Ms. Jenkins. That wasn't my calling. It can't compare to smoky bars and … and this …"

"Miss Lillian."

"Miss Lillian, Ms. Jenkins." And Teardrop took Miss Lillian and held her in his hands.

And from the study's window, Arlene watched this, what her father did, taken hold of Miss Lillian, whom he cradled in his hands. Arlene had been at the window for over an hour, watching them, Teardrop and Ursula; her eyes trained down on them.

Teardrop stood. "Ms. Jenkins, let's say we, uh, take a walk. Let, why don't I show you something Teardrop Williams does daily—when I can, at least. Not in the winter. On cold days. And the winters are really cold in Walker City. Or on rainy ones. It's something I most love, enjoy doing." Pause. "Come, let me show you."

Ursula hopped out the chair, her sneakers practically bouncing up off the grass like rubber.

"Yesterday, you weren't dressed for it—uh, not with that lovely ensemble you wore—"

"And heels."

"But today, it'll work. I was happy to see you in casual wear, something more rugged. More suitable for what's in store for us."

Ursula laughed to herself. How "rugged" does one have to be to take a walk? Ursula thought. *She didn't get it.*

"Wouldn't let me help you with your chair, huh, Ms. Jenkins? That eager, are you?"

"That eager," Ursula laughed.

Teardrop waited for Ursula to join him. Then—

"Uh, Ms. Jenkins, aren't you going to bring that along with you? Your tape recorder?"

The tape recorder was still on top the lawn table. "Oh, yes, Mr. Williams, I can't, uh, m-mustn't forget that ... M-my tape recorder."

And Arlene watched from the window and was furious by what she saw, for she knew where her father was taking Ursula Jenkins: out into the woods, the thickly wooded area behind the house. His haven. His refuge. His private sanctuary, where he found his solitude. Neither she nor Jamal were ever invited, privileged to go along with him on this private, almost daily walk of his with Miss Lillian. This journey, it was more like a journey he took every day, Arlene thought. The woods had become off-limits to them; they'd accepted it, not inserting themselves into the process, knowing it was ritual now.

"We're not hiking, Ms. Jenkins. Just into the woods."

Ursula's excitement grew.

"You don't mind, Ms. Jenkins, do you?"

"N-no, not at all!"

Teardrop and Ursula entered the woods.

Teardrop and Ursula walked in silence, except for the cracking of the broken branches underfoot or peeled-off bark on the ground meeting the same fate.

"Now you can see why I come in here, Ms. Jenkins?" Teardrop asked, breaking the silence.

"It's so peaceful and quiet."

"Peaceful. I can think out here in this quiet."

"Musical thoughts, Mr. Williams?"

Teardrop stopped walking. "Easy to guess, I imagine?"

"Yes."

"Yes. Yes, it is."

The peace she talked of was really more like feeling one with nature. A cliché, she knew, but one worthy for what was happening to her in this wooded area.

Teardrop looked around at the tall, thick trees, birds chirping, and other distinct and distinguishing sounds filling the air as they moved deeper into the woods. The gentle life and gentle energy of it surrounding them in a way, for Ursula, was spellbinding, seducing the mind into easy surrender.

"It's out here where I compose."

"A lot of songs, Mr. Williams?"

"A lot, Ms. Jenkins."

"Songs—"

"No one's heard."

"Then that-that's sad, Mr. Williams."

"L-like, say, this one … ," Teardrop said, suddenly taking Miss Lillian and spinning this beautiful melody out her blue wood frame, his eyes shut, Miss Lillian's twelve strings singing abundantly as if he and Teardrop were back in the blues world again among patrons of the blues who dropped their heads and shut their eyes and shifted their bodies in a solemn hymn of recognition of a cultural history they knew and loved and behaved reverentially toward.

"Oh … Mr. Williams. It … it's so beautiful," Ursula said, her voice glowing. "So won—"

"Or … or, say, this one … ," Teardrop said ecstatically. "And there're words for them. Lyrics, but …"

"No, what you're playing is fine, Mr. Williams."

Again, Teardrop shut his eyes, and so did Ursula as he switched over to another blues tune, and yet still another to stoke the fire he'd built.

Ursula was emotionally dizzy-headed.

Teardrop's back was up against a giant oak tree, and one leg stretched backward. His boot scuffed the oak's brittle bark.

But then as quickly as he'd started, he stopped.

"That, the last one, Ms. Jenkins, I made, just made up, composed on the spot. Spontaneously, I might add. J-just now."

"You did?"

"Yes."

"Everything was so wonderful. To hear someone play like that," Ursula gushed. "Thank you, Mr. Williams. Thank—"

"Miss Lillian too—don't forget her."

Ursula laughed. "Of course, Miss Lillian. Of course, Mr. Williams, Miss Lillian too."

"Miss Lillian means everything to me." Pause.

"By the way, this wasn't taped by the recorder, was it?" Teardrop asked, looking at the tape recorder.

"Oh no. I turned the recorder off. Even if, at the time, you startled me, Mr. Williams."

"With my unplanned, uh, impromptu blues rhapsody. Totally unplanned."

"Yes."

"I don't know what overcame me," Teardrop said, looking into Ursula's dark penetrating eyes. "I'm not usually so impulsive."

"But spontaneous."

"Yes, when it comes to my music. It's what any good musician worth his salt is: spontaneous. It should be any great musician's attribute. Their calling card, you could say."

Now Ursula stood and stared at Teardrop as if he were going to play Miss Lillian again, but in her heart, she knew that the moment had slipped away. No, not that.

"Ms. Jenkins," Teardrop said, his back coming off the oak tree, "are you ready to head back to the house?"

"Oh, yes, Mr. Williams. T-that would be fine."

"Then follow me!"

While they walked, Ursula felt so refreshed and practically mindless that she was really beginning to capture Maurice "Teardrop" Williams, his portrait sprouting in her mind like fresh flowers.

"Mr. Williams, there's so much music left in you. Greatness, genius ... however one wishes to describe it. Why did you leave the music business when you did? Retire in the first place."

"That question had to come up, it was inevitable. I knew it would the instant I agreed to do the interview, Ms. Jenkins. M-Mac told me about it."

Was he stalling? Ursula thought. *Was Teardrop Williams actually afraid to answer the question? Was it that direct? Was it that intimidating? Maybe confrontational?*

They'd stopped walking. And now Ursula saw what was this palpable conflict in Teardrop Williams, the weakness in his shoulders—shoulders that just seconds ago seemed so strong and willing.

"No one knows, Mr.—"

"Yes, people know, Ms. Jenkins. Oh yes, people know all right. They haven't been left out. Just not the public." He shut his eyes. "My family knows. Shorty Boy, Twelve Fingers, McKinley Scofield—my inner circle of friends know why I left the music business. They're not in the dark."

"And now, don't you think the public—"

"Should know?" Teardrop's eyes opened.

"Your genius—"

"Without a soul? A soul? Feeling? Conviction, Ms. Jenkins?"

"But—"

"But what, Ms. Jenkins? Just what?"

"I, just minutes ago, I just heard—"

"But that was just Miss Lillian and me. Out here in the woods, alone, in this peaceful setting. Not on a stage, a bandstand, looking out, playing to ... for an audience of people. Trying to take them on a journey, through an experience, the music and I, Ms. Jenkins, and my heart's not in it, not with them—a part of the journey. Me missing from it. Entirely from it."

"I don't understand."

"But I do, Ms. Jenkins. I do. The artist does."

"Then please help me to understand, Mr. Williams. Explain it for me. Please. Please."

"It's too much. Just too much."

"I know you were married."

"Maureen. Maureen, Ms. Jenkins. Maureen Williams."

"And seven months after your wife passed, you—"

"It was colon cancer. My wife died of colon cancer."

Ursula knew this. She'd done her research. It was thorough: Maureen Williams, a grade-school teacher.

"Just took her, my wife, Maureen, from me. She and I smart, educated, sophisticated—just not thinking to do our checkups regularly. The things we should have been doing at our age, medically, healthwise. J-just plain irresponsible. It's what it was. Can chalk it up to."

"But, Mr. Williams—"

"Have you lost someone, Ms. Jenkins? Really lost someone?"

But before Ursula could respond, Teardrop said, "No ... you're so young, so young, Ms. Jenkins. You're ... you're so young ..."

And then Teardrop began walking, was almost at the edge, the beginning of the woods, the footpath.

"I ... I don't mean to be condescending, but ..." Pause. "But ... but ... you are so young."

"Yes, I am young, and—"

"I lost someone I loved desperately, Ms. Jenkins. Someone who I love now. The memory of my lost world. The memory of Maureen!"

And it's when Teardrop's strides quickened, and Ursula tried to keep pace with them, but when they came out the wooded area, Arlene saw this visible, deliberate separation between her father and Ursula Jenkins, the agitation and upset in her father's face.

"Mr. Williams, you owe the world—"

"The world ... I owe the world nothing. But the memory of Maureen, my wife, my everything!"

"Yes, yes I know, Mr.—"

"You don't know, Ms. Jenkins. You don't know. God, you don't. That's the problem: nobody knows! Nobody, Ms. Jenkins. Nobody. Nobody but me knows!"

The separation between them lengthened.

"Then ... then I understand, Mr. Williams, I—"

"Understand what!" Teardrop said, quickening his steps. "Understand what!"

"Dad. Dad!" Arlene screamed, running out the house.

"I can't go on with this, Arlene! I can't go on with this! I can't go on with this!"

Arlene ran to Teardrop; he held on to her with what seemed total desperation and fear. Ursula stood in silence. And then a flood of tears shot out Teardrop's body, and Ursula suddenly realized who "River of Pain" was written for: Maureen Williams, Teardrop Williams's wife.

"Dad. Dad, you go inside the house, Dad. Now, Dad. Now. I-I'll handle this with ... with her, Ms. Jenkins, Dad."

"Yes, yes, Arlene, the—"

"Please, Dad. Please!"

Teardrop released Arlene, and when he did, he didn't turn to Ursula but hustled up the stairs with Miss Lillian strapped to his shoulders, onto the deck and through the house's kitchen door.

"I knew this wouldn't work. From the start."

"I hoped it would," Ursula said firmly.

"You reporters—after a story. It's all that matters. Nothing more than a story."

"I was doing my job, Mrs. Wilkerson. N-nothing more. Only my—"

"And it's over, thank God."

"O-over?"

Arlene glared at her. "You upset my father and have the gumption, n-nerve to stand there and think that it's not! That it'll continue? The in-interview? That I'll allow it to continue!"

"Yes ... I, we, your father, Mr. Williams and I just touched a sensitive—"

"Ms. Jenkins, I don't want you back in my house. It's over. O—"

"But please, please, let me talk to your father, Mrs. Wilkerson. Mr. Williams, I, see if we can—"

"He doesn't want to talk to you. Don't you have the good common sense and, and decency to see that? My father did not need this interview with your magazine. It, he shouldn't have approved it. It should never have happened. Been consented to."

"I ... I have to get home, back to the boarding house, Mrs. Wilkerson. Can I go, at least go into, inside the house—may I at least call for a cab? Use the ... the phone. Your phone. Call f-for someone to come and get me for I can get back to Ruth Ingram's—"

"No. No. Ms. Jenkins. No. You go to the front of the house. That's what you can do. Where you can go. Not in the house. You go around to the front of the house, and I'll get my car keys, and I'll drive you back to Ms. Ingram's place, Ms. Jenkins."

"D-drive me—"

"The sooner the better. The sooner you're gone, Ms. Jenkins, the better."

Arlene turned and then quickly ran back up the back porch stairs.

Ursula was in front of the house, her body trembling. She was looking at the house, mostly looking at it blankly, thinking all of this happened so fast, without any warning, preparation.

Arlene was on the porch.

"Are you ready, Ms. Jenkins? Ready to leave?"

What am I supposed to say? Ursula thought. *What!*

"The car door's open," Arlene said; she and Ursula stood at the car. "This is not New York City. We know our neighbors in Walker City."

Ursula was in the car. When she shut the door, she looked straight ahead. Arlene started the engine and the drive to Ruby Ingram's began.

The passenger-side window was already rolled down, so Ursula didn't have to do that. She figured, assumed, Jamal was probably the last person in the car, that he'd rolled the window down. *Where was Jamal?* she thought. She and Jamal got along. Where was Jamal during all of this mayhem? She and Jamal got along well.

And now she began noting things in Walker City she'd not noted before, the real color of it, how the trees stood in the ground, how the air really smelled—things she would always remember about Walker City, Iowa: how the long road rolled ahead as if endlessly, without consideration of ever ending somewhere at some defined point.

And the silence inside the car continued. Arlene Wilkerson refusing to look at Ursula Jenkins. Ursula Jenkins refusing to look at Arlene Wilkerson.

And now Ursula could see Ms. Ruby Ingram's boarding house and the days in Walker City. And the car that hadn't topped the thirty-mile-an-hour speed limit began to brake, and within seconds the car was in front of the old wooden boarding house that sat like a barn in the wilderness—a lonely figure to be sure.

The car braked. Arlene's head swung around to Ursula.

"You will not write your article, Ms. Jenkins. You will abort this weekend. Forget it ever existed. I forbid your magazine to write the article. You have done enough emotional damage to my father, to this family. Three years my father has lived with me, my son and I. And you, in one stroke of a pen, an afternoon, will not undo what we've done in three years."

"And what's that, Mrs. Wilkerson?" Ursula asked challengingly.

"Th-this is where your story ends. Right here and now in Walker City."

The Impala's engine idled. Arlene swung her head away from Ursula.

"Don't come back to Walker City, Ms. Jenkins."

Ursula opened the car door and then shut it.

"Ever again." Pause. "You're not welcomed here. Not under any circumstances."

And it's when the car left the front of the boarding house, and Ursula watched the car with tears swelling her eyes.

Ursula was in bed, under the bedsheet, shivering.

She felt like a monster and wished she were home, in Queens, not practically three quarters of the country away from New York City. But before she'd felt like a monster, like she'd done this reprehensible crime to Teardrop Williams, she'd felt humiliated. The drive home in Mrs. Wilkerson's car, the treatment from her. The way she spoke to her in the house's backyard and then when she dropped her off, before she left, driving away. *Where was the fight in me, my guts, the stubbornness, the steel spine everyone knows I have?*

But why did she expect that from herself when ...

Ursula reached for the pocketbook on the floor, her fingers fumbling the metal clasp open until she pulled out the tape recorder. She turned it on.

"Oh ... oh ..."

And the music wound out the tape recorder. It was put atop her chest.

No, Ursula had not turned the tape recorder off when Teardrop Williams played out in the woods, had startled her; she wouldn't do that, not when he propped himself up against the oak tree and his lithe fingers began lifting music from out Miss Lillian's silky strings and her ears suffused with surprise and wonder.

"How did I know the loss of Teardrop Williams's wife meant the loss to play music? And how her death brought him back to live with his daughter and grandson."

Her thoughts weaved back into the music, wanting Teardrop Williams to soother her, what he was playing so tenderly and warmly on Miss Lillian—like he could never be angry with her, not in a thousand, million years.

"But I know where his house is in Walker City. It's still in his name. I ... I have it. What I mean is I have it on the notepad in my pocketbook—I mean, in my head ... I know it, all right. He can't live there, can he? Not without her, Maureen Williams. Without her there with him.

"What a love story it must've been between them for those years. But no one's to know, are they? Only Teardrop Williams and Arlene Wilkerson."

Ursula's flight out of Walker City would be tomorrow, not Tuesday as planned. It was 9:10 p.m. She smelled something come out Ms. Ingram's common kitchen. Just the thought of food, for her, turned her stomach. Just the thought of it turned her stomach upside down.

"I can't eat. I won't eat."

And then the song, the one Teardrop Williams had "spontaneously" composed today, right on the spot out there in the woods, played out the tape recorder. And she listened to it as she did the first time, during its initial offing, and she could have sworn, at the time, that Teardrop Williams was composing it for her (out his heart for her). She'd had that much sheer conceit and vanity, at the time, in her. It's why her eyes shut more deeply with him, feeling some kind of incredible vibrations quivering from Miss Lillian.

"And if there were lyrics to the song, what would they have said, I wonder?"

But there were no lyrics, just the melody and the great series of arching chords breaking through the clouds, charming as the sun.

CHAPTER 8

Ursula was back home. She'd been moving through her apartment with little patience. A lot was on her plate. There were a lot of decisions to make. And instead of the flight back to New York being pleasant, which was normal, she felt trapped in the sky.

But the first thing she had to do was talk to Dan Gottlieb of *Currents* magazine.

"Dan …"

"Ursula, you're back."

"Yes, I'm—"

"Great. Great. Hold, could you hold on, I've got Tim Murchinson on the other line, and you know who—"

"Yes."

"Give me a couple of seconds."

Ursula barely swallowed, when—

"Ursula, I'm back." Pause. "So the story, Maurice "Teardrop" Williams story, Audrey's all hot to trot on this one. So am I. So when can you get the article—"

"There is no article, Dan. There is no story. It's why I called."

"Ursula, ha, don't pull my—"

"It's been killed, Dan."

"Killed? Who killed it! Not me!"

"Not you."

"Teardrop Williams, he approved, agreed to the, to the interview with the maga—"

"I know. I know. But everything in Walker City ... everything went wrong."

"Wrong?"

"Disastrously wrong. I upset him, Dan. The past—it was too much for him. Too much for Mr. Williams to handle."

"It can't be that simple, Ursula. What you're saying, telling me. It can't—"

"The story's dead in the water," Ursula said forcibly. "It's where it stands now."

"I'm stunned by this. Shocked—if you want, really want to know the truth." Pause.

"But how much did he want me to know, the public to know, I keep asking myself."

"He wanted to keep stuff, personal things to himself then, is that it?"

"Mr. Williams knew I'd eventually tread over sensitive, personal ground."

"Yes, sure, was smart enough t-to understand that much. What an interview is all about. Especially one of that size, uh, magnitude."

"Yes. And maybe at the time, when he granted me the interview he wanted to get it out his system. It's what he'd hoped to do."

"At the time. When he went along with it. B-but when the moment of truth came, what? He stiffened? Just plain—"

"Bolted, Dan. Bolted. Mr. Williams—"

"What did you say? Ask?"

Long pause.

"Ursula, you're not going to answer me?"

"It's not that ..."

And Ursula wasn't going to tell Dan Gottlieb what really happened, the *real* story, for she felt she'd be saying too much, opening up a can of worms—that she'd found out far too much about Teardrop Williams (she felt she owed him that much of her loyalty for those two days he gave her).

"Then ..."

"It was his daughter, Mr. Williams's daughter, Arlene Wilkerson, who took over. Who anticipated his position, his unwillingness to continue with the interview."

"His daughter is some kind of—"

"She's an economics professor at a local university down there. A brilliant woman."

Then Ursula remembered the drive from Arlene Wilkerson's house to Ruby Ingram's boarding house, her humiliation—like she was the enemy. It felt ground in her like dirt.

"But you—did you get, come away from this car wreck with a story? With something?"

"I—"

"Something that maybe we can use, cobble a story out of? I still feel Teardrop Williams's music is great. Would like this great bluesman to still receive his due."

"No, it's a dead story. Dead. My notes—I discarded them. G-got rid of them. I—"

"Ursula, I've never known you to be meek under fire, only feisty. Never taking no for an answer. Fighting tooth and nail. It's how you got the Maurice Teardrop interview in the first place. Come on, there's got to be more to this than what you're telling me. I'm hearing from—"

"More? No, there's not any more—no more to this. It's just that if you're going to do a story on someone like Teardrop Williams, you have to get to his soul. If you don't, then you have nothing, Dan. Absolutely nothing to account for your effort. A ... a skeleton. It's worthless.

"You had to learn that from *River of Pain*. And it's much more evident, clear when you meet Mr. Williams personally, Dan."

"Then you came away, I mean, what you're saying is that you came away from the interview even more of an admirer of his? More persuaded of his genius."

"Yes, with a far deeper admiration, appreciation of Mr. Williams. Yes, Dan, I did."

"Well," Dan sighed heavily, "I didn't expect this. This unfortunate turn of events—that's for sure." Pause. "O-okay, let's drop it for now, but ... but who knows ..."

"Yes, Dan ..."

"Mr. Williams might have a change of heart. O-okay, just send your expenses in. Ha. Ben Phillips, the bean counter over here, will be happy to hear that."

"Sorry."

"Don't be."

"B-but I am."

"Look, Ursula, I feel sorry for Teardrop Williams. It's who I feel sorry for. He doesn't know what he missed out on. Had no idea what a great, great writer you are—what kind of bang-up job you'd do. Fantastic, simply fantastic. Award-winning journalism. Stuff, if you'd been given the chance to tell the Maurice Teardrop story.

"Decisively, with certainty. It's Teardrop Williams's great loss."

Ursula shut the bedroom blinds.

The room was dark, and for now, she felt little consolation regarding what Dan said in basically concluding their earlier conversation. How Teardrop Williams was in the best of hands with her, this top-rung journalist. And of course she hadn't discussed her notes, only to say she'd discarded them, since there were no notes to begin with—everything sticking to her brain like Velcro, there for instant, immediate recall.

"There's not one word of Teardrop Williams's t-that I don't remember."

But now, all of a sudden, Ursula felt as if she were protecting Teardrop Williams, as if he had to be protected, such a great, wonderful man. And suddenly, too, she empathized with Arlene Wilkerson.

"Her love is so pure, so real. I love my father no less than she. I … why wouldn't I do the same for him, what Arlene Wilkerson's doing, is doing, has done for her father? Keep the 'real' world from him. Not let it touch him. People, people like me from him. The mob." She sighed.

"His wife, I could feel her yesterday. When he said Maureen Williams's name, as far as I was concerned, she was in the yard, out in the backyard with us, Mr. Williams and me."

Ursula shut her eyes and laid her head back gently against the pillow.

"How I wish things had gone better. How I wish … Then he wouldn't be Teardrop Williams, would he? He wouldn't have this great beauty in him. What makes him special."

Five days later. A Friday night.

Ursula, Byron, and J. C. were in Ursula's living room. Ursula had invited them by the apartment. J. C. was supposed to bring his girlfriend, Ramona Gaines, but something, at the last minute, came up; so she had to cancel out. The living room's TV was on, but no one was watching it. The TV was an old Zenith model with an antenna, of all things—looked like something out of a bad '50s sci-fi movie.

"You know you could've told me sooner about the Teardrop Williams fiasco, Ursula."

"Don't tell me we're back to that again?" J. C. said disgustedly, crossing and then uncrossing his leg.

"I mean, what are friends for?" Byron said, ignoring J. C.'s remark. "And y-you're still hurting," Byron said, sitting next to Ursula on the couch, taking her hand, looking into her eyes.

"I'm a big girl, Byron."

"But that doesn't mean you can't hurt, Ursula. Sweetie." Byron fidgeted. "It's why you asked us by tonight, J. C. and me, isn't it?"

"Yes."

"For company."

Ursula nodded her head. "Yes."

"Yeah, what you need right now," Byron said. "For sure."

"Uh-huh."

Then Ursula reached for J. C.'s hand, taking it, holding it.

"Helluva thing Teardrop Williams did to you. Helluva stunt—backing out the article the way he did, like that. Thought he'd have more class, style than that. Shit."

"Byron, I told you something, but I didn't expect you to make judgments. Go ... go wild with them."

"How, but how can I not, Ursula? The man did you wrong, downright wrong out there in Walker City. Hell ... that's plain as day."

"Ursula, Byron's right. The man did do you wrong, and there's no two ways about it."

Ursula looked at both of them. "You wouldn't say that if you'd met him."

"Stringing you the hell along like that. Having you fly cross country, all the way to some remote, off-the-wall place no one's heard of. For what, w—"

"Byron, did you hear what Ursula said? Just ran down to us, man?"

"Sure, J. C., but Ursula's always out to give somebody a break. And now, in this case, Teardrop Williams, in my estimation, doesn't deserve one. The dude—"

"If you had someone you loved for thirty years of your life suddenly die and you had to choose between preserving their memory, living with it day and night, or your music, continuing with it—"

"The present, the present—hey, Ursula, you've got to live in the present. You've got—"

"But what about your heart, Byron?" J. C. said. "What about that shit? What, cut it out? And only use it when you have to? I mean, that's the deal? What's up with that? What we're talking about Mr. Williams doing, right, man?"

Byron reached for the Wise potato chips in the plastic yellow bowl on the coffee table, scooping up a handful and then, inadvertently, a few falling out his hand and onto the brown-and-yellow patterned area rug.

"Oh, uh, sorry, Ursula," Byron said, scooping up the chips off the rug. "Look, that's a sad situation, uh, lamentable, losing someone you love … What, thirty years you said, Ursula? They were married. Thirty?"

Ursula nodded her head.

"Damned lousy luck. A raw deal. But, uh … the way I look at it, the only way to free yourself from the past—not all of it, mind you, but the bulk of it—is to live in the present. Present tense. Not past. Go full throttle. Full blast—"

"Until what, Byron, you fizzle out? What, man, shit, you were so busy running from it, until it, all the shit catches up with you eventually and you have to face it anyway? Run into a brick wall?"

"I, what do you have to say, Ursula, on the subject, sweetie?"

"I don't know, Byron. I don't know," Ursula said, shaking her head.

"Shit … ," Byron said. "Shit …"

Pause.

"You know what, you guys. I think we're too young, all of us, to know what kind of pain, grief—what Mr. Williams is apparently going through because of his wife's death."

"True. True, J. C. I'll grant you that. It's like a life experience thing. Yeah, I'll concede you that," Byron said, munching on a potato chip.

"He had to be devoted to her, right, Ursula?"

But before Ursula could answer J. C., Byron said, "Right. But the guy was out on the road all the time. Probably two hundred times a year. It's a hustle, a stone-cold hustle. I have a few musician friends, it's how they make their scratch, man, cash—it's the only way, in fact."

"I know a few too," J. C. said. "It's true, it's strictly a hustle game. Everything's up for grabs."

"And so, if he's out there on the road all the time"—pause—"just how much family life does the dude actually have when it's all said and done,

J. C.? At the end of the day. When you actually add the whole shit up? Do the math."

"Not much, that's for sure."

"So it stands, it stands to reason—"

"Stop it! Stop it! The two of you!" Ursula said, fuming. Her body flew off the couch. "I … I didn't ask you by, ov-over here to discuss, talk about Teardrop Williams!"

"Sorry, Ursula. J. C. and I know how much this thing meant to you. S-sorry."

Ursula stood by the glass door leading out onto the apartment's veranda. No one said anything for a good full minute. Ursula had stepped onto the smallish veranda. She was looking down onto this eastern section of Jamaica Avenue, retracing her walk through the woods, in her mind, knowing what Teardrop Williams had probably done that activity today, gone into the woods, Teardrop Williams holding Miss Lillian, him supported by the tall oak tree, the music riding on the afternoon's air. New music, old music—no matter which.

It felt so peaceful out there with him, Mr. Williams. Quiet as we both noted.

Her back was turned to Byron and J. C. They sat on the couch, each still looking at her, the TV an afterthought.

"Mr. Williams has a daughter who loves him. A grandson who adores him. It's a beautiful family Mr. Williams has," Ursula said privately to herself.

And since it was late evening on Jamaica Avenue, there wasn't near the hustle and bustle, the struggles and stresses of the day, the honking of cars, the street-level energy—Jamaica's solid racket dominating things before they wind down to a crawl and welcomed strain of civility and city life, gentleness that survives as long as it can until daybreak and the new/old beginnings awaken.

When Byron looked at J. C., J. C. knew all too well *the* look.

"Well, it's late, Ursula. J. C. and me got to book outta here. Right about now."

And since Byron had driven this time around, J. C. was at Byron's mercy.

"Thanks for the invite—enjoyed it as usual," J. C. said.

Ursula turned. "Oh, yes. Thanks, thanks for coming by—I … I enjoyed it too," Ursula said, fixing her face into a smile. When she got to them, she put herself in the middle, Byron's arm wrapping around her waist, J. C.'s around her shoulder.

"Chips were good."

"And the booze," Byron laughed.

"Are you sure? Maybe you should hand J. C. the car keys, Byron."

"Hell no!"

"Hell yes!"

"Two bottles of Heineken ain't gonna lay me out, Ursula. Rock the boat. No way. No … can … do, momma!"

They laughed.

"That's it, girl. Laugh a little. Take the weight off. Damned thing off your mind," Byron said. "Before, it was like you were still spaced out. A part of you still a part of that story. Don't let it get you down. Ain't healthy—you know that, Ursula. I know your heart was dead set on doing the article, but another one will come around just around the corner."

"Yeah, Ursula," J. C. said. "That you'll feel just as passionate about."

"I suppose so," Ursula said bravely. "Thanks, guys."

"Smile," Byron said. "That is a smile, isn't it?"

"Yes," Ursula said, her dark eyes brightening, seemingly genuine for now.

"Looks damned pretty on you, girl!"

J. C. kissed Ursula's left cheek, Byron her right, simultaneously.

"Just keep it that way."

"Okay, Ursula?"

"Thanks. I … I don't know what I'd do without you two. R-really. My two buddies."

"Hey, you're always there for us, right? When me and J. C. hit a speed bump."

"Talk to you soon."

"Know we will, J. C.," Ursula answered as J. C. entered the apartment's plain-walled hallway.

Byron looked up at her and then whispered in her ear, "Love you," while rubbing her hand. "Love you like a sister, sweetie."

Ursula watched them as they reached the elevator. When it finally did come, the three waved and then Ursula shut the apartment door. She walked into the living room, picked up the bowl of chips (there were but a few left in the bowl), glanced down into the bowl, and was about to head for the kitchenette when she lost it again, her emotions as raw and painful as a loose nerve.

The bowl of chips meant little to her now as she put them back down on the coffee table and headed for her bedroom, back to where her small tape recorder was—where she actually thought it awaited her. And in it was Walker City, the woods, Teardrop Williams's voice and the song, and Miss Lillian playing it, and them together in that setting—and another night she couldn't fight, try to win, but was too weak to not give in to him, the music she still felt he had written for her and only her that day before trouble thundered out of nowhere.

Thirteen days later.

Ursula had submitted an article, op-ed piece, to a magazine and was to begin another one this week (she had to pay the rent!). She'd just gotten in from grocery shopping. She was checking her machine calls when, suddenly, she stopped, caught herself, for she knew just what it was she was about to let herself do, think, slip her mind into it, but then got back to what she was doing—back on track.

"Nobody wants me today, huh? I pity them!" It was a hardy laugh. "But I've been so busy since t-the 'Teardrop Williams fiasco,' as Byron coined it."

And the following morning, after submerging herself back into Teardrop Williams's world, the homemade tape, and *River of Pain* CD, she came out on the other end of it better, as if she could fully function close to 100 percent again.

"Now for the mail." She'd brought the mail up from the apartment's lobby but hadn't looked at it. "It's that time of the month when Uncle Bill wants to get paid. Wants to put me in the poorhouse. Makes … w-what's this?"

She scanned the envelope. She couldn't move. "It can't be. W-Walker City, Iowa. T. Williams. It says T. Williams on the envelope."

And there was more fear than shock in her, this letter just showing up, springing up at the top of the envelope unannounced—atop monthly bills.

Ursula got up from the kitchen table as if she were going to run off, as if she were looking at a letter that sat there, as if it contained words that could make that tiny kitchenette blow up and, with it, her.

"It was Mrs. Wilkerson—Mr. Williams just running to his daughter," Ursula said, her eyes red, her feelings intense and fretful.

"She said she'd take care of every ... me. Take care of me, and it's what she did. Told me not to come back to the house. Not ever. Ever again. And now it ... it's your turn, Mr. Williams? Is ... is it y-your turn to rant? To hate me too? I don't know. I don't. Don't know!"

And it was that rush of emotion that pushed Ursula to pick up the letter, to zip it open using her fingernails with the efficiency and severity of a sharp letter opener.

"What!" she screamed angrily, confused, letting her pain explode. She slumped in the chair and then stubbornly sat up like she refused to succumb to any fear she might have or imagined to have in what had become this war of wills.

Then and only then did she begin reading the letter from Maurice "Teardrop" Williams.

Dear Miss Jenkins,

If I had known how to begin this letter to you, it would have been written much, much sooner. How do I defend my actions of a few weeks back? None of this was your fault. You were not to blame. You did nothing to overstep the boundaries of journalistic good taste or what I had already carefully calculated would come from your interview with me. My own personal assessment.

And I had carefully calculated events in every possible detail before you came. Making myself the interviewer. Forcing my mind to think like one. Putting myself in your shoes. Asking the hard questions. Putting myself on the griddle. I had to make sure if I committed myself to the interview, that I could do it. See it through. Not be able to stand up to exacting scrutiny by you.

But instead, I came apart. I failed. I don't know why (it's not what this letter to you is about). I simply want to apologize to you for my actions. My bad manners. To let you know my intentions were pure all long, as pure as rain before you flew here to Walker City to interview me for Currents *magazine. That I enjoyed your stay here— everything about you, in fact. That is to say, your professionalism, your courtesy, how you approached me and my family from the start. When we went into the woods, it felt very special to share that moment of time, that daily source, that especially rejuvenates me when I come out of there, with you.*

This was not to turn out this way, with such a promising beginning but rude ending. I wish to apologize not only to you but Currents *magazine. I will send a letter of apology to them. To Dan Gottlieb. You told me of his great support of my music.*

One other thing, Jamal was upset over this (rarely have I seen him that upset). Not knowing the circumstance, of course he wondered why his mother and I let you leave that day without him having an opportunity to say good-bye. We explained it to him as best we could, but, of course, it wasn't truthful, a miserable failure, for what, if anything, can one really tell a ten-year-old so that he might understand adult things when oftentimes it is we adults who do not understand these things ourselves.

And as for my daughter, Arlene, I let her do my dirty work for me. It woke me up, that's for sure. It really woke me up. Arlene did what any daughter would do under the circumstances, I would agree. So many people I have to apologize to. Sorry, Ms. Jenkins.

I wish you continued success in your journalistic and personal life, of which there should be much.
God Bless you,
Teardrop Williams

"Mr. Williams, Mr. Williams, I forgive you! I forgive you, Mr. Williams! I do!"

Ursula's hands were shaking. Her body felt as light as yeast. "I must write you back. I ... I must write you back as soon as possible. Right away!"

Hurriedly, Ursula got into the bedroom. She took a yellow notepad out her smallish desk drawer and sat. She was going to write the letter out in longhand first and then computer type it. And now it's when she laughed, for she was no better off than Teardrop Williams because she didn't know how to begin her letter to him.

"And ... and I'm a writer," she said mockingly. "How shameful when I do this kind of stuff for a living. Every day." But Ursula knew this was personal, that this letter was to be so personal that it ached her insides like an overripe toothache.

"Okay, okay"—Ursula began checking herself—"if Mr. Williams can, I surely can. If a bluesman can write such a beautiful, touching letter, yes, I know I can!"

Dear Mr. Williams,
I just received your letter today. It was on top my bills.

"What a beginning. But I don't know if I'll leave that in or edit it out. Later. But either way, it is a start … isn't it?"

CHAPTER 9

It was a hot day in Walker City, Iowa, today.

Teardrop scratched his arm. "Is it the insect repellent or me?"

Whatever had caused the itch, Teardrop itched.

Teardrop was ready to go into the woods. This was the time of year when you needed bug repellent, July. It's when the Walker City bug population sought its revenge on the human species (at least most folk in Walker City thought so, what it would tell you without asking).

"I hope it's not me."

Teardrop entered the woods with Miss Lillian, and his chest filled with exuberance; and even now, in this afternoon walk of his, he was playing Miss Lillian. She hung down in front of him, the right side of him, lazily. And what he was playing was the song that came out his fingers when Ursula Jenkins was in the woods with him and Miss Lillian, the day he invited her into the woods to participate in this huge part of his life, daily routine. And it was really a song without words yet. For Teardrop was yet able to put words to the song or an appropriate title, but his fingers knew it like the song was older than Mother Earth.

But as he found such relief in the woods, entering into it, this grand setting of nature, there was a certain degree of anxiety in him, something Teardrop knew even the woods could not cure.

"I'm sure Ms. Jenkins, by now, has gotten my letter. I'm sure of it."

He let the words, seemingly, travel through the woods, as if to echo.

And then Teardrop played a cluster of notes on Miss Lillian as if to hear what Miss Lillian had to say on the subject.

"Uh … you agree, Miss Lillian. Agree with me then."

More notes, in a flurry, came out of Miss Lillian's sturdy blue frame.

"Ha. I know. I'm nervous too."

But then a somber look folded back into Teardrop's handsome, taut face.

"I'm just hoping the letter to Ms. Jenkins was enough for her to forgive my egregious behavior."

Teardrop looked up to the trees' branches that looked like long arms stretching up to heaven for more prayer for his benefit.

"I felt so young, alive that day. Around Ms. Jenkins. She really enjoyed it out here, it seemed."

Teardrop played a flurry of notes on Miss Lillian and then waited for Miss Lillian's reply.

"Say something, Miss Lillian. Anything. Come on, say something—or do I have to coax it out of you."

Next day.

"Morning, Teardrop."

"Good morning, Sid."

Teardrop was out on the front porch. Sid Turner was the mailman. It was 10:03 a.m. Sid was on time, as usual, with the mail. Sid Turner was tall and angular, his frame slanting to the right, the same side he carried the mailbag on in all his years of postal work.

"Hot already," Sid said, handing Teardrop the mail.

"Have you got your sun lotion on, Sid?"

"Now you know black folk don't need no sun lotion, Teardrop. Not 'less they're light as white. Of the white variety."

"What about insect repellent?"

"Now that's horse of a different color. Don't know why insects like to feast on black folk skin so much. Skin must got a ingredient nobody else got—or want." Pause.

"So, uh, so see you tomorrow, Teardrop."

"Tomorrow it is, Sid."

"Same time, same place, tomorrow?"

"Right, Sid."

"Wish I could get paid for saying that, Teardrop, every day."

"You and me both, Sid."

Sid Turner was off the porch, moving farther and farther away from the house, when he said, turning back to Teardrop, "By, uh, by the way, Teardrop, got you something from New York in that stack. Put it on top. Didn't want you to miss it. Seeing it's from New York."

Teardrop gasped, covering his mouth. "T-thank you, Sid. T-thank you," he said under his breath.

And now Teardrop was looking at the envelope, and it *was* from New York, for up in the upper left hand corner it said that and—

"Ms. Jenkins. Ms. Ursula Jenkins."

And Teardrop had to stand to work the sweat, the nerves out him. *Surprise, surprise,* he thought. And for now he was thanking Ursula Jenkins for writing the letter, whether good or bad, positive or negative—at least he no longer would have to go to bed at night wondering about her. Worry so. So many days of that was a long time when totaled.

He sat back down on the porch. His anxiety had lost its muscle.

"Now for the moment of truth, Ms. Jenkins."

Dear Mr. Williams,
I received your letter today. It was on top my bills.
"You, you don't say, Ms. Jenkins."
Better your letter than bills, any day …

Teardrop had read through Ursula Jenkins's letter, and his head was back against the top of the chair, and his body felt like a cool breeze had just blown into the hot Walker City day and he was its lone recipient, not anyone else in Walker City as privileged—just him on the porch with Ms. Jenkins's letter in his hand.

"What a beautiful letter. A beautiful person who wrote this letter. Such beauty has to be from within—it can't be intellectually thought out. Nothing as lovely and handsome," Teardrop said, shaking the letter softly in his hand, his eyes again admiring so many of its words.

"Thank you, Ms. Jenkins," Teardrop laughed. "It's all I can say. What a relief this is."

It was 2:20 p.m.

As soon as Arlene got out the car, she looked up. "Dad, you, why you startled me."

"I did?"

"You weren't there when I drove up in the car."

"No, uh, I guess not. I ... I wasn't."

"Dad, you weren't. I can assure you. There isn't any reason to guess."

Teardrop kissed Arlene's cheek.

"I lectured those students today until their ears practically fell off. There's nothing worse than summer school, but I'm relentless. If they want to be on summer vacation, then they shouldn't've taken my course this summer. They picked the wrong professor."

"That a girl, Arlene. Give them heck!"

"What's that, Dad? A cleaned-up version of Harry 'Last Buck Stops Here' Truman?"

"Why not."

Arlene looked up into Teardrop's eyes. "Dad, there's something going on with you ..."

"What ... what do you mean by that, Arlene?"

"I know that look, what it means. It's full of possibility, mischief, to be precise."

They were on the porch. Teardrop was opening the screen door for Arlene; she was about to step into the house's vestibule.

"Guess who I heard from today?"

"Uh ... who, Dad?"

"Ursula Jenkins."

Arlene's body locked. "Ur-Ursula Jenkins?"

"In today's mail. I received a letter from her."

Arlene seemed flustered. "W-what in the world did she write you for? Does she want from you, Dad? Not, not that story again. Not another story a—"

"Hold it, Arlene. Hold—I was the one who wrote Ms. Jenkins, honey. I initiated contact. I couldn't leave things the way they were—in that kind of mess. Condit—"

"Why not, Dad? What price did Ursula Jenkins have to pay? The loss of a story for her magazine? What's the comparison to what you lost that day, trying to get at your pain, your suffering, for the sake of her story? For it could be written out and told as if it were a pound of flesh sold to the public. For public consumption."

"Is that what you think, Arlene? Ms. Jenkins was doing that, really? No, no, Ms. Jenkins was only doing her job—what makes her the extraordinary writer she is. You should read her letter."

Arlene walked into the living room and sat down on the couch.

"So you didn't tell me, Dad, of this, this correspondence of yours," Arlene said, crestfallen. "You writing Ms. Jenkins."

"Did I have to?" Teardrop said assertively. "Oh … I'm sorry. Yes, yes, I should have told you, honey. In hindsight. But I still feel so guilty about what I did, making you the villain. The fall guy that day. Not living up to my responsibility."

"Dad, you were distraught, too overwhelmed to do otherwise. And besides, I smelled trouble that day. As soon as Ms. Jenkins walked into this house. The minute she got here."

Teardrop sat. "Why, I didn't know that. H-had no idea at the time."

"Somehow, it was in the air."

Teardrop sat there and contemplated what Arlene had said and then thought no more of it.

"I must write Ms. Jenkins back."

"W-write her back?"

"The things Ms. Jenkins said, I must write her back. I owe her that much."

"Dad, haven't you done enough? E—"

"You know I told her how upset Jamal was when he found out she'd left the house. Not being able to say good-bye to her."

"You told her that?"

"Of course. I thought it important she know. Jamal was disappointed. He really liked Ms. Jenkins's visit here."

"A-and how soon are you going to write, to write, Ms.—"

"Tonight. I'm eager to. Very." Teardrop rubbed his arm. "The magazine article, if I had let Ms. Jenkins finish it, would've been wonderful, exceptional, Arlene. I, yes, I can say it unequivocally. There's such simplicity and beauty in her writing. Understanding, depth, humanity—from someone so young, Arlene. So young—and short on living."

Arlene didn't like this feeling, but it was back permeating the household. And it was because of Ursula Jenkins, Arlene thought, wrapping the magenta robe around her—hard into her solid frame. For Arlene was back spying on her father, watching his every move.

What had he done? Where did he go after he'd told her how "eager" he was to write Ursula Jenkins? He'd put insect repellent on and had gone out to the woods. He and Miss Lillian (of course he took her with him). When he came back, he did something with Jamal's bike (something to do with the bicycle chain), and then the two sat on the front porch for a while until she called them to dinner, eating out on the porch's deck (pretty much standard fare).

"And then what did … Dad and Jamal did the dishes and I went to my study. And now I'm here in the bedroom, and Dad finally reached his bedroom, and I heard the bedroom door close, and I thought I was going to die when it did."

She knew the day had to settle in him. "Eager," yes, but he would get everything right when he wrote Ursula Jenkins. She knew he was a perfectionist; he was a great musician, creative person. He always put perfectionist demands on himself.

"Everything has to be just right, doesn't it, Dad? It's how you do things. Execute them."

She'd been around him all her life, enough to know, observe him. Hear things through her mother, see things for herself, how a great mind, musician, man thinks. Loving him as much as any little girl can their father. His absences long but worth his return, to just be around him. His willingness to keep at it, stay at it, his music, the blues business, through good and bad times, her mother's support never waning, never having second thoughts, never second-guessing, failing the genius of Maurice "Teardrop" Williams.

"Oh … Dad, Mom loved you so," Arlene said, her hand covering her face, looking like someone stricken with grief and memory.

"What does Ursula Jenkins want from you, Dad? The story's dead. There is no more story. It was killed. I … I told her not to come back to Walker City. Not ever to return to Walker City. She's not welcomed here. T-there's nothing here for her. Nothing at all here for her."

The horrible death of a woman, still young, vital, still in the prime of her life—but debilitated and suffering, her physical beauty dissipating, making the horror real, the colon cancer, the disease. The Williams family there to take its stand against such tragedy; but, of course, in the end, losing, not able to change anything—losing its hope for better days, but only at the end, not before it came.

But better days had come slowly the past three years. Her father moving into the house with her and Jamal, Arlene thought. Their lives solid as wooden posts dense in circumference, secure in the ground. And suddenly this interloper …

"And Dad's in his room, bedroom, writing her. Right now. I know he is." Pause. "It's supposed to be over, done with. All of this foolishness. Maurice "Teardrop" Williams is not on the road anymore. He's not out playing blues music anymore. He's given it up, turned his back on it. His life is me and Jamal and … and, it's me and Jamal and …"

They had this perfect thing, Arlene thought. *It was perfect harmony.*

"I don't like this. Not at all."

And Arlene knew her father was in the room writing his perfect letter to Ursula Jenkins, making it read exactly like his music, something that always touched a nerve in you, set it off in some ecstatic, visceral way.

"Dad doesn't need to be writing Ursula Jenkins. Corresponding with her. Why is he? W-why should he?"

CHAPTER 10

One and a half months later.

Ursula and Byron were talking over the phone.

"Y-you've been doing what, Ursula?"

"Corresponding ... writing Mr. Williams."

"You have? What for? For how long? Since—"

"Slow down, slow down, Byron," Ursula laughed. "One question at a time."

"So ... what's the deal? Going on with you?"

"It started with Mr. Williams's apology. The letter he sent me."

"And you didn't tell me about it."

"No. I chose not to."

"For any reason?"

"No ... well ... I just figured it ... it was a personal matter. I guess— but I'm not sure, really sure."

"So why now? Now, then?" Byron said. "Are you doing it now?"

"I guess, suppose, because, it's because it's been such a surprise. So much fun—this correspondence with him. C-can I say that?"

"I don't know. Can you?" Byron said like he wasn't about to let Ursula off the hook that easily (not as easily as it seemed she wanted him to).

No reply.

"Threw it right back at you, huh? Threw it right back at you, didn't I?"

"I know. I'm sorry about keeping you in the dark, Byron, all this time."

"But, ha, in a way, you're not," Byron said in an easy tone.

"It seems this conversation's going in circles, like my reasoning—a dog chasing its tail."

"J. C.'s going to be pissed, I know. Pissed off. Know if you're just letting me in on this, telling me, you haven't spilled the beans to J. C. yet either."

"No, I haven't."

"Don't worry, I'll tell him. Beam him up. I was going to call him later anyway."

Pause.

"Okay, sweetie, so what really gives? What do you and the old guy talk about? You and an old blues player who ain't out there working, talk about?"

"Everything, Byron. Everything."

"Come on, Ursula. Be more specific. 'Everything' covers a lot of ground."

"Well, we do."

"I mean the guy lives in Walker City, Iowa. Damn. Been out the loop for a long time, basically … Come on. He's back being a hick. Someone who's letting life pass him by. Probably thinks swatting a fly with a fly swat—"

"It's what you think? Honestly think of Maurice 'Teardrop' Williams?"

"Pretty much. Pretty … Yeah, yeah, it's what I think. Ain't ashamed to admit it."

"It's a simple life, that's what, Byron—"

"Ha. Right. Right."

"All … all. An … an unrushed life. Un-unburdened. That's all."

"Lovely, Ursula. My dear. Very nice. I love your semantics, girl, the pitch and tone of your words."

"Said with condescension. Well, say what you want to—"

"That Teardrop Williams is a great bluesman but a big bore? Okay? Crapped out on life just when it meant the most while serving his gift to make music, the most. Wife dying or no wife dying, Ursula. It's my take on the guy. Yeah. Wife dying or … or no wife dying …"

Byron's comments jolted Ursula, caught her totally off guard. There was a load of dynamite In it, what he'd said—a load, Ursula thought.

Denis Gray

"No comeback, Ursula?"

"No, no, Byron. I'm tired."

"Hey, now look, you did call me, sweetie, don't forget. You called me."

Ursula laughed. "I know."

"So don't lay that heavy guilt trip on me. Shit!"

"No, Byron, I am tired. Really."

"Been a long day, huh?"

"Yes."

"For me too. You ain't the only one. Ambition, drive—I hope it's going to pay off, worth it at the end of the rainbow."

"T-that's how—"

"I mean, let's get back to Teardrop Williams, Ursula, shall we? Look how things turned out for—"

"Byron, I *am* tired. I wasn't joking. And for one night, I think Mr. Williams's name has popped ... come up more than enough in one conversation?"

"So this weekend, what, your parents' place, huh? Over to Jersey?"

"Uh-huh."

"Hey, tell them I said hi."

"Will do."

"Saturday and Sunday as usual?"

"Saturday and Sunday, as usual."

"I don't think I'll bother with J. C. tonight. Call him. You don't mind, do you?"

"No. Uh-uh."

"Call him tomorrow. Tell him about your new ha—pen pal in Iowa: Teardrop Williams."

They bade one another good night.

Ursula got up. She was in and out the bathroom, having run bathwater. Then she walked back into the bathroom and sat on the edge of the tub, watching the water fill out the tub.

"I do have to agree with Byron on one point: it was quite powerful but ultimately explosive if not handled properly, the right way. But it's like life blew up in Teardrop Williams's face. Crapping out on life ... It's a crass ... maybe crude way of putting his life in perspective. Honest, but not accurate. But his genius jelling. It was always there in the early recordings—but, of course, age deepened it as it should."

Ursula had received a letter from him two days ago. But as usual, she wouldn't answer him right away but let his words soak through her as she would let the bath water in the tub do once it was filled with warm water and she would add the sweet smelling bubble bath and the water would soak through the pores of her skin and it would feel so good—just right for her.

Each letter had its own personality, its own spark, never boring—almost too energetic, bursting with life.

"I have yet to mention my parents, but I will the next letter. I'll let him know they live in Jersey City, New Jersey. Mr. Williams probably has never heard of it—like I'd never heard of Walker City, Iowa—but then again, maybe he has in his travels, being that it's just across the water from New York City. A close cousin."

It was one of the things she would talk about in her letter, along with a lot of other things.

"Like I told you, Byron, Mr. Williams and I talk about 'everything.'"

Ursula's water was ready and so was she. She dipped her hand down into the bubbles, bursting them and away from the water's surface, her fingers entering the depths of it. And suddenly she felt a chill but realized it would soon pass—and she would let it.

Then she was naked, and she stepped into the water. Already, in her mind, she'd composed a letter to Teardrop Williams. A letter as alive and animated as his letters were to her. It was there set in her mind about to snap at her like a turtle.

Arlene had driven Teardrop into town. Teardrop went into town for a haircut and to do some personal shopping. It was 9:30 a.m. that they got into town. They'd both checked their watches, synchronizing them, laughed, and Arlene asked, "What time do you want me back, Dad?" "Hmm … how about eleven thirty, honey?" "Eleven thirty it is." And so that was that.

It was ten o'clock. Arlene was standing outside the house looking at the red Impala intently. *Should I wash it?* she thought. *I have roughly an hour and fifteen minutes.* And before she gave herself time to carry on a great, windy Lincoln versus Douglas debate, Arlene had the long green garden hose in her hand and was giving the red Impala a good old-fashioned hosing down in the driveway.

It was 10:03 a.m. when Arlene saw Sid Turner, the mailman, and waved to him. He was approaching the house slowly—due to his age and feet and his long, dedicated service with the US Postal Service.

"Hi, Sid."

"Hi, Arlene. Look kinda good with that hose of yours. Sure you're a college professor over at Walker State U teaching students?"

"Oh, I just do this, wash cars, to make extra money. After all these years, Dad won't increase my weekly allowance."

"Shame, ain't it? Anything I can do about it?"

Arlene smiled.

"Uh, talking about your father, where's he? Usually here to get the mail."

Arlene stopped hosing the Impala. "I drove him to town to get a haircut. Then found out he had other things to do in town."

"Can always say, Arlene, Teardrop Williams and me use the same barber, old Josh Perkins. And Josh tells me we tip about the same too."

"Ha."

"Put the mail on the stoop?"

"That'll be fine, Sid. Thank you."

Mischievously Sid looked at Arlene. "And now you can get back to work. Don't want no one to say I held you back. From doing your chores, Arlene. Rumors to get around Walker."

"See you, Sid," Arlene said, about to turn the hose back on.

"Oh, by the way, your father got a letter from New York. On the stack, there."

Quickly Arlene stopped what she was doing.

"Same person as usual. Always announce it to him too. Been a lot lately."

Arlene panicked. *A lot? A lot!*

And seizing the moment, she ran to the stoop and got the letter and looked at it and saw "U. Jenkins," and she called out to Sid Turner who hadn't gotten far.

"Stop, Sid. Stop!"

Sid turned. "Yes, Arlene? Yes. Uh … uh something wrong?"

Arlene ran up to him. "I want you to understand something, Sid," Arlene said, catching her breath.

"Yes?"

"If only, if only you knew what these letters do to my father. H-how upset he is when he gets them from New York. Depressed w-when they're delivered to the house, Sid."

Sid looked bewildered.

"Yes, they're from New York City, all right. A reporter up there who … who a few months back came to Walker City to—"

"Was out here doing a story on your father, Teardrop. From a magazine. Know all about it, Arlene. Ruby Ingram told me. Was all ginned up. Ruby was."

"Yes. Yes, Sid. Ms. Ruby was exactly right."

"Heard it don't go so hot. Between them. That New York lady and your father."

"Then you heard right." Pause. "B-but she won't take no for an answer, this person. Woman."

"Reporter. New York reporter," Sid said, squinting, and not because of the sun.

"Yes, Sid. New York reporter. She's been harassing my father. Upsetting him to the point where it's depressing him. But she won't take no for an answer. Give—"

"Writes him enough times. See it for myself. But he don't seem upset over it, uh, at the time I tell him. He gets them. Uh, his face, manner, Arl—"

"But you know my dad, Sid, you know how he is. Y-you know him."

"Sure do. Don't like to upset nobody else's day. Ain't in Teardrop. Disposition, personality to upset nobody else's day. No matter the trouble in his."

"Yes. Yes." Pause. "But, Sid … there, but there's—and there's nothing Dad can do about the letters, but … but maybe, just maybe we can, Sid. We, we can."

"W-we can, Arlene?"

"Yes, you and me, Sid."

"Oh … yes, you and me. Arlene. You and me. Thought it's what you meant. Was saying."

"You see, we can intercept it—"

"What, your father's mail? Teardrop's—but there's laws. Strict federal laws on the books," Sid said. "I gotta abide, a mail carrier gotta abide by with the postal service."

"I mean just this letter, Sid. This one," Arlene said, her disgust evident. "The letter from New York, from that, uh, pushy New York City reporter up there—nothing else. No other items will—"

"How do we do that? What, you got an idea about, what to do?"

"So ... you're for it?"

"If it's upsetting Teardrop then of course I am. All for it. He don't need that. He's too special a man around here. Man needs his ... but how do we work this out between us, Arlene. You and me, since your father takes in the mail out on the porch most days I deliver?"

"Easy, Sid. Easy. You'll just withhold that letter from him, that's all."

"A-and do what with it, Arlene?"

"Call me at the school. The university. I'll give you the number. That's no problem. And then I'll pick It up. Better still, rip it—"

"Uh, well, I would appreciate it if you read it first, Arlene," Sid said with a worried look on his face. "No telling, never can tell if there's something in it might change in importance. No, uh, telling," Sid said, grimacing, seemingly not at all pleased by what he'd heard from Arlene.

"Yes, I meant to say, read it first. Sid," Arlene said, under better control. "The letter first. There, yes, there's no telling about that, Sid. You're right. Dead right."

"Even though I'm sure nothing's gonna change with them folk. New Yorkers up there."

"Sure, I'll read the letter through first. It was just that I am so upset myself by the person's per—"

"Don't have to bother to explain it again, Arlene. Ain't gotta. Just to make me more mad than what I am."

"Then, uh, uh, it's a deal then, Sid?"

Sid stuck out his hand. "Let's you and me shake on it, Arlene."

"Shake, we will, Sid. Shake on it!"

Arlene grabbed Sid Turner's hand.

"Signed, sealed, and delivered. And don't worry, Arlene, you can count on me. Anything to save Teardrop from something unpleasant as that. He don't need. You ain't gotta worry about me doing what's right by Teardrop. You got you a ally, Arlene."

"Thanks. Sid. Thanks."

"Oh, well ... let me get moving along. Ms. Earlwell down the road sets her clock by me every day. Gotta really hustle now in order to make up for lost time! Ha. And this hot sun don't help any. Don't want it to get on my record. No telling what old Bertha Earlwell might do or say against me!"

Sid scooted off as both he and Arlene laughed uproariously.

"Thanks, Sid," Arlene said under her breath. "Thank you so much."

Arlene sat at the bottom of the white stoop, looking up to the top. She walked up the steps and then sat. She picked up the letter and then stood, opened the screen door, and then wandered through the house, finally, standing by the study's wicker waste-paper basket.

"Now let's see what you have to say to my dad, Ms. Ursula Jenkins. What's on your mind? What seems to be so damned important in New York City that you have to write him!"

The letter was out the envelope, and Arlene was speed reading through it.

"W-who wants to know about your parents? Your mother and father? Why would my father want to know—need that kind of information? For what purpose? Don't make me laugh. S-so you're working on this and that—you're a freelance writer, nothing more … What do you expect? The world's not going to bow to you, Ms. Jenkins. It's what, only what you should be doing. The—it's what your professional work is. How you make a damned living."

It was a two-page letter, front and back.

"So … you can't wait to hear from my dad … can you, Ms. Jenkins?"

The letter was stuffed back in the envelope, and then Arlene ripped the envelope in half as if possessed.

"There'll be no reply. It's over. Done with. My father will never hear from you again!"

Arlene said, dumping the torn envelope, its shreds, in the waste-paper basket adjacent to the desk.

Two weeks later.

Teardrop came out the woods distraught.

"I … I haven't heard from her. I don't want to ask Sid. What did I say in my last letter?" Teardrop looked up at the clear blue sky, perplexed. "I … I don't know. I don't even know, Ms. Jenkins."

He'd been giving her the benefit of the doubt up until today: busy, so busy with her writing, her journalistic assignments, schedule that she just hadn't found the time to sit down to write him.

"She's not sick. I hope Ms. Jenkins is not in any way ill. With the pace she apparently maintains. The demands of her profession. B-being always on the go. Running around."

Or maybe she was just tired of him—writing this man, middle-aged man who was more than double her age.

"Maybe Ms. Jenkins said enough's enough. Maybe it's what she finally said. At … at last."

But Teardrop knew he'd still be looking for a letter in the mail from her tomorrow. He felt he didn't want to give up this easily; he wasn't like that—it was not the nature of his personality.

Ursula was sick to her stomach.

"Why hasn't Mr. Williams answered me? Hasn't written me back? Why haven't I received a letter from him?"

Ursula stretched her body out in the bed, and it was not only her stomach but her head that was agitated. She couldn't understand this delay in communication. No communication for now. This gap. But for her, it felt more like a gulch rather than something as innocuous as a gap.

"Is … is he sick? I keep asking myself. Wondering. Is Mr. Williams ill? Is … is he?"

Ursula had a new story to finish, a deadline to meet—it was important. And there was someone who was to call her tonight. She was to interview someone vital to the piece, but right now, for now, she was back to thinking about Teardrop Williams, worrying over him.

It began four days ago, and now it no longer drizzled down on her silently. She felt it now, this sudden change in her life, like a rain burst.

"Have our ages finally made a difference? Caught up with us? Am I beginning to sound like, too much like a foolish schoolgirl and not a woman?"

It's how Ursula was feeling, had begun to think. Maybe the age difference between them *did* matter, had finally caught up with them and passed them by.

"*Why am I writing to this young lady?* Is that what Teardrop Williams asked himself when he got my last letter? How he evaluated it? Did he question why I mentioned my parents, as if they would play some vital role in our future for us?

"No, he wouldn't take it that far—for … for I haven't taken it that far. We're writing each other because …"

Because, Ursula thought. *Because of what? What? Because of what?*

It's when Ursula suddenly didn't like the way she was talking to herself—the way she was thinking. She was putting herself out there—somewhere she'd never been. Somewhere on a ledge, where it felt dangerous, where she felt unsure. For she didn't understand her heart, it beating like crazy, too fast. Maybe she was acting like a schoolgirl and not like a woman. Maybe Teardrop Williams had seen through her (so transparent), had broken this whole thing off, looked at it for what it really was, saw it, shattered it into bits and pieces—the one smart enough to do so, his years of experience valuably revealing itself.

Teardrop didn't care. On this night, he didn't care. He was going to write her, Ursula Jenkins. Step out of this dark shadow he felt he was in, that he didn't like. So what if she didn't write back—there was no law in the universe to dictate or argue she must. The letter writing didn't have to follow a precise pattern, routine: I write you, therefore, you must write me back. And to write her would change the pattern as it stood now, Teardrop had decided. It would make her communication freer, much freer, open it up, loosen its rigidity, predictability.

This was good, Teardrop had thought. He didn't take to rigidity, unspontaneous events, not in his music, not in anything. There was nothing wrong with routine, discipline, but not when it came to the soul, the spirit; it must feel free, ride on the wing of a wave—always.

Teardrop was at his small desk (it looked more like a flat-surfaced table with tiny drawers on either side than a desk).

"I have to write you, Ms. Jenkins. I have to."

Dear Miss Jenkins,
Since I haven't heard from you in some time, I have assumed you've just been busy, unable to write. Your professional career is continuing full steam ahead. Which is always good news. But be as it may, as you can see, I'm writing you. And there's much to tell you since little water has run under the bridge.
First …

She was in the lobby, down in front of her mailbox. She'd gone into her mailbox. And when it happened, it was like an explosion, the letter was ripped open, torn open right there on the spot. It was read right there, in the lobby—after her heart had quieted. Of course. Of course. (She wasn't a quitter. She was never a quitter!)

Ursula was upstairs in the kitchenette trying to make sense out of things, standing between the stove and the refrigerator.

"You haven't heard from me? You haven't heard from me ... but I wrote you last month. The letter wasn't returned to me, the *sender*. Someone has it, it's somewhere. Has to be, Mr. Williams."

Could it have been lost? Ursula thought. Just rotten luck? Everybody having to depend on delivery systems that sometimes break down are not efficient—have failures too. Why not a letter suffering the same tragic luck.

"Why not," Ursula laughed. "It could happen to anyone—might as well've been me. Law of averages. There's nothing so special about me or my letter to the post office."

Ursula continued to laugh, for she felt so happy. Gay. Giddy. Happy that this communication between her and Teardrop Williams had not ended. And in her heart, all along, she knew it hadn't. It just wasn't for a person of his character to do something like that—end something with no words spoken. Silent communication. First and foremost, Maurice "Teardrop" Williams was a gentleman.

"So ... there it is—it's how it happened. The post office. US Post Office. Rain, sleet, and snow—it's their motto. The mail must go through. D-delivered. Well, it didn't this time around. But it will next time. It couldn't happen twice in one month. Suffer the same unkind fate. The odds of it happening again are too great, uh, extreme. It would be like hitting the lottery for a million dollars twice in one month—mathematically impossible!"

Ursula got up out of bed. She was going to soak in the tub's bathwater and then get to her desk. She would mention her parents in her letter, but everything else would change, that and her rant against the United States Postal Service (and it wasn't going to be pretty, she'd already decided).

Ursula picked up the letter, sticking it in the envelope. "Let me hurry up and get started!"

Jamal wheeled the bike into the backyard.

"Granddad, I guess I won't be riding my bike much longer."

Teardrop was sitting on a back porch step. "You've got another good month left, Jamal, before it turns bitter cold."

"It's what I figured, Granddad. About another month."

"Early October. But when I was your age, it didn't matter. I rode until the first snowflake fell. My friends and I." Pause. "Don't want to say we were of a sturdier stock then, but then again …"

Jamal hopped off the bike, leaning it against the stair's post. "Then it's what I'll do, Granddad. But Armon—"

"He might not see it your way."

Jamal's head wheeled around to Teardrop. "Granddad … d-did you and Miss Lillian go into the woods today?"

Teardrop's head flopped to the side and then he said, "No, I didn't. Miss Lillian and I, Jamal. Not today."

"T-two days in a row. Straight, Granddad?"

Teardrop failed to answer him.

"Gran—"

"Uh, I heard you, Jamal. I heard—I guess Miss Lillian and I need a break from our routine. S-sometimes I think we do."

"She's complaining, Granddad?"

"Oh, nothing, nothing like that. As serious. No, Miss Lillian's not complaining. It's me …" Teardrop looked away from Jamal. "Don't worry, Jamal, it's temporary. These, uh, things are temporary." It's when Teardrop looked back at Jamal. "Life goes through these little cycles, like the change of season we were just talking about."

"If … if you say so, Granddad."

Pause.

"Be right back," Jamal said, grabbing hold of his bike, hopping back on it. "I forgot something—left it over at Armon's house!"

"Okay," Teardrop laughed. "Okay, Jamal. Okay."

"Be right back, Granddad!"

Jamal sped off on his bike.

"Yes, just enjoy the simple pleasures of life now, Jamal, while you can," Teardrop said wistfully. "Until they become complicated … too … Why hasn't she written me! Why hasn't Ursula Jenkins written me!"

Teardrop said, storming to his feet. "W-what's gone wrong between us? This relationship we have?"

Teardrop began walking what seemed in a nervous fit, when he stopped halfway between the house and the woods. "What have I done, Ursula? Tell me, what!"

And it's when Teardrop realized it was the first he'd called Ursula Jenkins "Ursula." This young lady he was beginning to know, become acquainted with. The first time he'd been so informal with her as to call her Ursula.

"Could this communication I thought we both were enjoying, were thoroughly engaged in, c-could it be over? Was it one-sided? One ... just how busy can she be? Ms., Ms. Jenkins be? Why not a note, a postcard if she's always on assignment, writing assignment. Something."

And now Teardrop felt furious with himself, that someone of his age, fifty-five years old, had been strung along by a twenty-five-year-old. He felt foolish, not just old. Naïve, to the point of feeling vulnerable, exposed, letting his heart guide him—not stopping it like he ought to, not deferring to earned and respected wisdom.

"Now she has two letters of mine to read. Who ... who knows what she's done with them? Who the hell knows!"

Teardrop was crying. He'd broken down. And he wanted to feel himself cry, the tears, the hurt in him—for it would be the last time. His final time for this. He promised himself it would be the last time that he cried over Ursula Jenkins, what had happened between them. Something he'd originally started and she'd followed up on. Something they both seemed to find enjoyment in, fun in—speaking to one another through letters.

"I'm sorry, Maureen. I'm sorry for this. T-this preoccupation with this. This foolish, reckless escapade of mine." He shook his head. "It was beginning to feel like an obsession. I was beginning to let it turn into one. I'm sorry," Teardrop sobbed.

"Only you belong on that throne. No one else. No one else could be as honorable, as loving as you ...

"This was just a mistake, a miserable mistake. A ... a temporary lapse in judgment, my senses. I ... I wasn't seeing clearly. Thinking the years have taken their toll. Your death. I gave Ms. Jenkins too much value. There was a void in me I was trying to fill. I see that now. B-but Ms. Jenkins ... I will not write to her again. It's over." Pause. "I mean that, Maureen. It's over. All ... all over between us."

CHAPTER 11

Ursula was frantic. *How much more of this could she take!* It was up to twelve days now (how could she count the days?). Twelve days ago she'd mailed her letter off to Teardrop Williams, and there'd been no reply. As soon as she knew the mail, this morning, was delivered, down in the mailbox, she was down in the lobby to check, to see if it'd gone from eleven to twelve days.

How could it have happened a second time? she'd been asking herself for the past few hours. Her thoughts had been interrupted, had disrupted her work. She couldn't think, or maybe she was overthinking. Whichever it was, her nerves were as tight as piano wires. She really, really felt frustrated and downcast.

Ursula hopped onto her feet. "But now I'm going to take matters into my own hands!" she said to herself. She had advised herself against the tactic. *But what choice do I have?* Ursula thought.

"I can't stand pat any longer. This has gotten to be far too serious. What appears out of my control."

Jamal was in the kitchen. Teardrop was on the deck reading. He wore a Windbreaker on a September day. The sun wasn't out. It was sixty-seven degrees with a warm sun yesterday. Today it was fifty-six degrees with no sun and a brisk northwesterly wind.

Ring.

"I'll get it, Granddad," Jamal shouted from the kitchen.

"Okay, Jamal."

Teardrop continued reading his book. It was an Abraham Lincoln biography. Teardrop wanted to know who freed the slaves—if not Lincoln, who (whose revisionist history)? Of course, needless to say, there was more to it, theoretically—the emancipation question—than that. Teardrop enjoyed reading the biographies of great men of history. He was interested in seeing the making and shaping of leadership, subtle in some instances, dramatic in others, but always absorbing to observe in the panoramic context of this enduring struggle in human history as it advanced forward.

But then Teardrop rested the book on his stomach. And as always, only one thought subsumed him: Ursula Jenkins. Teardrop couldn't shake her out his mind no matter how hard he tried. He just shut his eyes, seemingly satisfied with that, that awareness—his face reflecting no overt emotion, his breathing, not at all mirroring his real state of mind.

"Granddad, Granddad, the phone, Granddad!"

Teardrop opened his eyes, was startled, the phone having rung, seemingly, hours ago but knowing it'd been minutes.

"Granddad …"

The screen door flew open.

"Yes, yes …"

"It's for you, Granddad! It's for you, sir!"

"Jamal, calm down," Teardrop said, getting out the deck chair slowly, reluctantly. "Why the excitement? Who's on the phone? W—"

"I'm not to tell. You see, it's a surprise. S-supposed to be a surprise."

"S-surprise?"

And it's when Jamal caught himself. "Oops, almost slipped, Granddad."

"Almost, but not quite."

"But you've got to hurry!"

The phone was dangling; it was about a two-foot-long cord running down the wall.

And as Teardrop entered into the kitchen, Jamal exited. "I'll be around, Granddad."

"Somewhere in the house—"

"Or outside."

"I know. I know, Jamal."

Teardrop paused and then looked at the phone mysteriously, as if the person on the other end were responsible for it, the way it dangled.

Teardrop placed the phone to his ear. "H-hello."

"Mr. Williams, it's me, Ur-Ursula Jenkins."

"Ursula Jenkins. Ms. Jenkins!"

"Y-yes, Mr. Williams. Ur-Ursula Jenkins!"

"How … how are you, Ms. Jenkins?"

"Fine, fine, Mr. Williams. J-just fine!"

"Of all the …" Teardrop's voice dropped off.

"Of course I told Jamal—"

"Not to tell me who was calling me on the other end of the phone."

"In fact, I heard everything that transpired between you, Mr. Williams."

"Yes, Jamal was quite emphatic, wasn't he?"

"Quite."

Pause.

"Uh …"

Both had said it simultaneously.

"No, you first, go first—by all means, Ms. Jenkins."

Teardrop waited.

"You do have the floor, Ms. Jenkins. Still—"

"D-did you receive my last letter, Mr. Williams?"

"Your last letter? Why that was quite some—"

"The second one, to explain that the first one, the last one that I'd written must've been lost in the mail."

"Lost? Lost in the mail?"

"Yes, it's the only explanation I suppose is reasonable. The post office didn't return it. The letter to me, the sender, so it's what I was left to assume—that it got lost in the mail. So I wrote you a second—"

"Ms. Jenkins, pardon me, but let's go back, backtrack. You mean you've written me two letters—"

"Within the past month."

"You … you have? And I've failed to receive them In the mail? Any of them?"

Pause.

"But you received my letter—"

"About a week and a half ago—"

"Which gave no indication you'd received my letter. And so I wrote you immediately. That night, in fact."

"And … and you mean I … I never got it? That's hard to … but Sid, Sid Turner. I … I always, oh, he's the mailman. The mailman around here. For need of explanation.

"And as it's routine for me to do, I take in the mail every day—since I'm home all day. And so as I said, Ms. Jenkins, Sid hands me the mail, so how could this happen?"

"I ... I don't know, Mr. Williams. I—"

"N-not once but twice."

"When it happened the first time, I didn't think it could happen again. A second time."

"But it did. Strange ..."

"That it would be mathematically improbable."

"It ... it would certainly seem so."

"No matter how bad I am at math."

"Uh, right, Ms. Jenkins. I remember you telling me that."

And then both their minds went to work, attempting to get to the bottom of something each knew would frustrate them more.

Shortly, things were refocused.

"I, may I be perfectly honest with you, Ms. Jenkins?"

"B-by all means."

"I ... I'd begun to think the worse. That you had not decided to write. To continue. Broken off all ... all communication with me."

"No, no, not—but it was what I'd begun to think too, Mr. Williams, from your end. W-when I didn't receive communication from you, that it'd been broken off by you."

"But then we're better than that, aren't we? We handle our affairs, personal matters, far better than that, don't we?"

"It's what—how I thought about it too, Mr. Williams. B-but only when you are frantic ..."

"Yes, frantic, Ms. Jenkins ..."

And there was a long pause, for both were aware they'd suddenly shared something very important and telling with each other.

"But I kept putting it off. Putting it off."

"What, Ms. Jenkins?" Pause.

"Calling you, Mr. Williams. I didn't want to take the chance."

"Chance?"

"S-suppose your daughter answered the phone. Not you or your grandson, Jamal, but Mrs. Wilkerson—your daughter."

"Ar-Arlene?"

"Yes."

"But Arlene's polite. Courteous. There'd be no problem with her. I told her I'd written you, apologized for my bad behavior when you were here."

And then, smartly, Ursula asked, "And that we're corresponding, Mr. Williams? Ex-exchanging letters? Did you—have you told Mrs. Wilkerson that?"

And it's when Teardrop's voice became barely audible. "No, no, Ms. Jenkins. No, I haven't."

"Then—"

"I sense my daughter doesn't like you."

"Yes. And her feelings toward me had nothing to do with the incident between us. It didn't instigate them. I sensed it far before that—her coolness towards me."

"Sorry."

"It's why I was cautious, worried, downright scared, in fact, about calling you. I guess if she had answered the phone—"

"Well, Arlene didn't, Ms. Jenkins. But if she had, would you have tried again?"

"You bet!"

"Now that's good to know. It really is."

"I think I would have kept trying until I got, eventually got through. I know I would."

"Stubborn, huh?"

"It's what everyone tells me. It's a trait of mine."

"A good one," Teardrop said in voice surfeit with admiration.

"I'm so glad I got a chance to speak to Jamal."

"By the expression on my grandson's handsome face, so was he. You should've seen it, Ms. ... uh, but did he ask about—"

"No."

"He's probably already forgotten about the incident. I try to remember how it was at that age. When time flew by so fast."

"Me too."

"But for you, Ms. Jenkins, it wasn't that long ago. Now correct me if I'm wrong."

"No, I suppose not."

"Something I can't say."

Ursula heard what was said but preferred to ignore it.

"Do you want me to tell you over the phone what I wrote in my letter, the last one, Mr. Williams?"

"You don't mind throwing your money away? You mean freelance writers command that much money nowadays? No, I don't want your phone bill to skyrocket to new astronomical heights—and then you blaming me. My poor judgment."

"But if I write you, Mr. Williams—"

"It—how could it happen again? How? This—I mean, just that it's occurred twice. To us twice. On two ... I ... I ..."

And both felt frustrated again or hamstrung or—

"Ms. Jenkins. Ms. Jenkins ..."

"Yes?"

"Don't think I've gone, I'm forward or ... or gone crazy, loony, because I haven't. But ..."

"But?"

"W-what I mean ... what does your schedule look like in the next ... say, next several days? It's Tuesday."

"Right."

"This weekend, at least ..."

"This—"

"Fly here. Fly down here. To Walker City, Ms. Jenkins!"

"There? This weekend!"

"Yes, yes! Why not? What do you say? Are you game? Are ... are you f-for it?"

Ursula was twirling as fast as a top. She was getting dizzy, giddy, light-headed. She couldn't believe what she had agreed to, this spur-of-the-moment, impulsive, whimsical, exciting thing she agreed to do.

She had agreed to fly to Walker City, Iowa, Saturday morning. Teardrop said he would pay for her airline ticket, charge it to his credit card, since, of course, it was his idea, not hers, being the only gentlemanly thing for him to do. She agreed. He would book the flight and then call her with all the necessary information.

She said she would stay at Ruby Ingram's boarding house again. He thought it perfect. It was Tuesday, and Ursula was busy packing a lot of clothes for her two-day stay (in her mind, that is). Envisioning herself in different outfits, combinations. She was playing Teardrop's music off the tape. She was listening to the song he'd composed on the spot, out in the woods—the one Ursula swore was for her, took some credit for.

"I wonder if Byron's at work?"

There was only one way to find out, Ursula thought.

"Hi. Busy?"

"What, for you, dear lady? Never. Was just bouncing numbers around in my head."

"It's all you have to do?"

"And looking at mountain peaks and valleys on the screen."

"The vicissitudes of the stock market."

"But it's all good. All good, Ursula, you know that." Byron cleared his throat. "So ... what's up? Why the call out the blue?"

"Byron, do—I have exciting news for you ..."

"But ... you'd rather I guess first, right?" Byron laughed, interpreting the cause of Ursula's silence. "And of course I won't be able to since it's so exciting, stupendous—so well beyond my imagination."

"Yes, kind of."

"Then you're up for a Pulitzer prize in—"

"How I wish!"

"Wouldn't talk to me then. Not a damned word."

"You can say that again."

"I know. I know."

"No, no. I'm flying to Walker City this weekend. It's all been arranged."

"Whoa ... whoa, Ursula, Walker City, Iowa—it's all been arranged? Back up, back up, I need a playback on—"

"To visit Teardrop W—"

"Don't tell me you're back on that story again? *Currents* magazine again? Dan Gottlieb? Ursula, my advice to you this time is don't waste your time. Burned once. Not twice. Get too close to the fire again. Man, I wouldn't trust Teardrop Williams with an interview. A second one. Hell, he'll probably back out again. Like before. You and *Currents* should just move on, cut your losses while you can, with that guy. It's not—"

"But it's not what my visit's about, Byron. *Currents* isn't sending me— is no way connected. I was invited by Mr. Williams to Walker City to, to visit him."

"Visit him!"

"Yes, this is a personal visit."

"Personal!"

"Yes, personal."

Ursula could hear the rumble in Byron's voice. "All this from you and Teardrop Williams—this letter writing you and him are doing?"

"Yes."

Long pause.

"Even though there's been some kind of awful, drastic mix up the past month. My last two letters never got—"

"I don't want to hear about it. It doesn't matter." Byron took his time. "What, so what's this guy, Teardrop Williams, up to? Huh? What's this guy, some ... some kind of Lothario, Don Juan? Dirty old man? Cradle snatcher? What the hell's this old guy after?"

"Af-after?"

"Hell yes, after!"

"Byron, you're not trying to turn this into some kind of cheap, perverse—"

"Is it, Ursula? Is it?"

"What, and you expect me to answer that!"

"What, you can't?"

"Answer it to defend myself, Mr. Williams? No ... I'm happy, glad to say I don't, Byron. Because Teardrop Williams and I are above that."

"So why are you flying off to Walker City for?"

Ursula reined in her emotions. "And why are you so upset by all of this?"

"Why ... why, I'll tell you ... B-because you're my friend. That's the hell why. And ... and I don't like to see old men ... especially middle-aged men like that, him, play out their fantasies, sick, perverse, cheap fantasies on young women like you. Damn, Ursula, I saw a friend of mine get hung up that way, like that when I was eighteen. Fall for an older dude. She played with dynamite like that. Plus, you hear about it all the time—old guys chasing after young girls, babes. Old dudes trying to retain it. You know ... shit, you know what I'm saying, trying to say, sweetie."

"Then ... then you don't know Teardrop Williams."

"And so you do?"

Ursula didn't answer him.

"A few letters through the mail, right, right? What, and then what, a couple of days with Teardrop Williams in Walker City, Iowa, interviewing him for that article, and what, Ursula? A talk on the phone, and you—"

"Everything starts somewhere. Someplace. Has its origin. Beginning."

Byron calmed down. "Ursula, you're so smart, intelligent, and, well, both of us are so young. We have to, we should remind ourselves of that. Constantly. Put the brakes on sometimes. You know"—Byron sighed—"we've tread over this ground before." Pause.

"Like right now, I'm sitting up here, on the thirty-third floor, in my office, trying to put two and two together, but Mr. Sol Abrams, a few doors down the hall, who's been with the company twenty-five years plus, is probably looking at the same thing I am, raw set of data—and probably already has a solution. And has moved on to a new set of data, not in the least rattled.

"Experience. It's all about experience. Of seeing things before. Stuff we have to think extra hard over, take time with in order to accrue … gain what they've already got. You see, it's about knowledge. Knowledge, Ursula. Knowledge."

"I have to go this weekend, Byron. It was never a question of *would* I go when Mr. Williams asked, no matter how surprised I was. It was only that I was going to go."

"And now I'm back to square one, back to what I asked you before: to find what, Ursula? Out what?"

"T-there's a lot I have to find out about myself. A lot I don't know about myself. Questions I still need to ask myself."

"And that could be, ha, rough, with you being a journalist. Very rough. Hard on you, girl."

"Darn tootin' it could!"

"Yeah. Yeah!"

"Ha."

"O-okay, lookit, Ursula, I've got to get back to why they're paying me the big bucks. But you let me say my piece. I've put my reservations out there big time, and as I said, well … that's what friends, good friends are for. Nothing but."

"Right, Byron."

"And having said that, I wish you a good, safe trip … okay? And the best of everything in Walker City. Luck. And t-talk to you when you get back. Back to the city, okay, sweetie?"

CHAPTER 12

Walker City was quite nice to look at today and not because of the sun making the temperature soar up to seventy-four degrees, where it'd been ten degrees less the past few days, but because of the topography of the few drifting clouds and the pleasantness of the soft blues in the sky. But Ursula had boned up more on Iowa's history, its past, and what she discovered was not as serene as the blue skies and drifting clouds when it came to black life in Iowa (this was historical fact). Iowa fought for the Union during the Civil War but still, in the 19th century, believed in white supremacy; and as a reasonable person, she could only wonder how such extreme opposite views could seamlessly coexist in the hearts and minds of the average citizen of that era.

Ursula had been in Walker City for no more than an hour and in Ms. Ruby Ingram's boarding house on Marble Lane for no more than twenty minutes. She felt settled in, and all she had to do was wait for Teardrop Williams's phone call.

Three minutes later.

Ring.

"Yes …"

"Hello, Ms. Jenkins?"

"H-hello, Mr. Williams."

"S-so you're here. In Walker City. Safe and sound. Thank you for coming. Have you settled in yet? Collected yourself?"

"Yes, yes, I have."

"Then it's all right to send Bert by to pick you up?"

"Y-yes, Bert—by all means."

"Uh, f-fine then. I'm sorry it has to be this way."

"B-but I understand, Mr. Williams."

"But I still want to a-apologize to you. But ... uh, well, Bert should be there in a few minutes. How's that?"

"Fine."

"Bert will know where to take you off to."

"Thank you, Mr. Williams."

Ursula continued looking at everything she could see in Walker City, the Trinity section, as if to memorize them, as if she were writing an article requiring images that dripped free with them. So the old trees and old grounds were being looked at as if they were new Iowa harvests for big-fisted men, farmers who worked as hard as the farm animals they trained and their sweat golden sunbursts paying homage to that vested past.

And now the taxi turned off Dawkin's Road and then soon onto the gravel driveway, riding over it like a languid, unwinding day just past summer, and up to a big house still looking like a summer house near a lake in the fall, in front of where small boats docked in its rear. Immediately, Ursula loved the house: white in color, full of robust, outgoing character, sweeping you into its grandness without even winking once in any overt effort to seduce you but knowing it had, with ease.

Bert's blue-flame taxicab stopped.

"Here we are, Ms. Jenkins, 18 Dawkin's Road. But ain't nobody around, looks like—not Tear—"

"I'm early by a few minutes. Mr. Williams and Ms. Wilkerson—"

"Arlene?"

"Oh ... yes, they're due any minute now. So then ... let me pay you."

"Seven dollars will do it."

Ursula handed Bert ten dollars.

"Thank you. And your—"

"It's yours."

"Thanks again, Ms. Jenkins."

Bert got out the taxi, opened Ursula's door, and she stepped out. She stood facing the house.

"Now you sure you don't mind standing out here alone, Ms. Jenkins? Not that there's anybody to worry about, to do wrong by you in Walker City. Not in Trinity, this neck of the woods, ma'am. But you always try to do the right thing by folk no matter—since it don't take much."

"I'll only be out here a few minutes, I'm sure," Ursula said, glancing at her watch.

"Yeah, you can see Arlene's red car ... Well, okay ... Welcome once again to Walker City. Hope you enjoy your stay. Teardrop Williams is a legend 'round here, you know. A living legend in these parts."

The taxi began to move from the house and then left the area.

Ursula's back was to him; she was facing the house, just looking at it, him fast approaching her with Miss Lillian out the case, hanging in front of him as loose and easy as a blues rhythm being tossed out to the breeze.

"Ms. Jenkins." Ursula turned. "Why hello, Ms. Jenkins."

"Mr. ... Mr. Williams. Where ..."

"From out the woods. The wooded area from my daughter's house extends here. Over to my house."

"Your house. Your house—I love your house, Mr. Williams."

"So do I."

Teardrop liked the way Ursula was dressed: slacks, jacket, loafers. His attire was pretty much similar, a plaid shirt, casual shoes with a smudge of brown dust on them (from the woods)—clothes that were very much up-to-date, modern looking.

"It has such a peaceful atmosphere to it. A sweet nature."

"It has a lot of years in it, Ms. Jenkins."

Ursula's body whirled around. "And the grounds ..."

"I have someone do them. A Mr. Kelly. Of course the leaves will be falling off the trees soon. But fall, it has such a magnificent splendor to it."

"And I bet in Walker City, in a beautiful setting like this, every year it's special."

"Special, yes. Iowa brags about its superior beauty all the time. Without fail."

And then Teardrop looked intently at Ursula again. "Thanks again for coming, Ms. Jenkins. For flying in from New York. For doing this."

"Thank you for inviting me."

Finally, it's when Teardrop saw Ursula not only had her shoulder strap pocketbook but was also holding on to a rather large manila envelope; only, she made no mention of it.

"Uh, would you like to see what the house looks like from the inside? Since, ha, there's so much to see."

"Oh … oh, would I!"

"Then if you will …"

Teardrop took Ursula's hand, and she proceeded up the front stairs with him. Teardrop went into his front pocket and pulled out the house key. In a way, it seemed he was teasing her with it as she laughed.

"Ex-excuse me, Ms. Jenkins," Teardrop said as Ursula moved to the side of him. "Since now it's time, it seems, for the grand unveiling."

It's when Teardrop inserted the key into the lock and then pushed the door open. As soon as he did, he switched the hall light on. It's when Teardrop turned to Ursula, and Ursula entered the hallway too, and the house didn't smell musty or stale like she thought it might but pleasant and nice like any ordinary house that was being lived in.

Ursula studied Teardrop's face, curious to see what she might find in it, but his expressive brown eyes seemed to be focused only on what she was doing—her being the only reason why the front door of the house was unlocked in the first place.

"Now for the grand tour … Ms. Jenkins. Or am I repeating myself?"

Ursula laughed.

And already, in the living room, Ursula saw the white sheets covering the furniture. And already, she began to think that there must be mystery in every room of the house, big, large, looming, giant ghosts hiding, sleeping under neatly starched white sheets—a blanket of sheets like a still, frozen river.

Ursula and Teardrop were out in the house's backyard.

"Quite impressive."

"It is, isn't it, Ursula?"

And it's when Teardrop looked at her, and she at him, and there was something that happened very naturally between them, not uncomfortable like before, but much more of something.

"Mr. Williams, I-I'd like to call you Maurice, if I may?"

And it's when Teardrop's body trembled, and his eyes turned totally from her.

"Maureen called me Maurice," Teardrop said; his eyes were back looking into hers, the two standing only feet apart. "M-my wife."

Of course, when they were in the house, Ursula wasn't shown Teardrop and Maureen's bedroom. The bedroom door was shut. It was pointed to. Referred to. But the bedroom was not opened nor was it shown. Ursula had anticipated this.

Teardrop just looked at Ursula for the longest, wondering what her thoughts were. He took her hand into his.

"I'd feel honored ... honored if you would. If you would call me Maurice."

Ursula never felt so warm, so flush.

Teardrop laughed. "So now that's settled, done with," he said, like he and Ursula had cleared yet another huge hurdle. He let go of her hand.

"Maurice ..."

"Yes."

"M-may I share something with you?"

They were standing directly in the sun at its hottest at two forty-eight in the afternoon in Walker City, Iowa.

"Maybe. First, we should step out the sun." The house's overhang provided great shade, and like Arlene's house, there was a deck with lovely furniture. "The sun, particularly at this time of day, can be brutal."

Teardrop pulled the chair out for her. Then he sat facing her at the wooden table. Ursula put the manila envelope on top the table.

"Better, Ursula?"

"M-much, Maurice."

"It ... it sounds much better than Mr. Williams—"

"Or Ms. Jenkins."

"Doesn't it?"

"Yes."

"Yes, yes, Ursula, you were saying?"

"I ... I simply have a confession to make."

"Which is?"

"There was a night when—it's hard, difficult to find the right words, but I brought this for you. Here, Maurice," Ursula said, handing the manila envelope to Teardrop.

Teardrop examined it and then looked at Ursula as though he were asking for a clue, some idea as to what was in the rather large envelope. But not really fearing anything from it, not for a minute, but still somewhat apprehensive about it, the idea of it.

Teardrop opened the envelope, and his fingers drew out several sheets of typed paper.

"Ursula, w-what is it?"

"Something for you to read."

"Yes, I can see that," Teardrop said, now looking at the papers, not just holding them.

Teardrop's eyes fixed onto the first page; Ursula's eyes shut.

"How did you know so much with so little time spent with me?"

She simply shook her head.

"Yes, it wasn't just missing Maureen but the special joy of coming back to her from the road. Playing the blues gigs. That's what killed my spirits. It was the loss I suffered. Made it impossible for me to go out again and then come back. The melancholy I had."

"Again, Ursula, how did you know that? Intuit it?"

"I don't know. Maybe I tried to put myself in your situation."

Ursula had written the article on Maurice "Teardrop" Williams as if compelled to. What she'd originally come down to Walker City, Iowa, to do. It was the next night, when she'd come back to New York, Jamaica, Queens, when she told Dan Gottlieb at *Currents* on the phone that the Teardrop Williams story was dead in the water. But it was not dead for her, not inside her—it was very much alive, raging as if she had to write it before her rage consumed her.

"You, literally, it's as if you burrowed inside me."

"I wanted to."

"You did?" Teardrop said, reaching for Ursula's hand and then taking it.

"Yes," Ursula said. "Yes! Yes!" Ursula said, her hand dropping down on the table, Teardrop wanting to get up to go to her, hold her, but not knowing how to do this, not even knowing if this is what he wanted.

Ursula's head came off the table, and she was sobbing. "I didn't want to lose those two days with you. T-they were too precious. And I would have if … if I hadn't written the article."

How potent that sounded, Teardrop thought. *How potent.*

"For … for someone to be so young, so—you to be so sure of things. Things around you. You're in the presence of."

"I … I don't know," Ursula said, wiping her eyes dry.

Teardrop stood. "More than me."

"W-what do you mean by that, Maurice?"

"I wanted to come to you just now, hold you, but I didn't— couldn't."

"I know. I could feel it in your hand."

"Ha."

"What, Maurice?"

"Let me say something, young lady. You're dangerous."

Ursula smiled.

"Ursula," Teardrop continued, "I didn't know how."

Her eyes lifted to Teardrop and then dropped back down. "But you did want to?"

"I did, yes."

"Then it's something, Maurice."

"I ... I don't know what it is."

"I'm just glad you liked, feel comfortable with the article."

"It's a masterpiece."

"It's yours."

"Thank you," Teardrop said, pressing the envelope's lid shut.

"Even if I could publish it, I wouldn't. Would not do it."

"Even if I begged you to?"

"No."

"Why?"

Nothing came back.

"W-we're fighting powerful feelings, aren't we, Ursula?" Teardrop asked, sitting back down. "Emotions."

"Yes, we are."

"Powerful feelings ...," Teardrop said, as if to himself. "Emotions ..."

"I still don't know why my friend Byron wanted me to hear the CD, where we occasionally meet."

"To lead you off to, onto this adventure. Something we yet know about."

"But how do we make this work?"

"Yes, how, Ursula?"

"And ... and especially with—"

"Ar-Arlene, my daughter."

"Mrs. Wilkerson."

"Ursula, you make her sound so old."

"No—remote. Someone I could never touch. Would ever let me touch her."

"I ... I feel impotent, powerless. But it is a problem. A real problem. It's why we're meeting this way ... she, Arlene thinks I'm—"

"Out with Miss Lillian."

"Right. Walking the woods with Miss Lillian, as usual. The damned woods with Miss Lillian, not with you! What am I? A fifty-five-year-old man who has no control over his life? Who's afraid of his daughter? His own daughter? Her shadow?"

"You're not afraid of your daughter. Don't say that, Maurice. You respect her. Respect her for all the things she's done for you."

"Arlene ..."

"Who would know better the great love you had for your wife, Maureen, than her."

"A-and now you. You."

"Yes, and now me."

Now Teardrop wanted to go to her and hold her, kiss her, but again, he felt this terrible restraint in himself not to, so afraid to do so, that maybe he didn't know how, that maybe this bright black woman was more fantasy than real, an illusion; and if she were real, could she ever feel toward a fifty-five-year-old man what he felt toward her?

Ursula looked at his lips, Teardrop's softly sculpted lips, and imagined him kissing her ... or her kissing him—one or the other.

"Ursula, we shouldn't have to meet like this. Veiled. Not like this. In secrecy."

She agreed.

"To repeat this tomorrow, in this same way. I ... this is such a small town."

"Gossipy, I bet."

"Oh, is it."

"Were you watching me get out the taxi when—"

"No, but I saw Bert's car drive away. I didn't want him to see me. I ... I must admit that."

"But how will I get back to Ms. Ingram's place without—"

Teardrop pushed himself up to his feet, troubled. "I don't know. I don't know. I don't have that part, any of that figured out yet, in my mind yet!"

Ursula laid her head down sideways on top her hands; she had a look of befuddlement too.

"I'm sorry, Ursula," Teardrop said, turning to her. "But I've never had to deal with something like this before."

"Me either," Ursula said, measured.

"This is just the beginning, and already we're running into obstacles. Com-complications."

Ursula pushed herself up from the table, standing. "But didn't we anticipate this—the foreshadowing of these problems to come?"

"Oh, yes, oh yes … Yes, we did."

"Then why are we surprised? Should we be surprised that it should be difficult, and at the first sign of trouble—"

"We, I feel helpless, to the point of giving up too quickly on us."

"Maurice, we don't have to answer to Bert or anyone else in this town, if we don't want to."

"Yes, it's none of their, anyone's damned business!"

"Why, not at all!"

Hysterically they began laughing vigorously, as if it would relieve them of everything. It was therapy, a tonic for the soul, for everything they'd felt and been through the past few months, the feelings each had pent up in them—feeling it together.

"Maurice …"

"Yes?"

"Would you kiss me? Kiss me? Hold me?"

And Teardrop walked to her and held her in his arms. He kissed her forehead, and even with that, he felt her skin shiver. And then Ursula's eyelids. And then Ursula's head tilted back just enough, and her mouth opened, and she and Teardrop kissed in the shade as if it were in the hot sun not yet fading from the sky, on the white house's solidly supported deck.

A call was placed for a taxi. It was after four o'clock. They'd sat for a little over two hours on the back porch.

"You're sure this is okay with you?" Teardrop asked. Both sat on the house's front steps, waiting for Bert's taxi.

"Yes, Maurice. I'll be busy with work I brought with me for the rest of the day. "

"Tomorrow I'll come by Ms. Ingram's. How's that? Give Ruby something to talk about. Really shock her speechless."

"She doesn't like me."

"Why?"

"Do … do I need to tell you why, Maurice?"

"No. You're that reporter … that troublemaker from New York City. A northerner."

"Yes, word got around, it seems, in Walker City from my last visit."

"It always does. In a small town. Your secrets are not your own. Not unless you share them with fifty other people or the six o'clock news. Pick your poison."

"Now that's an exaggeration, I know."

"I know—but not by much."

"But—"

"Don't worry, Ursula. I'll clear up that perception of Ruby's with her tomorrow."

"But can you in a small town? I mean, once the die is cast, the perception of someone is made …"

"Small-town folk are stubborn, granted, thrive on gossip—suspicion too. Small things. But Ruby's a good person. I'm confident you'll win her back. Clear your name. Small-town people have a deeper understanding of human nature, the human heart, than most."

"Profound …"

"We're just more in touch with nature out here—much more, that's all. Not like big-city folk. Crickets even confound us."

"Crickets?"

"Do you know that at one time there was great superstition regarding crickets around here? Having a cricket in the house brought good luck. They—why here comes the taxi."

"B-but, Maurice …"

"I'll continue with the, my cricket story, resurrect it for another time," Teardrop said, taking Ursula's hand.

"Y-you'd better. I'm curious now. All fired up."

"A reporter's instinct."

"Awakened."

"Ursula, looks like you have Bert again."

"How charming," Ursula giggled. "But how … how can you tell from here?"

"Bert makes the speed limit, thirty miles an hour in Walker City, seem exceptionally fast!"

Teardrop and Ursula were standing in front of the house, when, from a good distance off Dawkin's Road, Jamal and Armon Robinson rode by on their bikes. But Armon was looking straight ahead while Jamal was looking at his grandparents' house when, suddenly, he spotted Teardrop and Ursula, Ursula's head ducking into the taxicab, Teardrop not closing the door but keeping it open.

"Ms. Jen—"

"Hey, Jamal. Why're you stopping?"

Armon was at least twenty-five yards ahead of Jamal, past the house. "What's wrong?"

"Oh nothing," Jamal replied. "N-nothing at all, Armon."

"Looks like you just saw a ghost. I swear, Jamal."

"No, no," Jamal said, pedaling again, rejoining Armon to narrow the gap.

"You act like it's the first time you've seen your grandfather's house."

"No, no, I … I—"

"Let's take our favorite shortcut home, Jamal. What you say? Game?"

"Yes, uh, sure, Armon. Game. I'm game."

Armon's slender upper torso leaned over his bike's bull-horn-shaped handle bars and then rocketed off on Dawkin's Road full steam ahead.

"Granddad and Ms. Jenkins. I … I know they didn't see me."

"The last one back to your house, Jamal, is a rotten egg!" Armon yelled in a high-pitched voice.

And Jamal rode off on his bike as if he didn't care who got to his house first, who was called a rotten egg, him or Armon, not after seeing what he saw.

"Okay, Ms. Jenkins."

"All right, Mr. Williams."

"I really appreciate your visit. Too bad Mrs. Wilkerson had to leave early, unless she would've driven you home. Back to Ms. Ingram's."

"Uh, Teardrop, there's room for three, you know."

"No, Bert, I'll skip on it. Miss Lillian and I—"

"Is gonna walk through the woods, right?"

Ursula laughed. Teardrop sneaked a wink at her.

"I'm afraid so, Bert," Teardrop said with an air of boredom. "Miss Lillian wouldn't have it any other way—especially on a day like today."

"Teardrop, I betcha there're times when you wished you played the piano. Well, I'll get Ms. Jenkins back to Ms. Ruby's all right. Don't worry none. You know how slow I drive."

Teardrop winked at Ursula a second time. "Yes, that I do, Bert."

"Good day, Teardrop."

"Yes, good day, uh, Bert."

Ursula and Teardrop smiled strongly into each other's eyes and then seemed to be longing for tomorrow.

"And good day to you, Ms. Jenkins."

"And to you, Mr. Williams."

Miss Lillian and Teardrop had tread through the woods. He had played a lot of old songs off of Miss Lillian's strings, mostly ones he'd written but some of Shorty Boy's and Twelve Fingers's songs as well. He'd heard from both just last week. Shorty Boy called and then put Twelve Fingers on the phone. Currently, they were playing a gig in Cincinnati, Ohio, at the Thunder Clap blues club.

They were doing fine. They had a new guitar player, Allan "Lima Beans" Green, in the band, a pretty good one, they said, young, full of fire; but they were breaking him in slowly, hoping he'd work out. After three years, Lima Beans Green was the band's seventh guitar player.

The band was going by the a new name (it hurt Teardrop a lot, the news), courtesy of McKinley Scofield: The Royal Blues Rollers.

"Chemistry," Teardrop said. "Being a chemist myself. Chemistry," Teardrop said more cryptically. "What makes things work and other things not work? Blend or toxic. Two compounds, elements, entities …

"Am I talking about Ursula and me … or … it's clear that I am. We work together. Age or no age. Young enough to be my daughter … something so outlandish, outrageous, but it works. Our ages not blowing up in our faces. We're a good mixture. G-good chemistry."

In a matter of minutes, Teardrop would be out the woods.

"I'm looking forward to tomorrow. With all my heart. Today ended too quickly for both Ursula and me. But what were we supposed to do? This isn't a pipe dream but real. And as far as her being a mature woman, she is—an extraordinary one.

"And the article she wrote (it was back at the house on the kitchen table), there's so much in it that's right about me."

Teardrop was out the woods. He was in the opening glancing up at the house. Now he was wondering how he was going to spend the rest of the day without repeated thoughts of her, as if it would be all he'd do was think of her.

"Now how am I going to be able to manage that? Tell me."

Teardrop saw Jamal's red bike flat on the ground, not upright, since Jamal rarely used his kickstand. Either the bike leaned against something or lay flat on the ground, its current state.

Teardrop chuckled. "I guess I didn't have the time to use my bike's kickstand either at Jamal's age.

"Oh how the human race progresses ever forward, daringly," Teardrop said sarcastically. "From one generation to the next." Teardrop was a quarter ways to the house. "He must've been out riding with Armon."

And now at the house, on the periphery of it, Teardrop began thinking of tomorrow with Ursula, having a keen feeling that it would top today's meeting. He was still scared to death, but so far Ursula Jenkins had made it simple for him.

"It's her charm and grace. Her ways."

Removing Miss Lillian from his shoulders, he just held on to her as he proceeded up the wooden steps. When he got in the kitchen, he went straight to the refrigerator, took out a large pitcher of water, took a glass out of the cabinet, poured, drank, and then returned the pitcher of water to the refrigerator. He continued drinking his water, when he heard—

"Dad."

"Arlene," Teardrop said from the kitchen, "I didn't know you were in the living room. Not when I got through the back door."

Teardrop took another drink out the glass, nonchalantly proceeding into the living room.

Arlene was standing, looking out the window, out onto the front yard.

"I didn't hear you, Arlene."

"I've been standing here, looking out the window."

"Oh."

"How was your walk in the woods?"

"Oh ... fine, fine. Nothing unusual for me to report."

Arlene turned her head. "Nothing?"

He drank more water. "Yes, just the usual routine."

"You and Miss Lillian."

"In the woods."

"Oftentimes, Dad, I must admit, I wish I could find a sanctuary like yours. Like you and Miss Lillian have had the past few years. A perfect place to turn to. A retreat. Something shrinelike. But more importantly, you and nature, two divine, creative forces in spiritual communication. Nature's music, the birds, the insects, the ...

"And then your music. A symphony of sounds ... and then silences, when nature retreats to contemplate herself, her soul ... and you yours.

No wonder you and Miss Lillian go in the woods every day without interruption."

"Arlene, I'm flabbergasted. How beautifully said, put ... uh, persuasive. R-really. I know you're brilliant, and not because you're my daughter, even if I'd still like to take some credit, your mother too, but that was a brilliant take into what Miss Lillian and I do in the woods—commune with nature, I suppose, if summarized. The setting is shrinelike. Nature at its most intense, energetic force. It is remarkable. Balanced to perfection."

"It's interesting that you should bring Mom up."

"How so?" Teardrop decided to sit, since the conversation was beginning to feel it had some apparent length to it. "For what reason?"

"W-why, Dad? Why?" There was a hardness yet, at the same time, a brittleness in Arlene's voice. "For what reason—you want to know why?"

"What's wrong, Arlene?"

"Wrong?"

"It's there hiding in your voice."

"I guess I can't hide that from—"

"No, not that."

"No matter how hard I try. Not with my father, nor Mom. My mother."

"School?"

"Oh, no, not school ... school."

"Oh, I thought it might be, relate to—"

"Jamal was riding his bike—"

"Jamal's all right, isn't he, Ar—"

"Jamal's fine, just fine. It's just that—"

"That's good to know," Teardrop said, the glass of water sitting better in his hand. "He and Armon were out riding, you say?"

"Yes, the usual. Usual, Dad. Everything's as usual."

"A boy and his bike. My best friend, at Jamal's age, was a boy named Gerald McFeaster. The McFeasters moved out of Walker City when Gerald was thirteen. I'll never forget that day, not to this day. Was a very sad one for me. I believe they moved to—"

"Riding, riding their bikes, when, guess what, Dad?"

"What, honey?"

"Talking about hiding things again. But this would be better described as deceitful, plain deceitful ... It's when someone is untrustworthy, isn't it?"

"What, Arlene? Armon and Jamal are having problems between them? Something happened? There was a lie told or—"

"A big lie, Dad," Arlene said, looking more sharply at Teardrop.

"But boys will be boys, Arlene. You—"

"No, it's what Jamal saw, Dad. It's what he saw on Dawkin's Road when he passed by the house, our house, today, Dad: you and Ursula Jenkins at the house."

The glass of water toppled over and out Teardrop's hand and splashed onto the carpet.

"I ... I ..."

Teardrop, when rising to his feet, his right foot kicked the glass on the carpet, knocking it against the coffee table's wooden leg.

"She came down from New York. She came down from New York! For what! What did she come down from New York for!"

"T-to ..."

"It ... it was arranged, wasn't it? Wasn't it!"

"Yes, yes, I—"

"You what, Dad, you what!'

"It ... it was my doing, not Ms. Jenkins's. Ur-Ursula's ..."

"Ursula! Ursula! You're calling her, that girl, w-woman, Ursula now!"

"Yes, Arlene. Yes—why ... why not? Shouldn't I? Why in the world ... I ... I don't know why I shouldn't," Teardrop said, somewhat dazed by this sudden, unexpected, blistering attack.

"From Ms. Jenkins to—"

"Ursula. Ursula."

"And how does she address you? What are you to her now? Teardrop? Tear—"

"Maurice."

"Maurice? Maurice! Why, Mom called you Maurice! Mom. Mom. Mom called you Maurice, Dad! Mom! Mom! She called you Maurice!"

"I know, I know ... but ... but ..."

"And you let her? You ... you didn't try to d-dissuade her, d-discourage her? Tell her not to call you Maurice under any circumstances, under any—that that was ... is ... is sacred, d-divine, that only your wife called you Maurice. Mother. Mother. No one else."

Teardrop retreated; he looked behind him, back to the sofa he'd been sitting on and then back down to the floor where the glass had spilled its contents, water and ice, and now the ice leaking, seeping into the carpet. He bent down and picked up the glass, holding it in his hand, on its sides and its bottom. Teardrop's fingertips rubbed into the glass in a slow and, what seemed, methodical grind.

"It felt natural. W-when it happened. S-so natural for her to—"

"Natural!"

"W-when Ur—Ms. ... Ms. Jenkins said, called me that—"

"Maurice ... ," Arlene said, disgusted. "M-Maurice ..."

Teardrop did not respond.

"You never know, do you, Dad? Who's watching, do you? You never know, D—"

"Watching?"

"Jamal ran into the house. To tell me everything. He ... he was exploding with ex—"

"Watching, watching? You used the word 'watching.' Watching, Arlene. I don't care who was watching! Why should I care who's watching!"

"You don't? Don't?"

"No, Arlene, I—"

"Then why did you and Ms. Jenkins—see how I used the name Ms. Jenkins and ... and not Ursula—not ... meet at the house today, Dad, and not here? The way you did. Not here? Meet here, at the house? Where it would be normal to meet?"

Teardrop shut his eyes; it felt like they were burning.

How could he argue with her, Teardrop thought, argue with anybody, when they would beat him at every turn, when he had no defense or way to defend himself? He was naked for insult, for any attack waged against him in this context he, by no means, could control.

He opened his eyes. "I can't defend myself, Arlene. I ... I won't—simply won't."

"Yes, of course you can't, Dad. She came all the way from New York by whose invitation?"

"Mine. Mine."

"By phone, Dad?"

"Yes."

"You called her from here?"

"Yes, Arlene. From here."

"From this house?"

"Yes."

"For how long is she to—"

"Until tomorrow."

"T-tomorrow. And she's staying where? No, don't answer that. Why should you have to? Ruby Ingram's boarding house. It's where Ms. Jenkins is staying."

"Yes."

"Right, right, Ruby Ingram's boarding house. Where else in Walker City would she stay? Where else…," Arlene said as if her heart had stopped. She walked over to a nearby chair to sit.

Teardrop felt awful, ashamed. His eyes moistened.

Arlene sat in the chair limp, as if there was no more for her to say. As if her body were saying it all for her, first starched by anger, now wounded and crushed by injury.

"I'm sorry, Arlene."

Arlene's body remained limp, motionless.

"I didn't mean to hurt you. This wasn't meant to reach you, this information. What Jamal saw today. A-at, out at the house."

Arlene's disposition hadn't changed.

"You see—"

"And you've planned, you and Ms. Jenkins plan … plan to do the same tomorrow? Meet at the house?" Arlene said, her eyes suddenly keen again. "Tomorrow—it's what you and … and Ms. Jenkins plan … plan to do? T-to meet at the house again."

"Yes."

"You took her inside?"

"Yes, Arlene."

"The house?"

"Yes. Yes."

"Yes. Yes. Why else would you take her there? To the house. If not to take her inside. For she could see it. Share another part of your life with her. Another part of your personal history. W-why wouldn't you … ?"

"It … it is my house, Arlene. I have no reason to—"

"And I … I thought … thought I'd broken this thing up," Arlene said, seemingly unconscious to what she'd just said, her body shaking.

"Had … had broken you two, t-this thing up."

"Broken it up? This thing up? How—"

"I … I tried. S-so hard to, dammit. Dammit." Arlene said, seemingly in a blurred, anxious state of mind, still shaking. "I tried so hard to."

"To break us up? Ms. Jenkins and me up?" Teardrop said, his body leaning forward on the couch. "How, Arlene? What do you have to do with this? How could you possibly do—"

"Break … how …" Arlene now appeared conscious as to where she was but not necessarily to what she'd said.

"How could you possibly break Ursula, break us up? In what way—"

"Did … d-did I say that? I … I …"

"There was no way in which, that you could do that, Arlene. No—"

"Right. Yes, oh yes. Right, Dad. I … I—"

"But why would you say it? Say it so forthrightly, so—"

"You had no right to write her! No right!"

"But I told you why, Arlene, I told you. I, we, I'd decided to correspond with Ms. Jen—"

"Back and forth. Back and forth! Her letters coming to you … ," Arlene said, again transitioning into that blurred state.

"The letters coming to the house the way they were. It had to stop. It had to!"

"You, but I …"

And he'd gotten letters, but not as many as Arlene seemed to be suggesting, making it sound "back and forth, back and forth"—no, there'd been an interruption in his letters getting to Ursula but Ursula's letters not getting to him, A postal mix-up, it'd seemed, he and Ursula assumed, something both couldn't explain away no matter how hard they'd tried. It's why they had to be with each other this weekend—to make sure nothing went wrong for them, this hex that seemed to have, out the blue, afflicted them.

"Stop it, Arlene? Break this thing up between me and Ms. Jenkins—"

"Up."

"Yes, up, Arlene—"

"And I thought I had. It was over. Done with. That Sid and I—"

"Sid? Sid, Arlene? How does, what does Sid Turner—"

"I … I …" And It's when Arlene transitioned out her altered state of mind again for a second time.

"You and Sid did what with my mail? What … what did you do with my mail, Arlene?"

"J-just Ms. Jenkins's mail. Just Ursula Jenkins's mail. Just her mail. Her mail. Her mail."

"Just! Just!" Teardrop thought he was about to lose it.

"D-Dad, you mustn't be upset with me, Dad. W-with me, you … you mustn't!" Arlene said as she began pacing back and forth in front of Teardrop. "I … I had to do it for … for your own good. Your … your own sake. Protection. I had to protect you from her. This woman. I had to Dad, I …

"It-it's why Sid, I told Sid to hold on to anything mailed by her. Y-your New York mail, as I called it. I told him why … why she was writing you. Sid knew about the story. T-the article to be written by her. The upset, enormous upset it'd caused. S-Sid—"

"This small town."

"This small town has its advantages. Ones that—"

"My mail … confiscating my mail?"

"It was for your own good. Done for your own good. Your own—"

"Who's to say it was for my own good? Who, Arlene? Who? You?"

"But you called her. Called her—"

"And I'm glad I did."

"And now, Dad, now you aren't even willing to appreciate what I was trying to do. How I—"

"No, Arlene. No. Only curious. Did you read them? Read the letters too? The letters from Ursula too?"

"How dare you!"

"Dare me? Dare me!"

"How dare you! How dare you say such a thing! Say … say, accuse me of such a … of … of doing such a thing. Yes, yes, how dare you!"

Arlene ran out the living room and the hallway and then up the staircase, when she whirled around to Teardrop, shouting.

"You will not talk to me like that! In … in that manner! Do you hear me! Do you!"

"Well, did you! Did you, Arlene! Did you! Did you open the letters, read them, stoop that low too!"

And both were stunned into silence—Arlene at the top of the staircase, Teardrop at the bottom—for Jamal was out on the second-floor landing, had appeared, what seemed, out of nowhere.

"What's wrong? What's wrong, Mom, Granddad? Why are you yelling at each other? Like this for?"

And Arlene turned to Jamal, rushing to him, holding him to her, squeezing him, crying.

Teardrop stood at the bottom of the stairs, looking up at them, feeling a bitter pain in him.

"I've never heard you and Mom argue before, Granddad," Jamal said, looking directly at Teardrop. "Not ever."

CHAPTER 13

Ursula had waited to shower at 1:15 p.m.

She wanted to feel fresh for Teardrop.

Since yesterday, all she could think about was when Teardrop kissed her. How it'd happened, when it'd happened. She'd never been kissed like that before. And if he had gone on, continued kissing her, she would've let him. But it had ended at one kiss, Ursula thought.

Of course, yesterday, mixed in between her work, there were other thoughts, impressions she had of Teardrop Williams. What lingered. How he smelled. How quietly his eyes held you in their gaze. How her hand felt in his. It felt all too lasting for her, all too real, the awareness of it.

And Teardrop was to be at the boarding house at two o'clock—it's what he'd said. It was 1:48 p.m.

"I know Maurice is punctual. I wonder if he and Miss Lillian have walked through the woods yet? I don't think I've been happier than today. What's happening to me now."

It was two o'clock.

Ursula responded to the knock on the door.

"Maurice."

"Good afternoon, Ursula."

"Good afternoon, Maurice."

Teardrop shook Ursula's hand; Ursula expected more. She liked the way Teardrop was dressed, but there was something that was not right about him, something shadowing him.

"Ursula, may I sit?" he asked, quickly, looking at the chair by the bureau. The other chair was across the room, off to the side of the window where the mix of green, purple, and white plaid drapes hung, but the window was open. The sun was out shining today, warm, just not through that single window yet but through the boarding house's front window for maybe forty-five minutes.

Looking at him, Ursula thought Teardrop looked anxious, unsettled; and this look was new to her, brand new.

Teardrop looked at this beautiful young woman sitting there with her short-cut Afro (not a bush) and felt he was losing paradise, that it was crumbling right before his eyes.

"Maurice, if you're not going to say anything, then I will. "Y-yesterday made me so—"

"Ursula, Jamal was riding his bicycle yesterday. Near the house. Dawkin's Road. Jamal saw us. He saw us at the house together."

And the way Teardrop said it, Ursula thought, it was as if he'd been stabbed in the heart by a phantom.

"He ... J-Jamal did?"

"Yes."

"I didn't see him."

"I know, but Jamal saw us."

Now for Ursula, it sounded as if they'd been spied on and caught doing something that was considered, by anyone seeing it, condemnable, illicit, unconscionable.

"And now Arlene knows. Knows you're in Walker City."

Again, Ursula felt as if some horror had happened, been committed, but also knew how fragile they'd suddenly become.

"I'm sorry, Maurice. What a shock it ... it must've been for you."

"It was," Teardrop said, seemingly wanting to finally get it out his system, this thing confronting him.

"Jamal told her."

"Of course," Teardrop said bluntly, as if not wanting to share more.

"Of course he did."

Pause.

"I wonder why he didn't say—"

"Does it matter? Matter what Jamal did or did not do?" Teardrop said in a scolding voice. "He was out riding with his friend Armon. They were riding their bikes. It's probably why."

"Oh."

"I'm sorry, Ursula—I'm, but this has got me so upset. Be-beside myself. I'm sorry."

"Yes, I can imagine. Well—"

"Can you?"

"Yes, w-why yes. Because this is something we didn't want, desire in anyway, in—"

"And especially like this."

"What did she say, Maurice? Arlene?"

"Why ... it-it's the first time you've called her that—Arlene, and not Mrs. Wilkerson."

"D-did I?"

"Yes."

"I ... I didn't ... didn't—"

"Ursula, it was Arlene, my daughter. She was why I wasn't receiving your letters. She was responsible for it. She had them intercepted, confiscated—if that's a better word to use for what became of them."

"Mrs. Wilkerson? B-but why? Why would she do that! S-something—"

"Isn't it obvious? She claimed she wanted to break up this thing between us."

Ursula shook.

"It was her idea, intention to do this."

"Just like I suppose she never could imagine you wanting to see someone. To see a woman. Correspond with her," Ursula said.

"No. No, Ursula. Not at all."

"T-then both of you did what was unexpected. Totally out of character."

"But for my daughter to stoop so low. To that level. To interrupt your letters ..."

"You argued?"

"Yes."

"Something—"

"We've never done before. Not in the past."

"Of course. There'd never been any reason to before yesterday."

Silence.

"This morning—"

"Nothing's been resolved from where we left off yesterday. Between us, Ursula. Absolutely nothing."

"No?"

"No."

"Mrs. … She knows you're with me now. At Mrs. Ingram's?"

"Arlene knows. I came by taxi. I'm in these clothes. Dressed this way. There was no deceit from me. On my part this time."

"Why are you clouding what happened, what we did, Maurice, by using the word 'deceit,' deceit, when all you were trying to do was protect Arlene? Protect—"

"If I hear that word one more time. Just one more time, then I think— it's why Arlene confiscated your letters to me, she claimed, in order to protect me from you. To do what she felt was good for me. What was best for me.

"It seems … e-everyone seems to be protecting everyone else, and all that's coming out are lies and deceit, a far cry, far different than anyone of us is used to. Normal for us."

"That is what we were doing."

"And it was what Arlene was doing. And we're all guilty. Stand guilty in this. Are holding the bag. Every last single one of us."

"Only, because of hindsight, Maurice. Not because we were deliberately trying to hurt anyone."

"I don't know what Arlene was thinking of at the time. I just know our motives were pure. I know that much. Out, but this situation, my grandson's been affected by it, Ursula. Jamal. This thing … whole thing has infected him now."

"J-Jamal?"

"The exchange between Arlene and me was—"

"Oh—"

"Heated. Yes, heated, very passionate, intense, loud, ex-explosive. Jamal ran out his room. He got in the middle of it—"

"No—"

"This thing between Arlene and me, Ursula. Ar-argument. It's as if we forgot Jamal was in the house. As if we were waging a private war, but Jamal was there—caught up in this nasty confrontation. He wasn't spared either, from the fallout."

Ursula stood.

"Do you mind if … if I go into the bathroom, Maurice? I … I have to go to the bath—"

"No, Ursula. Y-you go ahead. Go right ahead."

"Excuse me."

The bathroom door was to the left of the room, about twenty-five feet from where Teardrop sat.

Ursula opened the bathroom door and then closed it behind her. The room was dark.

"What have I done?" she asked herself. "W-what have I done?" There was this nascent fear in her that she felt unable to control, not under its current relentless attack.

She backed herself against the bathroom wall and then imagined the wall as some barrier.

Teardrop looked down at his hands, every line in his palms, some leading somewhere, some disconnected, broken off, fading into smooth uninterrupted skin, as undetermined as to their fate as what seemed to be to his. Trying to read your life before it's made up its mind, like gypsies and palm readers say they're doing—reading tea leaves, your future, knowing how your stars hang in the sky, what's next for you when you see only mystery and doubt lying ahead.

Ursula was out the bathroom. Teardrop stood in reaction to her entrance back into the room.

"Ursula … I think we have to put a stop to this. Whatever it is we've gotten ourselves into at this point, we have to put a stop to. Draw it to an end."

Ursula walked to the chair off by the side of the window. "Yes, I think so too, Maurice," Ursula said softly, her hand holding the back of the chair firmly.

"It-it's affecting too many people. What we're doing."

"Your family, Maurice."

"It wasn't supposed to produce this kind of result, negativity."

"No, no, it wasn't."

"I'm not cut out for this. N-never was."

She turned to him.

"With Maureen and I, it was easy. It was meant to be. For … for us. We only brought happiness to others—not this. Friction between Arlene and me. Jamal's too young to understand why. What it is adults fight over, can be so passionate and strident about.

"To cause the house we live in together such—this kind of tension and chaos."

"I ... I just want to know, Maurice, one thing. Was it a mistake how you kissed me yesterday?"

"No, it wasn't."

"Yesterday was my dream. Last night."

"Y-you'll get home safely, won't you?" Pause.

"Yes, I promise."

Teardrop opened the room door.

"No more letters, Maurice?"

"No, Ursula."

"Good-bye, Maurice."

"Yes, good-bye, Ursula."

Ursula closed the door behind Teardrop. She stood at the door as long as she felt capable.

"How awful that sounds."

CHAPTER 14

Two days later.

Ursula was lying across the bed. She was crying aloud. She didn't care. She didn't care about anything since she'd gotten back to New York. Nothing mattered. The smells of New York. The sounds of New York. What did she care about New York when she was in love with someone in Walker City, Iowa? In New York City it felt as if she were fighting the world.

She'd read so much about love. Books. Novels, classics, plays. The human heart—tormented, beaten down, so eager to find love, adventurous, know it, feel it, want it. And when love fails, falls out the sky, the light of day, that which makes it bright, shine—joyful—then love cries in many ways that are strange, unnatural, exaggerated, twisted, and cynical.

"I love him. I love him. I love him."

And not to have the love returned was driving her crazy.

The machine was on.

"I know you're there. Come on, girl. Answer. Pick up the phone. Pick it up, Ursula. T-this is the umpteenth time I've called since Monday. Since you got back. In town. You're trying to avoid me? That's what you're doing? Come on, sweetie, pick up—"

"By-Byron ..."

"I knew you were there. Back from your two-day trip to Walker City." Pause. "What gives? Why haven't you picked up the phone? Or at least returned any of my calls for the past—"

"I ... I couldn't."

"Couldn't?"

"I just couldn't."

"Ursula, oh no, things didn't go well in Walker City. B-between you and Teardrop Williams, did they?"

Silence.

"Ursula, I'm not going to let you, listen, hold on, I figured I'd buzz your ear, nothing more, b-but this is serious. Let me get over to my office. Hold on. Don't go anywhere."

"I ... no, no I won't."

"Stay ... stay on the phone."

While Ursula waited for Byron to move from wherever he was, it felt like an eternity, like if she could tear time's heart out its chest, she would—her fingers could, in a fiendish fury.

"Okay, Ursula. I'm in my office. Uh, set ... wait a minute, a sec—let me do one more thing then, okay?"

Ursula heard movement, like her ears could hear any sound injected into the world.

"Just wanted to get that pile of papers, work in front of me. From staring at me." Pause. "What did he do to you, that old man do to you in Walker City to cause this?"

"I'm in love with Maurice 'Teardrop' Williams. That's what he did to me."

"In love with him? That's what this shit's about, all about? This shit?"

"Yes, Byron."

"You went out to Walker City and fell in love—"

"I knew I was in love with him before I went out there. I knew it all along."

"You did ... I mean you did?"

"Yes."

"And this weekend, your visit, did what? Confirmed it?"

"Yes." Pause.

"And now where does it go from here?"

"N-nowhere," Ursula replied tersely.

"Nowhere?"

"Yes, nowhere."

"Damn!"

"No—"

"I don't understand, damn—I know Mr. Williams, he—"

"He loves me."

"He—did he say that? Tell you that?"

"No … but I know he does. Maurice does."

"Mau—you call him—"

"Maurice."

"N-not Teardrop. The guy's—"

"No, Maurice."

"Why not Teardrop?"

"I don't know why not Teardrop, Byron."

"And he calls you Ursula? What—"

"Yes."

"Did you tell him you love him?"

"No."

"But—"

"He knows."

"Like you know he loves you?"

"Yes."

"And so something went wrong."

"Everything went wrong. Everything."

"What—"

"It's a long story. A very long story. It's just not me and Maurice—"

"That sounds funny. Still sounds funny, Maurice. Teardrop sounds better. Much—"

"It's just not me and Maurice in this. It's family too."

"The daughter, Mr. Williams's grandson."

"We're not alone in this."

"You make it sound so grim, ominous, Ursula. I mean, shit …"

"It's gone beyond that, Byron. Well, well beyond that."

"How?"

"By-Byron, can we discuss this at another time? Just not tonight."

"How, Ursula? How?"

"I'm tired. I'm really, really tired. I … I picked up the phone because I had to talk to someone. And … and I knew, sooner or later, I would have to talk about it. It's the only reason why I—"

"Since you knew I knew why you went to Walker City."

"Uh-huh."

"You made it seem as … well, we talked around it, but I knew. Read between the lines. In what was little confusion to me, at least." Pause. "Are you at least working, getting on with your life?"

"It's been different. I shut down. At times … I do shut down."

"The guy means that much to you, huh?"

"That much."

"Damn, Ursula. Damn. Damn. Damn."

Silence.

"Man ..."

Silence.

"All ... all right. Okay. S-so we'll talk about this at a future date. T-time then."

"Right."

"Ursula, do you want J. C. in on this?"

"No, it's not necessary. I don't want this thing bandied about right now, picked over—even though you two are my best friends. I love you two guys, but this is too personal, Byron. I have never loved anyone before, and the first time I do, it has nothing to do with me or him but with other factors that have split us apart."

"But ... only think it through. Maybe you and Mr. Williams are giving up too easily."

"Maybe. But it's all Maurice and I can do for now. Nothing ... we must take a selfish view, hurt ourselves before we run the risk of hurting others."

"Self-inflicted."

"Give up our relationship while we're able to."

"Yeah, that makes sense. Good, solid sense."

"S-so I'll be talking to you."

"Uh, sure ... sure thing, Ursula."

"Byron, thanks for being so persistent."

"As always."

"Ha. As always."

"A stock trader's trait. We're a breed apart."

"A journalist's trait too."

"Yeah, sure—to see something through to the end."

Days later.

New York and Jersey City are separated by a big body of water: the Hudson River. You must go through either of two tunnels to get to Jersey City from downtown New York, the Lincoln Tunnel or Holland Tunnel.

Jersey City is in the state of New Jersey, but it is so close to New York, at times it thinks it's a part of New York (Siamese twins joined at the hip) and not New Jersey. For the most part, it suffers from wishful thinking. For Jersey City's always been a small city full of big-city ambition, like New York City, but with little to show for it in way of any real, substantial success.

Ursula was raised in Jersey City, New Jersey. She attended public school there (Snyder High) and did her undergraduate studies at Columbia University's School of Journalism. So she was strictly an East Coast product who was now taking up residence in Jamaica, New York. But a few of her friends still lived in Jersey City, along with her parents, Iris and Harry Jenkins.

Working as a mortician for over twenty years, Harry Jenkins was a funeral director. His reputation in Jersey City was well earned. He owned his own funeral parlor, eponymously named Harry Jenkins's Funeral Home. Harry Jenkins was so good with dead bodies people in Jersey City often said his funeral parlor did the "best bodies in town." So if you wanted your deceased family member to be "done right," look good in his or her casket, 183

look good on their way either to heaven or hell or wherever it was they were going, you, by all means, should send them to Harry Jenkins's Funeral Home. Harry Jenkins was your man, a man who had a certain genius with formaldehyde.

Iris Jenkins was a grammar-school teacher, and an excellent one at that.

It was a Saturday, and Ursula was visiting her parents for the weekend. She'd rented a car and driven it through the Holland Tunnel connecting New York to New Jersey. The car was on Forest Avenue, her old block, and though she knew it was her old block, it felt much like a new one to her. Her parents' home was just up the block, an old house still retaining its charm but nestled between a changing neighborhood, its economical equilibrium no longer middle class but poor and crime ridden.

The Jenkinses refused to be run off (their house burglarized twice), still believing the block one day would return to its former glamour— what had been, for them, better days. But it still worried Ursula, her parents' personal safety, that even optimism, hope, can be defeated by a community's overwhelming despair and reasoned opinion of itself.

"No, Mother, I can't outcook you. Admittedly. Wouldn't even try. Tell such a fib."

"When are you going to let your father and I find out, Ursula? Firsthand?" Iris asked, putting her napkin down, glancing over at Harry Jenkins, who'd just taken her hand.

"New York, Jamaica, that's off-limits to you guys. Only one Jenkins through the Holland Tunnel at a time—and that's me."

"Ursula, your cooking can't be that bad."

"Close, Dad."

The Jenkinses had finished eating. They were sitting in the dining room. As habit, they'd sit at the table for a while but would soon drift, as creatures of habit, off to the kitchen.

Iris Jenkins was brown skinned with height. She was becoming but not pretty. It was her great personality that made her feel pretty.

"Well, at least you took your father and me out to dinner when we came over to see your apartment when you first moved in."

"Yes, Iris, that was a great treat."

"And If I remember correctly, Ursula, the food was excellent," Iris Jenkins laughed.

Harry Jenkins's skin was about as black as black piano keys. Ursula looked every bit the same as him, meaning, Harry Jenkins was a striking-looking man. He'd just begun wearing glasses so had yet adjusted to them and, from time to time, showed it by getting an irritable look on his face, one that challenged patience.

"You look happy, Ursula."

"Thanks, Dad."

"You are, aren't you, darling?"

Ursula paused. "What would make you think otherwise, Mom?"

"Oh … I don't know … ," Iris said. "Being a career woman …"

"What I think and haven't asked is are you seeing someone? A special young man?"

Ursula was surprised. "Where, I mean, did that question come from?"

"Ursula, don't you think your mother and I give thought to these things? These matters when it comes to you dating men?"

"Sure, Dad. Sure … but … but …"

"You do share everything with us," Harry said. "At least you seem to make us think that you do. We're left to believe that."

"Is there someone, Ursula? A young man you're involved with?

And it's when Ursula felt Maurice "Teardrop" Williams storm through her.

"Excuse me. I ... I have to go to the bathroom. Excuse me." Ursula left the living room.

The house had two bathrooms, but Ursula chose to use the one on the second floor, not the first.

When she came down from the bathroom, she walked back into the living room. She didn't expect her parents to be there but in the kitchen. She knew, by now, both were in the kitchen washing and drying the dishes. They enjoyed washing the dishes together, and now was that magical hour.

Ursula was still hurting; it's why she was in Jersey City—to visit her parents for the weekend and out of New York and her apartment. She was hoping to take her mind off things, a change of pace and routine. She was trying everything possible that made sense, to get her head back on straight, to cure her heart. She and Byron still had not broached the reason why she and Teardrop Williams had reached a fork in the road. She still felt she wasn't strong enough to discuss it in detail with anyone—it was still how much she was hurting.

She stood and walked down the hallway and into the kitchen. Iris and Harry turned to her, both standing at the dated kitchen sink, Iris much the taller than Harry but Harry seemingly comfortable, unbothered by it, standing beside her.

"Your father and I heard you come down the stairs, Ursula."

"You and Dad have always been a great team," Ursula said, seeing them doing the dishes.

"When we can. You know how my schedule is. How grueling it is."

"Teachers have days off, whereas your father, funeral directors, morticians—people expire every day, are in grave need of your father."

Simultaneously, Iris and Harry turned back to the sink and the dirty dishes.

Ursula sat at the kitchen table. When she was in the bathroom, she'd wanted to cry but fought it off, thinking that if she did, it would surely show in her eyes when she got back downstairs, that it would be to her ruin, detriment, that her parents would surely realize that she was unhappy, that there'd been a misstep, mishap, that something had gone badly wrong in her life. She hadn't come home to take risks bordering on any kind of revelation or self-confession.

But as Ursula sat in the chair and watched her parents work together, doing their chore as one, the more she felt saddened—absorb the gracious surroundings as if she were back in the woods with Maurice "Teardrop" Williams, at least that one time when both were in harmony with something, in the moment with it, like her mother and father seemed, maybe just going through the motions of routinely washing the dishes, unfettered by cause or result but involved in something so generous and refined and meaningful it reflected all that was good and available to whom they were and meant to each other, thereby defining them.

"Well, Iris, let me put this—Ursula, Ursula, y-you're crying. Crying!"

Iris turned. "What's wrong, darling?"

Her hands were reaching out to them.

"Do you want us to know?"

"Yes, Dad. I ... I do."

Iris and Harry sat.

"I'm in love," Ursula began.

"S-since when?" Iris asked.

"S-since July, I guess."

"Four months, Ursula?"

"Yes, Dad."

"And it didn't work out, or are you two having a lover's spat? Quarrel? A separation of some kind? Is that it?" Harry asked.

Ursula stared straight ahead. "No. It's over, Dad. The relationship."

"That fast? Sudden?"

"Like a comet. Yes. A comet flashing in the sky and then plunging to Earth!"

"Ursula, why that's not like you to—"

"No, no, it isn't, Iris. That's not our daughter talking like this. Using that kind of hyperbole."

"Cursory. That doesn't sound like love, Ursula," Iris said. "Something for someone to cry over. To feel in such deep pain over. What it, apparently, is doing to you now."

"It's how I want to think of it now."

"Then it's not over," Iris said. "It'll never be over if you think of it in those terms, darling. That it was fleeting—when it wasn't."

"Your mother's right, Ursula. You have to face it head-on—like you do everything, if you want to get over it."

"Then … then I don't want to get over it. Then I don't want to get over it. Ever!"

"Ursula …" Iris's face suggested serious concern. "He's not … is-isn't married, is he?"

Iris's question didn't rattle Ursula. "No."

"Oh, I thought … thought I'd only ask," Iris said, looking at Harry, both appearing relieved. "Clear the air."

"It's something I'm careful about when I date. Even though I know it can happen to anyone."

"Yes," both replied.

"If you're not careful. But no, I haven't fallen in love with a married man. That's not the obstacle."

"Do you care to talk about it then? With your mother and me?"

"No, Dad. I came over this weekend to the house t-to avoid the subject. Stay completely clear of it. If I could—it was possible."

"Do you think it's done any good, Ursula? You were just cry—"

"I have to find my way through this muddle, mess, that's all, Mom."

"And there's nothing you care to tell us about him? Who he is? What he does? How you met him?"

"Not now, Mom. Not for the time being."

Again, Iris glanced over at Harry, not in the least sure as how far to take this matter with their precocious daughter. "No help in this from your father and me, Ursula? Advice? None?"

"No, Mom." Then Ursula looked at her father. "Dad."

Patiently Harry removed his glasses, wiped at his eyes with his hands, and then put the glasses back on. "Okay, Ursula. All right then. We'll … all right."

Seconds later Harry took a look at his watch. "Iris, let's finish up the dishes. You know where I have to go."

They got up from the kitchen table.

"Being a mortician's wife all these years—I'd better!"

The Jenkins family had been to church and back. They ate at four o'clock, an early dinner for them. It was for Ursula's sake, for she was ready to head back to New York City, Jamaica, the Holland Tunnel, in her rented car. Ursula and Iris were in casual attire; it was only Harry who was still in suit and tie. He was going to clock in at the funeral parlor as soon as Ursula left the house.

They were standing out on the brick stoop.

"So when will we see our daughter's beautiful face again, may I ask?" Iris said.

"Soon, Mom. You know it's nice to get a good home-cooked meal now and then."

"And a couple of slices of baked apple pie to boot," Iris joked.

"Two days' worth," Ursula shot back.

"And you do look gorgeous these days, Ursula," Harry said.

"Thanks, Dad."

"It certainly doesn't hurt your father's ego when everyone, including me, since birth, says you look just like him. The spitting image of your father."

Ursula kissed Harry flush on the lips. "No, it doesn't."

"All I have to say," Harry said beaming, "is that's my girl!"

She kissed Iris flush on the lips. "Love you two."

She skipped down the stone steps.

"Call when you get in."

"Will do. As usual," Ursula said, now standing in front of the rented car. "It's still here!"

"Yes, the neighborhood has changed. Jersey City, in general," Harry said.

"But of course we've gone over that before like a broken record. It is sad, but your mother and I don't know if we'd be happy anywhere else other than here if we moved."

"Dad, I don't think so. I think your and Mom's hearts are right here in Jersey City. On this block—like you said."

"Yes, she *is* your daughter, all right, Harry."

Ursula was in the car. Before pulling away from the curb, the car's horn honked twice.

Harry's arms wrapped around Iris's slender waist. "Ursula will be all right. I know it's what worried you in bed last night. This morning too, Iris."

"I know, Harry. I do have complete faith in her."

When Ursula came up off the Van Wyck Expressway, she knew that in a matter of minutes, she'd be home. She also knew she had four rooms to contend with. The same four rooms. She would call her mother as soon as she got in the apartment, for sure. And then what to do? she thought. Her life felt empty without Maurice "Teardrop" Williams in it.

The past two days in Jersey City, with her parents, she'd accomplished nothing, absolutely nothing, she thought. Just distraction, delay, interruption, buying some time—but nothing meaningful that could make this night before her feel any kinder, gentler. Oh, yes, Ursula thought, she did have her mother's baked apple pie in the bag (she carried over from Jersey City) to look forward to—and was looking forward to. She could put a scoop of Breyers chocolate ice cream on top, and if she felt in the mood for more, she would have a second serving, have it with another scoop of Breyers. Really, a pie a la mode.

CHAPTER 15

Teardrop stood outside the study door. Teardrop felt the time had come. He entered the study.

"Arlene, are you busy?"

She looked up from the desk. "Not so busy that I can't find time for you, Dad."

They'd patched things up between them. It took a few days of contemplation on their part, but Arlene was a person who could easily forgive, as well as Teardrop.

"Arlene, I've been trying, but this isn't going to work. I've tried. Really tried—but I'm miserable. Just plain miserable."

"You're not—"

"Ms. Jenkins, Arlene. Ursula Jenkins."

"Her again?"

"Yes, Ursula Jenkins again. Ursula."

She stared at him.

"Shut the door, Dad. J-Jamal …"

"Of course, the door …"

Teardrop closed the door.

"We … we mustn't argue. I don't want us to argue, you and—"

"You come in here with this, this piece of informat—"

"These are my feelings—besides my life I'm talking about here."

"Your life?"

"Yes, my life, Arlene. It's my life, and I should be in control of it—as I've always been. Not you. Someone else but me, as you're in control of yours."

"And Ursula Jenkins, she means what to—"

"I have powerful feelings toward her. Feelings that won't go away—not that I expected them to. Our friendship, relationship, whatever one wishes to call it, didn't break up because we wanted it to. We did so, Arlene, because we had to."

"Because of me."

"You."

"Am I to feel guilty because of it? Am I to feel—"

"No one's trying to throw blame or guilt around—"

"You—"

"Let me finish. Finish this. No, not blame or guilt your way, but it is me who has to decide what's best for me, not you or anyone else—and that's the case here. And I'm going to change it, Arlene. I am. That's—"

"Starting when, Dad?"

"Tonight."

She took her eyes off him. "Well ... if that's all you came into ... came in here for ..."

"I don't want trouble. I just don't want trouble. Any—"

"Trouble?" Arlene replied. "Trouble?"

"I want respect, Arlene. It's all I want. Something I've always had from you: your respect."

"What about your respect for me, Dad? Your respect for our home?"

"I will not bring Ms. Jenkins into this house if it should ever come to that. If Ur-Ursula hasn't completely forgotten me by now. If that's your concern. Your wish."

Arlene looked at Teardrop and she was more angry. "Dad, I do have to get back to my schoolwork." It was said dismissively.

"If this thing should get off the ground again, Arlene, I do want you to respect Ursula and me."

"Am I to call her Ursula? What, Ursula, Dad?" Arlene asked flippantly.

Teardrop didn't reply.

"But I won't see her anyway, if, as you say, this thing should get off the ground."

Teardrop turned to the door, took a few steps in its direction, and then turned back to Arlene.

"There won't be any deceit this time. Pretense. No dishonesty from me. Not this time. Everything will be conducted above board. No secret … clandestine meetings at the house. If Ursula and I are to have a relationship, it will be conducted in daylight. I want to give it every opportunity to work between us."

When Teardrop left the room, Arlene stood. "Respect. Respect, huh, Ursula Jenkins? Never!"

Ring.

"I don't want to talk to anyone. Let it ring. I'll let the machine come on."

Ursula was lying in bed. It was well after nine o'clock. She'd had her slice of apple pie.

Ring.

She'd topped the pie with Breyers chocolate ice cream. The second slice was wrapped in the refrigerator for tomorrow night's dessert.

She was lying in bed feeling drowsy, totally wiped out.

Ring.

"Ursula, it's me, Maurice. I thought you might be home. I'm disappointed that you're not. Are-aren't. But I will try again later to—"

"Maurice! Maurice!"

"Ur-Ursula, is that you?"

"Yes, Maurice. It's me!"

"I … I—"

"You called!"

"Yes."

"You actually, actually called … It's like I've been waiting, Maurice. Waiting …"

"I'm sorry about all of this. What I've put you through. Of giving up on us so quickly, without putting up a better fight."

"But how could you, Maurice? C-could you have?"

"Well, that's over, done with, because I cleared the air with Arlene tonight."

"How?"

"This is my life. Not someone else's. And I still must live it, conduct it my way—do what's best for me, not someone else. I've lived this way my entire life. And to change it now would be silly."

"But Arl—"

"We mustn't worry about Arlene for now. Just us. Our focus should be on us. Not on anyone else. Something like this happens once in a lifetime. We must take advantage of it. Not because of someone else's opinion or perception of us.

"I ... I think we almost made that fatal mistake. Took the focus off us and put it on someone else. I've missed you. God how I've missed you. With all my heart I have."

"When do you want to see me, Maurice?"

"Why as soon as possible. As I can."

"I've never been so miserable. So ... so ...."

"Ursula, you don't have to tell me. Not me."

"I thought I'd never get you back."

"We ... we both—then we both thought wrong." Pause. "Miss Lillian told me to keep the faith though."

"She did?"

"Uh, well, sort of. I didn't really seek out her opinion on this one. Not really. They say it's better to listen to your heart—it has most of your answers."

Ursula was as giddy as Teardrop. They'd been talking for a while.

"And now, Ms. Jenkins, can we pin it down? Put this thing? Set it in stone? The date you fly into Walker City."

"Well, I'll have to look at, check my calendar. Hmmm. Next weekend. By all means, next weekend, Maurice!"

"Oh if the Lord ain't good!"

"Maurice, I've never heard you talk—"

"Well, I can, when I know I'm going to see my favorite girl next weekend!"

"I'm to stay—"

"At Ms. Ruby Ingram's."

"Where else?"

"Yes, where—"

"Maurice, are you sure it's the only boarding house in Walker City's populace?"

"Well, it's the one closest to me."

"Then Ms. Ingram's is perfect!"

"And as usual, I'll arrange the care of everything."

"Maurice, there goes that word again."

"Yes, it is becoming quite burdensome, isn't it?"

She sighed. "This will work out this time, won't it? Won't it, Maurice?"

"It will. I think any relationship has to be tested at one time or another. There's always something. Something we'll have to weather."

"You and Maureen—"

"Of course there were things. Like I said, there're always things. Things that try to get in the way. You have to hurdle."

"And Arlene, can you rest easy with that?"

"I can and will. I'm not happy, not by a long shot. But it won't affect the household, Jamal, in any way. Neither Arlene nor I want that. We were careless before, let our emotions get the better of us. Override caution. But there'll be no blowups this time around. Arlene knows my intentions, where to draw the line—who's now in my life."

"That sounds so good, delicious."

"It does, doesn't it?"

CHAPTER 16

Ursula arrived in Iowa under a gray slate sky that threatened rain. No, there was no tornado on the horizon that was about to touch down, at least the Walker City's weather service reported there wasn't—and, mostly, it was unusually right for such a small operation of weather providers.

It was Saturday afternoon, 1:23 p.m. to be exact. Des Moines International Airport in Polk County was in the car's distance. The terminal, as usual, was busy, something Iowans were proud of as a reflection of just how booming the state's economy was performing, that its industries received worldwide attention.

"I really like this car," Ursula said, brushing her hand over the car's lush leather seats.

"It is a beauty. It's rented out until Monday."

"When you called to tell me you'd pick me up from Des Moines International, Maurice, I kind of lost track of whether you owned a car or not."

"It feels really good being behind a steering wheel again."

"You do look quite handsome too—if I must say so myself."

"And you don't look too bad sitting over there either. So ... I guess the trip to Walker City is becoming old hat for you? Can we say that without trepidation?"

"You may. Old hat," Ursula said smugly.

"It's just so good to see you," Teardrop said, taking Ursula's hand, kissing it. "Knowing you're here."

"You'd better be careful, Mr. Williams. I might just make you pull over to the side of the road—"

"And do what, Ms. Jenkins?"

"Make you kiss me—what else!"

"Like I did—"

"On the house's back porch."

"You mean you still remember that kiss?"

"Remember? How could I ever forget. It's not every day a woman gets kissed by Maurice 'Teardrop' Williams."

"Or a man gets kissed by Ursula Jenkins."

"Maurice, I need a nickname."

"And so what's your middle name?"

"Jeanette."

He laughed. "It's not every day I get a kiss from an Ursula Jeanette—"

"I'd still rather have a nickname. Something as original, striking, strikingly original as Teardrop."

"I suppose it has its advantages. A bluesman has to entice his public. Whet its curiosity when possible."

"Jeanette certainly wouldn't."

"No, not Jeanette. That is, uh, stretching it a bit."

"But back to that kiss."

"Was it—"

"Don't worry, Maurice, you know how to kiss a woman, all right. It's one thing I won't have to teach you!"

They'd reached Ruby Ingram's boarding house at 2 Marble Road.

"Looks like I'm going to have to be on my best behavior while I'm down here with you."

"M-me too," Teardrop laughed. "Since Ruby will be seeing me as often as she will you while you're here." Pause.

"Well, I'm glad you took my advice and pulled out your woolen coat. Brought it along with you for the weekend."

"The weather's about the same in New York—chilly."

"It's just that Walker City probably will get snow before you do."

Teardrop got out the car and then opened Ursula's door. She got out the car. She was in slacks, woolen jacket, and black leather ankle boots with a gold buckled side strap. Teardrop thought she looked smashing.

"Now for your bags."

Teardrop opened the trunk and pulled out Ursula's bags.

"When I was out on a week's tour, Ursula, I never carried this much luggage."

"Well ... a woman has to decide what to wear."

"Or what not to wear." Maurice could only chuckle. "Whichever is the case."

"Exactly."

"Well ... as long as we agree on that."

"If, ha, you couldn't charm the fur off a bear."

Ursula and Teardrop were in Ursula's room (they'd gotten past Ms. Ruby Ingram). It was the one and same room she was in the last time she stayed in the boarding house.

"Ursula, you were in this room the last two times down. Correct me if I'm wrong."

"You're not."

"Seems like Ruby can't rent out this room—"

"Not unless Ursula Jenkins from New York City shows up."

Teardrop waved his hands in front of him. "Coincidence, okay?"

"Of course," Ursula said as playfully as Teardrop.

"Well, tonight you'll finally—"

"Maurice, may I say it?"

"By all means. I want you to ..."

"I'll finally get a look at Walker City. Its metropolis, not just its outskirts."

"Hope you're not disappointed. You being a big-city girl."

"Why, Jersey City is hardly a big city."

"I'm just thrilled you're here. And 'here' can mean anywhere as long as you're there."

Teardrop took her in his arms, and all he did was look into this tall woman's dark, beautiful eyes.

"I'm going to kiss you, Ursula. Not like I did on the back porch of the house but much, much better than that."

"Y-you are?"

"Without a minute's doubt in my mind."

Dinner and the movies and then who knew what else, Ursula thought. The evening was planned out for her and Teardrop (exciting stuff, Ursula thought, even for Walker City, Iowa!).

Just minutes ago, she'd gotten off the phone with Teardrop, and he'd be there any minute. It's why her coat was on, and she was all set to step out onto the boarding house's front porch.

Standing on the porch, having bid Ms. Ingram good evening and receiving back a lovely reply, Ursula began thinking about how her life had gone from doom and gloom, disaster, to now this sparkle, gleam—all in a week.

And Teardrop was on time. He stepped out the car. He was dressed to kill. He and Ursula greeted each other. Gallantly, he opened the car door for her. And when he got in the driver's seat, Ursula said, "What, the same car this afternoon, Maurice? I thought sure you would've rented a new one by now."

"Oh, already I can see this is going to be a great evening!"

They'd eaten at the Walk-In Restaurant in the heart of Walker City. Teardrop had warned Ursula not to expect too much of Walker City proper but that it did have a post office with an American flag on a flagpole draping from it, a library (with the same American flag theme), police station, firehouse, mayor's office, and a small park with real, live gray-colored pigeons.

Of course Ursula saw much more than that in Walker City but Teardrop had tried to describe its quaintness without giving away too much of its old-fashioned sweetness and intimacy.

But now the date was well past the dinner stage and onto the cinema stage, where a multiplex, Evening Star cinema (three wide screens), had recently been built in the Walker City proper. It's where Teardrop and Ursula were, inside the cinema. They'd bought a super-duper box of popcorn (plenty of butter). They were holding hands and using them, on occasion, to eat the popcorn.

The movie was about ten minutes in, so they hadn't been in the theater long when, suddenly, Ursula felt a tension in Teardrop's hand; it was as if it'd come out of nowhere.

She took her eyes off the movie screen to glance at Teardrop, whose face was contorted and appeared to be fighting something. Then Ursula looked back to the wide screen.

But it was only minutes later when she did the same thing, repeated herself. Where they sat in the theater, there was no one to disturb, the theater about a third full, a scattering of people.

She whispered, "Maurice are ... are you enjoying the movie?"

Ursula felt the tension rise in Teardrop's hand, but he had not answered her. She didn't know what to make of it, so she looked at Teardrop again, not covertly but overtly, and saw a face that was not the one that had come into the multiplex nor the one at the restaurant nor the face she saw when Teardrop picked her up in the car from Ruby Ingram's an hour earlier.

"Ursula, f-forgive my rudeness ..."

"Yes, Maurice ... ?"

"But can we leave now?"

She looked up at him and then back at the movie screen and then back at him.

"Leave the theater?"

"C-can we?"

"Of course, of ... of course, Maurice. Of course."

Ursula took the quarter-eaten box of popcorn off her lap and stood. Teardrop, seemingly anxious to get out the theater, was leading instead of following.

When they got out into the theater's elaborate lobby, they didn't look like a couple, two people together, but more like two people who were trying to find separate exits out the theater. But they went out the same polish-buffed door anyway, out into the night air that had sting in it.

The car was parked behind the Evening Star, in its parking lot. They were walking, still separated, at lengths, in a way, from each other. But Ursula stopped as if she were going to stand her ground while still holding on to her box of popcorn.

Then Teardrop stopped and turned.

"Something just came over me. I ... I just ... ," Teardrop said incoherently, vaguely.

"Over you? What do you mean, over you?" Ursula asked, upset, her face hot, ignoring the air's chill.

"I don't want to insult you or ... or myself, for that matter. B-but something came over me ... and ... and let's leave it at, just leave it at that, s-shall we?"

"Then you don't know me very well, Maurice. Not as well as I thought, because this—I'm not going to stand for." Pause. "Dismissing it as if it didn't happen or cavalierly or ... or as if—"

"I'm your father."

"You said that Maurice, not me."

"But it still—"

"The age gap between us?"

"Yes."

"Well, I'm well beyond that. Well—"

"Well, I'm not. Just now, in the theater, holding hands, eating popcorn out a box ..."

"What?"

"It made me feel like a teenager out on his first date, and I'm not because I'm a fifty-five-year-old man, Ursula. So ... so I ... I had to stop, pause, and ask myself who am I trying to kid? It was a difficult question, but I couldn't answer it, and it ... it made me just the more angry—angrier with myself—that I had let this thing between us get this far."

"As ... as far as it has ... already. I am not a teenager anymore. So why am I—"

"Having fun? Enjoying yourself?"

Teardrop took a few steps toward her.

"But ... but ..."

"You were, Maurice. You were, until you began thinking. Thinking the fun out of the situation you were in."

"I can't shut that part of me down," Teardrop said. "Turn my mind on and off. And why would anyone expect me to?"

"No, you can't. But I thought, when I interviewed you for the article, you said you played your music, the best music came out of you and Miss Lillian when you lived in the moment."

"It's what I said. Absolutely. There's nothing to think about," Maurice laughed. "Yes, when I live in the moment with my music, then nothing's been done before, and everything's possible."

"So I wasn't wrong."

"No."

"So by living in the moment—"

"It's when you are who you are. Truly. The best of you."

"Your character and what? The music's too, Maurice?"

"Yes. Yes, Ursula, yes!"

"I know the feeling too. When I'm lost in my writing, the moment, when it happens to me. When all things are possible and nothing is impossible. But there's a total joy ... Full, personal awareness of it. Isn't there, Maurice?"

Teardrop drew nearer to Ursula and then walked past her.

"Well, are you coming?"

"Coming?"

"Back to the movie?"

"I—"

"Film critics says that the first ten minutes of a movie, it's what counts. The rest, you can catch up with."

"They do?"

Teardrop looked at the box of popcorn. "And don't worry, I'll buy you a fresh box of popcorn when we get back inside the movie. I know that one's gotten cold."

"With extra butter?"

"Extra butter."

Teardrop began walking, and Ursula, in a burst, scooted behind him and in line with him and then put her arm around his waist.

"Ursula, you do have the ticket stubs, don't you?"

"And if I don't?"

"Well …"

"I thought you were the one who told me that everyone in Walker City knows you."

"Uh … well they do, for the most part, up to a point. But that young lady at the Star's ticket window looked awfully young?"

"The blues hasn't reached her yet?"

"The legend of Maurice 'Teardrop' Williams."

"Bluesman, par excellence!"

Having seen the movie, Ursula and Teardrop were back in the car. Ursula realized she'd defused something earlier but didn't know if it'd been entirely eliminated: when the age issue might come up again. She wasn't afraid of it but would always want to deal with it directly, not duck it but stab it enough times to kill it—make certain it was dead and buried for good.

"Maurice, one day we'll be equals."

"Ursula, you've been sitting there in the car seat thinking, haven't you?"

"I have."

"Any silence around you is not good, I see."

"Now you're catching on."

"Then we're back to outside the theater, aren't we?"

"Uh-huh. Right."

"I'm glad you don't let things roll off your back. I really like that about you, al-already. That you're willing to see things through."

"Since they were your feelings, Maurice, they shouldn't be taken lightly or for granted. They're creditable."

"And it probably won't be the last time. I still find this all too incredible to believe. Ex-extraordinary, Ursula. I'm still in that 'pinch me' stage of this. Pinch me and I'll wake up and find out this isn't real. This isn't happening to me. T-to find someone as incredible, beautiful as you."

"Beauty means a lot to all of us, doesn't it?"

"Probably to every society, every culture on Earth. It's intrinsic to—"

"And you're the most beautiful man I've ever seen—if I may be liberal with that word."

Teardrop smiled. "You may be, Ursula. As liberal as you'd like."

"But you are, Maurice. I'm serious."

"So it's not only me seeing it in you—"

"But me seeing it in you. See, we're equal when it comes to that too. I find you incredibly beautiful, and I sometimes want to pinch myself to make sure this isn't a dream, that it'll all be snatched from me when I wake. I am no better off than you, Maurice."

"Are all the Williams men—"

"We hail from Virginia. My grandfather, Beauchamp Williams, was a strikebreaker in a mining town in—"

"The Consolidation Coal Company. You're talking about the town of Buxton, Iowa."

"Amazing, Ursula. How'd you know that!"

"I did my research."

"You have. Well done." Pause. "Buxton, uh, was a black utopia for us here in Iowa at the time. It really was, compared to Virginia. Buxton was integrated—"

"By mostly immigrants. Swedes, Welsh, the Irish …"

"Men striving to make it in this country too. Came with expectations—"

"To gain an economic foothold here. To live the American dream."

"Yes, much like any immigrant group arriving here. With that goal in mind."

"Even if our experiences here are totally different than theirs, Maurice." Ursula had to laugh sarcastically. "How we arrived to these shores."

The conversation continued.

Minutes later.

"Well, Ursula, one day down and one more to—"

"Tomorrow, Maurice, can we go into the woods?"

He frowned. "Ursula, I don't know—it might be too chilly for—"

"Have you and Miss Lillian been going into the woods in this weather?"

"Yes," Teardrop said, turning the car to the right. "We have."

"It's something, I must say, I was looking forward to before coming down here, going into the woods with you."

"To see the big bad wolf!"

"Ha. Yes!"

"B-but we'll have to go in from the other end. Side."

"I know."

"From my house."

"I know."

"It's a shame, Ursula. It really is."

"One day we'll work that out too, Maurice. Find a resolution."

"You think so?"

"I do."

"I love, just love your natural optimism. Something that's not based on any pretense or false presumptions. You're sure of things. But most importantly, yourself."

"Arlene ..."

"I've noticed lately that it's Arlene now, more and more, and not Mrs. Wilk—"

"My friend Byron noticed it too."

"It—that's progress."

"It is."

"Using the name Mrs. Wilkerson, I think you were giving my daughter far too much power."

"You did mention it."

"You know it's good to reduce things down to size. Down to scale. It doesn't frighten you as much." Pause. "But Arlene, my daughter, she's going to be a tough person to buck. T-to deal with."

"Probably more than I'd like to imagine."

"That's good not to underestimate anyone."

"Not someone as brilliant as your daughter. I wouldn't do that with her. Be so careless."

"You do respect her then?"

"I have the utmost respect for her. For what you've said she's accomplished."

"A lot."

"Especially a black woman."

"You know, she could be teaching at a big, prestigious university if she chose to. She certainly had enough offers. But chose, instead, to teach at Walker University. A predominantly black college. Founded by black educators. She's full of idealism, my daughter."

"I sensed that. It came through, even if the conversation, at the time, was one-sided, directed solely at you."

"Idealism, making sure black students don't get shortchanged. Aren't cheated out their education. Not get a second-rate one. At least not under her tutelage, they won't."

"Admirable."

They'd gotten back to the boarding house.

"Coming in for a nightcap?"

"Ursula," Teardrop said, braking the car, "I hope tomorrow doesn't sail along like today."

Ursula sighed. "Coming in?"

And Teardrop stepped out the car to join her.

CHAPTER 17

Three weeks later.

Ursula had arranged her schedule in order to spend a weekend in Walker City with Teardrop. She was doing more and more op-ed pieces, and with her trusty laptop by her side, night and day, she'd have no problem in meeting her writing commitments.

Recently, she'd written a fiction piece that was grabbed up by the *New Yorker* magazine and would be published next month (that took care of at least four months' rent!). Ursula had other fiction pieces she was toying with, stories exciting her and couldn't wait to write. It'd just become a matter of which one to start first, plotting out her agenda.

Teardrop had asked for more time together with her, and she was tickled pink to accommodate him. So her response was yes. She'd be in Walker City for a week, but if she could have carved more time out for him, she would have. Her visit three weeks ago seemed like one of those sun showers that last only for a few minutes, not like a downpour in April.

Arlene and the red Impala were away from the house—north of it, away from the city, away from any possibility of her and her father being on the same road, passing by each other what would be purely by accident, mistake. She knew Ursula Jenkins was back in town and what Ursula Jenkins and her father and Jamal had planned for today: lunch at the Walk-In Restaurant.

Teardrop informed Arlene Ursula was flying in from New York City to spend the week with him. He told her up front. It's the way it'd been between them, the current status of their situation since their initial confrontation, getting off on the wrong foot. He'd asked if it was all right he took Jamal along with him since Ursula liked Jamal so much, since the feeling was mutual. She'd asked about him many times, it seems, and Jamal the same.

Arlene said yes. She wouldn't get in their way. It's how she fought her personal battles, strictly on her own, certainly not utilizing Jamal as a pawn. She made no bones about it to Teardrop she disapproved of what he and Ursula Jenkins were doing. Mentally, she was still fighting them at every turn, tirelessly. She kept wishing her father would come to his senses about this woman, Ursula Jenkins—what she was thinking now while putting distance in the car between her and the house.

The lunch was supposed to be for 11:30 p.m. She knew by the time they sat down and everything, the lunch got into full swing, it'd be closer to twelve o'clock. At bedtime, Jamal was excited and when he'd arisen this morning, Arlene thought. He said he got little sleep.

"It's such a big thing to him," Arlene said, looking out onto Elk Road, a lonely-looking road. She hadn't traveled over it for some time; actually, she couldn't remember the last time she was turned in this northwesterly direction in Walker City.

"I just know I don't want to see that woman. But she's becoming more and more of a nuisance. Aggressive. More sure of herself every day. Confident ... isn't she?

"The freedom she gives herself to range like this. To go wherever she wants. Whenever she wants."

And when Jamal got back to the house, of course he'd tell her what a fabulous time he had, and why shouldn't he? Arlene thought. *He'll burst through the house's front door, if I'm home, sweep me up into his day. He'll know I'm home. He'll see the car. And he'll hear me—I'll ... I'll stand no chance. No opportunity to get away from Dad or Ursula Jenkins.*

Moving forward, the red Impala gained greater speed.

"Ursula, they make the best banana splits. Want to try one?"

Ursula looked at Teardrop. "Why not?"

"Granddad, well ... he looks forward to his strawberry shortcake when we come here, so I'm not even going to try," Jamal said glumly at the round highly polished table. "Try to get him to order a banana split."

"But ask him, Ursula, how long it took him before he realized I was a pig stuck in mud. Wouldn't budge."

"How long did it take, Jamal?"

"Oh … about a year. Right, Granddad? A year, I'd say."

Jamal was sitting to Teardrop's right and Ursula to his left in the Walk-In Restaurant. Teardrop patted Jamal's shoulder. "But he put up a good fight. Didn't quit at the first sight of blood."

"Right, Granddad. I gave it my all." Pause. "They put whipped cream on it, Ursula, uh, with a cherry top, of course."

"Of course," Ursula and Teardrop said in unison, laughing.

"Ursula I … I just can't resist it."

Jamal was in the rented car's backseat.

"Granddad, why don't you just buy a new car instead of renting one each time Ursula comes to visit? You can afford it, sir!"

Ursula took Teardrop's hand, threw it up in the air, and then laughed mightily while covering her mouth.

"My financier back there, in the backseat. My financial planner. Jamal," Teardrop said, looking into the rearview mirror, "don't you want me to save money for your inheritance?"

"Aww, Granddad, you'll have plenty by the time you go. You're going to live to be a hundred anyway. Wait and see."

"I'm with you on that one, Jamal," Ursula said. "I totally agree."

"I don't think Miss Lillian would let him die anyway, Ursula."

"Now who told you that, Jamal? Miss Lillian?"

"No, Granddad, but—"

"Jamal, I think you had too much of that banana split back at the restaurant."

Ursula winked at Jamal. "It was delicious, wasn't it, Jamal?"

"It was … umm … it sure was, Ursula," Jamal said, rubbing his stomach. "Granddad doesn't know what he's missing out on."

"I think he does, Jamal," Ursula said, now winking at Teardrop. "But he just doesn't want to admit it. Give in, right, Maurice?"

"Ursula, uh, why … why do you call my grandfather Maurice. My grandmother was the only one to call him that. I mean, that I know of."

Teardrop didn't want to look at Ursula nor she at him to draw greater attention to themselves, thus drawing greater attention to the actual depth of Jamal's question.

"I just never thought of calling your grandfather anything else, Jamal. By any other name, I suppose."

"Then Grandmother must've felt that way too. I … I guess. Same as you."

"Jamal, I think you're right," Teardrop said.

"S-suddenly I could go for another banana split. What about you, Ursula?"

"Sounds good to me, Jamal."

"Well, you'll both have to suffer, since this car is pointed in one direction and one direction only."

"Not unless there's a mutiny aboard ship."

"W-what's that?"

"Yes, why don't you explain it to him, Ursula," Teardrop said. "For I can prepare myself for the worst to happen. A blood-thirsty munity."

Ursula glanced over her right shoulder; Jamal was all ears.

"Yes … Ursula?"

Arlene was back from her drive. She just drove and drove and drove until she knew she'd have to drive back, covering the same ground, recording the same mileage.

There was no rented car in the driveway; of course it was the first thing she saw, the first thing she looked for—the shiny black four-door sedan her father rented for the week.

"Why did I expect them back from their lunch?" Arlene said, parking the car. "No, not at all."

And now it would mean that Jamal would come bursting through the front door, practically tearing the hinges off it, bowling her over with his enthusiasm, excitement, kindled by the lunch, the time spent out the house. It was guaranteed now, not an imaginative possibility but real.

"And I'm going to have to prepare for it," Arlene said, pulling the key out the car's ignition. "I resent this," she said, furious. "I resent this whole damned thing Dad's doing to this family. Our family!"

The car door slammed.

She looked at the sizeable house. "If I could hide in it, I would. If I could just hide in it …"

And to think she was talking this foolishly, thinking this foolishly, she thought. She resented even more that her life had taken this turn, and there was no one to blame but Ursula Jenkins. That there could be no one to blame but her.

"I ... I-I've never hated anyone. I don't think. The word is abnormal to me. Not in my vocabulary. I'm a Christian. My s-spirit's honorable. Clean, pure, I don't love my enemies, but I do pray for them. If they offend me, I pray for them. Do pray for—"

Arlene stepped up onto the porch, angled out to the front of the house, looking out onto the yard, expecting snow to come soon and coat the yard in white, piled at least a foot high. The word "hate" banging in her ears. She'd said it over and over out on the road, in the car, hoping she'd left it there, out on the road—done with it and its capacity for ill.

But here I am, Arlene said to herself, *Jamal's not here, Dad's not here, they're with Ursula Jenkins.* Spending the day with Ursula Jenkins. And the more Arlene used Ursula Jenkins's name, the more she didn't question herself, this introspection, account she was taking of herself on a day she hated.

"I feel this way. I don't want to feel any other way toward her. How can I have any other feelings when she's trying to steal my family from me? W-who'd expect me to?"

But she didn't know how to fight, that was the thing, Arlene thought, without looking like she was the bad person in the scenario.

"That's her advantage. And she knows it. Ursula Jenkins knows it."

Cunning. Cunning, Arlene thought.

"You're so cunning, Ursula Jenkins, aren't you?"

And how could she say something bad about someone she didn't know and not look foolish for it during the process.

"How." Pause.

"I teach my students about the rules, protocol of argument. How you must have a model, premise, your argument, polemic must be based on something solid. In economics, its trends, cycles, benchmarks, paradigms. I don't know Ursula Jenkins so ... so ...

"I don't know her, so how can I argue against her to make sense? Be ... be logical. These are personal feelings based on nothing. It would be said, argued, that she'd done nothing to me. Against me. To harm me. It's how it'd be argued."

Arlene 's eyes shut.

All I can do is hate her, Arlene thought. *Continue to hate her. Not stop. Not give up. It's all I can do. All ... it'll be to my advantage over her. To hate her. For what she stands for. For who she is. For what she's done. It-it's enough reason, argument, l-logic for anyone to hate someone.*

Ursula Jenkins.

꧁

It was the fifth day of Ursula's stay in Walker City, Iowa.

Two days ago it'd snowed and then rained, washing the snow away. Now the ground was dry, at least, in most spots.

Ursula and Teardrop were spending most of their time together in Teardrop's house. Ursula was feeling more comfortable in the house. Teardrop was feeling more comfortable in the house with her. Because of the weather, they hadn't done much in the way of getting outdoors. Around noon, Teardrop was picking up Ursula from the boarding house.

They'd spend so much time talking or reading. Ursula, her material; Teardrop, his. The time would fly by, something they thought was incredible that two people could spend so much time together, but it would turn out that it was still not enough. That really surprised them.

"Ursula, I still can't believe this day, can you?"

"It's a far cry from the past two."

"The sun, it looks like it'd like ... is going to work overtime today."

They'd driven to the house.

"It's even warm."

"Midfifties."

"Maurice, that warm?"

Teardrop braked the car.

"Maurice, may I say something ... ?"

"Which is?"

Ursula looked back to the car's backseat.

"Oh," Teardrop laughed, "Miss Lillian."

"Miss Lillian. Miss Lillian," Ursula said, "you haven't played Miss Lillian—"

"In, what ... ?"

"Three days."

"Oh ... so you've been counting?"

"You bet I have!"

"I guess Miss Lillian has too. Knowing her. She is about things."

"It's the woods, isn't it, Maurice? Not being able to go into the woods because of the weather the past few days."

"Exactly."

"Oh no you don't. No you—"

"I can't get away with that one, huh? Not on my life?"

"I won't let you," Ursula laughed.

"Okay, okay. But normally, usually I play Miss Lillian in the house during winter. So …"

"So?"

"I mean, I haven't been doing even that. So it does mean I've been distracted by something or someone, doesn't—"

"But not today," Ursula said, stepping out the car, opening the car's back door, picking Miss Lillian up off the car seat, watching Teardrop open and close the door and then get to her.

"Here … ," Ursula said, handing Miss Lillian to Teardrop. "We're going into the woods today, Maurice. Miss Lillian, you, and me."

"You really are something," Teardrop said, holding Ursula by the waist.

Ursula and Teardrop had been in the woods for about an hour. There were damp spots in the woods, quite a few the sun had yet dried. They were hungry so were heading back to the house. They were about eight to ten minutes from the house.

Teardrop's arm was around Ursula's shoulder and hers around his, not until a tree or a low branch blocked them, and then they'd undo themselves but then reattach.

"Oops," Ursula said, and she and Teardrop broke apart. "Maurice, the branches."

It's when Teardrop mildly took Ursula by her shoulders, halting her. "Ursula," he said, standing behind her, Miss Lillian strapped to his back. "Uh … Ursula …"

Ursula turned. Her body was relaxed, expecting Teardrop to kiss her. Instead, he hugged her to him, smothering her body with his.

When they broke off the embrace, it's when Teardrop looked into her eyes, waiting to feel them like a black fire.

But as Ursula looked into his clear brown eyes, she didn't know what she saw. Fear? Joy? The presence of each juxtaposed in her eyes' cornea, him not blinking once as if some eccentric pulse drove him.

And suddenly, without warning, Teardrop dropped down onto one knee.

"Maurice!"

"Hear me out, Ursula. Hear … bear with me. Please. Please bear with me. A … a second more."

"But you're on your knees, and I heard a squish. You hit a damp spot. You're kneeling in water, Maurice. Water. No matter how much—"

"I … Ursula, I don't care for now, right now. In fact, I could care less."

"But your pants, Maurice!"

"B-but my nerves, Ursula. My nerves!"

"Nerves?" Ursula said, looking down at him as the crown of his head took on a sweaty fix.

"Ursula, uh, this is tough enough. Tough going enough. So please don't make it more, tougher than—"

"Tough, what's tough—"

"This. This, Ursula. This."

It's when Teardrop breathed heavily and then took in one final breath.

"Ursula, Ursula Jenkins … will you marry me?" Teardrop said, switching over to his other knee and then slipping his hand inside his Windbreaker and pulling out the dark velvet blue ring box.

"Maurice! Maurice! Maurice!" Ursula shrieked again and then dropped to the ground with him, presently getting her jeans wet, spoiled in the damp soil too.

"I'm handing you my heart, Ursula. All of it."

Ursula and Teardrop came out the woods. Things had pretty much calmed down for them. The engagement ring fit Ursula's left finger to a T. The ring sparkled. Ursula loved it; she thought it exquisite. She and Teardrop were holding hands, but Teardrop was not holding the hand with the engagement ring on it.

"I still can't believe it fits … fits perfectly."

Teardrop's smile was probably as bright as the diamond ring. "Lucky, I suppose. Uh, guess." Then he looked down at her knees. "Ursula, sorry about your jeans."

"Oh that's okay, Maurice. No one told me to get on my knees too."

"You did shock me."

"Look who's talking about shocking someone," Ursula said, snuggling up to Teardrop, anchoring tightly to his arm.

"I'm just glad you said yes. Otherwise—"

"And so you're going to tell me, what, you lacked confidence, had reservations when you know how much in love I am with you?"

"Ursula, would you say, repeat that again, please? One more time for me."

"What?"

"You know what, without me—"

"I love you, Maurice. I love you."

Then she broke free of him and spun in the browned, flattened grass.

"I love you, Maurice 'Teardrop' Williams!" She yelled out at the top of her lungs in the wooded area. "I love Maurice 'Teardrop' Williams!"

He laughed and then ran up to her, let her body spin like a top again, and then took her in his arms, and it's when they paused to catch their breath before kissing.

"Maurice, if we hadn't come out to the woods today, then—"

"I would have proposed to you the in the house. Ha. But don't worry, you would've been proposed to. Somehow, somewhere ... Probably in the kitchen."

"Far, far less romantic. The kitchen? Good thing I got you and Miss Lillian out to the woods. Now I really have a story to tell my friends."

Ursula couldn't take her eyes off the engagement ring. "Plans, plans, plans."

"Yes," Teardrop said soberly, "it's what's next."

"There's so much to work out, isn't there?"

"Yes, quite a lot. For us to square away."

"And a date. Do—"

"How about in the spring? Say late May?"

"There'll be no argument from me. The sooner the better."

"Oh ... Ursula, you're a girl, truly, after my own heart!"

"Only—"

"Yes, baby?"

"Oh ... I like that."

"It came, did come naturally. Out of me naturally."

"Like me calling you Maurice." Pause. "Arlene, Maurice. Arlene."

"It's what you were about to say?"

"Yes."

"She won't be happy."

"That, I'd say, is an understatement."

"Oh sure ... sure it is. Is."

"We're going to turn the world upside down with our announcement."

They were back at the black car; both leaned against it, folding their arms in complete accord with each other.

"Maurice, when are you going to tell her?"

"Tonight."

"Jamal, he'll be—"

"Thrilled."

"Are you going to tell them separately or together?"

Teardrop squirmed. "I, Ursula, I haven't quite decided. D-don't have the foggiest idea right now."

"Oh."

"But I'm not worried. Mentally, I've crossed that bridge."

Ursula stood in front of him and then, softly, fell into him.

"I wish I could be there with you. I really do. That it could be a happy occasion we both could share in."

"But that would be asking for far too much."

Ursula pressed her cheek against Teardrop's shoulder.

"You're not going to let this upset you? Dampen your spirits, are … are you?"

Her head came off Teardrop's shoulder. "Not at all, Maurice. No, not at all."

"Because this day is our day, belongs to us. And the tomorrows ahead, all of it, Ursula."

"It's how we must think, isn't it?"

Teardrop shook his head. "No, Ursula, it's how we feel. Feel … feel inside. It's nothing cerebral, baby."

"Maurice, y-you said it again."

"I did, didn't I?"

"I feel so good in your arms. So protected."

"Mmm …" Teardrop hugged her more to him.

"When we're like this …"

"Sssh … Ursula, you've said too much already."

"Things I don't need to say."

"Uh-uh. It doesn't get any better than this. The love we have, baby."

Since Ursula's stay in Walker City, Arlene and Jamal ate dinner together. With Teardrop and Ursula having dinner at the house, of course this condition had become a matter of course.

Teardrop had just come in the house. As usual, Arlene and Jamal were chatting in the kitchen. But once in the kitchen with them, he'd need their undivided attention. No, he wasn't going to tell them separately about his and Ursula's engagement; he would kill two birds with one stone. On his way back to the house, he'd decided it'd be easier on him this way, telling them together.

"Dinner's over?"

"Over, Granddad. You don't know what you missed."

"Smothered pork chops, Jamal. I know what I missed."

"Mom, that brown gravy, Mom ..." Jamal's long legs wiggled beneath the table.

"If you say it one more time, Jamal, I'll package and retail it. Market it around here."

"An economics professor, practicing what she preaches, huh, Arlene?"

"Right, Dad," Arlene replied perkily. "It would serve as a first for my calling."

"A new precedent for economic professors."

"I don't know about all of that, Granddad. I just know Mom's—"

"You like your mother's brown gravy a whole lot."

"Yes!" Jamal's legs stopped wiggling.

Teardrop sat down at the head of the table (where he would have been sitting if he'd eaten with them).

"Dad, you must admit, Jamal *is* consistent."

"He is." Pause. "Well ... ," Teardrop said, lacing his fingers together. "I ..."

"Granddad, excuse me, sir, but Mom and I were talking, just talking about me getting a new bike next year," Jamal said, clapping his hands.

"Really, Arlene?"

"Yes, that's where my money for my recipe fortune will be—"

"Oh, come on, Mom."

"Okay, okay, Jamal. He's ... lately your grandson's been twisting my arm, Dad. Dropping little hints here and there. Cleverly, I might add."

"Cleverly placed and timed, huh, Jamal?"

"Been working on her, Granddad. Real hard."

"Persistently softening his mother up. With no letup."

"You don't say, Jamal."

"Have to keep the pressure on her, sir. And I think she's finally cracked."

"Jamal does need a new bike though."

"See, Granddad?"

"So I see, Jamal. So I see."

"He is too big for the one he's riding."

"Especially, ha, with those long legs of his. Spider-Man legs, Arlene. It does look like he grows an inch taller by the day."

"If not more, sir."

Arlene was to the left of Teardrop. Her hands were flat to the table. Teardrop touched her right hand.

"So let me buy it, Arlene. Like before."

"You want to, Dad?"

"It's what grandfathers are for—our calling."

"Wow! Wow! Thanks, Granddad! Thanks!"

It's when Jamal jumped out the chair and began acting as if he were going to boost himself to the moon.

"L-let me call Armon! He talked his parents into getting him a new bike too!"

But when Jamal rounded the kitchen table, it's when Teardrops stopped him. "Jamal, before you do, can you sit back down in … in your chair? There's something I'd like to tell you and your mother, together."

"Uh, now … now, right now, sir?"

"Now, Jamal. Yes, now."

Jamal, whose body had been tumbling with excitement and was now being asked to bring it under control, asked. "Uh … it can't wait?"

"Jamal, Armon can wait. I'm sure your grandfather must really have something special to tell us. One it seems he can't keep under his hat."

"It sure does, Mom."

"I know your grandfather. When he gets like this," Arlene sighed, "one can only imagine."

It's when Jamal scooted back over to his chair. When he got there, he sat alertly.

"Well … Granddad?"

Teardrop looked at Arlene first, and then at Jamal.

"What is it, Granddad?"

And it's when Arlene felt some level of tension build in the kitchen.

"Arlene, Jamal, I've asked Ursula … Ursula Jenkins to marry me."

"Wow! Wow! Wow! Great, Granddad. Great, great, that's great!"

And Jamal flew out his chair again and ran to Teardrop, throwing his arms around him.

"Married. Married. Married to Ursula! To Ursula! Wow! Wow! Wait until I tell Armon. T-that's even better than a new bike. Better, much, much better than a new bike, Granddad!"

And Jamal ran out the kitchen at top speed so he could call Armon. And it was Teardrop and Arlene who sat in the kitchen, at the kitchen table, alone.

And then the silence pervaded. Arlene was shaking. Teardrop not looking at her. Arlene seemingly landing into a clutter of thought. Teardrop still was not looking at her, not until the back leg of the chair scraped the kitchen floor.

"Arlene ..."

"What do you want me to say? What?"

Teardrop's head dropped. "Nothing, Arlene, I s-suppose nothing."

"I'm going to my study. I have work to do."

"Of course you do, Arlene."

Arlene had cleared the kitchen.

"I'm ... I'm sorry, Arlene."

"For what? You're happy."

Arlene was out the kitchen.

"Happy ... ," Teardrop murmured. "Yes, I'm happy."

"Granddad," Jamal said, whizzing back into the kitchen.

"Oh, oh, you're back," Teardrop said, looking up.

"Granddad, I ... I told ... told Armon all about the bike you're going to buy me next year—"

"Good, Jamal. G—"

"And ... and Ursula. About Ursula. Your marriage to Ursula!"

And then Jamal sped up the kitchen's back stairs before Teardrop could reply—if it's what he had in mind.

He got up from the kitchen table. His walk was perceptibly different, knowing pretty much, certain, how this part of the day, for him, would go.

"Ursula."

Teardrop had just called her.

"Maurice." Pause.

"How did it go, Maurice?"

"As expected."

No reply.

"I told them everything. Arlene and Jamal together. I guess I was a coward. I couldn't tell Arlene alone." Tears were in his eyes.

"You're crying."

"Yes. It's difficult. It is. But it's done. Over with." Teardrop tasted the tears in his mouth.

"Jamal, Maurice?"

"Happy, happy as a lark hearing the news. Thought it out of this world."

"I'm happy t—"

"But we knew he would—Jamal, all along."

"I'll be his friend."

"You can't be his grandmother."

"He only has one grandmother, Maurice."

"Maureen, Ursula."

"Maureen."

Long ago Ursula knew she would accept her role if it ever got to this point in her relationship with Teardrop.

"Maurice …"

"Yes?"

"This might not be the right time to say this. My timing might be off, way off."

"No. No. If there's something on your mind, air it out. Please."

"There is—I … I mean during the midst of all of this unpleasantness, I was thinking …"

"Come on, out with it."

"Sure." Pause. "Maurice, you haven't been to New York City to visit me. My part of town."

"Ha. No, I—"

"I want you to meet my parents. How's that?"

"Your parents, yes, I forgot about them, your parents, uh, Ursula."

"Now that we're engaged, getting married in—"

"May."

"May."

"Yes, I forgot all about them, baby."

"And you'll love them, Maurice, just love them. And it'll be mutual, don't worry. They'll love you too!"

"And this little brainstorm of—"

"Like I said, in the midst of all of this unpleasantness. I tried thinking of something positive, besides how happy I am."

"You know, it's what Arlene said, the only thing she said. When I apologized for hurting her … I said I was sorry."

"And she said …"

"Happy, Ursula. That I'm happy."

"Y-you are, aren't you, Maurice?"

"Yes. Yes, Ursula. More than happy."

"Whew …"

"Now you're not having second thoughts about that are you—when I'm about to sign up to come to New York to see the big-city lights—"

"Where you've been before but not with—"

"And to visit your parents in where, again, Ur—"

"Jersey City, Maurice. Jersey City, New Jersey, New Jersey. It is on the map, you know, like Walker City, Iowa."

"Jersey City. Yes, Jersey City, just a hop, skip, and—"

"Jump—"

"From New York City."

"Maurice … I was thinking …"

"Now what are you up to? What little scheme have you hatched, are about to unleash on the world? Is this how it's going to be between us when we're married? Ursula Williams, the woman full of surprises? Ideas? A woman of a thousand faces?"

"Could be. Could—but I do have a plan."

"Not a scheme?"

"O-okay, all right, if you think I'm so devious … that devious then. Scheme."

"It does, it is far more appealing, intriguing, don't you think?"

"I agree."

"Out with it then. I know it's killing you."

"Okay, okay, Maurice are you prepared … Because it goes like this …"

CHAPTER 18

"Ursula, I can't believe this."

"Me ... me either. Me either!" Ursula said, squeezing Teardrop's hand, sitting in the plane seat next to him.

"It's a good thing Josh Perkins cut my hair this week. I have a fresh haircut, unless this trip to New York would've been put off until next week," Teardrop laughed.

"Not on your life. You were coming, returning to New York with me, or else!"

"Now, if that doesn't sound serious."

"Serious, Maurice. This is serious business, all right."

"My in-laws-to-be."

"Iris and Harry, you mean."

"Iris and Harry. Not 'Mom and Dad'?"

"No, no, Maurice, I'm afraid not."

"And they know about me?" Teardrop asked searchingly.

"Yes."

"Everything?"

"Yes," Ursula responded, knowing what Teardrop was hinting at, was building to.

"They do, and there's been—"

"Maurice, age is a number."

"And you've picked a high one."

"The one thing I know, am certain of, is you'll get along with my parents fine. That we'll be ha—"

"Don't say it, Ursula. Please …"

Ursula couldn't stop laughing. "One big, happy family." Pause. "Maurice, I can't wait!"

"Well, I'll say one thing, I feel good about all this already. The whole idea, trip, already."

Ursula eased her head back on the seat, and so did Teardrop. And when he did, Teardrop thought of last night and this morning. Arlene keeping busy in her study. Telling her last night about something else she didn't want to hear, that would upset her even more. Him standing at the study's door this morning before she went off to her first class at Walker City University, Arlene looking like she'd lost sleep. Sadness squeezing her like an octopus.

He wanted to be a father, but she had to get used to this as well as him. It's what blocked him, kept him in place, at the study's door—saying good-bye to her before she left for school, not knowing if she would come into his room when that time came, having sudden doubts.

"Why, I like it, Ursula. I really do!"

"And it's mine. As long as I pay the rent, my landlord, every month. On time."

"Which you do."

"Undoubtedly. The fifteenth of the month."

"It is modern, chic."

"I like to think so," Ursula said, putting her laptop down on a chair. "I call it flea-market chic."

"And where am I to sleep, my dear one?"

"On what you're sitting on now. Uh, it folds out into a bed. It's a La-Z-Boy converter."

"So it's something I might as well get used to?" Teardrop said, patting the cushiony leather pillow behind him on the oak-brown La-Z-Boy. "My new and best friend."

"Everything has been thought of and taken care of."

"Good. Good," Teardrop said. His suitcase was parked over in the corner of the small living room, by the chrome floor lamp with a lovely blue shade in various shades of blue, reminding the viewer of a Picasso painting during Picasso's Blue Period.

"Maurice …"

"Here it comes."

"Oh …"

"I could feel it. It has a certain—"

"I might as well tell you, since you've never asked. I'm not much of a cook. I mean, uh, not like you or my mother. Mom, Maurice, but I try. Really try."

"Don't worry, baby. I'll do most of the cooking anyway when we're married. So don't—"

"No, because I want to become a better cook."

"Then all you have to do is keep trying. Put out the pots and pans as often as possible. A cook isn't born overnight—it's not how it works."

"Uh … yes, I guess."

"Don't look for a miracle."

"N-now I like that advice. Want something to drink?"

"Fine."

"Coming right up!"

Teardrop felt right at home in Ursula's four-room apartment. The quarters were tight, the space lacking size, he thought, but cozy for a single person. And she was right about "flea-market chic," for it wrapped him like a fuzzy blanket. But it was a brilliant balance between old and new furniture, bridged by how well each maintained their own individual personality and function within the small space. She was a neat-minded person, as was anticipated, Teardrop thought. The room clutterproof. There was a sprinkling of books; he expected more. But in all fairness, he hadn't seen all of the apartment yet, no matter how small it was.

"Oh aren't you efficient?" Teardrop said, taking the glass of Coke from Ursula. "Thanks."

"Now it's time for me to spoil you, since you spoiled me for a week."

"My pleasure. Anytime."

Ursula looked at her watch. "Oh, let me call Byron and … and J. C. to let them—"

"Who—"

"They're my boyfriends."

"But I thought I was your fiancé."

"Oh, Maurice, you know I've mentioned them, Byron and J. C., to you a thousand times by now."

"Of course. I'm not jealous. There's not a jealous bone in my body."

"They should be at work."

She rushed to get to the phone. "I'll invite them by tonight. They can't wait to meet you—finally meet you."

"Sounds like a fun evening. My first night away from Walker City."

"Uh, Byron is a cutup, J. C., well … he is too, but he still has to take a backseat to Byron whenever he's around, which is all the time." Ursula picked up the phone. "Excuse me."

Teardrop nodded his head.

"Byron, Byron. Hi. Yes. I'm back. Back from Walker City with good news: Maurice and I are getting married! Married, yes, I said married! Married, you heard right. It's what I said. It's what I said. Married, Byron! We're getting married!"

Ursula buzzed Byron into the apartment. He hopped onto the elevator. During the four flights up, his temperature was rising. But he stood in front of Ursula's apartment door, his heart beating a mile a minute, and he needed to just knock on the damned door and now, right now! This was Ursula with a new life and him suddenly wondering what role he'd play in it.

Knock.

"Byron!"

"Hey, Ursula!"

"Come in, come in!"

"You look fabulous, girl, just—"

"Maurice, Byron, Byron—"

"P-pleasure's all mine, Mr. Williams."

"No, please call me Teardrop, Byron."

"Sure, sure thing, Teardrop. W-will do."

Ursula's arm was around Teardrop's waist and vice versa. They let Byron sit, but it seemed, at least to Byron, that neither wanted to sit for fear of ungluing themselves.

"Aren't you guys going to sit, or should I stand too?"

"Oh … ," both said, looking puzzled, confused, and then embarrassed. When they sat, it's when they held hands.

"W-when Ursula told me you two, uh, this afternoon, were getting married, Teardrop. I … I have to be honest with you, really, really. I was floored. F-flipped out."

"Yes, I was here when Ursula was on the phone, wasn't I, baby?"

Ursula rubbed the top of Teardrop's hand. "You certainly were, Maurice."

"In fact, Byron, I was sitting here thinking at the time that either you were hard of hearing, even if I knew you were younger than Ursula by a few years, or you needed a lot of convincing when Ursula kept repeating it over and over the fact we were getting married."

"Guess it was roboticlike. Uh. Uh, yeah. To be able to repeat one, only one word. Married? Married? Married! Ha."

"It's what the water does to Walker City women, Byron—make them want to get married," Teardrop laughed.

"Uh-uh, Teardrop. Walker City's water's not taking credit for this little-to-do hitch up. I played the role of cupid in this scenario. For you two. Bought Ursula your CD *River of Pain*. I shot the arrow in the lovely lady's heart. Cupid. Byron Jeffries. No one or nothing else is taking credit for that but me, Teardrop. Yours truly."

"He's right, Maurice."

"Then I defer to the truth, not fiction."

"Congrats, Teardrop. You're getting yourself quite a gal. Ursula's quite a catch for anybody at any a—uh …"

"It's all right, Byron. Ursula and I have been through all of that. Even on the plane, I'm sure some passengers thought she had to be my daughter, not until Ursula and I—"

"Kissed, to prove to them otherwise."

"Look, I had my moments with it too. The age factor, I must admit. Got bent out of shape over it. Totally."

"You wouldn't be a good, true friend, I don't think, if you hadn't."

"We had our drag down, drag-out fight, Maurice."

"Didn't we though, Ursula, didn't we though?" Byron laughed defensively. "But the girl, she suffered when—"

"Byron, you—"

"Let him finish, Ursula. The man finish. I'm enjoying this."

"As we say, she thought she was being 'dogged,' Teardrop. Dogged. Seriously, she was in pain. Heartbreak hotel. The sister was bluer than the blues, man."

The three laughed.

"But she wasn't the only one, Byron. I was in that heartbreak hotel right along with her. Renting out a room."

"It's what convinced me. Taught me a lesson: love is love no matter what the ages are. Between people." Pause. "I mean, if you don't mind, Teardrop, you're one handsome-looking guy. Person, uh—"

"Middle-aged man. It's all right, Byron."

"Just, ha, trying to pretty the whole thing up a bit. Clean it up some."

"I don't blame you."

"And now for the big test, huh, Teardrop?"

"Byron, don't frighten Maurice."

"Over the phone, Ursula, you mentioned you were calling them. Your parents. Right?"

"I did."

"So?"

"Sunday. Sunday dinner."

"With the Jenkinses. Man oh man," Byron laughed, "doesn't that sound cozy, delightful. Like a Sunday massacre!"

"Oh ... uh, excuse me, uh, I'll be right back. The bathroom ... ," Teardrop said, getting up from the couch. He left the living room.

"Yeah, Ursula, J. C.'s going through some changes right now. Uh ... c-complications. It's why I told you to call him about tonight. Ramona's got him doing cartwheels lately. Really putting pressure on him. Tightening the screws. I think she wants to get married too. Tired of playing the 'wedding game' with no ring on her left finger.

"Yeah, she's definitely turning the screws—practically every night these days. Command center."

Teardrop was in the bathroom. He was nervous. Earlier he'd called the house, before Byron came, to say he'd arrived in New York safely. He spoke to Jamal. He told Jamal to pass the information onto Arlene.

"Today's Friday, and look at me. Just look at me. I'm a mess. A physical and mental mess."

He was afraid of Sunday. He was frightened by the prospect of it. He knew Ursula's parents to be somewhere near his age, possibly younger than him (he hadn't asked) since Arlene was eight years older than Ursula.

"I'm asking their daughter's hand in marriage. S-suppose the shoe were on the other foot. S-say Arlene was bringing home someone who was older than me ... C-contemplating marriage. Marrying her. How would I react? Take to the news? T-to such an idea ...

"Not well, I don't think. Not well at all. I could think of a hundred reasons to disapprove. Find fault. For being upset, turned off by the whole thing. A hundred reasons why an older man, thirty years older, shouldn't marry my daughter."

"Hey, welcome back, Teardrop."

Teardrop smiled as best he could (actually it was forced). He sat, taking back Ursula's hand.

"I was admiring Ursula's rock, Teardrop. Nice. Nice piece of ice, if I must say so myself."

"T-thanks, uh, Byron."

"Mrs. Jenkins, Iris Jenkins, Ursula's mom, of course, can burn, Teardrop. I … I mean really work it in the kitchen. You'll see Sunday what I'm talking about, Teardrop," Byron said, bouncing up to his feet, joining Ursula and Teardrop.

"It's going to be one hell of a day. Sunday with the Jenkinses."

"There're no traffic jams in Walker City to speak of, Ursula. At least not anything compared to this. Of this magnitude."

Ursula and Teardrop were on a Lower Manhattan street that was but one of the many entryways into the Holland Tunnel.

"Don't people have better things to do on a Sunday afternoon in New York City than sit in traffic?"

"It's about a twenty-five-minute, uh, thirty-minute delay, Maurice. Estimated. It's always a slow stretch, where I always hit a snag. Predictably."

"Well, at least everybody appears calm for now."

"At least until the first horn blows. Then it's a chain reaction. A series of desperate pleas on everyone's part then."

"Don't make me laugh," Teardrop said, even if he was doing just that, laughing as he peered out the windshield and up to the street sign. "Broome Street, huh? Cute name."

"Maurice, now that we're stuck here, or at least at a snail's pace, I have something to ask you. Something that's been on my mind f-for quite some time now, b-but I didn't feel it my place to ask. But now that we're engaged—"

"Nothing's off-limit. Nothing, Ursula."

"Me too. The same applies to me too, Maurice. My life."

Teardrop smiled.

Ursula straightened out her arms and gripped the steering wheel. "Arlene, Maurice, Arlene. Where's her husband?"

"Now isn't that something—it's not come up, has it? Between us. I never thought about it either. Shocking. I guess I'm so much, so used to Arlene's situation, she and Isaiah have been apart, divorced for so long."

"Isaiah."

"But don't let the name in any way fool you. Its biblical origin. Isaiah Wilkerson was far from trustworthy. He's a college professor too. Brilliant like Arlene. He was one before Arlene, a history professor—Western Civilization.

"He cheated on her. Arlene caught him—those are the plain, unblemished facts. He was remorseless. There was no second chance. Arlene dumped him. They were married for two years. Jamal was a year old when they divorced."

"And is Isaiah Wilkerson still in Arlene's and Jamal's lives?"

"He's a professor at Indiana University. He's since married. It's all any of us know."

"He ... he ..."

"He's absent from Jamal's life. He wanted nothing to do with him. Arlene didn't look for alimony or child support. She, well, frankly, just wanted him out her hair, her life when he said any contact with Jamal, his son, would cause him too much emotional trauma—it's how he put it. So he thought better not to communicate with him at all. For no reason."

"How horrible, Maurice. Insensitive."

"Ursula, you can be smart, brilliant, in fact—but what rationale people can come up with, devise as device, at random, is incredible."

"No, Maurice. Isaiah Wilkerson's just plain heartless."

"Yes, baby, heartless ... heartless—and a coward."

"And Jamal?"

The question made Teardrop visibly twist and turn, his face frown. "Naturally there were questions, inquiries made, voiced at the time. But now who knows, Ursula? Whoever really knows about these matters, after all, with young people? What's at the heart of them."

"He just seems so well-adjusted."

"He is. That's not fake or anything on his part."

"And so Arlene didn't change her name back to Williams. From Wilkerson to Williams."

"Ursula, you didn't put that in the form of a question."

"Ha."

"No, she didn't want to confuse Jamal. She wanted him to have, what she felt, was his legal ... right name: Wilkerson, not Williams. That he has a father. That he wasn't born out of wedlock. That she and his father were married. So it remains Wilkerson."

"Does she date? Has there been someone else since Isaiah Wilkerson?"

Teardrop squirmed again, more than the Broome Street traffic was doing. "No, it's all work with my daughter. All work and no play. When Maureen was alive, she tried encouraging her to date but gave up. Me too, to be honest. The little input I had since I was out playing on the road. Her devotion to her work, of course, is admirable, especially for parents who are college grads. Maureen and I, but sometimes I worry—"

"About extremes?"

"Anything done to extreme, to excess, as we know, is not healthy. Can lead to problems."

"How hard did Arlene take her mother ... Maureen's death?"

These were tough questions, Teardrop thought. Very tough.

"Hard, very, very hard." He looked at her. "Ursula, what are you trying to do? Understand her?"

"Yes."

He examined her more. "Y-you are, aren't you?"

"I want to, Maurice. I really do."

"Even if it means you might get hurt."

She shrugged her shoulders. "Yes."

"Somewhere down the road, baby?"

"Yes."

He hesitated and then said. "Brave girl."

"Maurice, now look, I'm no Pollyanna."

"No, we don't want that. That, ha, would be regrettable, most regrettable."

"I just think, in time, there'll be something in the future to pull us together. S-some event. After all, we have so much in common."

"And what's that, my beautiful, lovely black maiden?"

She threw a kiss at him. "We both love the same men."

"That's true," Teardrop laughed, encouraged. "By the way, Jamal would just love to hear that."

Conversation had flowed so fluently between Ursula and Teardrop that he'd almost forgotten the mission he and Ursula were on, he thought, as he could feel, instinctively, that Ursula and he were drawing closer and closer to her parents' house (just something in his gut told him); for conversation had, abruptly, become spotty, intermittent, starting at exact points and breaking off at others. But it was him with the nervous stomach, the twitching insides, Jersey City streets narrow and cramped, nothing like those in New York, or Walker City, for that matter. A gutted-out store here, a fire-charred store there, and then a standing store occupying Jersey City's rough, tough landscape pocked by fancy graffiti art. He saw Jersey City's city government not at work but asleep at the switch and indifferent in creating this social malaise. His eyes took it all in as a bluesman with Miss Lillian in his hands and him about to rip off a blues tune for whatever observation there was, detailing, distilling it with an appropriate lyric, personality, and a sharp blade to the soul to exhume its truths—sometimes something messy, awful for the psyche to smoothly digest.

His mind drifted, him now letting it imagine what the Jenkinses looked like, Iris and Harry. They'd produced a beautiful daughter, Teardrop thought. Father? Mother? *Which does Ursula look like, I wonder. Arlene favors her mother. Why, Ursula does too!*

"What is it, Maurice?"

"N-nothing, Ursula."

"Don't be nervous, Maurice. My parents will love you. All right?"

How did Ursula know? Boy, we've got a harmony going between us. Elegiac. Hear each other's heartbeat. Be quiet, Teardrop. You're beginning to sound silly, fool ... I'm no kid. I'm a fifty-five-year-old man, sane of mind, have years of experience under my belt—will not knuckle under pressure, nor ... Not Maurice Williams, not—they ... Ursula, say something!

"Maurice, guess what? We're about there. P-practically there. A block—"

"Block?"

"A block, a block and a half, and we're there. Can you believe it?"

Seconds passed.

"There it is, Maurice. That's it," Ursula said, her finger pointing to the house.

"Where you were born, baby."

"Yes, where I was born."

The house was solid, standing there as if it were resisting change. Teardrop had seen most of the neighborhood. It said a lot about the Jenkins family, about who they were as people.

Ursula parked the rented car maybe twenty feet from the house. Quickly the key came out the ignition, her joy unimaginably high and lighthearted and gay.

"May I, before we get out the car?" Ursula asked, her body leaning toward Teardrop's.

"You certainly may."

They kissed.

Then her fingers ran lightly along Teardrop's lips. "No traces."

In due time, they were on the house's front porch. Ursula had her house key but was going to ring the doorbell. Make it official, she thought.

As for Teardrop, he was sweating. It felt like most seconds before a performance so many musicians go through, not before they strike that first note on their instrument (in Teardrop's case, Miss Lillian). It's how he felt, like he was out on one of his blues gigs with Shorty Boy and Twelve Fingers, especially when they were about to play a new blues composition. But this was a different kind of music he was about to face: the Jenkins. This tandem. Two-person front. Ursula's parents.

"Ready, Maurice?" Ursula asked, holding on firmly to Teardrop's hand.

He cleared his throat. "Ready as I'll ever be, I suppose. Uh, for this."

Ursula rang the doorbell.

Then she raised her hand, looked at her engagement ring, and then sighed.

Teardrop laughed then, quickly, but stopped once he heard the front door of the house begin to open at a slow rate.

"Ursula!"

"Mom!"

"Mr. …"

And the pause seemed to have its own life, drama, so it seemed to Teardrop, spinning in the air like a bullet.

"Maurice, Mom. Maurice."

"Mr. Williams."

Ursula got into the house by going up to her mother and hugging her while Teardrop entered the house from behind her.

"Where's Dad, Mom?"

"He, Harry, you—t-they're here. Ur-Ursula and Mr. … Mr. Williams, Harry," Iris said. "They … they're—"

"Yes, I heard them," Harry said, charging down the staircase and then suddenly stopping short.

She didn't tell them! Teardrop thought. *Ursula didn't tell her parents about me! She never told them about me!*

"H-Harry," Iris said, turning around to him. "It's Mr. Williams. Mr. Williams and … and Ursula."

"Y-yes, I see, Iris. I … see," Harry Jenkins said, now proceeding farther down the staircase, to the landing.

"Hi, Dad."

"H-hello, Ursula."

Ursula hugged and kissed him.

Now both Iris and Harry's eyes were addressing Teardrop when Ursula went to him, taking hold of his hand.

"Come, Maurice, let's go into the living room where we can relax."

"W-we'll be eating shortly," Iris said. "Are … are you hungry?"

"Famished, aren't we, Maurice? We had breakfast but very little. We, Maurice and I, decided to save our appetites for dinner this afternoon."

"Oh," Iris said.

"I talked so much about your cooking to Maurice, Mom. Actually bragged about it. Praised it to high heaven."

"Why, thank you, Ur-Ursula. Darl-darling."

"Even though Maurice is an excellent cook. And I should know, since he cooked dinner for me the week I was in Walker, spent in Walker City with him."

"Oh."

And suddenly Teardrop realized he'd not spoken a word to the Jenkinses, as if he couldn't talk or had been stifled, or Ursula's nervous, busy energy was, up till now, making it impossible for him to talk—catch up with her in her race to seemingly want to "right" things.

"I'm a bluesman."

This bit of unsolicited information from Teardrop seemed to jolt Iris and Harry even more emotionally.

"I go by the name of Maurice 'Teardrop' Williams. Teardrop, needless to say, is my stage name. But I've retired from the stage, from performing. I retired seven months after my wife died close to four years ago now. So, I, of course, am a widower.

"How I met your daughter was serendipitous. She was trying to resurrect a dead bluesman, I suppose. An article for a magazine. *Currents* magazine. It's how our paths crossed in Walker City, Iowa—where I was born and still live. It was a lucky day for me. Very," Teardrop said, looking into Ursula's eyes.

"Oh, oh, I see," Harry said. "Uh, y-yes, I see."

"Well, let me do my duty—get up from here and back into the kitchen if … if we're going to eat. H-have dinner, that is."

When Iris got up to leave the living room, Harry looked over at Ursula and Teardrop. "Uh, excuse me, please. Uh, let me help your mother, Ursula. In the … ex-excuse me."

Teardrop stood, and when he did, he looked down at Ursula once realizing Iris and Harry were a safe distance away. "You didn't tell them, Ursula? You never told your parents about me."

"N-no, Maurice, no," Ursula said, biting her bottom lip.

"Why didn't you? Why?"

"I—"

"This is like shock treatment. Ambushing someone. It was neither fair to them or me."

"No. No, it wasn't, Maurice, it wasn't."

"I trusted you, Ursula. I … trusted you," Teardrop said, disappointed.

"I know you did, Maurice. I—"

"Then why?"

Ursula stood and reached out for Teardrop's hand, only for him to rebuff her—didn't want any part of this thing she was doing.

"Yes, you should be angry at me, Maurice. I did mislead—"

"You lied, Ursula. Lied. Flat out lied. There's nothing ambiguous about this. Out and out lied to me. Because I asked you directly, on the plane, specifically—"

"You did, yes, yes, you—"

"On the plane if you told your parents about me, 'everything' about me. And you knew what I meant. My age, Ursula. My age."

She sat back down on the couch. "Yes, I lied. Was dishonest. Any … any word you wish to choose. Use, Maurice, is appropriate."

"Is that something I should begin to look forward to? Worry about. Prepare myself—"

"Oh, no, no," Ursula said, quickly coming to her defense. "I … I was going to tell them, but …"

"But!"

"They … without meeting you, seeing you, Maurice …"

"Well … they're still in shock. You put them in shock. Were totally unprepared for this."

"But if I told them over the phone, I mean at least now, now we'll be able to … able to iron this thing, smooth this whole thing, matter out before the day's over. Do it face-to-face. Spend time together, Maurice. In one another's company. They have to know, get to know you—be around you. F-first."

"You say that as if I'm some sort of magic person, man, Ursula. And I'm—"

"But you are, Maurice, you are."

"No, I'm not. These are your parents. They only have your best interest at heart—it's the same for any parent. Their concerns. Private concerns. I share their anxieties, worry. Fear. I have a daughter. I have Arlene—"

"I know, I know," Ursula said, fighting herself. "I only did what I thought was best at the—"

"Best?"

"Yes."

Ursula's hand reached for Teardrop's again, and this time Teardrop took it. He held it.

"Yes, you … you were only trying. Only trying, baby."

Ursula slumped. "Yes, I was, Maurice. I really was."

Teardrop kissed her hand. "This is all new to you … We're in virgin territory, charting totally unexplored territory right now. You and me."

"I can't believe it, Harry. How could she?" Harry helped Iris over to the kitchen chair. "How could Ursula do this to us!"

"H-he's …"

"Our age, if not older. He has to be!"

"Right, yes, right. Maurice Williams is," Harry said, sitting, his slight frame already tired, listless. "We asked so little yet assumed so much."

"But nothing like this. Who would've expected this? Who? Certainly not me. You and I."

Harry's head was swimming. He removed his glasses but did nothing with them.

"What's come over her? Our … our daughter?" Pause.

"Do y-you think they're in love? Actually—"

"I—"

"Can they be in love?" Iris said, reframing her unanswered question.

"I don't know. I—"

"A bluesman though. A … a bluesman …"

"But he speaks so intelligently. In such a refined, erudite way. His speech. The way he speaks. I … I mean—"

"I know what you mean," Iris said, tenderly taking Harry's hand and then releasing it. "You don't have to explain yourself. We're not snobs. And you're not in the least bit stereotypical. There is that image of a bluesman. The pervasive image of one."

"Now, Iris, how—tell me—how are we going to handle this? Take care of this? Tell me for … for the life of me, I don't know."

Harry reentered the living room. The tension he felt was palpable.

"Oh, Ursula, your mother would like to see you back in the kitchen."

"Y-yes, of course, Dad. I'll … I'll go right in." Ursula turned to Teardrop and kissed his cheek. "Won't be long. Gone long, Maurice."

She passed her father, faintly smiling at him.

Before, when he got into the house, because of the rapid unfolding of events, Teardrop wasn't able to make a clear impression on Harry Jenkins, and now that he was walking the floor to be seated, impressions of Harry Jenkins flew fast and furious at him. Short. Proud. And Ursula was the spitting image of him. As they say, Harry Jenkins had literally "spit" her out.

"This is better, wouldn't you say, Mr. Williams?"

"Much," Teardrop said.

"And If I may be honest with you, uh, above board, uh, you know my wife had no need for Ursula. Not in the kitchen. At any time. Being it's her domain. That it was a ploy."

"Of course," Teardrop said.

"By the way, Mr. Williams, what instrument is it that you play?"

"Guitar."

"Oh, like B. B. King."

"Except B. B. King calls his guitar Lucille. I call mine Miss Lillian."

"Now is that some sort of standard practice for a bluesman, Mr. Williams. In giving their instruments nicknames?"

"Generally speaking, I'd say, Mr. Jenkins. Yes, It could be considered a matter of common practice."

"I'm a mortician. Funeral director."

"Yes, I know."

"And Iris, Mrs. Jenkins, a schoolteacher."

"Yes, I know as much, Mr. Jenkins."

A frown creased Harry's handsome dark-skinned face. "There's a lot you know about us, Mr. Williams, but so little we know ... my daughter's told us about you."

"I shocked you. Or, I should say, Ursula shocked you. I tried to understand too why she didn't tell you and your wife everything about me. I thought she had."

"Your age, Mr. Williams."

"Yes, that."

"It plays a big part in this particular situation we're in. Us, my wife and I, our views on your relationship with Ursula. My daughter."

"Yes, your daughter." Teardrop was beginning to relax more. "I have a daughter myself. Arlene. She's thirty-three, eight years older than Ursula."

"How does your daughter feel—"

"She doesn't approve of us. Ursula and I. She's a college professor. Economics. I have a grandson, Jamal. He's ten. I'm fifty-five years old, Mr. Jenkins."

"I'm fifty-one. So is my wife."

"I'm thirty years older than your daughter, and when I would say it, think it—this has all happened so suddenly, rapidly ... my doubts were as keen and well-placed as I'm sure yours and your wife's are.

"For your daughter came into my life like a storm, not gently, mind you, Mr. Jenkins, but like a storm. I loved my first wife. Loved Maureen. Was lost after she died." Teardrop took a deep breath. "Devastated. Emotionally, physically. Yes, it's why I gave up my music career and returned home to Walker City, Iowa. But not to my home but my daughter's.

"It became my refuge, Mr. Jenkins. My daughter's home for three years. From the world. A shelter. It's been three years that I've lived with my daughter and grandson. Walking back into my house, coming off the road"—Teardrop's body shuddered—"the thought of Maureen no longer there. In the house. Greeting me when I came off the road. Thirty years of loving one woman all my life. Someone as loving, dear as Maureen ... ," Teardrop said, his body shuddering again without any sign of him trying to stop it.

"It must have been. I-Iris, Mrs. Jenkins and I have been married twenty-seven years, Mr. Williams. Our marriage must be identical with what was yours with your first wife."

"Friends more than anything else."

"But this is a different time and age we live in, Mr. Williams. Sex gets mixed up with love, and love with sex—and friendship—"

"Ursula is my friend. I guess it's what makes all of this so remarkable to me. When I think of it. What happened for a second time in my life."

"It's how you perceive my daughter, Ursula? Do you? As a 'friend'?"

"Yes, a friend. She—"

"Excuse me, but she was heartbroken a month or so back."

"I, yes, I know just what you're referring to. The incident."

"Depressed. Down in the dumps. She visited us on the weekend. More so, I suppose, to get away from her problems—more or less. She hadn't heard from you, it seems."

"No. Ursula and I got to the bottom of it. We were able to clear that obstacle."

"She was so unhappy, Mr. Williams. I'd never seen her so unhappy before. As an adult. D-did I say heartbroken before?"

"Yes, ha, y-yes you did, Mr. Jenkins. You cer—"

"Ha. I did. I did, didn't I … Something like that, my wife and I—it's something you don't soon forget. It does leave a quite a strong impression with you."

"What happened between Ursula and me was upsetting. Something we really agonized over. It drew, seemed to draw our relationship totally, fully into question. Its foundation. Especially all of my self-doubts as whether or not this thing of older man, this whole notion, category of older man–younger woman could work. Be able to, well … that we could work our way through it. Something I never would have thought before—"

"Not until you met my daughter."

"Yes."

"My daughter, Ursula," Harry Jenkins said proudly.

"Someone who's one of a kind."

"Precisely, Mr. Williams. Precisely." Pause.

"You know I'm a chemist," Teardrop said.

"Chemist?"

"My degree's in chemistry."

"Chemistry, why I thought—"

"Chemistry and the blues?"

"Yes, chemistry and the blues, Mr. Williams. But as far as the chemistry goes, maybe you and I could trade notes, put our heads together," Harry laughed. "Maybe you know of a better way of preserving my clients, deceased clients, better than I do."

From cheek to cheek Teardrop's smile grew.

"You know, I'm from a small town, Mr. Jenkins. And everyone calls everyone else pretty much by their first name in Walker City, Iowa. Are on a first-name basis."

"Harry," Harry said, standing up, crossing the room.

"Teardrop."

They shook hands.

"You know, Teardrop, I didn't shake your hand when you walked into the house. It was rude of me. I apologize. It was inexcusable of—"

"Not under the circumstances, Harry. Not at all—in the least."

"I ... I suppose. And when Iris gets back in here, we'll reintroduce the two of you." Both sat back down. "Get you off to a fresh start. By the way, Teardrop, Ursula calls you Maurice. Any significance to that?"

"Maureen was the only one to call me that too, Maurice too. No one else. It's just a wonderful, uncanny coincidence. The entire thing with that. Ursula, oddly, had no prior history of it either. Not a clue on her part."

"And now, Teardrop, you must have a thousand and one stories to tell me about your days as a bluesman. Playing the blues circuit. 'Out on the road,' as you say."

"Ha. Well ..."

And it's when Ursula and Iris reentered the living room. Iris with her red-and-white polka-dot apron on and Ursula with a look as anxious as anyone wishing the world to tell them of all its hidden treasures with one quick burst of breath.

Harry winked at Iris.

"Teardrop was just about to tell me of some of his many adventures as a bluesman. Uh, weren't you, Teardrop?"

"Y-you were, Mr.—"

"Teardrop, Iris, just call him Teardrop. Ursula's the only one who calls Teardrop Maurice. And, of course, Maureen."

"Maurice's first wife's name, Mom," Ursula said. "Deceased wife, Maureen."

"Well, men, it's dinner time!"

"Music to my ears. What about yours, Teardrop?"

"Why yes, yes, Harry. I *am* hungry. And have I ever been looking forward to your cooking. This dinner this afternoon, Iris."

"Oh ... Teardrop," Iris laughed, "Ursula does have a tendency to exaggerate. But, ha, I won't quibble, will I, Ursula?"

"No, Mom," Ursula said, going over to Teardrop, taking his hand as Harry walked over and took hold of Iris's.

Then the four walked toward the dining room area that was appropriately prepared for a feast. The setting of the food and plates, spectacularly done.

"Teardrop, what instrument do you play by the way?"

"Guitar, Iris."

"Oh, I play piano."

"Piano? Any blues?"

"Uh, no, but given a little encouragement, I think I could try. Fit the blues on for size." Iris's smile had that of a bluesman's who'd just squeezed the last drop of the blues out a turnip.

It was chilly out on the porch, but regardless, Iris and Harry were waving at Ursula and Teardrop.

"Don't forget to call the minute you and Teardrop get back to Queens, Ursula. Don't forget. So we'll know you got through the tunnel safely, darling!" Iris yelled at the top of her lungs.

"Will do, Mom. Will do. Bye, Dad. Good-bye!"

"Good-bye, Ursula, good-bye!"

The car moved from the house.

Honk. Honk.

"This is going to work, Iris. I'm telling you. This marriage of theirs is going to work!"

"They're so happy, Harry."

"Their relationship's electric. I don't care if Teardrop is a hundred and two as long as Ursula's happy. My daughter's happy. It's all a father can ask for. Want for his daughter."

"And he's handsome too, to boot," Iris said without skipping a beat.

"Why twenty-seven, twenty-seven years we've been married. And it's the first I've heard you call any man, another man, handsome, besides me."

"Ha. Because, Harry, I'd never met anyone before quite as handsome as Teardrop Williams."

"Well, I'm glad he's taken," Harry said, opening the porch door for Iris as each stepped out the cold.

"Has imminent plans for himself."

"May, they say."

"May it is. And it'll be here before we know it."

"Harry, the weather—"

"Will be perfect—just pitch-perfect that day. Day in May. I suspect."

"I told you you'd win my parents over, Maurice, I told you. I never had a minute's doubt," Ursula shouted out in the car, getting to the end of Forest Avenue. "No problem at all."

"You're something else, Ursula. Such an optimist."

"And I should be. I have every reason in the world to be."

"So far, I can't argue with you."

"You wouldn't win anyway."

"Don't I know it. I see the light."

"They love you, Maurice, Iris and Harry Jenkins."

Teardrop looked at Ursula, her two hands bracing the steering wheel, driving properly. "Ursula, how do you keep your Afro so neat under fire? That's what I'd like to know. Can't seem to grasp."

They were back in Jamaica, Queens.

"So how does Iris sound, long distance? New York to New Jersey? Through the tunnel?"

"Funny, funny."

"Your mother's some cook."

"Better than you?"

"I don't know, baby. The jury's still out."

"Yes, I quite agree. I've been eating my mother's cooking for twenty-five years, and yours—"

"Really, for just a week."

"So I can't declare a winner—"

"Until what, Ursula, twenty-six years from now?"

"Umm, you'll be—"

"Eighty-one."

"That was quick math. And I'll be—"

"Fifty-one."

"Still in love with you."

"You'd better!"

Teardrop was on the La-Z-Boy where he'd slept the past two nights and where he would sleep tonight. He'd be leaving New York tomorrow.

Ursula stood in front of him and, in her pants, straddled Teardrop's legs. He held her back, drawing her to him, this slender, shapely young woman with her supple back and shapely legs and breasts that still seemed to be budding whenever he kissed her like he was now and her nipples swelled round inside her cotton blouse.

They kept kissing, mouths open, tongues searching for evidence that this was the time for them to have sex, something they'd not done in Walker City for the seven days Ursula was there, or the Friday or Saturday night they'd been in New York together.

"Maurice, Maurice … ," she said, biting his neck, his flesh turning a purplish-brown.

She stood to undo her blouse; it's when her fingers unhooked the bra. When Ursula's bra fell away, Teardrop saw two beautiful breasts and nipples that throbbed with a pulse and language, what seemed, of their own. She unbuckled the dark gray pants. When done, the belt slid out the pant loops, and quickly, Ursula undid the pants' inside button. She pulled the pants' side zipper down. Her hands rode the side of her hips, and so slowly she began shimmying the pants down her legs, and what Teardrop saw were pink panties, but her eyes were shut and her mouth open as if anticipating what was to come, Teardrop's mouth enveloping her breast.

"Ursula, no, no, we mustn't do this, not this, not now," Teardrop said quietly but forcibly.

"B-but why, Maurice, what—"

"Be-because I … I …"

"I'm not a virgin, Maurice. You know that. Understand that."

"Yes, I—"

"Then why?"

There was no reply.

"It's not Maureen, is it? It's not—"

"No."

"W-was she a virgin?"

"Yes."

"Then—"

"Don't think that. Don't. I'm not comparing you and Maureen. My dead wife with you. Or the past."

And Ursula felt embarrassed and emotionally devastated and cold— and now aware of her partial nakedness.

"Don't cover yourself, you don't have to. Y-you look beautiful, Ursula, b—"

"What do you think this is, Maurice? A freak show? Some kind of freak show?" Ursula said, suddenly running out the room and for her bedroom, her blouse and bra lying down on the living room floor.

Teardrop stood; he picked up Ursula's blouse and bra from off the floor, looked at them lying in his hand, and then carried them with him into the bedroom.

She was on the bed sobbing, her body curled up. She was holding herself.

Teardrop was at the bed. He sat.

He was still holding on to Ursula's blouse and bra.

She kept sobbing. She wouldn't look at him. Her fists were balled, now protecting her eyes.

"I love you so much, Ursula."

"Then why, Maurice? Why? When I want you so much. To have sex with you so much."

Pause.

"Because e-everything's been so special. So unique. So unexpected. I told your father you came into my life like a storm."

Her eyes opened.

"If I had to describe it again, maybe I would say you came into my life like a quiet storm. Not only your beauty, Ursula, but your dignity and sophistication and intelligence sweeping me along off my feet, if I care, choose to be less poetic about it and more down to earth."

"Maurice ..."

"It's ... that's the power you have over me. And I want it to continue to build, keep building in me until our honeymoon. Our wedding night. That ... that night we will make love until there's no end. The night will never end. And the day, it'll never come. Never for us."

"Oh, Maurice!" Ursula said, grabbing him. "I love you! I love you! I ... I was so—"

"Sssh, sssh. You're a woman. A red-blooded black woman. Enough said."

They kissed, and Ursula became undone again, her full, smooth-skinned breasts exposed, the tips of them back alive. And when Teardrop handed her the blouse and bra, his hand trembled noticeably.

"Ursula," Teardrop said, shaking his head, "it must take an awful foolish man to do what I just did. One who needs his head examined."

Ursula put the bra back over her breasts, and her fingers trembled when she fastened the bra's clasp back from the back.

CHAPTER 19

"I missed you, Dad. How I missed you," Arlene said.

The three days Teardrop had spent in New York City had taken a toll on her. Her life felt much, much different without her father in the house. It wasn't gradual but sudden.

Arlene had not spoken to Teardrop since he'd left for New York. Only Jamal had, by phone. *Was he deliberately trying to avoid me?* Arlene thought. Did he feel that uncomfortable about things between them and it'd reached that stage?

And right now it hurts just to think that thought, Arlene thought.

"But how do I get out of this mess, malaise? How, Dad? How do I right this? Our relationship? Father and daughter. Get ourselves back on course?

"Darnit, what a word to use: 'course.' Back on course like we're vessels, ships, or something. Wooden. I'm sick with this. This is making me sick. I'm losing my father!

"A-and I know I can't blame Ursula Jenkins—n-not for everything. Not for all that's happened, because I could have chosen to do things better. I could have ..."

And if this was a self-confession, if this was soul-searching, some kind of bearing of her soul, that her soul needed it. She needed to think things through, to look at this part of her life that made her whole, Arlene Wilkerson, the woman she was, Maurice "Teardrop" Williams's daughter, the bliss of being his daughter, him helping her reach this point in her life.

Again, Arlene paused, and last Friday came to mind. For what came in the mail but a letter from Stanford University (Stanford!) saying they'd like for her to come in as a visiting lecturing professor. Walker University's president, Avery Washington III, just loved the news, something giving Walker U prestige, cachet, national exposure, its residual effect.

"I was thrilled when I got the letter, Dad. I wanted to share the news with you. But you weren't here. You were in New York with Ursula Jenkins. It almost felt as if I'd chased you away. Even though, in that instance, I hadn't—took no part in that."

It was late afternoon, 5:24 p.m., and Arlene knew Teardrop would be home from International soon, no later than six o'clock. She'd cooked his favorite meal, meat loaf, mashed potatoes, smothered cabbage, and homemade biscuits.

"It's the least I could do, Dad."

Maybe I've carried this thing too far with Ursula Jenkins, Arlene thought. Maybe to the point where I am either going to be perceived as the villain or the fool. And Arlene knew Jamal, at the dinner table, would have so many questions to posit for his grandfather about the New York City trip. Jamal's enthusiasm would be boiling, brimming, probably, practically to the point of tedium. To the point of wearing things thin, down to a nub.

"And I will be around that. Bound to it by my presence in the kitchen. A-and I won't dismiss myself from it, excuse myself s-so that I may avoid it. No, I won't do that. I want to be in the company of my son and my father. I won't make it an option. Not, not at all."

I just want to make it better between us, Dad and me, Arlene said to herself. *I won't lose him. I won't lose my father. When he walks into the house, I want to start winning him back. But what do I do, say, how do I begin doing, going about doing that?*

Arlene had been in her study all this time. She got up. She looked down at the book she'd been reading, shutting it.

"I'll begin heating things up for Jamal and Dad. Their food. Dad's favorite meal."

"Okay, Bert, will do. Thanks again," Teardrop said, closing the creaky car door, the blue-flame taxi, with Bert in it, pulling away from the house as slow as a *lazier-than-sin turtle*.

Teardrop looked at the red Impala and knew Arlene was home. Hot blood rushed through him. And he couldn't wait to see her, to hear her voice.

He gripped his suitcase, looked around the front yard, and then got up on the front porch. Teardrop was about to open the front door, when it opened, instead, much to his surprise.

"I love you, Dad. I love you!"

"I love you, Arlene!" Teardrop said, dropping his suitcase, grabbing Arlene, feeling his blood boil over.

"Let your grandfather eat, come on, Jamal. Enough's enough."

"Ha. It's all right, Arlene. All right. Jamal's imagination's on fire. It's probably been running wild the past few days, so he's not going to leave one stone unturned, right, Jamal?"

"Uh … whatever … whatever, Granddad. Now what about Ursula's apartment, Granddad? Is it big, fancy? You know, the furniture and gadgets and—"

"Yes, Jamal, your imagination *is* really at work."

"I know, but—"

"Jamal, Ursula lives like you and me. There's no—"

"But, Granddad … Granddad, Ursula lives in New York, sir."

Arlene and Teardrop laughed at what was Jamal's innocence.

"Yes, New York—it is quite different from Walker City, that's for sure."

"More exciting I bet, just bet, Granddad."

"Much."

"Wow … wow. I thought so."

Teardrop cut his meat loaf in half and then speared it with the fork.

"Granddad, where are you and Ursula going to live when you get married? Here or New York City, sir?"

And as if his bones had been cracked by a sledgehammer, and Arlene's too, Teardrop let go of his knife and fork and looked at Arlene with this stunned yet beleaguered look on his face, one that sat on Arlene's too.

"I don't know, Jamal. Honestly don't know. Ur-Ursula and I haven't discussed it. That's something, isn't it? It hasn't come up until now, you asking where we'll live."

"You'll live here, Granddad. It has to be here. In Walker City."

"I don't know, Jamal. Ursula and I will have to discuss it, something we haven't done. Something we'll have to do."

Arlene was in her room and didn't have a firm grip on things. Even she had forgotten to ask the most basic, fundamental question: where her Dad and Ursula Jenkins were to live after they married. Ursula Jenkins is a writer, Arlene thought. Her career is in New York, not Walker City, Iowa, but in the hotbed of New York.

"But she's a freelance writer, one with solid connections. She's established herself. A freelance writer has the freedom to roam. To make their world their home, wherever they're at, if they choose. They're not tied down to anything. They just have to remain current, similar to what I, as a teacher, am required professionally to do."

Arlene sat and then stood again.

"She's going to live in the house. They're going to live in the house. And I'm going to have to get used to it. Mom and Dad's house."

Arlene looked at the air as if she saw her words still hanging in it, not delighting in hearing them but rooted to them.

"So I must prepare myself for that inevitability. For Ursula Jenkins to live in my mother and father's house."

And it's when Arlene felt this delicate dance, just how delicate everything must be from now on when it came to her father and Ursula Jenkins, the feelings she was beginning to feel before her father came home today.

"The word is coexist in some abstract way with Ursula Jenkins. In some totally removed, detached way with Ursula Jenkins. Co-coexist. For I will not have contact with her, but Dad must never feel I'm at odds with her or them. There mustn't be any friction between us of any kind.

"Never. N-none. Yes, yes, coexist is an abstract … removed, detached sort of way. Dad must feel free to talk to me, tell me everything that's going on between her and him, t-them. Trust me. That's right, trust me.

"I mustn't drive him away. Put a wedge between us. Not again. Just telling him about the Stanford lecture series was the best reward I could receive. And if Mom were alive. Mom, if only she were alive."

Arlene went into her pocketbook, opened it, and had her wallet. Holding the wallet for some time, she opened it. There were pictures of her mother in the house, living room, study; but just holding the wallet in her hand, looking at her mother at her best, her youngest, in her prime was still emotionally overpowering for her.

"Mother, you taught me to be strong like you throughout your life. Throughout your sickness. With the ovarian cancer. I'll do anything, Mom, to hold on to Dad. Anything at all. I won't lose him. I won't let it happen again. A second time to me, Mom."

CHAPTER 20

Many holidays and birthdays had passed. Thanksgiving, Christmas. And then there was the New Year. Ursula and Teardrop spent the holidays with family, choosing to do so as some final tribute to past tradition. But New Year's they spent together, Teardrop flying to New York to bring in the new year with her.

Arlene had gone off to Stanford as a guest professor lecturer, and now Duke University had called her for the same lecture assignment. Her reputation was budding in her field, in the hallowed halls of academia. Teardrop took care of Jamal during her absence.

Teardrop and Ursula *would* live in Walker City, Iowa. It never became an issue between them, not that Teardrop or Ursula, once prioritized, ever thought it would. Ursula, by all indication, seemed to be looking forward to living in Walker City, as if she could blend effortlessly into its décor like a grasshopper hiding in tall Iowan grass.

And because it was March 2, it was time for Ursula and Teardrop to set their wedding in motion. The wedding was set for May 23. It would be performed in Jersey City, in the Jenkinses' house. Ursula and Teardrop wanted it this way: small, intimate, just family and close friends. For the past few months, Teardrop had flown pretty regularly to New York. He and Iris and Harry Jenkins had become great friends. A strong bond had been built between them.

Today Teardrop picked Ursula up from Des Moines International Airport. It marked Ursula's first return to Walker City since the marriage proposal.

"So, Ursula, how does Walker City feel? You being away so long?"

Ursula took a quick glimpse of Iowa's rolling landscape. "Like home."

"That's nice to say, baby. But how does it really feel?"

"Maurice, I'm not putting on an act. It does feel like home. I like it here. I feel comfortable in this part of the country."

"New York—"

"I'll always love New York. And you said we'll be flying back and forth on a regular basis to see Iris and Harry."

"Fresh."

"Yes."

"You know it's all I can do to contain Jamal. You being here and the wedding. Be prepared. He's a live wire."

"It's another reason why I can't wait to live here, Maurice—Jamal."

"And do I have a surprise for him!"

"Don't you though."

"To ask him to be my best man."

"When Jamal probably doesn't even know what a best man is. I'm just thankful there's been no resistance from Arlene. That she—"

"No, everything's been fine between us the past few months. Her schoolwork, Jamal and me, her family—she's kept everything in perspective. Not like before. She's accepted this reality. I suppose she had to, uh, in a way."

"F-forced to. Maybe forced to, Maurice?"

"Why not, shouldn't we choose the word, Ursula. Strong as it is. Force. Our relationship was forced on her. Of course it was. Since she was an unwilling participant. But when I went off to New York the first time and came back, her attitude changed. And for us, it was like a fresh start, a new beginning, something it seemed we both wanted and badly needed."

"Well … as long as she's at the wedding, it'll make both of us happy."

"She'll be there—if not for us then at least for Jamal's sake." Pause.

"And now for us, my darling lady. Your surprise, Ursula—before this conversation gets too far afield."

"The one you have mentioned before."

"And, by now, drummed through my head a thousand times."

"And sung and played—"

"On Miss Lillian. Ursula, you're as silly as me!"

"And more and more in love with you each day."

"And let me tell you, baby, this is going to be some surprise all right. So be prepared!"

"I'm belted in, Maurice."

"Tight, I hope."

And it took Ursula only ten minutes before she began questioning things, seeing mistakes in the car's route, remembering correctly how things should be to get to point A and B and so on and so forth.

"Maurice, what are you doing now!"

"All you're doing, Ursula—honestly, and I'm being honest with you— for the past few minutes is complain. Really, baby."

"And I've—there's a reason. I know my way around this place, part of Trinity, and don't for an instant think I don't!"

"Oh … the wrath and fury of a woman hath no equal. No comparison. Oh, I hope we never have to cross swords. My heart should suffer such mortal … mortal wounding!"

"Oh, baloney, Maurice, baloney. You're up to no good. And you know it! So don't even try that with me. Act out that drama. It won't get you anywhere. It went out with Hamlet!"

"Oh ha … Hamlet, Hamlet, my dear fellow Hamlet!"

"Now you really have my curiosity piquing."

"I … I do? Really do?"

"It'd better be good. Your surprise. Something awful special, Maurice."

"Don't worry, it is."

"Then hurry up. Step on it!"

"I'm already doing five miles over the speed limit. For these parts. Want me to get a ticket from Charlie Bradshaw? He cruises the Trinity area, you know. Uh, in his black-and-tan squad car, and if you didn't, well, he does."

If Ursula could topple over from laughter, she would. But she kept a straight face and her lipstick on straight.

"Small towns."

"And their thirty-mile-an-hour speed limits!"

"Maurice … ," Ursula said, looking at the house as the car rolled toward it off Dawkin's Road with little *umph* behind it.

"You mean you had no idea?"

"None."

"You're staying in the house. After all, we'll be living here. So you might as well get used to living in it."

"Oh, Maurice!"

"No Ruby Ingram's boarding home for you, when this is your home."

"But, so you're, you'll be staying at Arlene's?"

"Yes, for appearances. Appearance's sake."

Ursula laughed. "I agree. Very much agree. For appearance's sake."

"The other day—"

"In the woods?"

"Of course."

"With Miss Lillian?"

"Of course. I gave it a lot of thought. I—"

"I just want May 23 to get here so fast, Maurice. So fast. I'm so anxious. For there will be just you and me. The mornings. The nights."

"What about the afternoons?"

"I don't know about them right now. Right now, it's a toss-up."

"We'll play them, what? By ear?"

He looked into her eyes. "As long as I can wake up with you each morning and go to sleep with you each night, Maurice, I'll be happy. Feel complete."

They looked at the lawn's grass as they sat in the car.

"Soon, I'll begin fertilizing the lawn. Keep the grass high for about a month once it starts growing again. It produces stronger roots when it's not cut right away. Too early on."

"Oh … I'll have to remember that. File it away."

"Don't worry, we'll make a small-town girl out of you yet," Teardrop said, turning to her.

"You're sure you'll be all right?"

Standing in the house's huge hallway, they were holding hands.

"Here you put me up in this luxury hotel." Ursula grinned. "And now you're worried about me?"

Teardrop blushed. "This was my idea, wasn't it?"

"I'll be fine, Maurice."

"Not a—"

"Afraid?"

"Can … it can get a little spooky out here, Ursula. Especially at night, so—"

"Not, you don't mean ghosts, do you?" Ursula said, mocking fright. "G-ghosts? Really!"

"Okay, okay, baby. I'm way off base. I'm convinced you'll be fine. Can't—"

"You'll call though?"

Teardrop held her. "How many times is too many, do you think?"

They got to the front door.

"It is quiet out here, isn't it?"

"Yes, I love it."

"But too much quiet can be—"

"Just love it."

"G-good … ," Teardrop said, seemingly relieved, but then he added, "I … I don't want you to be bored, baby. In any way."

"Never."

"M-Maureen, she grew up like this. In this environment. It's all she knew, this lifestyle. This everyday pace. One day to the next like a straight, unbroken line."

"Maurice, I'm adaptable. And quiet … I've been thinking about writing a book."

"A book!"

"Or a series of short stories. I haven't decided which yet."

"Why, wouldn't that be sensational?"

"We'll have to see."

"So … I'll call—"

"As soon as you get back?"

"Ursula, young lady, I love you so much."

She kissed his cheek and then chin and then looked at him for the longest time until she kissed his lips.

"I'd better let you get to the car unescorted, or you'll never get out of here."

Teardrop was in the car.

"Call you!"

"All right!"

"Let you know if I navigated the two miles between here and the house," Teardrop said, his head hanging out the window, "without catching a stoplight on the way."

Ursula giggled.

Ursula stepped back into the house.

"No, I'm not afraid out here," Ursula said, shutting the front door, turning to walk into the house. "It's just that there are so many memories in this house for you, Maurice. So many things I don't know about. Things that you and Maureen and Arlene do.

"I'm not afraid of them. I just know they're still here in the house."

Teardrop laid Miss Lillian in her guitar case.

He was in his room. Arlene and Jamal were in the kitchen eating dinner. Of course he and Ursula ate at the house. He cooked. Teardrop was upstairs. He attended to Miss Lillian by polishing her. He'd found a distraction, something to take him away from the real chore ahead: telling Arlene Ursula was staying in the house for the next two weeks, not Ruby Ingram's boarding house but at the house. Something that had not been discussed in advance.

"I told Arlene I'd be honest with her. Completely above board, and I haven't. Not with this new situation staring at me."

Teardrop knew the time had come, for now it was deep in the day, timewise. The deed had been done. What a word to choose, Teardrop thought. And now the consequences of such a deed must be dealt with between him and Arlene. It's just that Teardrop didn't know how to break the news to her, really felt helpless considering this part.

"It's after the fact, n-not before. Arlene was excluded," Teardrop said, looking down at Miss Lillian. "D-deliberately. On purpose."

But what Teardrop found odd, upon reflection, was that Ursula hadn't asked if Arlene was told of the new development.

"Maybe Ursula was so surprised by this. Taken off guard. Eu-euphoric."

Maybe it's why, Teardrop thought.

"But Ursula's usually so involved in everything, every aspect of it. It's her mind, her journalistic training. Usually both are reliable. How'd she overlook the question, something this obvious?"

But now he was faced with telling Arlene. Letting her know about something he never thought could happen: another woman staying in the house. Someone he loved with all his heart. *A woman who had replaced Maureen.*

Teardrop had gone downstairs by way of the back stairs in order to access the kitchen. A staircase used practically, exclusively, by Jamal these days, not by Arlene or him. He heard Arlene and Jamal talking animatedly and then stopped, and suddenly, when his foot came off the last step, he became the center of attention.

"W-what's—"

"Granddad …"

"What, Jamal?"

"The backstairs, Granddad. That's what. You used the backstairs, sir."

Teardrop turned and looked behind him. "Uh … I did, didn't I? Y-yes, I did, Jamal."

"Wow … ," Jamal said.

Arlene was removing the plates from the table. "Quite unusual, Dad."

"Boy, I'd say, Mom," Jamal said suspiciously. "Since I'm the only one in the house who—"

"So I did," Teardrop said, now questioning his own motives.

"Out with it then, Granddad—"

"Jamal, I … I …"

"Don't try to explain, Dad. There're things, just some things that can't be explained away logically, I suppose, at times."

Edgily, Teardrop laughed. "And this has to be one of them, Arlene. F-fit, must fit into that category."

"I can't wait to see Ursula, Granddad."

"And don't worry, Jamal, the feeling's mutual. Ursula said the same about you."

"She did? Ursula really did?"

Teardrop pulled out the chair. "To a T."

"And she's going to be here for two weeks this time, right, Granddad?"

Teardrop nodded his head.

"And so lunch like before, sir? S-same thing as last time she was here?"

"Like, of course, like before, Jamal."

"At the Walk-In Restaurant so Ursula and I can have our banana splits?"

"Where else, Jamal?"

"I'm glad she likes them too, Granddad. So much."

"Like you."

"Uh-huh, like me."

"I'm still sticking to my strawberry shortcake."

"I know, sir. You don't have to tell me. It's impossible with you, Granddad."

"I don't know why you keep trying, Jamal. Your grandfather won't budge. Not a chance."

"I don't know why either, Mom," Jamal groaned. "But I guess I'm young, uh, I guess."

"Smart, ha, Jamal, very smart to realize that," Teardrop said.

"You always, you and Mom, tell me I'm too young to understand things, so …" Pause. "And then it's back in the rented car to Ms. Ingram's boarding house to drop Ursula—"

"Only that, that's where you're wrong, Jamal. Off base. It's where you're totally—"

"Wrong? How? We do drop Ursula off at Ms. Ingram's, don't we, sir?"

And it's when Teardrop realized what he'd said, how he'd allowed this to unfold the way it had.

"How could I be, Granddad? When Ursula's staying at—"

"The house, Jamal. The house," Teardrop said, looking directly at Arlene. "My house this time, Jamal. It's where Ursula is … is right now. At the house."

And Arlene kept looking at Teardrop until she burst into tears and then ran off to the back staircase and then up it.

"Mom. Where are you going, Mom?"

For Jamal didn't see Arlene's face; it was only Teardrop who had.

There'd been contact between Teardrop and Arlene since what occurred in the kitchen but only briefly. Arlene'd not gone into Teardrop's room. She said she didn't want to talk to him then but later, when Jamal was in bed.

Jamal was in bed.

It'd been, according to Teardrop's estimation, about ten minutes. He'd called Ursula; it was after the incident in the kitchen (he had to). He didn't bring it up, the incident, but would tomorrow, how it happened and its resolution.

"Dad," her voice was cold as ice. Teardrop felt it freeze over him. Arlene stood outside the door.

"Yes, Arlene?"

He walked to the door. It's when Arlene began walking away and toward the study. Teardrop watched her walk into the study and then began walking down the hall, stopped, and then walked inside the study.

Arlene stood in front of her desk, a desk that looked messy, unruly—atypically so.

Long pause.

"Jamal's in bed."

"Yes."

"I don't want to discuss this in here," Arlene said tersely, her eyes not looking at Teardrop but into the white built-in bookcase across the floor. "Not anywhere in the house."

"He must not hear us."

"No." Pause.

"I have my coat."

"I'll get mine."

She tipped her head.

"Where do you—"

"The front porch."

"We'll go for a walk and talk about this, Arlene. T-talk this through, honey."

Arlene was mute.

Arlene was on the front porch, her hands down inside her pockets, waiting for Teardrop. The front door opened. Teardrop was out on the front porch with her.

They stood there motionless. The night air was cool. March weather in Walker City, thirty-one degrees.

"Are we going to walk and talk, Arlene? Is that what you want? Do you—"

"I want to sit in the car. I don't want to go off too far from the house." Arlene looked at the red Impala.

"Okay, honey." Teardrop said. "I see no problem with it."

Arlene went into her coat pocket and pulled out her car keys but then realized the doors were open, that no one in the Trinity area would steal the car, that it'd been a momentary mental lapse on her part.

They were inside the car, Arlene behind the steering wheel, Teardrop in the car's passenger seat, his long legs sitting high up.

"So when were you going to tell me?"

"I came down to the kitchen to tell you."

"You'd waited till then? After the fact?"

"Arlene, let me explain—"

"Explain?"

He appeared uptight and then tried to unwind himself, pull himself together, but then, a second time, appeared uptight. "W-why this happened this way."

"I thought we were to be honest with each other, above board about, regarding Ursula Jenkins."

"Yes, but—"

"It was her idea, wasn't it? Ursula Jenkins's grandiose—"

"No, it was mine. I shocked Ursula as well with it."

"And it came with a lot of thought from you, didn't it, Dad? And why am I asking such a question? This, when I know the answer's yes. Of course it did. It's your modus operandi. How you operate. You're not rash, impulsive. Not in your thinking or your habits."

"No."

"So it'd been a couple of days that you kept it from me. It'd been your quiet little secret to keep."

"Ursula … we're getting married, Arlene. In May. In two months. A little over two months from now, we'll be married—"

"Man and wife."

"Ursula will, yes, Arlene. Ursula will be my wife. She's a guest at the house. My guest, in concept."

"Concept?"

"It's how I—"

"You're rationalizing it? This?" Arlene said, shifting her body toward Teardrop. "Now?"

"Now?"

"You mean to tell me that until now, right now, you didn't have a totally different take on this? Up … right up to this instant. Give it a totally different rationale?"

"Let's not complicate this, Arlene," Teardrop said defensively. "Layer this. Make it more—"

"No, no, let's not. Let's dare not do that, Dad. No, we mustn't."

The dark sat in the car; the windows rolled up, airtight.

"It's taking on some kind of insidious residue."

"Has it?"

"She's going to live there. In the house, Arlene. It's going to be our … Ursula's going to … what harm can two weeks do? Mean to anything, anyone?"

Arlene switched on the car's overhead lamp.

"Do you remember her, Dad? Your wife? Your wife, Dad!" Arlene screamed, her wallet in her hand. Her finger stabbed like a dart at the picture in the wallet, inside the protective plastic, Teardrop looking at it, his heart as well as hers running away from them.

"Do you? Do you!"

"I love your mother, Arlene. I love your mother!"

Arlene's finger still stabbed at the picture repeatedly. "And this is how you show it? S-show it to my mother?"

"I-I've done nothing wrong. Nothing. I love your mother, but now—"

"What are you going to say? Some cliché? Something trite but psychologically soothing, healing for you, like 'But I've moved on with my life?' Or how about, about this one? 'Forward. Forward. I've moved forward with my life'?"

Teardrop wasn't pleased with this, for he was willing to yield some ground to Arlene, let the leash stretch some, accept most of the brunt of their disagreement but not to the point where his daughter openly mocked him, practically to the point of personal humiliation, ridicule, if this was her intention.

"Grow up, Arlene. It's time you grew up. And If my falling in love with someone else has been a jolt to you, then it's time you get over it. It's not going to change. Vanish. Ursula's in my life to stay. And nothing will change it, nothing, Arlene, absolutely nothing."

Arlene's eyes squinted. "Are you having sex! Y-you two having sex together!"

"Why … why that's none of your business. None of your damned business!"

"Well, are you! Is it why Ursula Jenkins is down here in Walker City? To have sex in your and … and my mother's bed!"

"How dare you! Y-you say something like that, implicate me in that! Your father! Your father, Arlene!"

And in the car's light, Teardrop's veins punched through his skin.

"You are!"

Teardrop's fists clenched. "You're showing me no respect. None, as your father."

"And … and my mother? What about my mother!"

"I won't discuss this with you. Not any longer, Arlene," Teardrop said, opening the car door. "Not like this. With—"

"No, no, it's over, Dad. It's over. Finally over. I want you to leave. I want you out the house, Dad. Leave! Leave! Leave my house!"

"L-leave? Leave? Leave your—"

"Go! Go! I want you out. To go. Out the house! Tonight, Dad! Tonight!"

"B-but—"

"Stay with her, Ursula Jenkins. Stay with her. The next Mrs. Maurice Williams. The future Mrs. Maurice Williams. I don't want you in my house. Living in my house. Under my roof. With me. I don't want to be around you!"

"But, Arlene, Arlene, we must talk a—"

"About what, Dad? What? Talk, yes, ha. Like we did before Ursula Jenkins came to town, down here to—for her two-week visit. To stay in your house. My mother and father's house. Like that, Dad? Do you mean like that? What, s-similar to that!"

"I didn't know it would hurt you like this, not this much, Arlene. Like—"

"You didn't. You didn't. Well, it's too late now. We have nothing to talk about, nothing."

"But two adults, r-reasonable, intell—"

"Tonight, Dad. Tonight. I want you out the house tonight. Immediately. Right now. Go. Go, Dad. Leave!"

"But what about people around here, Arlene? Our neighbors? A-appearances—what will they say? T-think?"

"And what, I'm—"

"Yes, I can see your, I can see your condition. Y—"

"You are a disappointment, Dad. A terrible, terrible disappointment to me."

The car door still hung open. He was still holding on to the car's inside door handle.

"And Jamal, Arlene? What about Jamal? What … what are you going to tell Jamal in the morning? How are you going to explain it to him?"

Arlene looked away from him.

"My absence. Why I'm not there? In the house?"

Arlene looked at Teardrop and then to her left, away from him, her eyes looking through the window, out into the darkness surrounding the car, and then back to him. "I'll tell him something. Think of something." Pause.

"Something like—how about Ms. Jenkins was frightened by something in the house. Yes. Ha. Maybe a rabbit got into the house or … or a field mouse. How's that? How—and so … so she called you because it frightened her. Yes, right, frightened her. And you had to go charging off, run off, ha, to … to save her. Rescue her like a knight in shining armor. Her hero … T-that sounds good, Dad. Sounds good, doesn't it? Suf-sufficient enough, doesn't it?

"And now you've decided on staying there the two weeks she's here for fear of a future event, e-emergency, unfortunate incident, as unnerving as they are, these things are to Ms. Jenkins, Ursula Jenkins, of … of them repeating themselves.

"And then you said, innocently, remarked, what the heck, Arlene, I'll be married to her in another two months anyway, so I … I, why I might as well move back into the house. Reacclimate myself to the old house since my new wife and I are going to live in it, spend the rest of our lives there.

"How's that sound, Dad? T-to you. Reasonable. Reasonably intelligent, Dad?"

"Fine, Arlene. Fine." Teardrop was out the car. He reached into his jacket that had all his keys, both house and car keys.

Arlene got out the car.

"You brought this on. You. You. Onto yourself. You caused this, not me. So don't blame—"

"I know, Arlene. I agree," Teardrop said despondently.

And suddenly Teardrop did something completely unexpected, something that shocked Arlene, for he'd advanced toward the car he'd rented for him and Ursula that was parked directly behind Arlene's Impala and opened the door.

"But I'm asking you to leave, Dad. Tonight. It's final. Go upstairs to your room and get, and pack your belong—"

"I'll do it tomorrow, not tonight. Don't worry, you'll be gone, you and Jamal. I'll get my clothes, things then—everything will be out the house," Teardrop said, entering the car, starting it, turning the car's lights on, Arlene blocking her eyes and then stepping out the light as the car shifted away from the property slowly, Arlene not turning, seemingly startled that everything had happened so abruptly without any further rancor or discord or unpleasantness abetting her ultimatum.

From outside the house, Teardrop saw there was one light burning inside.

He shifted the car into park. He turned off the car's high beams. His head felt fuzzy, but he was glad he'd gotten to Dawkin's Road without difficulty.

His head lay back on the car's padded headrest. All he wanted to do was shut his eyes just for a second before going into the house.

He put his key in the door lock, opened the door, and turned on the lights.

"Ursula. Ursula!"

From the second-floor landing, Ursula soon appeared in bra and panties.

"Maurice, what's wrong? Why're you back here?"

It's when Ursula realized her state of dress, or undress. "Let me get my robe!"

"Of course."

When she returned, Teardrop was no longer in the hallway.

She ran down the staircase, and when she got into the living room, Teardrop was sitting in a corner chair, the antique gold drape hanging in back of him. Just one room lamp was on.

"It's one of the saddest days of my life, Ursula," Teardrop said. His head was back against the chair. He was looking up at the ceiling. His eyes were shut.

Ursula sat.

"Maybe I knew it would be. Maybe … I don't know …"

Teardrop let the thought settle. "Who am I trying to fool? Of course I knew."

"Me staying here in the house."

His eyes opened. "Why didn't you ask me before?"

"I don't know why. Maybe I was afraid too."

"It was my responsibility to tell Arlene you were staying here. At the house for two weeks. To make wedding plans."

"Maurice, what happened?"

"Maybe I was asking too much of her. That Arlene finally had accepted us. Not that there were any outward signs saying she had, but I know how decent my daughter is. How Maureen and I raised her," Teardrop mumbled.

"When I heard the house's front door open, I—"

"Sorry, sorry. I didn't mean to frighten you. But I didn't go back to the house after Arlene and I sat in the car, after we talked. We, you see, Arlene told me ... I ... I wasn't going to go back into the house, Ursula, not for anything or anyone. I wasn't."

"So I couldn't prepare you. I just got in the car. Drove over here."

"It's all right, Maurice. It just frightened me for that brief instant, since I didn't expect—but then I heard your voice."

"Cry out to you? Is ... is that how it sounded, affected you?"

"Yes, Maurice. It did."

"She threw me out. My daughter threw me out of her house. Arlene, Ursula."

Ursula gasped.

"She doesn't want me to stay there. I'm no longer welcomed in my daughter's house."

"Tonight? T—"

"We talked about you staying here, in the privacy of Arlene's car. Away from ... so ... so Jamal wouldn't hear us. She'd found out earlier. But we talked later. Needless to say I knew she would be upset ... but not this. Not to this extreme."

"Yes, this is a shock."

"She showed me a picture of Maureen. Pulled out her wallet. Asked me did I know who I was married to."

"I-I'm sorry, Maurice, so—"

"She also asked me if we were having sex."

"She ... she ... you ... you told her no ... no, Maurice, didn't you? You told her no, Maurice. By no means are we! Not under any circum—"

"I told her it was none of her business. It's what I told her: that it was none of—"

"But why? Why that? Why didn't you tell Arlene we're not having—"

"Because it's none of her business what goes on between you and me. Even though she openly accused us of having sex in ... sex in her mother's bed."

"And you let her get away with that without denying it? You saying it's not true?"

"She can think what she wants. If that's what she thinks of me, has such little respect for me these days, then ..."

"But what about me, Maurice? You ... you should have considered me, my reputation in this. It's given her reason, j-justification to hate me. Hate—"

"I would not yield ground to her, Ursula. I wouldn't," Teardrop said strongly. "I'm sorry, but she will not read motives into why you're in this house. I won't let her tread on our privacy or our dignity. Not like that. This is a different Arlene I'm looking at, not the one I know Maureen and I raised. I don't know this Arlene. Have no sane, rational idea of who she is."

"Everything's so different for us. Right now."

Teardrop got up and walked over to the couch. "Care to join me?"

When she sat down next to him, Ursula nestled into Teardrop's arms. He rubbed her arm gently through the robe. "I was angry ... so damned angry with her."

"What about Jamal, Maurice? Tomorrow? In ... in the morning?"

He kissed her forehead. "Arlene has a story worked out. I'll tell you about it, so if Jamal should ask, you'll confirm it." Teardrop sighed. "Nothing's to be in conflict. Disharmony."

"No."

"It's something suggesting you were frightened by a small animal that entered the house. He'll name it for us. So I ran over here tonight and then thought it best I stay the two weeks, the duration with you."

"Oh, I see," Ursula said, not at all surprised by Arlene's inventiveness. "And when I leave, leave after the two weeks are up, Maurice, then what?" Ursula asked, her forehead knotting.

"I'll just say, at that time, that it was planned, planned out this way. For me to move back to the house a month before the wedding."

She straightened herself. "What, Ursula?"

"I ..."

"What ... ?"

"What about the wedding, Maurice? Arlene and Jamal being there."

"Damn this is difficult, Ursula. Damn, damn if it isn't!"

Now Ursula was holding Teardrop, for he'd grabbed onto her.

"You wanted Jamal to be your best man. It's what you'd planned on."

Teardrop was crying.

"Will everything be different by then? D-do you think between you and Arlene by then? By the time of our wedding, Maurice?"

CHAPTER 21

Arlene woke. And now she felt guilty for sleeping, for she'd had so much on her mind. It was those things that made her know sleep, last night, would not come easily for her; and if it did, it would be somewhat like a miracle. That she'd found some steel will in her to sleep. But now she felt guilty that sleep had come to her, that she hadn't spent the whole night thinking.

"But I did what I had to do last night no matter how much it hurt. If ... how devastated I feel by it now. Dad is wrong. I love him, but he's wrong, all wrong, what he's doing. He's misguided. He asked too much of me."

Arlene looked at the alarm clock on the nightstand. She knew Jamal's alarm clock would be going off at any minute now.

She got up from the bed. She was in her robe. It's how she'd slept, in her robe, on top her bed in her soft slippers. She'd rolled up her hair, slowly, but it was done—she did it.

She was out in the hallway.

"Dad's clothes are still in the closet, aren't they?" Arlene stood in the hallway, staring down it. "It's going to be like when he went to New York that first time. It's going to be like that.

"It's going to feel like that, I think. Similar. Around the house now. But it had to be done. For Mother's sake. No one is here to protect her, the past, but me. I'm the only one left who has not forgotten her. How ... just how beautiful and wonderful everything was ... un-until her cancer came. Took her from her family. Us.

"And now Jamal must know his grandfather's gone. That he'll have to get used to this, the feeling of him no longer around, in the house. With us. That's something he'll have to get used to, that's all."

Jamal's alarm clock went off.

Jamal's awake.

Jamal's door sprung open.

"Good morning, Mom." Jamal was in his cotton pajamas.

Arlene was midway down the hall.

"Good morning J-Jamal. I was waiting until your alarm came on. Went off. Before I—"

"Oh, that."

"There's something I must tell you about your grandfather."

Jamal yawned.

"What, Mom? That you need to tell me?"

Then Jamal stretched his arms well above his head, arms that had length to them.

When Teardrop opened the door, it's when Ursula opened hers, as if they were wired to the same morning.

"Good morning, Ursula."

"Good morning, Maurice."

"You were waiting for me to—"

"Yes."

Teardrop was at the head of the hallway, Ursula at the back. He'd slept in his bedroom, Ursula in the guest room.

"I've been up for some time now." Pause. "Care to use the bathroom first?'

"It's all right?"

"Of course, baby."

"Thanks."

"Oh—"

"Be right out."

"No, don't—no need to rush."

"You know how I am anyway, Maurice."

"Yes, from my New York experience. You're no slowpoke. Can't very well accuse you of that."

"No, not in a million years."

"A journalist tied to a computer or laptop or newspaper. In a rush to dash off the next copy."

Ursula winked. "That's me, all right."

Teardrop had washed up as well as Ursula. Teardrop was preparing breakfast, nothing special on the menu: bacon, eggs, sausage, hash browns, biscuits. He'd told Ursula he'd be down in the kitchen. He was still in pajamas and robe.

Teardrop turned. "There you are," he said as Ursula entered the big kitchen, one you could make an echo in. "Missed you."

"You did … ," Ursula purred. Then she walked over to him, kissing Teardrop's cheek.

"Now I'm awake. Fully. Totally."

"Ha. Me too."

She was still in her robe with a nightgown beneath it.

"The house stays warm, doesn't it, Maurice?" Ursula said, sitting at the kitchen table.

"It does. Some old houses are drafty but not this one, I'm glad to say."

"Last night, Maurice …"

Teardrop laid the spatula to the side of the iron-cast frying pan. "It was rough. Very difficult. But it's over. The storm. I'll sleep better tonight."

"I tossed and turned too."

He picked up the spatula. "No doubt you did. It doesn't surprise me that you would."

"I guess my principle—main concern, Maurice, is your future relationship with Jamal. How that's going to be handled, will play itself out."

"Yes, it's so apparent, isn't it?"

"E-especially since you said, you feel you no longer know Arlene. How all of this has changed her."

"Agreed, but to think she'd get in the way of Jamal and me. Stand in the way of our relationship. No, not that. She wouldn't carry it that far."

"Oh … I'm glad."

"She's not trying to hurt me. P-punish me in any way. She's only trying to preserve what was the past. Is unwilling to move forward. She still sees me only as her father, loyal to family, an ideal, but not as a man."

"A man who can fall in love again."

"Just a common, ordinary man."

"I wouldn't want to think I'd stand in my father's way if my mother died and he was proposing marriage to another woman."

"Not even if the woman were as young as you, Ursula?"

Ursula's facial expression changed.

"You mustn't forget that. Arlene, to be honest, probably, deep in her heart, feels I'm being foolish about all of this. I'm sure that feeling still permeates her feelings. And the fact that I couldn't possibly love you or you possibly love me." Pause.

"Still three strips of—"

"Make it four this morning, would you, Maurice?"

"Okay. And one—"

"No, make it two—"

"Sausage?"

"I really am hungry this morning."

"So ... uh, what? More of everything then? This morning, you're loading up on everything then?"

"Please!" Pause.

"But we're not foolish, Maurice. We'll never be foolish!"

"Ursula, I'm the last person on Earth you have to convince of that."

"I mean, because look at us, Maurice. Just look at us—you in your robe and me in mine."

"What ... ," Teardrop said, turning to her, "like an old married couple? Is that what we look like now, together, these days?"

"Yes and yes."

"A year removed from their honeymoon."

"And completely settled."

"We're so good together, Ursula. What do you think?"

"You make it so darn easy, Maurice," Ursula said, walking over to him.

"Let me," Ursula said, taking the spatula out Teardrop's hand.

"Just don't burn anything, baby, okay?"

"Maurice, I do know how to fry bacon!"

"Uh ..."

He stood behind her, holding her from behind. "Here, let me help you," Teardrop said, taking hold of Ursula's hand with the spatula in it, Ursula leaning her body back against Teardrop's, the four strips of bacon frying in the pan, soon to be flipped.

$\mathcal{M}$

Three days later.

Teardrop had been in touch with Jamal. It was Saturday. Yesterday, Teardrop asked Arlene if he could take Jamal into town to Josh Perkins's barbershop for his haircut, something Arlene normally did. Arlene agreed. It's how the conversation between she and Teardrop was conducted— cleanly, efficiently, only the request brought up for discussion.

"Granddad's here!"

"He said he'd honk."

"I can't wait to see him!"

Arlene and Jamal had been sitting in Arlene's study, Arlene doing schoolwork, Jamal quietly biding his time until Teardrop arrived. This strong tug of nerves for both Jamal and Arlene, only, emotionally opposite.

"Mom, aren't you—"

"I'll see Dad, uh, your grandfather when you get back from your haircut in town, Jamal. Tell him I send ... uh, would you do—"

"Aww come on, Mom. You can tell Granddad—"

"Jamal, you'd better get outside before your grandfather honks the horn again. You don't want that. God forbid, honey."

"Okay, Mom!" Jamal ran over to Arlene and kissed her. "See you when we get back!"

When Jamal got to the door, he looked back at her.

"Go ahead now. Hurry up. The horn. The horn, Jamal. Remember the horn."

When Arlene heard Jamal heading down the front stairs, it's when she got up from her desk. She turned the room lights off. Then with her arms folded in front of her, she walked out into the hallway and waited to hear the car gain momentum away from the house. And when it did, she said, "Ah ... they're gone."

Arlene lit down the stairs, opened the hall's closet door, pulled her jacket off the hanger, turned, and ran out the front door, turned, locked it, and then ran off the porch and off to her Impala.

It was 12:35 p.m.

On her yellow pad, Ursula was writing in longhand. Her laptop was upstairs in the guest room. She was stringing together information for a new article that thrilled her. Since staying in the house, she enjoyed working at a large, smooth-surfaced wooden table. Great natural light from the outdoors poured through the kitchen's wide-set windows. Just by angling herself to the right, the outdoor's golden light settled nicely onto the yellow-lined writing pad, even, heavenly at times, Ursula often thought.

But for now she was giving thought to how Teardrop was handling this crisis with Arlene. Bravely, she thought. Bravely.

"I know why I love him. I'm so lucky."

She stood, moved to the door to go out on the back porch, when an idea struck her.

"That'd be great. Great for the—"

The doorbell rang.

Ursula looked one way and then the other. "I won't forget," she said confidently as she headed for the front door. "I wonder who's at the door."

By saying that, Ursula checked the time by glancing at her watch.

Ring.

Ursula was at the door when the doorbell rang a third time.

"Impatient, are ... Ar-Arlene, what are you doing here?"

Arlene's brown skin reddened from the question. "Maybe I should ask you the same."

"Maurice, your father, you know he's just picked Jamal up. From your house. They, to take him for his haircut, so ... so—"

"I came here to see you, Ursula, since it now seems we're on a first-name basis these days."

"I-I'm sorry but—"

"You know me so well by now, don't you? D-don't you? Strictly through indirect sources though, I might add."

Ursula's body sagged.

"Aren't you going to invite me into my own house?"

"Yes, yes, forgive me. Come, by all means, p-please come in."

Ursula didn't offer to take Arlene's coat. She knew it wasn't to be that kind of visit.

They were in the huge hallway.

"So where were you when I rang the doorbell?"

"Oh ... uh, you rang the doorbell ... ," Ursula said, still in a daze. "The kitchen. W-working on an article. A new article of mine."

"The kitchen. The light … in the kitchen provides great light, doesn't it? Great light."

"Yes, yes, it does."

Arlene walked into the living room.

"There's so much about this house I love. The house I was raised in," Arlene said, sitting.

"Yes, there is."

"Nothing's changed. It's just the way my mother left it. Nothing's changed."

Ursula didn't wish to tussle with Arlene, only to lose.

"Yes."

Ursula sat.

"Just think," Arlene said, looking sharply at Ursula, "I haven't seen you since, ha, the first time you arrived in Walker City. Just think. Came to Walker City to visit."

Ursula's insides had turned sour.

"Walked into my house with such an innocence. S-such a charm about you. I say 'charm,' because you charmed Jamal right off. He was smitten by you. Ms. Ursula Jenkins, a reporter from New York City. All the impressive credentials in order.

"Oh, by the way"—Arlene paused—"how much has Dad told you about me, Ursula? I know you've asked by now. With your reporter's training. How much of my background, life, has he shared with you? Revealed? Don't worry, you can tell me, Ursula."

"I—"

"You've had to ask, inquire … How about who Jamal's father is?"

"Isaiah Wilkerson. Yes, I know who h-he is."

"Professor. Philanderer. Isaiah Wilkerson. My ex-husband."

"I-I asked," Ursula said. "Your father, M-Maurice told me. But it was—I made inquiry as—"

"And so you got that little piece of business out the way. Out your system. Revelation. You peeking into my life. My personal life examined and shared with a stranger. Bits, pieces of my personal history."

"But soon I'll be family. I'll—"

"What do I know about you?" Arlene asked sternly. "About you, Ursula Jenkins?"

"There's nothing to hide, nothing at—"

"There isn't?"

"What do you want to know? Know about—"

"Nothing. Absolutely nothing!"

"Then why are you here b-because I'm not going to fight with you, if that's what you're after."

"Fight? Why we're both intelligent women," Arlene said coyly. "And two intelligent women don't fight—they just discuss things that ring with truth, aren't hollow. Things with meaning, substance. That's not fighting, Ursula, not in my vernacular. That's simply getting to know each other better."

Ursula eased back in the chair as if she didn't need to hear any of this, the way she was being talked to.

"So ... by the way, where do you sleep around here, Ursula? In whose bed? Just where?"

"If you came to insult me, o-offend me, I won't let you. That I won't let you do. Not to me you won't."

"In my mother's room? In my mother's bed?" Arlene's voice was strident. "Is that where you and my father have sex too? In my mother's bedroom?"

Ursula glared at Arlene and then stood and began walking toward the kitchen.

Arlene hopped to her feet.

"No, you don't ... you don't get away that easily!"

"Then leave. Leave!" Ursula said, wheeling her body around to her.

"This is my father's house. This is my mother's house. This is my house. It'll never be your house. It'll never be your house! You can sleep in my mother's bed, but my father has loved only one woman in his life! Is ... is in love with one woman ... only one woman ..."

Ursula broke down; she was crying.

Arlene went into her coat pocket; her wallet was out. She walked up to Ursula and stuck the picture in her face.

"Y-you've seen her before. You've seen this beautiful woman before, haven't you? H-haven't you? This ... this kind, n-noble, loving woman before ... haven't you? It's the woman Dad loves. It's the woman he's never stopped loving. Not since her death. Maureen Williams. You'll never be Maureen Williams no matter how hard you try. No matter what you think it'll take. You'll always be Ursula Jenkins no matter what. Ursula Jenkins. Never, never Maureen Williams Never, never Maureen Williams!"

"Leave, Arlene! Go!" Ursula said, pointing to the door, her face a mask of tears. "Leave, leave, leave!"

"The marriage will be a sham. A travesty. And all that goes with it. Dad is lying to himself, and he's made you his accomplice, un-unwitting accomplice."

Ursula stood there, weak, near collapse, waiting to get away from Arlene's invective—Arlene's face, once a pretty thing to her but now rolled up in hate, her mouth, this twisted-up, horrid monstrosity of skin and bone and indecency.

Arlene put the wallet away.

"And now I'll leave. You know now what will stand in the way of your happiness. Of ever being happy. You saw the 'real' Mrs. Williams today. What Dad and I carry in our hearts every day. Every day that we live and breathe. You can never accomplish that. Create that in my dad. That kind of special love. Not you, Ursula Jenkins. Only my mother can."

The front door opened and then closed, and it's when Ursula felt her heart drop to the floor.

Ursula told Teardrop everything.

"I love you, Ursula."

"I … I know you do, Maurice," Ursula said, dabbing her eyes with the tissue. "I don't doubt it for a second."

"If my daughter only knew how much I love you. But how could she, when all she's wanted to do is hurt you? Denigrate and hate you."

"S-she does … she really does, Maurice."

"And it's her hate that won't let her see what we have. You and me. Is blinding her. The love between us. Something that's grown without any mystery or mistake. Not from us."

Pause.

"Ursula," Teardrop said, "I have something to do. Will you be all right?"

"Fine, I'll be fine, Maurice."

"It won't take long, baby. I promise."

Ursula smiled. She squeezed the tissue in her hand.

Teardrop walked up the staircase, his hand holding on to the banister. When he got to his bedroom, he walked straight off to the telephone on the nightstand. He picked up the phone and dialed.

"Hi, oh, hi, Jamal. Yes, me too. May I speak to your mother? Okay. Yes … talk to you soon. V-very soon."

Teardrop waited.

"Yes?"

"Arlene, as of today, I'm ashamed to call you my daughter. As of today, Arlene."

"I said what I had to say to her. I'm satisfied. Completely." Pause. "And now I'm going to hang up the phone, Dad."

And Teardrop heard what was a deafening sound to him, one that could fill up the big bedroom like it was a big ocean of water.

CHAPTER 22

May 23. Saturday. Exactly 12:30 p.m.

Teardrop stood in the Hilton Hotel's luxurious lobby at the Avenue of the Americas in midtown Manhattan. The black stretch limo pulled up to the Hilton Hotel's blue-uniformed, gold-braided doorman as soon as the other limousine departed. The doorman stepped into the hotel lobby where all the glitz and glamour was, the brilliant mirrors and crystal-clear chandeliers, and the picture of money as green as Irish lassies and laddies on St. Patty's Day in New York City parading in perfect splendor up Fifth Avenue.

"Mr. Williams, your limousine has arrived, sir."

The doorman opened the thick, sparkling double-glass doors, and Teardrop followed him like sheep follow a shepherd. The doorman opened the stretch limo's side door.

"Harry!"

"Teardrop!"

Teardrop hustled into the limousine. It's when a twenty-dollar bill was slipped into the doorman's palm.

"Thank you, sir," the doorman said, not peeking to see the size of the tip.

"Teardrop," Harry said, "I thought we agreed that everything's on me today. Is my expense, not yours. To include the doorman's tip."

Teardrop grinned guiltily. "Let me splurge a little bit on my wedding day, Harry. Share the wealth with the world, some."

"Right. Right. How are you doing, by the way? Holding up?" Harry said, shaking Teardrop's hand and then hugging him warmly.

"Fine, Harry. Fine."

"Up to it?"

"How about you? You're the father of the bride."

The limo pulled off into midtown traffic that produced a beast of sound.

"Something new for you."

"But I knew this day would come. Only, I didn't know when, especially at the rate Ursula was going."

"Ha."

"I figured, roughly, by the year 2010 she'd tie the knot. Well … far into the new millennium that's still a few years off."

Teardrop spread his long legs out. He was decked in a black tux, and so was Harry. The wedding was for three o'clock.

"You know, this is one of my new limousines, Teardrop."

"Is it?" Teardrop said, touching the leather seats.

"Used exclusively for funerals. For families of the deceased."

"Why thanks a lot. That's good to know. Awfully, awfully encouraging. Cheerful news. Symbolism."

"Just thought I'd let you know, son. Uh, you don't mind if I call you 'son,' do you?"

"Harry, you can call me anything you want today, and I'd answer. I'm marrying your daughter, Ursula!"

Harry winked from behind his glasses.

The limo's destination was Manhattan's West Side to pick up Byron. He was to be there outside his apartment building at 12:50 p.m. (traffic permitting). He was to be Teardrop's best man. Ursula and Teardrop explained their situation with Arlene to Iris and Harry, the estrangement extant between them.

Whatever Arlene had said to Jamal, Jamal was not to be at the wedding. Teardrop was game enough to take the disappointment in stride. His only objective, it seemed, throughout the entire painful ordeal was to get married to Ursula on May 23. He concentrated on that fact and that fact alone.

Byron was waving his hand at them (couldn't miss him in a tsunami).

The limo driver got out the limo to open the car door.

"Hi! Hi!" Byron said excitedly.

Teardrop made room in the backseat.

"Room for three?"

"There's plenty!" Harry said.

Byron was in a black tux too. The three men looked dashing. Immediately, they shook hands. And the shine on the tips of their shoes looked like they could light up Broadway from Forty-Second Street to 125th Street in Harlem.

"Your knees shaking yet, Teardrop? Do you think you'll make it to the altar?"

"Funny, Byron." Harry chuckled. "I asked Teardrop that, but he never answered me."

"What about you, 'best man.' How are your nerves holding up today?"

"I see he's not answering me either, Harry."

The limo pulled off into the Upper West Side traffic (and being Saturday afternoon, that opened its own Pandora's box for the limo driver).

"I think he's a bit nervous," Harry said as he and Byron jointly examined the man of the moment, head to toe. "I already called him 'son' to clarify his status, Byron. Once. Just once though. That, ha, seemed to pretty much petrify the poor guy. But in a way, I'm glad Teardrop didn't call me Pop."

"What a glorious day," Byron said.

The sun splashed across the car's hood.

"For a wedding," Teardrop said.

"Truthfully, Byron, in all my years, I've never seen a man so eager to get married as Teardrop appears to be."

"Your daughter, well, uh, to be honest, uh, totally, Harry … I just didn't have it. The right stuff, uh—that is. Was hot for her. Ha. What guy my age wasn't? But she cooled me down quick. Awful fast: like the air conditioner in this limo."

Teardrop and Harry laughed.

"Right out the gate, I didn't stand a chance—I've got to admit. Ghost of a chance from the get-go."

"Confessions of a—"

"Man, if I had just been a little more, bit more mature in my ways …"

"You, Byron?" Harry laughed.

Even Teardrop glanced at Byron with much suspicion.

"D-don't all of you gang up on me at once. Okay, okay. I'm not debonair, worldly, uh, or as s-sophisticated as you, Teardrop. But give me some time. I'm young, enterprising. Have a lot of upside. Growth potential, yet."

"Said like a true stockbroker, Byron. Talking about time though, we're making good time. We should get to the house say … oh, by no later than one twenty, one thirty at the rate we're going. But don't worry, Teardrop, we'll hide you away somewhere in the house. Ursula won't get to see you until she marches down the aisle. Uh, t-the steps—that is. "

"You sound a little teary eyed though, Harry," Byron said, looking over at Harry. "Somewhat spaced out."

"I am, Byron. Not every day something like this happens to a father."

"The father of the bride, Harry?"

"Exactly."

Teardrop held Harry's hand; he understood.

"Oh, I'm glad you passed on the family heirloom, the wedding dress I was married in, Ursula, and chose this one instead."

With little exaggeration, the wedding dress Ursula chose transformed her into an African queen in white. The white wedding gown set against her black skin was part of its enticing appeal; the other, the sophistication and elegance of the gown's ruffles gleefully dancing across the skirt and cascading diagonally downward toward the dress hem. The fitted bodice delicately cinched her waist, and combined with the thirty-six-inch-long wedding veil and Ursula's Afro, indeed, Ursula looked like she could conquer a continent, not just Teardrop's heart today.

Ursula stood in front of the bedroom's built-in wall mirror. She was admiring herself. "This is more than I could ever want, Mom, or ask for."

"I'm so happy for you, darling. Your life has taken on a glow. We're all bathing in it, your father and I. Teardrop has been perfect for you. S-simply perfect."

Ursula couldn't take her eyes off herself, and it wasn't because of who she was but, instead, of what she'd become, the journey to get to this day.

"And today is the official beginning. The crowning."

"Nervous, darling?"

"Am I. I have butterflies, Mom. I really do."

Iris hugged her. "It's to be expected, as long as—"

"D-do you know if Maurice has gotten here yet? Him, Dad, and Byron?"

"Are you kidding? Teardrop's been here. The three of them."

"Oh ... so he didn't chicken out. Get cold feet after all," Ursula laughed. "Didn't take Route 96 back to Iowa."

"Oh yes, Teardrop's here all right."

Iris, who was attired in a bright, flowing, light-colored green dress with lovely sapphires bordering the dress's hemline, took hold of Ursula's hand. "Your face, it's so beautiful, Ursula. It truly is. Oh, sorry for the distraction, but your father did tell me he's never seen a groom so eager to see his bride walk down the aisle. Even if it's just down the stairs, and the walk into the living room isn't long. Uh ... somewhat short, uh, to be honest."

And that pretty black skin of Ursula's was already a bright color red.

The music played rhapsodically.

"H-here they come, Teardrop. The bride and her father," Byron said under his breath. "Ursula and Harry. To be exact."

Teardrop shifted his eyes to his left as Harry brought his daughter to him.

And then Teardrop looked at Ursula as if he could see fully behind her white-laced veil, all the way into Ursula's eyes at this blessed moment before man and God. The preacher, Rev. Maxwell Lucas stood pleasantly in front of them to pronounce them man and wife after their exchange of vows and rings, the unveiling of the bride's face, the kiss—the happiness in the Jenkinses' home not only palpable but exhilarating in wishing the couple a bright future together.

The three-tiered white wedding cake with blue trim was cut.

Byron was licking the buttercream icing off his fingertips. He didn't use a plastic fork to eat his sliced cake but his fingers.

"Man, Ursula, I want to get married now. I ain't kidding. After seeing this," Byron said, licking the top of his thumb.

"Don't believe him, Ursula," J. C. said. "Ain't a bone in the brother's body that ain't lying."

It was the three of them standing around friends and relatives (it was like a beehive). It was as if this was to be the last time the threesome would be like this—old friends together. "I don't know, J. C., I mean me getting ready for this marriage business. I don't know. I'm thinking about it though, doing it."

"You, are you serious, Byron?" Ursula said, her eyebrows lifting at least half an inch.

"No, Ursula, he's just—"

"Keep that pose!" Teardrop said. "Don't move an inch, a muscle—any of you!" Teardrop was pointing the Canon camera at them. And they were grinning like mad hens.

Snap!

"And how about this one, Teardrop? This one!" Byron said, kissing Ursula's cheek.

"Great, Byron! Keep that pose. Don't lose it ... got it!"

Snap!

"And this one!" J. C. said, kissing Ursula's other cheek so not to be out done by Byron.

Snap!

"Except with me, Teardrop, you don't have to worry about being jealous around Ursula, your bride, but J. C., him, I don't know, man!"

"What do you say, Ursula?" Teardrop laughed. "Say about it, baby?"

Ursula's beautiful white teeth glittered when she said, "Not one of them stands a ghost of a chance against my husband, Maurice!"

"Aaah ... come on, Ursula. Give us poor saps a break!" Byron pouted. "Come on now, girl!"

Ursula was pouring punch into Byron's cup. "Enough, Byron?"

"Fine." Byron put his arm around her waist. "Are you ready for that kind of life back in Walker City, Ursula? I know we've discussed it before, but now that it's here, a—"

"I can't wait, Byron. Walker City's in my blood now. The town. The house. The—"

"The quiet ..."

"It's like a little universe I've discovered, Bryon, through the help of Maurice. A piece of me that I never knew existed."

"It's just that ... that it's not going to be the same, Ursula. None of it. I mean ... with you gone."

"You and J. C., we have been great, great friends, haven't we, Byron? O-over the years."

"Oh, Ursula, I'm so happy for you, but you are my best friend in life, Ursula. Damn, girl, you are."

"And we'll call and write each other. We will. Don't worry, Byron."

"Sure, sure. I ... I guess I would really be upset except for Teardrop being a great person. Probably the greatest person I've ever met. And to think, yeah, yeah, I thought you were crazy, out your mind when you told me you were in love with the guy. An older man.

"Man. Got all ... yourself all strung out over the dude. But you two got it going on. Getting down with it, Ursula. Shit. Make me wanna holler like James Brown doing his thing at the Apollo in front of a full house. Sold out. Ain't lying, Ursula. Not to my girl."

Teardrop and Harry walked to the back of the house where it was quiet. There was still a lot happening, festivitywise, but Reverend Lucas had left the house along with a few others like Dan Gottlieb of *Currents* magazine, but folk still abounded.

"It, everything went so smoothly, beautifully, Teardrop, from start to finish."

"I am truly blessed, Harry."

"It's just," Harry said calmly, his dark skin folding into a frown, "one question, thing I'd like to toss out at you, if I may."

Harry had Teardrop's undivided attention.

"And that is grandchildren. Iris and I have always bet on, uh, hoped for grandchildren in our lifetime. Are ... are there to ... will there be any in our future?"

It's as if Teardrop didn't know what hit him. He was floored.

"Sorry, Teardrop."

"No, it's all right," Teardrop said, loosening up. "Yes, by all means, Harry, by all means, grandchildren."

"Have you and Ursula, I mean, have you discussed it?" Pause.

"Uh, no. We haven't. Ursula and I haven't crossed that bridge. Is-isn't that incredible? Just incredible to say now that I think of it."

"In a way, I agree—it is."

"Harry, Ur-Ursula does want children, doesn't she?"

"I'm sure she does. She loves children."

"No doubt she would if asked." Teardrop winced. "But now the ugly monster raises its head again, Harry: my age."

"I am sorry, Teardrop. Really am."

"You needn't be. For what?"

Harry forced a smile.

"It, eventually it had to come up. Acknowledged, if not by Ursula, certainly by me sometime down the road." His hands went up to his head. "Ursula should want a baby, Harry. A child. A fulfillment as a woman."

"Your child, Teardrop."

"And it's not come up between us. Not once. Neither of us has raised the issue. Harry, what am I to make of it?"

They were up on the twelfth floor in the Hilton Hotel.

The bedroom lights were low.

Music was in the background (actually, it was Teardrop's CD *River of Pain* playing).

Miss Lillian was idle but in the bedroom too.

"Sounds familiar, Maurice," Ursula joked.

Ursula was in the king-size bed, in a red hot teddy.

Teardrop was simply taking off his clothes in front of Ursula, his tuxedo, one article of clothing at a time, immodestly stripping.

"So ... uh, you've never seen my chest before, have you, baby?"

"Only dreamed of it, Maurice," Ursula deliberately swooned.

Teardrop's shirt was off; he let it fall onto the thick bedside rug.

"Maurice, I love your chest, your shoulders. You hairy ape man!"

(Teardrop's chest *was* hairy, all right.)

He removed the cummerbund and unbuttoned his pants, and they too fell to the rug.

"And your legs, wow!"

"All those walks in the woods, I guess, uh, suppose, have muscled up my thighs, calves, pretty good." Teardrop laughed heartily. "I-I'd say."

"Me too!"

Teardrop, needless to say, was in his underpants.

"I just hope you like the rest of me."

Ursula laid her head back on the three pillows dreamily. "Come here," she mumbled, "and let me find out ..."

Teardrop hadn't removed his socks yet, but he didn't seem to take note of it while dutifully obeying his wife's urgent command.

CHAPTER 23

Teardrop and Ursula spent a four-day honeymoon in New York City. Today was their first day back in Walker City. All of Ursula's clothes plus personal items flew back on the plane with them. Everything was packed into a station wagon Teardrop rented, one currently parked outside the house on 18 Dawkin's Road.

"Home sweet home," Ursula said, stepping out the station wagon.

Teardrop was out the station wagon also. "Mmm … the air smells fresh, crisp too."

"Now, Maurice, New York's not known for its air quality."

"But it certainly does make up for it in other ways, doesn't it?"

"It does."

"I'm telling you, baby, it's a great city. Great for a honeymoon."

"We did have a ball once we left our hotel room, the Hilton, to find out what the rest of the world was up to."

"Ursula, you're something else. You really are," Teardrop said, winking at her.

"Look who's talking," Ursula said, winking back.

"I just can't help it, Mrs. Williams, when you're around me. My temperature begins—"

"Mrs. Williams," Ursula said, looking down at her 14k white-gold double-tier wedding ring. "Mrs. Williams. I could say it all day, Maurice, and not—"

"Ursula, please don't."

"Get tired of saying it."

"Well, I'm glad there are far many other important things for us to do right now. Distractions. Like moving your things into the house for starters."

"Oh ... yes, I almost forgot!"

"It's why I'm here to remind you. Your husband."

"Four days and counting."

Teardrop was back at the station wagon swinging the cargo door open, sizing up Ursula's personal belongings.

"Are you sure you don't have a twin sister that Iris and Harry don't know about?"

"I might be a poor freelance writer, Maurice, but I'm going to make sure I dress in style."

"Ha."

Ursula and Teardrop had gotten everything out the station wagon and into the house. It was all at the foot of the staircase, ready to be moved to the bedroom (most of it, that is). Teardrop wiped a nominal amount of sweat from his wrists. It was an eighty-four-degree day in Walker City. In fact, Teardrop sat on the second step of the staircase.

"Maurice, do you want me to get you a glass of water?" Ursula said, looking over at Teardrop who was looking down at a nebulous pile.

"Or do you think—"

"You have worked me like a mule, Ursula. No better than—"

"Do you want a glass of water or not? I can't stand a wimp!"

Teardrop shot up to his feet. "Oh ... so that's what you think, huh? It-it's what you think of me, huh? Well, I'll show you!" It's when Teardrop snatched a few boxes, carrying them in his arms, looking up at the staircase.

"Baby, follow me ..."

Ursula grabbed some of her clothes and began following Teardrop up the stairs, but when they got to the top of the landing, he said. "Uh ... ladies first."

And when Ursula got into the bedroom—

"Maurice!"

"It's new, Ursula. Brand new, baby. It's ours."

For the bedroom had a new bed in it. Teardrop put the boxes down on the floor. "That I wouldn't do to you. Not that. Have you sleep in the other bed. Not in a million years."

"Thank you, Maurice," Ursula said, laying her clothes across the queen-size bed. It was not only the bed Ursula saw but a new bedroom set.

"It's fabulous, Maurice," Ursula swooned.

"Maureen, our furniture, I donated it to a local charity in town. I wouldn't sell it. Someone in need should get some good out of it."

"The furniture had such character."

"Maureen bought it. Was quite excited at the time. And I was quite excited about buying this furniture for us."

She held him around his waist with both hands, and his lips came down to hers. After kissing her, and Ursula slowly melting into his arms, Teardrop said, "Don't start anything now, Ursula. No monkey business. You know how you get."

"Look who's talking, will you? You sure you don't want to break in the bed right now? Test the bedsprings out?"

"No, because I want to intrigue you into—let's go downstairs, you and me, baby."

"But I find it far more intriguing up here, Maurice. At the—"

Teardrop spun her body around. "March!"

He took her hand; it was like he was going to lead her through a field of jasmine.

The living room's furniture hadn't changed any. Ursula glanced around the living room, wondering why Teardrop brought her down there, what seemed this desperate rush to get there.

"Maurice, nothing's changed, has it? At least not to the naked eye. Let me … The—"

"That's it, that's it, exactly, as the new Mrs. Williams, it's yours. This house is yours to do with as you wish. Desire."

"Change it? The furniture, the décor, Maurice?"

"All of it. Breathe new life into it." Teardrop held Ursula's face. "I'm … look, I'm certainly not a millionaire …"

"B-but we'll be on a budget. A tight, strict budget."

"One room at a time. Over time, Ursula. Over time. Exciting?"

"Is it! Is it ever!"

"It should be a lot of fun for you."

"I'm going to have a ball, yes, a ball with this!"

"Not to the point where I regret it, I hope," Teardrop said like he was seeing dollar signs.

She dropped her head down on Teardrop's shoulder, these two tall people standing there in the large room.

"I've seen your eclectic taste. Your aesthetic, Ursula. So I'm sold."

"E-even though that was on a small scale—my apartment." (Ursula had to break her two-year lease and suffer a penalty with the owner by doing so.)

"But it was enough to sell me on the idea. I trust you implicitly."

"Oh … Maurice, the things I can do with this room. To this room. Just look around at it … ," Ursula said, her head popping off Teardrop's shoulder. "I already have ideas!"

"Remember, don't forget the budget. Our budget, baby. It already sounds like you're way over limit."

Ursula was wearing Teardrop's blue shirt and her lilac panties but no other clothing beneath her shirt. Her Afro was messed but not a wreck. Ursula and Teardrop were on the side of the bed. Ursula was straddling Teardrop. She was holding him around his shoulders, with him holding her around the waist.

"So you like the new bed, do you?"

"Do I!"

"I think we gave it its proper christening."

Ursula's breath heaved in and out. "Did we!" Pause. "My decoration plans certainly didn't get off the ground, especially once we got up to the bedroom."

"I guess you're going to blame me."

"And why not? Shouldn't I?"

"Because!" And it's when Teardrop fell off onto his right and he and Ursula became entangled on the bed.

"Oh, Maurice!"

"Ha!"

"I love you!"

They kissed and then lay there thinking how happy and fulfilled they were.

"Maurice …"

Teardrop could sense something major coming.

"Yes, baby?"

"Reality will come crashing back down on us soon, won't it?"

"Arlene and Jamal, you mean?"

She nodded her head.

"You're right."

"It's going to mean a lot," Ursula said, rolling over back into Teardrop's arms. "How we handle, this is handled by us."

"I agree. I want to say day to day—I want to say that, baby."

"Jamal is such a big part of your life."

"He wants to be a part of our lives. As much as he can. He's said as much."

"But if he senses tension, hostility …"

"It's so fragile, Ursula, the balance—everything," Teardrop said, coming off his back. "Going on here."

"I love him."

"We'll just have to wait and see. It wouldn't pay to force or demand anything. Any opportunity available to me, I'll take. Be thankful for."

"With dignity and grace."

"And as for Arlene, I love my daughter. She's done nothing to me to … for that to change. What she did to you in this house was reprehensible, but if she ever comes to her senses, I think the entire father-and-daughter relationship will grow. It will be a coming together of sorts, having given Maureen her due. Freeing Arlene and us."

Pause.

"Pragmatically, there will be a conclusion."

"Great class, Professor Wilkerson."

"Thanks, Aubrey. And your participation in discussions is improving, after our—"

"Little talk, ma'am. Something I needed. I'm starting to apply myself better. But it was just a matter of time, Professor Wilkerson. I mean, your lectures are always stimulating. Keep me on my toes. They really do, ma'am. Am not just saying that."

Arlene had left the lecture hall and was out on Walker University's sprawling campus with a briefcase in one hand and a book in the other. She was heading over to the university's library but then saw the vacant concrete bench, giving her the urge to sit.

The clouds sat in the sky like soft weights as students scurried about at the far end of the campus but not where Arlene sat. She was, basically, isolated from things. She was in a shaded area, under an elm tree, good for when the summer sun was hot and you sought predictable relief.

The library was about two hundred feet from where Arlene sat.

With effort she'd put the book down on the concrete bench. The bench was backless, so she tried firming her back, but she felt her back failing her as if splintering.

Arlene was in the dumps. Daily, her heart felt as if it were breaking. Like each day she felt it break more, or heard it—it just felt *crazy* what she was going through—she'd think. If it wasn't for her schoolwork, she'd often think she'd just die. She'd give herself unarguable reason to die.

She missed her Dad so much. Nothing or no one could compensate for him, not Jamal or her mother's memory—nothing. But how long had she come to the same conclusion? she thought. How long had the same thing been spinning in her head, just weaving its own tiny web there. And there was nothing at all she could do about it, nothing—not as long as Ursula Jenkins was around, still in her father's life, his new wife.

"There's nothing I want to do. Nothing," Arlene said bitterly.

She'd told Jamal that she and her father, for the time being, weren't getting along but guaranteed him that things would work their way out, eventually improve between them.

At first he took the news badly but, over the past few weeks, seemed to accept whatever relationship or time spent with his grandfather as what was best for them for the time being without complaint, without any signs of anger. Arlene was proud of him, the maturation he was exhibiting in handling these new set of circumstances, what surely was difficult on the family.

Family, Arlene thought, *family.*

Ursula Jenkins was more settled in her family now. More entrenched. She was reaching a new level of comfort—Arlene was dead certain of it. One day she would say a level of arrogance. It's just how many months away from now? Arlene thought. How many months away before she felt she was a true member of the Williams's family, changing it like she was changing some of the house's décor (so Jamal had told her), making what her mother had done in the house obsolete, something belonging to the past, no longer viable—ghostly memories.

She was back on her feet, picking up the book, edging her eyes off to the left to look at the library, the library standing erect and tall and imposing, students huddling around it as if the sun were out and summer sat in full bloom. More time had passed between the days, when students streamed into the library to learn and absorb information, and she felt draggy, practically lethargic, missing her Dad, knowing that Ursula Jenkins wasn't going to go away. She was using their name, now used to it, living in the house where she'd grown up, her parents raised her, slowly redecorating it, what was to be room by room by room—piecemeal.

Arlene wanted to scream out on Walker State University's campus—on that scale: a frenetic, delusional, chaotic, uncontrolled kind of a scream for all those on Walker State University's campus to hear and feel her madness.

CHAPTER 24

Months later.

"Ursula, don't forget the bug spray!"

"You know I wouldn't dare do that, Maurice!" Ursula hollered from the top of the stairs down to Teardrop.

"I don't want you to look like you have the mumps when we get back in!"

Teardrop was on the front porch with Miss Lillian. Then Ursula came out on the porch with her small canvas folding chair (weighing two pounds), small lightweight table (possibly two pounds), and laptop (weighing ounces).

"Ready?" Ursula said.

"Ready."

They wore shorts and T-shirts (not identical, distancing themselves from that newlywed stuff). Teardrop carried Miss Lillian, and Ursula her things, refusing to let Teardrop help—insisting on maintaining her independence. Since Teardrop had a free hand and she didn't, he put his arm around her shoulders as they walked toward the field of the woods' opening.

"Don't ever say we run out of beautiful days in Walker City, Ursula."

"It is beautiful. Another gorgeous day—"

"To be alive."

They had a favorite spot in the woods, since now they'd been doing this together for the past few months. It just happened, Ursula tagging along with Teardrop at first just to be with him in the afternoon. But now she was spending time in the woods to write. She simply unfolded her chair, table, and then got busy on her laptop, when necessary.

The area they favored seduced the senses. It was still untamed, seemingly a resting place for both man and nature.

Having reached this area of the woods, it's when Ursula unfolded her chair, and then her table, and put the computer atop it.

"There's a lot to do, Maurice. A lot of ideas to unscramble today."

Teardrop laughed. "Don't let me stop you, baby. Miss Lillian and I know how to stay out your hair. We'll just go on and do what we always do: play music."

"Uh ... just nothing too sexy—you know how I get."

"I didn't bring the blanket along for us—now you know why. In the house, I saw you seemed anxious about something. Was I right? Are you, Ursula, about something?"

"I think I might have a book floating around in my head."

"A best seller?"

"Close!" Ursula said.

"Then you'd better get started and fast. Please don't let me and Miss Lillian stop you!"

"I'm just going to diddle with it."

"It's what you writers call it? 'Diddle'?"

"Well, at least I do."

"Oh."

"Diddle with a few ideas, and then see how it works within plot design, structure, and—"

"Sounds like you're building a bomb, not writing a story. A nuclear bomb, at that."

"Oh ... Maurice ... ," Ursula said, waving her hand at Teardrop, "let me get busy with my story. I can't wait to be interviewed by Oprah!"

"Oprah Winfrey!"

"Oprah will make me a star!"

Time had marched by.

Teardrop had Miss Lillian. He'd wandered farther and farther into the woods, away from Ursula, about three hundred, four hundred yards, but Ursula didn't seem to miss them—she was thick in concentration.

When he got back to her, Ursula was seated. When he saw her full, absolute concentration (it was stunning), and knowing how that was, how it felt, he and Miss Lillian blended into the background with no notes being struck on her, seemingly contented to be there.

But after three minutes or so, Ursula snapped out of it. "Oh … Maurice, there you and Miss Lillian are."

"Ursula, baby, Miss Lillian and I have only been standing here for a good two to three minutes."

"Y-you have … ?"

"We took a walk."

"Maurice, I'm, I mean I'm so excited by the book idea."

"Care to share it."

"Share it? Uh … share it? Uh … not yet, if you don't mind. I just want to make sure, certain there're no holes in the story. You know, that my plotlines are solid, airtight."

"It must be some story you've got cooking up in that beautiful head of yours."

"It is, really is."

He checked his watch. "Want to head back to the house?"

Ursula appeared panicked and Teardrop took notice. "Maurice, uh … can … can we stay out here a little longer? S-slightly longer, p-please."

He walked over to her and put his hand at the nape of her neck and then kissed her forehead.

"Any reason why you're so, suddenly so serious?"

"Why nothing, Maurice. Nothing. It's just that it's—the day is just so pleasing. That's it, Maurice. Plea—"

"Oh … that's a new expression for me. 'Pleasing.' I don't know quite yet what to make of it," Teardrop joked, "but it does bemuse me."

Ursula sneaked a peek at her watch.

"I saw that."

"Oh … uh …"

"I guess it's time to go. Head back, right? From this 'pleasing' idyll."

"Funny, very funny."

"Not as funny as that word of yours—'pleasing'—before," Teardrop said, putting his arms around Ursula's shoulders. "I won't correct it. It will become a permanent word, fixture in how I'll describe a day in Walker City, in the woods when it's—"

"Pleasing!"

"Yes!"

They laughed as they began leaving their favorite part of the woods. "You and Miss Lillian wandered off?"

Teardrop quickly realized Ursula was after something.

"Just looking forward to tomorrow morning when Jamal comes over to spend the night with us, baby, that's all."

"He's such a joy to be around. I don't know who's more happy when he visits, Maurice—you or me."

"That new bicycle of his is beginning to register a lot of miles between the two houses."

"Maybe I should buy a bike. You know, it's not a bad idea. In fact it's a good one, don't you think?"

"What, and race Jamal around Walker City on it?"

"Maurice!"

"All right … okay. By the way … Ursula. I wanted to discuss that with you, that very idea."

"What?"

"The idea of transportation. Us getting around Walker City. How about we buy a car, a new one."

"Y-you want to?"

"It's time, don't you think? Bert has collected his last taxi fare from us Williamses."

"I've never driven in—"

"Don't worry, baby, I'll be here, around to remind you not to exceed the thirty-mile speed limit. That Walker City's not New York City."

"Maurice, I've seen you do … thirty-five."

"Well …"

Now in the sun, feeling it practically penetrate through him, Teardrop's mind circled back to the woods, back inside them, and wondered why Ursula had panicked as she had, her gorgeous face spoiling. It raised his curiosity. He was going to say something but looked over at her, at her clean, clear black skin, quickly changing his mind.

"Ursula …"

Conversation had been streaming between them, and when they got to the door of the house and Ursula stood to the side, Teardrop observed this indescribable look on her face, this thing that was so radiant within itself that it could knock the door down by itself if he didn't open it, Ursula's body bustling straight through it, so that hurriedly Teardrop opened the house's front door, and Ursula did bustle straight through it with her folded chair and folded table and laptop in tow.

"Shorty Boy, Twelve Fingers, we're here! Maurice and I are here!"

"Ursula," Teardrop said, stunned, "what—"

"Well, it's about time!" Shorty Boy Logan said, flashing before Teardrop's eyes like a cue card.

"Shorty Boy!"

"Yeah, it's about time!"

"T-Twelve Fingers!"

Teardrop looked at Ursula completely bewildered. Ursula smiled back innocently.

"Well ... ain't you gonna give your old guitar player and your old piano player a hug?"

"I ... I mean y-you have to ask, S-Shorty Boy?"

Teardrop, Shorty Boy, and Twelve Fingers hugged; and Ursula, with sheer delight, looked on.

Then when everything calmed down, Shorty Boy took a long look at Ursula. "Your voice over the phone, Ursula, was velvet to my ears. But seeing you here in person ... Well, I ain't kissed a pretty woman like you since ... well ..."

Ursula got over to Shorty Boy and he kissed her on the cheek.

"Shorty Boy ain't the only one talking to you that day, Ursula. Mental pictures don't even add up to describing what I'm seeing. Ain't even good enough."

Twelve Fingers's meaty lips got a hold of Ursula's cheek too.

"Now that everyone's had the pleasure of kissing my wife ..."

"Ha!"

"The telephone, a phone call?"

"Oh, but before we get—"

"Get into—"

"Teardrop, Ursula, sorry about that wedding up in New York."

"New Jersey, Twelve Fingers. Ursula and I were married in Jersey City, New Jersey. Let's set the record straight. Not slight it. Jersey City's probably been slighted enough, in its lifetime."

Ursula laughed.

"Was the road," Twelve Fingers said, twiddling with his suspenders, yellow suspenders at that.

"Always the road," Shorty Boy said, tugging at his pub cap with an irritation in his hand.

"Get in the way of a lot of important things. You know that, Teardrop. For a fact, man."

"Of course."

"Can't swing out from under it at times."

"Miss out on the cake, Twelve Fingers. Bet, just bet it—"

"But getting back to—"

"The telephone call … call from Ursula …"

"Yeah … that call a few days back," Shorty said, the four of them now in the living room sitting. "Ursula—"

"How, Ursula?"

"Oh, I called McKinley Scofield—"

"Mac?"

"He told me where to find Shorty Boy and Twelve Fingers. Where they were playing."

"Chicago, Teardrop. Annie Brown's Tea Cup," Shorty Boy said.

"Man, it's so good to see you, Teardrop!" Twelve Fingers said, clapping his hands. "And Miss Lillian too."

Miss Lillian was sitting out in a tufted chair in the hall where Teardrop'd left her.

"It has been a while."

"A long while," Twelve Fingers said wistfully. "Many miles and months, Teardrop. Before breaking bread together."

"Chicago, huh."

"Yeah, Chicago," Shorty Boy said. "Had us some good crowds in the Tea Cup. Ms. Annie shoe horn them in. Joe Taylor dead though. Dropped dead. Heart give out on him."

This wasn't good news. Joe Taylor was a regular in the Tea Cup, a man who lived the blues like the Tearmakers played them.

"So you was out playing in the woods, you and Miss Lillian—like before, Teardrop?"

"Nothing's changed, Twelve Fingers, for me and Miss Lillian. We still go out there to meditate. Listen to the air breathe, uh, if you will."

"Excepting two of you got company now, these days, "Shorty Boy said, grinning over at Ursula.

"Lemonade, anyone?"

"Great!"

"Wonderful!"

"Thank you, Ursula."

Ursula left the room.

"H-how'd you two get in the house anyway?"

"Ursula said she leave the front door open, Teardrop," Twelve Fingers answered.

"After all, Teardrop, this is Walker City. Ain't Chicago. Not even a close second."

It was 4:12 p.m.

"So you were to be here, by here … ?"

"Three thirty, give or take fifteen minutes. Bert got us here," Shorty Boy said.

"Remember us too, Teardrop. Nice not to feel like just 'nother fare on the stop. Suitcases back in a trunk of a car bumping along on a back road. Ha!"

"Congratulations, Teardrop. Congratulations," Shorty Boy said. "Ursula, I mean, when you told us her age …"

"But the two of you look swell together. Just swell," Twelve Fingers said. "Can't disguise that happiness neither."

"Ursula and I … well, actually we, it was a big problem, major problem for me at the time."

"But she loves you. Man, Teardrop, there ain't no mistaking that, man!" Shorty Boy said. "For nobody to see."

"See you two been decorating up the place though. Living room, this part of the house don't look the same as before, or are my eyes playing tricks on me, at my age?"

"It's Ursula's house now, Twelve Fingers. It was Maureen's before. But Ursula's now."

"Both got them excellent taste. Both, Teardrop," Twelve Fingers said, nodding his head, strumming his suspenders "Feels like what a home oughta."

Ursula was back with the glasses of lemonade, each taking one from the silver tray. They all sat back and took a sip of lemonade out their fancy-looking glasses.

"Ursula …"

"Yes, Shorty Boy?"

"Great taste."

"Thank you, but Teardrop made the lemonade, not—"

"No, talking about here, the living room, darling. Decorating. What you done to it. Moderning it up like you done."

"Oh … thank you. Thank you, Shorty Boy."

"Maureen have it going on too."

"Ha. I know."

"But you changed it up quite nicely."

Twelve Fingers had been looking at Teardrop—something Teardrop was unaware of—rather intensely for the past few seconds.

"Teardrop, guess you wondering why Shorty Boy and me paying you this visit, sit-down in Walker City. This neck of the woods, ain't you?"

"Yes, it has crossed my mind," Teardrop responded, looking at Twelve Fingers and then Shorty Boy and then Ursula in that order, but then back at Ursula with some keenness since she was the one who called them to arrange the visit.

"Yes, it has crossed my mind more than once since you've been—"

"Should, Teardrop. Should," Shorty Boy said.

"We fly down here—we want you to chew on something. Consider something big."

"Like how you put that, Twelve Fingers," Shorty Boy said.

Ursula was studying each expression on Twelve Fingers's broad, black, deep-wrinkled face.

"We been doing without you for a long time. And—"

"We want you back, Teardrop. We want you—"

"Back?"

"Back with us. With the band. On the road. Playing the joints. Blues again. That's what. With us," Twelve Fingers said. "The band, man. Why we here, come to Walker City for."

Ursula could feel the music, the blues in the air like some old-time gospel spreading its wings.

"What you say, Teardrop? Tell us, man?" Shorty Boy asked.

Teardrop had been rendered speechless, foggy headed, trying to gain control over his emotions, his thoughts but, instead, seemingly mired in them.

He turned to Ursula, who sat at his side, whose hand was on his leg, laying there for him to take if needed. "Is this why you called them, Ursula? T-to discuss this with them, baby?"

"Yes, Maurice. It was."

"Oh."

"Knocked our socks off too, Teardrop!" Shorty Boy said. "Ain't lying to you worth a plug nickel!"

"Come clear outta left field on us. For both Shorty Boy and me."

"Whew … Whew …" Teardrop was sweating.

"All you gotta say, Teardrop? To pipe out your lungs?"

"I feel myself sweating."

"You is … is," Twelve Fingers said. "And bad, man. Horrible."

Teardrop now took Ursula's hand. He held to it strongly.

"Sweating, probably, right between the cracks in your toes too," Shorty Boy laughed.

"And we did say 'consider' now, Teardrop."

"The polite word to use," Shorty Boy said.

"Don't take it to no more than that. Ain't gotta jump into the stew just yet. Still in the simmering stage, ain't cooked. Consider … it's all me and Shorty Boy asking now that your life's back in order, on a even keel again. You and Ursula gotta home here, family here for yourselves."

It was 6:42 p.m.

Dinner was served at five o'clock. Teardrop cooked.

"Best meal me and Twelve Fingers have in months, Teardrop. Still don't know how to drop beef out my diet. Mmm … hmm. Tender tasting." Twelve Fingers was picking his teeth with a toothpick.

"Shorty Boy, Teardrop's still king of the hill. Everybody else climbing backwards."

"Teardrop's second to none. The title's his, man."

"You do get to cook, practice some, don't you, Ursula? In the kitchen?" Twelve Fingers said, sucking his teeth.

"Not much, Twelve Fingers. But I do watch Maurice … a lot."

"Man, Ursula, you and Maureen. Maurice!"

Ursula and Teardrop laughed at Shorty Boy.

"Making the man sound important. Like he own something."

"Own the blues, Shorty Boy. Sweet as ginger."

Shorty Boy nodded his head in agreement at what Twelve Fingers said. "Uh, well that's true. Give the man some credit for that. King of the blues. Don't cost a penny for the truth. At no time."

"Afraid to get up, might topple over, ate so much, but—"

"I know, Twelve Fingers," Teardrop said, "but you and Shorty Boy have to go."

"Ain't nothing personal, Teardrop." Twelve Fingers glanced at his watch. "Only, got a flight to catch outta Iowa. Me and Shorty Boy."

"Put a call into Bert," Shorty Boy said.

"Let me," Ursula said, getting to her feet.

There was a phone in the kitchen, but for some reason, Ursula headed for the living room's phone instead.

"Oh, that girl's a angel, Teardrop! Dropped out the sky for you, man."

"Luckiest, I think the luckiest man on Earth, Shorty Boy."

"Sometimes when you down—"

"But I wasn't down, Twelve Fingers. Not at the time."

Twelve Fingers's face puzzled. "Or, say, riding along," Twelve Fingers said, seemingly offering a more wise, patient philosophy, "like a sunset waltzing with you in your path, then somebody come along, and you find out it all make-believe, wasn't what it appear to be, like there's more in one smile than a sunset make in five ... six ... seven."

"For her to toss this at me and Twelve Fingers, Teardrop. Put this dream back in us ..."

"Only, she was thinking of you first and foremost. All the way. Your happiness. Was right at the heart of what Ursula, your wife done," Twelve Fingers said.

"Bert will be here any minute now. He's in the area!" Ursula announced.

"Man, that tip must've worked with Bert fine. Big time!" Shorty Boy quipped.

"Shorty Boy's still loose with his money clip, Teardrop. If he ever make a fortune, ha, the world knock on his door from sunup to sundown. For real."

"Well ... at least half of it, Twelve Fingers," Shorty Boy laughed. "Half of it gonna be sitting pretty in my pocket, man."

Bert was there at the house with his blue-flamed taxicab in tow and raring to go.

Shorty Boy was in the backseat glad-handing Bert.

Ursula's head was through the front-passenger-side window. She was talking to Bert.

Twelve Fingers pulled Teardrop to him before getting in the cab. "I know you gotta lot to give up, Teardrop," he whispered. "But you gotta lot to gain too."

"Twelve Fingers, Bert's meter's getting hot as a branding iron, man!"

"Oh, it is, it is, right, Shorty Boy."

"Got here awful quick, Bert," Shorty Boy said as he watched Twelve Fingers climb into the taxi. "Don't worry, I got money to burn, Bert. This trip, no telling, just might help you with your retirement fund. Help retire you from the taxicab business."

Once the taxi was gone, Teardrop's arm wrapped around Ursula, pressing her to him. "So ... my darling little wife, what do you have to say to defend yourself now that our company's gone?"

"It-it's something I wanted to do so badly, Maurice. Y-you don't know. Even before we were married. Months ago."

"But why, baby?"

"B-because you're a great, great bluesman. A genius."

"I am, am I ..."

"You must know that. You can't feign modesty. You are a great communicator."

"You have put me in a fix though."

"I had to. I had to challenge you. Make it as difficult as possible for you."

"And you have, baby. You've succeeded spectacularly on that front."

"Maurice," Ursula said, looking into Teardrop's eyes, "it's okay to play in the woods every day, you and Miss Lillian for me. But don't you think you owe yourself more than that?"

"But it's, Ursula, it's not that easy. I'm happy. So happy with my life now."

Ursula didn't reply.

"I ... I have to give this serious thought, don't I? A ... a lot ... ," Teardrop said, holding his breath back.

"It was great seeing Shorty Boy and Twelve Fingers. The guys. They haven't changed—still look the same, great. S-so Jamal comes in the morning. Bicycles by. Yes, it's going to be great seeing him, being with him the next couple of days. He's growing at such a rate. At a fast clip. Like a ..."

Jamal and Ursula were in the kitchen. Jamal was chomping down on an apple. It was a big apple, but Jamal ate through any sized apple as if he were a moth eating through wool.

"Guess what, Ursula ..."

"What, Jamal?"

"Mom's going to buy me a computer," Jamal said, looking down at Ursula's laptop out on the kitchen table, a slice of sun beaming down on it, adding to its gleam.

"She is?"

"What she promised me. There's one in my classroom. I'm good at computing."

"That, I bet you are, Jamal."

"You know, on the ride over, I got a little winded," Jamal said, switching the subject completely.

"H—"

"I was so excited."

Ursula smiled. "Oh."

"I always get that way. Can't you tell?"

"Tell, oh, of course, Jamal. Of—"

"Ursula, it seems like Granddad has a lot on his mind."

Why, how perceptive of you, Jamal. For Teardrop had woken this morning without an answer for her, without having made a decision about his music—going back out on the road with the band, of calling McKinley Scofield to work contractual matters out between them.

"I can tell, Ursula. Granddad does, doesn't he?" Jamal was sitting next to her.

"He does, Jamal."

Silence.

"Aren't you going to tell me what it is all about?"

She didn't expect this sort of inquiry, but then again, why shouldn't she? *I am dealing with Jamal after all.*

"Jamal, I want your grandfather to return to his music. Go back to play—"

"You mean go back on the road?"

"Jamal, you know what, you catch on fast."

"Because you know what, Ursula, so do I."

"Y-you do, Jamal?"

"Yes. With all my heart. My Granddad's a great blues player, Ursula. He is."

"Jamal, you don't have to twist my arm."

"I know."

"So that's what's on your grandfather's mind today."

"It's why Granddad and Miss Lillian went out into the woods early today?"

"Precisely."

"Without you."

"Well, someone had to keep an eye on—"

"But I think Granddad would've gone out to the woods by himself anyway."

It's when she felt Jamal knew Teardrop better than she did, and the thought amused her.

"Wow. This is heavy stuff, Ursula."

"Heavy, Jamal. Heavy."

"Wow, I mean, he loves you so much."

And now Ursula felt like taking Jamal's hand and kissing it until it broke off, literally!

"It's going to be tough. Real tough on Granddad. Wow."

Jamal was doing wheelies on his bright red-metallic bike as Ursula and Teardrop watched on the front porch. Jamal was maybe 150 yards away. It was as if he'd created his own space, somewhere private, but was still being watched under watchful eyes.

"Hmm ..."

"Hmm ..."

"He's terrific, isn't he, Ursula?"

Ursula's hand's on top Teardrop's leg. "Hmm ... quite."

"I get tired watching him."

"Me too."

"Even though I could watch him all day."

"Me too."

And with that said, and out the way, Ursula and Teardrop continued to watch Jamal do his wheelies as Ursula's hand stayed attached to Teardrop's leg.

"Hmm ..."

"Hmm ..."

Three minutes later.

"Ursula, I'm going inside to call Mac. Finally. The day has finally come."

"Has it?" Ursula said abstractly.

"I'm going back on the road. Back out there with the band. With Shorty Boy and Twelve Fingers," Teardrop said, pressing Ursula's hand. "Thank you, baby."

When Teardrop stood, it's when Jamal noticed. And when Teardrop turned to go into the house, it's when Ursula's smile beamed out to Jamal, and Ursula's fingers made the okay sign that made Jamal signal it back— that everything was all right.

Teardrop returned to the porch.

He sat next to Ursula.

"Jamal," Teardrop said, motioning to Jamal.

Jamal sped over the grounds like a red streak on his bike.

"Yes, Granddad?"

"It's done, Jamal. Fait accompli."

Jamal's face squinched up.

"Mac was ex—"

"Thrilled, thrilled, you mean, Maurice!"

"Uh, sure, thrilled, Ursula," Teardrop said modestly. ""He knew you were up to something by contacting Shorty Boy and Twelve Fingers. But just what, he wasn't sure."

"Smart man," Ursula smirked.

"Only, you two aren't getting rid of me that fast. I informed Mac I'm still on my honeymoon with my new bride, plus, there're a few things we have to do, Ursula."

"Which are?"

"The car. Brand new—"

"A car, Granddad? You and Ursula are going to buy a new, brand-new car, sir?" Jamal was actually licking his lips at the prospect.

"That we are. That Ursula and I are!"

"C-can I go … go with you? Help? Can I?"

"You certainly can, Jamal."

"We're going to put Bert out of business. Uh, oh, by the way, Charles is Bert's—"

"Last name?"

"Finally remembered, Ursula. Final—"

"And ruined it for me. I had all kinds of fictional names flashing away in my mind."

"Me too, Granddad."

"Even if I like it. Bert Charles. It's better than anything I could've cooked up."

"Well, we're going to put poor Bert out of business. He's practically our own private family chauffeur these days."

"I'm going to miss him, Maurice, especially when he takes me to the Piggly Wiggly," Ursula giggled.

"A car, I can't wait until I drive a car," Jamal said, his hands bracing the bike's wide curved handlebars. "Vroom! Vroom!"

"But you have a beautiful red bike, Jamal," Ursula said.

"You like blue too, Ursula?"

"Uh … yes, Jamal."

"Then it'll be one of the colors we'll look for, uh, for the color of the new car we're going to pick out, okay, Granddad, Ursula?"

"Uh—"

"Just leave it up to Ursula and me, Granddad," Jamal said, hopping back on his bike seat. "We'll know how to handle everything when the time comes. Right, Ursula? At the car place."

CHAPTER 25

It was a month ago that Arlene got the news from Jamal, and it hit her like a ton of bricks: her father was going back on the road. She was all for it, 100 percent—no matter how much she despised Ursula Jenkins.

"It's high time," Arlene said, folding the clean clothes on the folding table in the basement. "It should never have happened in the first place. Dad giving up his music. Cutting it out his life, taking such a narrow view of his life."

In her heart, she had to appreciate Ursula Jenkins for that, for taking such a bold leap in forcing that kind of challenge onto him, where he was confronted with choices, prior to her, he'd made. He let Jamal tell her of his decision but then called and, when he was through talking to Jamal, asked for her. It's when he told her the whole thing had been Ursula Jenkins's initiative.

And now, in two days, her father would be back on the road with Shorty Boy Logan and Twelve Fingers Eakins—the blues band billed as Teardrop Williams and the Tearmakers again, no longer the Royal Blues Rollers. And tomorrow her father was to come to the house to talk to her, to say good-bye.

It was his idea, not hers, but she was all for it. She wanted to see him so badly. Lately, it was all she wanted, was to sit down and be with him. And now it was like a dream come true. But she knew too well there were still things blocking their relationship off, driving this distance between them, each living their own life on their own terms now.

"But I just want to see Dad, be with him—and all the other stuff I can deal with. Set aside. At least he's thought enough of me to want to say good-bye," Arlene said, patting Jamal's white sweat socks, assuring they were dry, "before he takes to the road." Arlene shut the dryer's door.

"I think things will go well for us tomorrow. I look forward to that."

Arlene stood behind the door; the door was partially open. When she saw the stylish turquoise Ford station wagon, she liked it. Jamal had tried describing it to her two weeks back, but seeing it in person, she liked it. Jamal said he and Ursula had the first and last say on the car; he'd really had an exciting day at the Ford dealership.

Arlene couldn't wait for her father to step out the car, and when he did, she said to herself, *Dad, you look terrific. So handsome.*

Then carefully, Arlene shut the door and made tracks for the back deck. When she sat on the deck, she wondered if her father would open the front door and just walk into the house or ring the doorbell and wait for her to answer it. There were options, she thought.

"Arlene, Arlene ... where are you?"

"O-out on the back deck, D-Dad."

"Oh ... so there you are.

Arlene stood.

"How are you?"

"Fine."

"Arlene, you look wonderful."

"Thank you."

Then Arlene looked away from him, dropping her head off to the side. "Sit. Sit, Dad."

He waited for Arlene to sit and then followed suit.

"Since you're in the back, you didn't see the new car. Want to go out—"

"Uh ... I'll see it when ... before you leave."

"Jamal ..."

"I wanted us to be alone. I will not, won't disguise that. I told Jamal as much, it's why he's at Armon's house."

"Yes, it's better this way."

"I think so."

"Well, I might as well get right to it. Tomorrow's a big day for me. Four years. It seems like it, and then again, not."

"How does Miss Lillian feel about it?"

"Funny you should ask. Now you know Miss Lillian and I see eye to eye on most subjects. But if you really want to know, Arlene, she can't wait!"

I love you, Dad! So, so much.

"Now tell me, Arlene, how do you feel about me going back out on the road? I deliberately avoided asking you over the phone. I wanted to see your face. Just what it looked like, and don't ask me why, honey. But it was important I do—extremely."

She looked to her left, onto the yard and then back to Teardrop, her eyes becoming childlike, practically twinkling in front of him.

"I am so glad. Happy about tomorrow. You and Miss Lillian going back on the road. Back to what you love."

"Thank you, Arlene. For that stirring endorsement. Coming from you it means an awful lot to me."

"It's what I wanted for you. Of course I loved the way it was. You always come first. But silently whenever I drew up the best possible case scenario in my head, Dad, for you—"

"You hoped—"

"One day you would return to the road. Rejoin Twelve Fingers and Shorty Boy. That Mother's death, the grieving part of it, would dissipate enough for you to go back to the thing you loved."

"In ... in my heart, it's what I hoped for too. But Miss Lillian and I kept going out into the woods, and it began to feel like it was all right to do, that it was enough compensation for a blues band. The music, honey. Playing before an audience."

"I can see how that could happen. The forces converge," Arlene said sympathetically.

"Yes, you, when you grieve like I did for your mother, you look for easy steps to take. Not difficult, painful ones. The worse you want to do is inflict more pain on yourself."

"Are you packed?"

"Pretty much, Ursula—"

"You're happy, aren't you? Aren't you, Dad?"

"Need I answer that?"

"No, no," Arlene replied, fidgeting.

"I married Ursula. And I am in love with Ursula, Arlene."

Arlene's eyes moistened, and it's when Teardrop recognized his insensitivity toward her.

"Arlene ..."

"Yes, Dad?"

"Mac says when I get up to Chicago tomorrow, get into Mr. Charlie's Blues Club, I'm going to be treated like some big deal," Teardrop laughed. "The toast of the town, Mac said. Royalty."

"D-did he?"

"Ha. Like the return of a blues legend, it's how they're billing it in Chicago. Radio and television interviews are on the agenda ... Aren't they though. My resurrection. *River of Pain*, the CD's still selling well. After all these years, people are still buying it."

"It's your best collection of work. By far."

"But I've written so much since. Just a store of songs. I sent a lot to Shorty Boy and Twelve Fingers to look at over the past month. They got back and told me they love them. So that's a big relief of mine."

"So the band will be going into the studio ... then?"

"Mac says soon, honey. But as you know, we like working out the songs first in live performances before they're recorded. Make sure they're in our blood."

Teardrop was happy to see no more tears banking Arlene's eyes.

"Ursula, Arlene, Ursula ..."

"What exactly do you want me to say, Dad? Want from me?"

"I'm not here to petition for her. But what, just what has she done to you, honey, tell me?"

"Dad, please, I will not discuss her with you. That I won't do!"

"But can't you see," Teardrop said, his arms completely outstretched, "how much, what all of this invectiveness on your part is doing to the family? You have to see—"

"Then so be it. Then let it stay the way it is. Where it is. For ... for we love each other, Dad—it's enough for me."

"But not me. For if you can't accept Ursula, then how can you accept me?"

"B-but I thought you just said you're not, aren't petitioning for her. Didn't you just say that? Yet it seems you're doing just the opposite."

"It's just that it means so much to me, t-to Ursula too."

And it's when, unexpectedly, Arlene felt as if she were holding on to something of enormous value—something that was actually hurting

Ursula Jenkins enough to make what she and her Dad had, this *great love* of theirs, suddenly, incomplete, not whole or bound tight.

"Nothing can, will be forced upon me," Arlene said smugly. "My life's in total balance. Perfect order. I won't chance anything upsetting it. Disrupt its flow in any way."

Teardrop stared at her with much irritation. "And you mean, it's how you really feel about this situation, Arlene?"

"I am a lecturing professor now, Dad. That you know. I am writing position papers, essays. I'm garnering great attention through my work, my—"

"Your dedication, Arlene. Fantastic dedication to what you do."

"It's been wonderful, exhilarating. Much more than I anticipated." Pause. "And I'm humbly grateful."

"You deserve it."

"Balance, Dad. All because I found my proper balance. Blend of things in my life."

And now Teardrop felt this sudden imbalance steering the conversation, almost to the point of tipping it into something else, almost too extreme and radical to comprehend, far beyond the realm of rational.

He stood.

"I'm leaving."

"Oh, you are?"

Pause.

"See … aren't you going to see me to the front door, honey?"

Arlene stood.

"No … uh, I'll say, just say good-bye here. The backyard."

"D-don't you want to see the car, Arlene? The new car."

"The car … oh, maybe another time. When you get back."

Sadly, Teardrop looked at her.

"Then, uh, let me kiss you good-bye, honey."

"Yes, Dad. Good-bye."

Teardrop held Arlene to him and kissed her cheek. Her arms stayed locked cautiously to her side.

"See you when I get back."

"I look forward to it," Arlene said coolly.

"By … by this time tomorrow, I should be in Chicago."

"It's two fifty-one."

"Yes, two fifty-one." Pause. "Rehearsing with—"

"Twelve Fingers and Shorty Boy."

"Yes, me and Miss—"

"Lillian."

"Arlene, are you sure you don't want to see the—"

"When you get back, Dad."

"Yes, that'll be fine. O-okay. Yes …"

Arlene turned her back to Teardrop and then walked off toward the deck's wooden railing.

"Good-bye, Dad."

"Good-bye, Arlene."

Arlene stood on the deck alone now that Teardrop had left. She drifted to the right and left and then settled in the center of the porch.

"She'll drive him to the airport like Mom once did. Mom always drove the car, the Oldsmobile, more so than Dad. The car was Mom's car, not Dad's. By … by default. He's never had any need for a car. It's Ursula Jenkins's car by right. It's who Dad bought it for: Ursula Jenkins."

Arlene turned and looked back at the back door. "Who's he trying to fool?"

Teardrop felt empty and distraught, but he wouldn't let Ursula see this come out him when he got back to the house, he thought.

Rain was falling, surprisingly (it wasn't forecast). Its drops marked the car's windshield, spotting it. Teardrop didn't turn the windshield wipers on; he just let the car roll along the dampening road, normally.

Teardrop's eyes, looking at the road, saw Arlene's body language, what it was saying to him when he thought she'd come out to look at the car, the distinct power it seemed to hold in it. It was the first time he really felt she was trying to hurt him, took an about-face, a 360-degree turn—had turned on him. For the other things, disagreements, were borne out of some principle, some belief, conscience, and her heart. But what she'd done today at the house, her reaction, was mean, deliberate, intentional, inspired, meant to hurt him, if possible.

He shook his head at all of this. He was emotionally drained from this roadblock, this ongoing obstruction blocking him off from Arlene. He so much wanted it to be like it once was. For all of this angst and sorrow to clear itself, to take their relationship from where it now was to where it'd once been, back to a happier time—to a time neither thought would change.

"No, Ursula will not see what's inside me today. I'll be emotionally dishonest. Inauthentic. Arlene has turned another corner with this. She's after my feelings now. To hurt me if she can. That I won't let happen. She has to know me, her father, better than that."

♪

Following day.

"Ursula, if I could have you turn this car around, I would."

"Maurice …"

"It's the first time—my nerves. The first time I went on the road, I was as nervous, petrified as now, but … I wouldn't dare let on to my parents, make them turn the car around."

"And even now, Maurice, you don't mean it."

Teardrop's head drew back. "No, no, I suppose not, baby. You're right."

"What are you unsure of?"

"I don't know," Teardrop said uneasily. "How about everything? Everything you can imagine. From the music through, straight through to you."

"M-me?"

"Two weeks. That's a long time away from you. From my wife."

"I'm prepared for it. I know it's the right thing to do. If I didn't stick to that belief in my heart then I think I would be a nervous wreck. A mess. Unfit to drive you in the car to Des Moines International today."

Teardrop laughed.

"Maurice, I'm serious."

"Baby, I know you are. I'm just glad Mac knows I don't plan to be out on the road with Shorty Boy and Twelve Fingers like before. Continuously. The past won't repeat itself. It's important he understand that no matter how many prospective bookings may come in, my comeback, if you will, generates. I'm willing to cut out some portion of my life for the sake of my music, but not all. Not like before. Not even close."

The telephone poles on the long extension of Iowa road stood tall. Ursula looked at them as their high-rise telephone lines stretched across to the other side of the road.

"I think we're going to be on the telephone an awful lot the next two weeks, Maurice."

"Me too, burning those wires up!"

"Melting them, you mean."

When Ursula parked the car in International's terminal, Teardrop grabbed her. "We'll kiss in the airport, Ursula, but this one, baby, well … it can only be done in the privacy of our car, unless I might not get to Chicago. Airport security might have to be called."

"It-it's going to be that—"

"Sexy, Ursula."

"Oh, I can't wait then. Not another second!"

Ursula was passing by those same telephone poles, the wires high above the car. *There'll be plenty of telephone calls, Maurice,* Ursula thought. *You can bet!*

Teardrop said she'd get a call as soon as he stepped into his hotel room, not a second later—that he missed her already. And right now, she missed him as if night had rolled into Walker City, and she was in the big house, in her bed, alone.

This is really going to test me, she thought. The two weeks Maurice is out of town. If she were in New York, of course, she'd have friends. *Real friends.* Down here, Walker City, she didn't. Frank, the mailman. Of course people at the grocery store, Chris and Roy at the gas station. People to say hi to, talk about the weather to, but not much else, socially, going on for her in the Trinity area.

In New York she had her parents and Byron and J. C. They were there for her, her social network—could always be counted on. But when she called McKinley Scofield, automatically she'd mentally processed what lay ahead if Teardrop bit at the bait, was lured back to his music by her and Shorty Boy Logan and Twelve Fingers Eakins. This was the "lonely" Byron at one time alluded to that fell on deaf ears, as if, abruptly, she'd become tone dead.

"I knew what I was getting myself into. Out the gate," Ursula said. "No one put a blindfold over my eyes. Arlene … if only things were different between me and Arlene."

She and Arlene continued to have so much in common, Ursula thought. So much to share between them. She could've been in the car with them today, her school schedule permitting, gone to the airport with them. She could've been a part of this new beginning for her father. And they could have commiserated, daughter and wife. They could become the best of friends. But maybe better than friends: emotional soul mates.

Only, Ursula knew it was wishful thinking. It would have to be her work that would have to pull her through the next two weeks without

Teardrop. And she was all set to start her book, postponing a few short story ideas until later. She would begin her novel, the first chapter of it today, and was buoyed by the thought.

It was raining.

The rain, no matter how slight, came as no surprise to the Walker City weather bureau. The car's windshield wipers were working. Yesterday when Teardrop drove onto the grounds (she was out on the porch), she saw he hadn't used the wipers, that the windshield was spotted with raindrops. At the time, she didn't know what to think; after all, he'd just come from Arlene's house, but she said nothing because when he got out the car he was upbeat, so she attached no importance to the wipers, but now she was.

"I'm beginning to see already that after you've done your work, all you really have at the end of the day are family and friends. I'm beginning to understand it more clearly. And with Maurice gone, I have neither in Walker City."

Ursula shut the front door, and it's when it sunk in, that she was alone and that she would have to make the best of it—whatever it took. Her laptop was in the bedroom. She took a look up the long staircase, and it's when the staircase began to feel like it was conquering her—that it was too much for her to climb.

Pause.

But it's also when Ursula laughed at herself. *I'm not going to go crazy now. This house isn't going to be the cause of a nervous breakdown either.*

In pants, Ursula then felt like taking the steps two at a time, springing up them like a pogo stick.

She laughed but then caught herself and began walking up the staircase cool, calm, and collected—ladylike, taking dainty, mannered steps.

Ring.

"T-the telephone!"

Surprised, Ursula had no idea who was calling.

"It's certainly not Maurice—"

Ring.

And Ursula didn't know which telephone to run for, to pick up, since she was halfway up the staircase but she was going upstairs to her bedroom for her laptop.

Ursula began taking two steps at a time (it's what she'd originally planned!).

Ring.

"Hello. Good afternoon."

"Hi, Ursula."

"Jamal?"

"Thought you might be lonely. With Granddad gone. Thought I'd call. So how are you doing, Ursula?"

Teardrop was in his hotel room, about to get to the phone.

"Hey, Teardrop, let us in, man!"

Shorty Boy and Twelve Fingers knew the room door was open but seemed dead set on letting Teardrop perform the distinct honor of opening it for them.

"Who said I wasn't going to ... Shorty Boy! Twelve Fingers!"

"Teardrop!"

They hugged rambunctiously but fondly.

"Why, thought this day was never to come, Teardrop. Never show up on the calendar!" Twelve Fingers said.

"There she is--

"The queen, Twelve Fingers. In all her glory, man."

"Yeah, Shorty Boy," Twelve Fingers said, sighting Miss Lillian out her black case and on the bed. "Sitting on her throne. Cozy. The magic's back, Teardrop. It's back ..."

"Back in Chicago. Back in Annie Brown's Tea Cup tonight," Teardrop said.

"Got in and don't look us up, huh?" Shorty Boy said accusatorily. "Was gonna be like that? Putting it down like that, was you?"

Teardrop shut the door. "Uh ... first things first, Shorty Boy. Uh ... pri-priorities. I have to—"

"You mean Ursula first, don't you, Teardrop?" Twelve Fingers said. "Your eyes could tell where buried hearts are, man. Easy."

"Ha. Yes, Twelve Fingers. You're on the mark. I had the phone in my hand."

Twelve Fingers looked at the bed and then at Teardrop and then at Shorty Boy. "Seen the wrinkles on the top the bedspread, that's all. Body impressions. Look real fresh. Awful new."

"Good detective work, Twelve Fingers," Shorty Boy said. "Must be Dr. Watson to your Sherlock Holmes, since I seen the same, man ... Uh, wrinkles that is."

"Well ... we ain't gonna keep you, Teardrop," Twelve Fingers said. "Ain't for long, that is."

"Wasn't our intention, Teardrop." Pause.

"So how we gonna play this, since you the boss man again. Calling the shots."

"Who was calling the shots before, Twelve Fingers?"

Twelve Fingers looked at Shorty Boy and Shorty Boy at Twelve Fingers.

"We was splitting it even, Teardrop, half and half … s-sort of. But mostly Shorty Boy's half. Ha. Trying to equal it out best we could between us. For the time."

"Wasn't easy with Twelve Fingers though. But you know that, Teardrop, without me drawing you a map."

Teardrop smiled.

"Was like fighting over pancakes or waffles for breakfast. Which one to eat. Splitting hairs down the middle, man. What was going down most of the time. Between us."

"Right. The two of you know the new music, right? Is … is that safe to say?"

"Now we do!" Shorty Boy said.

"Uh, let's not rehearse the songs then. Let's—"

"Y-you … you saying that, Teardrop? Teardrop Williams? As much as you used to rehearse us, man? Kill us. Bleed a blister dry."

"Let's do it differently tonight, Shorty Boy. I feel like—let's make it happen on the bandstand. Find ourselves on the bandstand. Do something … start off like that tonight."

"Just hit a groove, Teardrop. Stay there, don't stop," Twelve Fingers said with assurance. "Don't think of nothing but the music. It's taking us."

"Yes, Twelve Fingers, that. But more like we're spiritually reconnecting with the music as sort of grand architects, master builders, putting all the proper pieces in place."

Shorty Boy looked at Teardrop, astonished. "Yeah, man, we missed you all right. Like hell, man. Sure, sure do."

Twelve Fingers and Shorty Boy had left the room. Teardrop clapped his hands.

He picked up the phone parked near his elbow.

"Ursula!"

"Maurice!"

"Oh, baby!"

CHAPTER 26

Two weeks later.

"Oh, man, oh man. If this ain't been the greatest two weeks since we been playing. Since we been doing this here thing together."

"This is like déjà vu, standing in the lobby together though—like the last time we done it."

"But we was in Atlanta, Georgia then, Twelve Fingers. Bunky's place, man."

The luggage surrounded them like swamp water.

"And we wasn't bound for home, Teardrop who was."

"Well … can't say that this time around."

"Not at all, Teardrop. Not at all," Twelve Fingers said. "We all going home this trip."

"So Mac said in another three weeks, Teardrop?"

"Yes, Shorty Boy. LA."

"Where it never rains." Shorty Boy chuckled. "Not on no occasion I know. Sun out all day. Kissing the sky."

"Mac can expect to hear from Annie soon, if he ain't already."

"Brick of money we make for her in this club, man. Sink the *Titanic!*"

"I love you guys."

"Feeling's mutual," Twelve Fingers said.

"That it is, Teardrop. Love you, man."

Then their heads turned to look out the broad window for the taxicab, but they knew now the future stretched before them with a wide smile.

The plane was about to land down on Des Moines International's tarmac.

Teardrop now felt what he'd felt when Maureen was alive, but so much more with Ursula today.

I can't wait to see you, Ursula, Teardrop said to himself. *To get home, Ursula. Our home, baby.*

"Just … I'd better not find a speck of dust anywhere in the house, Ursula. I'm warning you," Teardrop said, taking his luggage out the station wagon's cargo area. "Not anywhere."

"You know it was so much quieter when you were gone, Maurice. So much … so less demanding. Just me and the owls and the birds and the bugs—"

"Mustn't forget them."

"And the—"

"Oh, so it wasn't like suffering through a cold winter storm in Iowa, as you so metaphorically put it?"

Ursula laughed while holding on to Miss Lillian. "Just using my artistic license. But …"

Ursula rushed to Teardrop, kissing him.

"If that doesn't tell me something!"

"Point me to the bedroom!"

"I'm all for it!"

Ursula's mouth was nibbling Teardrop's hairy chest. His eyes were closed; he and Ursula had made love this afternoon.

"Maurice … Oh …" Ursula shivered.

"Is that what two weeks does, Ursula?" Teardrop asked, his voice drowsy. "Does to you?"

"Yes …"

"God forbid then if Mac should ever book the band for a month!"

"T-then we'd kill each other! Literally!"

"Does sound absolutely, sinfully delightful, divine, though."

Ursula shut her eyes and laid her head flat to Teardrop's chest to listen through his pepper-gray tangle of hair for heartbeats racing to the surface. For she'd been thinking the past two weeks, her heartbeats racing up to the surface too, anxious to be heard, not because of any great sex but because of some great love for someone and the thoughts of fulfillment any woman wanted from the man she loved.

"Mmm …"

For Ursula's mouth was back to nibbling Teardrop's chest. But now her mouth traveled to his neck, finishing there—and she was raising herself up further to now where her eyes looked into his.

"Maurice, we have never discussed this, but I want a child. I want to have your baby."

Teardrop's body reacted like it'd been electrocuted.

"Ursula, Ursula …"

Ursula's hands were holding on to Teardrop's shoulders as if to steady him, root him down in place.

"I had this overwhelming feeling, sensation, when you were gone, Maurice. O-overpowering sensation. Of having your baby. Of carrying it for nine months. Of being a mother."

"Ur-Ursula, I'm startled," Teardrop said, taking in a deeper breath.

"Yes, you are. I've never seen your skin so red."

"It is?" Teardrop said, looking down at his hand, a hand that was shaking as badly as a leaf. "Red … red as a strawberry. But yes, we haven't discussed this. Such a—"

"But you've thought about it?"

"I, well … your father did mention, bring it up once, Ursula. Harry. Once—"

"He did?"

"At, it was at our wedding, in fact. I caught, I was caught off guard—completely that time too."

"You didn't tell me."

"No, I didn't. I don't know why in retrospect."

"So did it, did it frighten you? Is that it? Scare you that badly at the time?"

"I—"

"Does it scare you now? The thought of a child? A baby with me?"

"Yes. It did then and it does now. Must admit as much it does."

"Why?"

"Ursula, you know perfectly well why. It's no secret. Baby, you can't be that naïve."

"No, no, I can't."

"I'm fifty-six, fifty-six. If I live to be seventy-six, how many years is that in total? Not many. And if I should become ill, saddled down by illness, my health begin to deteriorate, in any way, just how fair would it be to you? Still raising a child while I … I mean me, all along, being enfeebled. Broken down. Relying on you. Depending on you every hour. For everything. Little thing there is.

"It … it has such dangerous potential. Such an enormous downside. It seems so overweighted, overloaded against us, Ursula."

"I want a baby by you, Maurice. I don't care. The future, it's ours. It's what belongs to us regardless of anything. I love you today and I'll love you tomorrow, whatever it may bring. There's nothing about that that will change."

And Ursula's dark skin was darker than usual, and even her short Afro took on a glow that could glow in the dark, if it were dark, Teardrop thought.

"You look beautiful, so radiant, stunning right now, Ursula."

"Maurice, it's how Ursula Williams looks when she wants her way."

"I can imagine, well imagine how beautiful you'll look when you carry our baby or babies. Who knows, we might have twins."

"Maurice!"

"Or possibly triplets."

After much discussion, the baby issue was dropped. Ursula and Teardrop decided not to rush things along too fast. After all, they were still on their honeymoon, and Teardrop was back to jump-starting this new chapter of his career. Maybe, they'd decided, they were trying to do too many things at once.

It was Ursula who pretty much advanced that front, that they should tone down things for the time being, but also said they would have a baby—but not just yet.

CHAPTER 27

May 23 marked Ursula and Teardrop's first wedding anniversary. They returned to New York and the Hilton Hotel to celebrate along with Byron, J. C., Iris, and Harry. They had a loyalty to the Hilton, feeling that it was where, for them, the magic began. The six went out to dinner with Teardrop footing the bill. They stayed in New York for a week.

But it was during that week Ursula was sure when it had happened. And today she and Teardrop were driving back from her doctor, Dr. Conolly Freely, with the good news.

Ursula would be steering the car with one hand even if she wasn't this excited.

"It had to happen in New York. In the Hilton Hotel. I'm positive it did!"

"I'm not arguing the point with you, Ursula. We're on the same page."

"It's time now, isn't it? To have a baby?"

"Yes, you'll do just fine with changing the baby's diapers."

"With a little help from my handsome husband."

"I'm great with diapers. Uh ... changing them, that is."

"We'll see, get to see just how skillful you are when it counts."

"Ye of little faith, I see."

"And the 2:00 a.m. feedings."

"Ha."

"A baby!"

"Ursula, the road, baby. You almost landed us in a ditch!"

Of course Teardrop was teasing, but there was excitement seemingly streaming out Ursula's every pore, and the same could be said of Teardrop even if he was trying to play the cool customer, seasoned by the years, marked by the ages; but if you saw his face, his smile, there was probably no other face or smile on Earth quite like his, that could quite possibly match it with the possible exception of Ursula's.

"It had to be the Hilton Hotel, Maurice. When I became pregnant."

"Is Jamal going to ever be in for a surprise when he gets here," Ursula said, zipping up her pants (she hadn't changed clothes since this morning). "Maurice, did you hear me?"

"Oh ... Jamal, yes, Jamal, Ursula."

Teardrop was standing at the bedroom window looking out.

"Maurice ... ," Ursula said, looking at him as if looking for answers.

"Oh ... right, Ursula. Right."

She walked over to him. He held her; they looked out the same window.

"I was wondering if it will be a boy or girl. Daydreaming about it. That's all."

"Boy!" Ursula said assertively.

"Ursula, h-how can you be so sure?"

"I don't know. You have a daughter, so this time you're going to have a son to carry on the Williamses' name."

"Oh, I see," Teardrop said sarcastically. "So this is the ideal mating, marriage of sperm and egg that will biologically produce a male species because the Williamses' name must march into the new millennium that's right around the corner?"

"Uh, something along that order."

"Ursula, a girl will be fine. Do me just fine, thank you."

"But it will be a boy."

"You and that stubborn streak of yours," Teardrop said, kissing her.

"You'll see. You will, Maurice."

Jamal sprang off his bike, leaning it against the porch railing and, in a jiffy, was in the house.

"Hey, anybody home!" Jamal was taller but with little new weight to add to his angular frame, so his pin-striped T-shirts never worried about their stretchability.

"No, Jamal!"

"Aah … Ursula … Then you wouldn't be answering me if you weren't!"

"We're in the kitchen, Jamal," Teardrop said. "Where you'll find us."

"Waiting for—"

"Shucks, don't have to be a rocket scientist to figure that out, Granddad," Jamal said under his breath.

"Jamal!"

"Hi, Ursula, Granddad!"

Jamal kissed Ursula and then hugged Teardrop, wrapping his thin arms around his shoulders.

"Sit down, Jamal, sit—"

"Because you just might need it," Teardrop said. "With the news we've got."

"Yes, we have good, uh, great news. A surprise for you, Jamal—to say the least."

"M-me, Ursula, G-Granddad?" Jamal said, grabbing hold of the kitchen chair.

"Your grandfather and I found out this morning …"

"What, Ursula? What!" It looked like heat was rising off the top of Jamal's forehead.

"I hope you're ready for this, because this is a big one. A big-ee, Jamal."

"I am, Ursula. I am!"

"Ursula does have a way for the dramatic, don't you think, Jamal?"

"Yes, Granddad, she can make you sweat it out, all right. And good." Something Jamal was visibly doing.

"So, Ursula, you'd better tell Jamal before I—"

"We're having a baby, Jamal. Your grandfather and I!"

Jamal's gangly frame did comical contortions in practically every which direction known to man.

"B-baby? Baby!"

"Dr. Freely told us this morning. In … in his office. Your grandfather and I."

Jamal charged out his chair; he kissed Ursula again and then hugged Teardrop again. Then he stood, folded his arms, and looked very serious (as if he'd planned this whole thing out last night in bed).

"Hmm … now how does this work?"

"Oh, in relation to what, Jamal?"

"Ursula, the baby is my—"

"Oh, I see what you're getting at," Teardrop said. "Well, if it's a girl, Jamal, she'll be your aunt."

"Not my cousin?"

"No, Jamal, aunt." Pause.

"But if it's a boy, he'll be your uncle."

"Jamal," Teardrop said, understanding the deep, underlining seriousness of this, "how do you feel about that?"

Jamal took his time. "It's great, Granddad," Jamal said, reclaiming his seat. "As long as she or he knows who's boss!"

Ursula and Teardrop looked at one another as if they wanted to fall to the floor face first with laughter.

"I think it's going to be nice having an uncle or aunt, Ursula, Granddad, around," Jamal said, grinning.

"A child! A sister or brother!"

Arlene shut the study door; she stood behind it. She felt faint, like she was going to drop to her knees if she didn't get over to the desk. And when she got to the desk, her hand slapped the stuff on it off, papers and the books flying off to the floor.

Her head was fevered. It'd been this way since Jamal told her the news. She put her head down on the desk like she wanted to bang it down on top the desk, knock her head off her shoulders—all the ill and sickness in it.

She was crying, sobbing, thinking the world couldn't do any worse to her than this or be more nutty, insane. Wondering what she'd done to it to deserve this. "This is her doing, not Dad's. It was her idea, through her persistence. Dad, Dad, my father—no, no, he wouldn't have any of this—none of it, none of it. He's too sensible. Too sensible. I … I know he is.

"Why? Why? At age fifty-six? This makes no sense, no damned sense at all. None. None!

"And Jamal, the baby, baby older than Jamal like … like some backward, ignorant, primitive backwoods family. Families with this odd, strange family arrangement, mix, mingling—assortment of … awkward range of ages to them made through strange alliances, odd, oddball behavior.

"And me … me … a half sister. At my age. My age … Having no voice in this. Having to accept someone's baby b-because of the situation. It's not fair. It's not in anyway, by anyone's standard, fair!

"If only I could die. Mother, if only I could die!"

Arlene's body tensed.

"Mother, why did you have to die? Pass a—look what's happened. A baby. A baby. Dad's gone crazy. This woman's having a baby by him, Mother."

A month later.

Teardrop, Shorty Boy, and Twelve Fingers were playing at the Blue Spoon for a week, and then two at the Play Book, two old established blues clubs in the San Francisco area. It's the first they'd seen each other since Teardrop's baby announcement via telephone.

"Teardrop, you is a rascal, man," Twelve Fingers said. "Skunk in the woods." Pepper green suspenders were the order of the day, Twelve Fingers tugging them downward.

"Shooting bullets like you still Wyatt Earp," Shorty Boy said.

"Taming the West," Twelve Fingers said.

"Have gun will travel, huh, Teardrop?"

"By the way, Shorty Boy, that was Palladin."

"I know, Twelve Fingers. You know me, like to jump around. Give everybody credit."

"But you certainly do rock us back on our heels, Teardrop, when we received the news."

"I know."

"Didn't Charlie Chaplin have eight, nine of them? Brood of kids. Started, I think, in his fifties too?"

"I certainly knew you guys would razz me. It was just a matter of how bad. But I'm prepared. You can lay it on me as heavy as you want. Ursula and I can take it."

"Hell," Twelve Fingers said, "Shorty Boy and me still come up short. Ain't but so much razing us two can do."

"Ursula, what she got to do with this? Was no pressure on her—was all on you, your shoulders," Shorty Boy said, tipping his pub cap to Teardrop. "And you come through with flying colors, man, I might add."

"Thank you," Teardrop said as if he were taking a commanding bow from the bandstand. "Well, it was put up or shut up, Shorty Boy, and when the time came—"

"If you ain't gloating, Teardrop. Sound like it. If this ain't the first I ever heard—"

"Well, he oughta, should, Twelve Fingers. If it was me, be filling orders out of one of them sperm banks they got going, man. Open up a damned clinic, full time!"

Teardrop picked up Miss Lillian. "We really are happy with this, Ursula and I."

"But you still got that fly in the ointment, don't you, Teardrop?"

"Who, Arlene, Twelve Fingers?"

"Uh-huh. Can't bring it to reconcilement, can you?"

"No."

Shorty boy's head flagged. "Shame it come to this. You and Ursula happy as a lark but still ain't all the way home. S-set things right with family."

"I just don't know how to get through to her. I pray. Honestly pray. So hard. But nothing's happened. Probably Arlene's resentment's worse than before now that we're having the baby. And all our attention, devotion given to, anticipating this event—I can't even think about Arlene f-for now."

"Well, she is a grown woman, Teardrop."

"Uh-huh. All the way grown."

"But she's still my daughter, Shorty Boy, Twelve Fingers. That hasn't changed."

"Was just angry, I suppose," Twelve Fingers said. "Never seen but what she want to see for your future. Was involved in education. You was involved in music. Seemed 'nough at the time. Life done set its route and nothing was to come later."

"But Ursula did come. Marriage. And now the baby. Our baby."

"Yeah, Ursula, marriage, and the baby—in that order."

"Talk to Arlene lately?"

"No, Shorty Boy."

"What, you talk pretty much through Jamal?"

Teardrop said sadly, "Y-you're right about that, Shorty Boy."

"Sometime there somebody in a family both sides can talk to. A go-between," Twelve Fingers said. "Keep both sides kind of current on things."

"That's my grandson, all right."

"Got it in my family too," Twelve Fingers said. "Most families do."

"Mine too, Twelve Fingers," Shorty Boy said.

"Arlene's doing so much these days. Taking on so much."

"What, with that lecturing business of hers?"

"Right, Twelve Fingers. Jamal said in a few weeks she'll be lecturing at Harvard U—"

"Harvard University?"

"In Boston?"

"Ain't but one Harvard, Shorty Boy!"

"Princeton too," Teardrop said.

"Oh, man, Arlene hit the big time, Teardrop," Shorty Boy said. "Still 'member when she was fifteen or so. Cute as the dickens. Pigtails. Nosy though."

"Inquisitive, Shorty Boy."

"Say what you want, Teardrop. Got her mind in your business. Ha. Stuck up in it. Just ain't got no idea how far at the time. Some of the questions I can't even answer, Twelve Fingers—begin to," Shorty Boy laughed. "P-probably can't answer to this day!"

"Yeah, it's a shame the way things go down. Look like bright skies all the way through when they that young and gifted," Twelve Fingers said softly. "Ain't no rain come on Sunday. Not on your side of the street—least. Sunny the whole damned day."

CHAPTER 28

Ursula withdrew her sunglasses from the glove compartment. The sun had just brightened. After putting the sunglasses on, she did only what had become natural: touched her stomach. "When are you going to start acting up, huh? Kicking and squirming like you want to come out of there. I can't wait."

And within minutes, the sky had turned gray, and there was a bolt of lightning and then a big boom, but she was back at the house. She'd driven to the Piggly Wiggly. But even with the stormy weather to come (the forecast said), she sat in the car, shut her eyes, and began thinking about the baby. Who it was going to look like, her or Teardrop? Or would it be a combination of her complexion, Teardrop's eyes or her eyes, Teardrop's complexion, her nose, Teardrop's nose. Oh, it could drive you crazy—mad! This baby thing!

"But it's so much fun guessing, isn't it? And yes, my darling boy, this angel tucked away in my stomach is giving me gray hairs, and each I'll take in stride. I'll try not to be too hard on him. Or difficult with him. Or spoil him."

When she and Teardrop told Iris and Harry about the baby, they went ballistic with joy. And Byron, he'd already put his bid in for godfather status over, of course, J. C's. strong objections.

"Our son might have, just have two godfathers. How's that? I don't know if that will set a precedent or not. But why not two godfathers? Our son's special."

Now Ursula felt like getting out the car, for she'd wrapped herself in that fuzzy blanket of happiness, and it was a warm day in Walker City. Even with the car windows rolled down, the air was sticky, awaiting the predicted heavy downpour.

In the house, even on a warm day, was comfortable. She carried her grocery bags into the kitchen. When she got in the kitchen, she looked at her laptop on the kitchen table and the yellow notepad to the right of the laptop. She let go a huge sigh and then began putting each bag's items, one by one, into the refrigerator.

She was doing well with her book. It was unbelievable how well the story was developing. She was gaining more and more confidence, momentum by the day. Teardrop had encouraged her in elemental ways, but it was coming from within her. She wanted to be a fiction writer so badly. She was beginning to digest the nuances of fiction, how her imagination worked, taking her from the known, the kind of writing she'd done before, nonfiction (basically knowing the shape and personality of the piece), to the unknown—the finding, seeking, and discovering.

Ursula put the last of the eggs on the shelf.

But there were times when the blank page scared her, Ursula thought. And at times she felt it was good to be scared, to have such fear; and at other times, not so good. At times when she was scared, her writing was great, and other times dreadful. And then the rewrites, the endless, miserable rewrites …

But the story was always there to challenge her. For her to make something happen on the page. For her to create something, she thought. To make a world, a world of people and ideas and human experiences.

Ursula, looking at the laptop, began circling the kitchen like her feet were thinking for her.

"Yes. No. Uh … that would work—I think … think so …" But as Ursula talked to herself, she began to slow down and, in no time, pulled out the kitchen chair and then sat in front of the laptop like it was her king and she its slave. But also, like she and it could conquer anything, anything at all that blank yellow legal pad tossed at them.

The rain smashed hard against the kitchen window, and Ursula yawned and then stretched. Her stomach growled, and she laughed, only because she'd been caught off guard.

"I'd better eat. Fix something, and fast."

Only, she felt mesmerized by the rain; it'd been raining for some time in Walker City.

"I did pretty good today, didn't I?"

This was a good day of writing for her and her yellow notepad and her laptop. This was Ursula's procedure now with the book, how she did her work.

There were intermittent patches of bursts of rain that rocked and thundered the sky with unbelievable force. Thinking of Teardrop and the baby, Ursula neglected what she'd intended to do—go over to the stove to cook dinner for herself—but, instead, was over by the hanging plants, looking out on the backyard that, by now, looked like it'd been pummeled by a small angry river. The ground was thoroughly soaked through, and heavy.

The phone rang, and Ursula sprang to attention.

"Coming."

"Hello, good evening."

"Is this Ursula Williams?"

"Y-yes, it is."

"This is Alma Brewer, Armon's mother."

"Yes. Yes …"

"I'm calling to tell you Jamal's been in an accident. Was hit by a car while riding his bike."

"Hit by a car? Riding his—"

"It happened this afternoon, late afternoon. I'm … I'm calling from Faraday Hospital, Mrs. Williams. Arlene asked that I call. To—I know the situation between you."

"Yes, but—"

"Right now, Jamal's unconscious. In intensive care, the intensive care unit. Arlene wants you to call Teardrop, Mrs. Williams. Call her father. She knows he's in San Francisco but not where exactly in San Francisco he's staying."

"Thank you, Mrs. Robinson, thank you!"

"I'll tell Arlene you called Teardrop."

"Yes! Yes, of course!"

When Ursula hung up the phone, she was a wreck.

"Hit by a car. Hit by a car. Jamal hit by a car … ," Ursula said, over and over as her forefinger punched through Teardrop's hotel's telephone number.

"M-Maurice …"

"Ursula?"

"Maurice, Jamal, Jamal's been in an accident. He was hit by a car while riding his bike!"

"What!"

"I just got the call from Alma Brewer. Just got off the phone with her. She called from Faraday Hospital. Jamal's unconscious. In intensive care. Ar-Arlene's there."

"Oh no, no. How did this happen!"

"I'm going to the hospital now right now. As soon as I get off the phone with you."

"And I'm taking the first flight out of San Francisco!"

The rain had stopped well over an hour ago.

When Ursula got to the Faraday Hospital, it's when she became the most nervous. "Jamal ... how could this happen, Jamal? To you ... ?"

It bothered her even more seeing two rain-drenched ambulances parked in Faraday Hospital's emergency entrance with their headlights still on. And Ursula couldn't help but wonder if Jamal had, earlier, possibly been transported from the scene of the accident to Faraday's emergency room by one of them.

She breathed spastically but then took a big breath to calm herself.

But the breath Ursula took was for Arlene's benefit too, for this would be the first she'd see Arlene since their confrontation (something which seemed long ago) at the house, before she and Teardrop married, during their engagement period, when Arlene told her who the *real* Mrs. Williams was—would always be.

And here this tragedy was, and she was walking into Faraday Hospital with twin fears: a fear for Jamal and a fear of Arlene—of just what her reaction toward her would be.

"I'll stay in the hospital though. Until Maurice gets here. Arrives from San Francisco." Already, her mind had been made up about that.

Ursula was at the lobby's reception desk, checking, finding out where Jamal was, room number and floor.

Ursula boarded the elevator. It carried her up to the third floor. When off the elevator, she followed Faraday's clearly marked bright-green directional signs. Even though people were in the corridor with her, she felt she was traveling the corridor alone. It was the weirdest feeling. When she rounded the corner of the corridor and looked straight ahead, she knew, instinctively, it was Armon Brewer's mother. It was her anguish she felt.

"Mrs. Brewer?"

"Mrs. Williams?"

"Yes."

"This is awful. Just awful, Mrs. Williams."

"J-Jamal …"

"No … his condition hasn't worsened, Mrs.—"

"Ursula. Ursula."

"Ursula, but …"

Alma Brewer appeared in her early thirties, around Arlene's age. She was short, stocky, light skinned with short, curly brown hair.

"Arlene's in the room with Jamal. Just family … family's allowed."

"Alma," Ursula said calmly, patiently, "how did the accident happen?"

Alma Brewer began crying. "Armon and Jamal were riding their bikes on Cliff Road. Ar-Armon said because of the road, pavement, c-conditions, the rain slicked the road, that his bike slid out of control, and when the oncoming car tried avoiding him, it's when it struck Jamal's bike. You see, J-Jamal was behind Armon.

"Oh , it was awful, Ursula!" Alma said, crying into her handkerchief. Ursula held her. "Just awful! Armon was in shock. He said Jamal flew off the bike and struck his head!"

While holding on to Alma, Ursula focused in on the closed door and knew Arlene was behind it. *Arlene and Arlene alone.*

"I'm going into the room, Alma."

Alma stepped back, and her hand felt for the bench behind her.

The room, when Ursula entered, had but one light burning—a soft one.

Upon entering the room, the attending nurse said, "Are you family?"

"Yes, she's family. She's my father's wife."

Arlene was bedside, and there Jamal was, breathing into an oxygen mask with the light centered directly above him. Only this sight wasn't what frightened Ursula, for what did was Jamal's immobility, seeing this spunky, peripatetic ten-year-old appearing practically lifeless in a sterile hospital room serving as, ironically, stimuli.

"How is Jamal?"

Arlene's hand was on top of Jamal's. "We don't know yet."

Looking at Jamal, Ursula felt helpless.

"You reached my father?"

"Yes, he's on his way."

"Armon's mother called. We came to the hospital together. She and I. Armon's with his father. Home. He feels awful about this."

And even in this slender shaft of light, neither had looked at the other, their eyes trained solely on Jamal, Ursula gaining confidence that no matter how serious this was, that Jamal was a fighter, that his spirit was still active and alive, serving him in this time of trial.

"His ankle's broken."

"Broken?"

"And bruises ... But thank God, nothing serious. It's the concussion we have to worry about."

"Y-yes."

"Concussion to worry about ..."

It's when Ursula wanted to hold Arlene the way she'd held Alma Brewer outside in the corridor just minutes ago.

Jamal's attending nurse continued to sit in the chair in the corner of the low-lit room.

"We'll have to wait. Wait."

Ursula sought a chair.

Hours later.

A new nurse was on duty. A night nurse. She'd sit a while and then attend to the floor's other patients and then come back to the room to sit more. Ursula still had not eaten (not since lunch). Her stomach hadn't growled. Maybe it was too nervous to. There were times in the chair when she'd actually dozed off but caught herself, scolded and fussed at herself that it wouldn't happen again, but this waiting for Jamal to regain consciousness was such a grim affair, and it was as if she needed something to relieve the tension. And she and Arlene had run out of words, their relationship grinding them to a halt, trenchantly reestablishing itself within so many words, gestures, and attempts at civility.

Alma Brewer had left Faraday for home well over four hours ago.

Ursula had stepped over to Jamal's bed basically to hear him breathe, and from behind she saw Arlene was still awake, alert—waiting for the moment when something medically miraculous, in the room, would happen.

This would be the third prayer Ursula would pray for Jamal. The other two were short. Her heart felt heavy and unclear. Ursula bowed her head.

When she turned, the room door opened.

Arlene, in silence, ran to Teardrop.

"Dad."

They all knew the kind of silence to be maintained in the room.

"Maurice."

Teardrop stood and looked down at the bed. Arlene grabbed him, and she cried into his chest. He kept his eyes shut, and when, finally, they opened, he laid his hand atop Ursula's shoulder, looking into her eyes.

The three stood outside Jamal's room door. The door was shut. With one arm Teardrop held on to Ursula, and with the other, Arlene.

"Dad, I ... can we ..."

Teardrop looked at Ursula. "Yes ... uh, of course we can, Arlene."

"I want to tell you how it happened, Dad. Everything."

Ursula took to the bench in the corridor. She wasn't angry. Her exclusion was expected.

Teardrop had the facts of the accident. While Arlene spoke to him, he'd glance over at Ursula and she the same and then smile, and at times, it would cause him to weigh the two tragedies equally.

"So ... Dad ..."

"We must go back into the room."

"Yes."

"Back inside. You, me, and Ursula, honey."

"Yes."

Teardrop held Arlene's waist.

The on-duty nurse was back in the room.

When Teardrop and Arlene got to Ursula, Teardrop let go of Arlene.

"We'll be right there, Arlene," Teardrop said.

"H-how's my son doing?"

The nurse stood directly over Jamal. "The same, Mrs. Wilkerson."

"Thank you."

"Your grandfather's here, Jamal," Arlene said, taking Jamal's hand. "For you. He flew in from San Francisco. From his engagement with Shorty Boy Logan and Twelve Fingers Eakins, honey."

"Ursula, I couldn't wait to hold you!"

"Me either, Maurice!"

It's as if they were crushing each other; their emotions were so high.

"I just wanted to get here. Be with my family."

"It's no one's fault, Maurice, the accident," Ursula said. "Not ... not Armon's or ... or Jamal's."

"No one's fault. These things—"

"The rain, it came with such force. I was watching it from the kitchen. It'd hit a dead spot but then teemed back down. It was ferocious."

"As you well know by now, Ursula, it's typical for around here. Walker City weather. It's just a matter of not getting caught in it."

"Maurice, we'll stay all night if we have to. That's what we'll do."

"Camp here if we have to."

"Everything's okay with the band?"

"Sure. In fact, I'm to call Shorty Boy and Twelve Fingers as soon as there's a chance." Pause.

"But the baby, Ursula, how's the baby, with all this ex—"

"We're doing fine. Just fine. You don't have to worry about us. Let's get back inside the room with Jamal."

"I'm so glad I have you, Ursula. At a time like this."

It was 2:16 a.m.

There was commotion in the room.

Jamal was in a fit. He'd just snapped out the coma. It was apparent he wasn't aware of his whereabouts.

The nurse rushed over to him. "Your son's out his coma! He's out of it, Mrs. Wilkerson!"

The nurse waited until Jamal's body normalized. It's then when she left the room to get the doctor.

Jamal was looking at Arlene, Teardrop, and Ursula; and you could see he was now conscious of who they were.

"He's conscious of us, Dad."

"Yes, he is, Arlene."

Ursula smiled at Jamal.

Dr. Zhu had been in the room for a while. The hospital room was fully lit.

"Yes, we'll put him through a battery of tests tomorrow," Dr. Zhu said. "With a good meal in his stomach and breakfast later this morning, I think he'll be fine. From what I can determine. It'll only be his ankle that will have to heal, of course. All in all, he was a lucky young man."

When Dr. Zhu left the room, Jamal's oxygen mask was removed.

"Mom! Granddad! Ursula!"

"Now, now, honey," Nurse Margery Hilliard cautioned, "don't try to do or say too much. Your body was in shock for quite some time. You take it easy now, okay … ?"

"Y-yes, ma'am."

The three walked over to him.

"Jamal …" Arlene was in tears.

"I know what happened, Mom. I … I remember everything, Granddad, Ursula."

"I'm going to get you a nice hot meal, Jamal. That's okay with you?" Nurse Hilliard said.

"Thank you, thank you." Then Jamal took a deep breath as if he were exhausted.

"We're here, Jamal," Teardrop said.

"I'm sorry, Granddad. I know you were in San Francisco, sir. Sorry you had to come back on account of me."

Teardrop let Jamal's comment pass, knowing it was his young grandson talking, who probably wished to express his feelings about what had happened to his family and chose him.

"You remember just what happened?"

"Yes, Granddad. All of it."

"Does it scare you now?"

"No."

They, Ursula, Arlene, and Teardrop, looked at each other relieved.

"Not a bit."

Arlene began caressing Jamal's dry-as-a-stick forehead.

"Feels good, Mom. It really does," Jamal said, shutting his eyes.

Nurse Hilliard, as promised, was back in the room with a tray of food. Ursula, who hadn't eaten in well over eighteen hours, felt a stab of hunger invade her stomach; it had to be because she saw and smelled Jamal's food, no matter how bland it looked on the tray.

"W-was that you, Ursula?" They were standing away from Jamal's bed.

"Sadly, yes, Maurice," Ursula said, embarrassed by her growling, overactive stomach.

"You did have—"

"Well, I was about to fix dinner, Maurice, for myself, but …"

"But?"

"Well, I got involved with my writing, and—"

"Oh, I thought it had something to do with me," Teardrop laughed. "Lonely, uh, while—"

"I'm well past that stage now."

"Then the honeymoon's over."

"Been over!"

"Let me feed you, if you don't mind," Margery Hilliard said. "By tomorrow, we'll let you do everything on your own. But for the first few hours, at least, Jamal, we like pampering our patients. Spoil them rotten for at least one day."

Jamal had eaten, and now it was just a matter of whether everyone would spend the remainder of the morning in the hospital, now that the crisis had cleared.

Jamal was in the room resting. Arlene, Ursula, and Teardrop were outside the room door.

"Dad, the two of you don't have to stay."

"But I want to, Arlene."

"Maurice, I think Arlene's right. Things do look good for now."

"And, Dad, I mean, I don't think you should, well, you are playing in San Francisco. Jamal feels guilty enough."

"Arlene, now that's unreasonable to ask of me." Teardrop looked at Ursula. "Y-you mean you agree with that too, Ursula?"

"I do, Maurice. It's just Jamal's ankle, Dr. Zhu said. Nothing more earth-shattering. And if he'd broken it and I'd called, you'd probably call him to console him. Certainly not hop on a plane and fly back to Walker City."

"Uh, yes, that makes sense."

"You know Jamal will understand. If anyone would, it'd be Jamal, Dad. Your grandson."

"Again, you're right."

Adoringly, Teardrop looked at Arlene.

"Yes, Arlene. Yes. It's a deal."

They hugged.

"I love you, Dad."

"I love you, honey."

"Have a safe trip back. And say hello to Shorty Boy and Twelve Fingers for me, will you?"

"You bet."

"I know they were worried."

"They were. But I'll call them when I get back to the house. By now, they must be on pins and needles."

Ursula was halfway up the hospital's corridor when she turned back to Teardrop.

"Coming, Ursula."

Ursula waited for Teardrop as he walked as fast as he could toward her.

$$\backsim\!\mathscr{M}\!\backsim$$

The car pulled away from the house.

"Back to San Francisco."

"It's one place I've never been but would love to visit one day.

"Ursula, you never told me that."

"Everyone who visits it says they love it."

"Including yours truly, baby."

"Four hours of sleep, Maurice."

"Does it look it?"

"No, not at all. It was just a comment."

"Y-you'll keep me abreast of everything back here, won't you?"

"I'm going to be there, at the hospital, every waking hour. Don't you worry."

"Ursula, the book. Don't forget about the book during all of this. Not fall behind."

"I'll carry my yellow notepad to the hospital, and laptop."

"And Arlene?"

"She'll just have to get used to me. She knows why I'm there."

"I'd like to say because of me, baby. Because I'm not here but in Frisco, but I know you and Jamal have something that's quite unusual. Remarkable between you."

"Whenever you're out of town, Maurice, Jamal's always been there for me."

"Comes through."

"Always. Jamal—now I'm going to be there for him. I look forward to it."

"And eating, you mustn't go so long without eating under any condition, Ursula," Teardrop said, touching Ursula's stomach, knowing the baby was what really worried him.

"I won't," Ursula said, not taking her eyes off Dawkin's Road. "That I promise, Maurice."

Ursula was back in Faraday Hospital. It was 11:10 a.m. She had her legal notepad and laptop (it was in a black leather case). Ursula opened the room door.

"Oh," Arlene said, looking up from the book on her lap. "Good morning."

"Good morning," Ursula replied.

Ursula saw Arlene had changed out yesterday's clothes.

"Jamal's sleeping."

Ursula looked at him. She smiled. "He's eaten?"

"Yes."

"The tests ..."

"They begin shortly, in about another hour, Dr. Zhu said."

"Oh."

Arlene and Ursula were the only two in the room. Arlene looked at Ursula again and then stuck her eyes back in the book, concentrating, what seemed, more than before.

Ursula moved over to the chair in the opposite corner of the room, where there was light too. She'd do her work there, she thought, keep pace with the book.

"M-Mom ..."

"Yes, yes, Jamal?" Arlene was out her chair.

"Ur-Ursula?" Jamal said, now sighting her.

"Good morning, Jamal."

"Wow, Ursula, you're back."

Ursula got out her chair. "That I am, Jamal."

Ursula and Arlene were on opposite sides of the bed. "I drove your grandfather off to the airport this morning then circled back here."

"Back to San Francisco for Granddad. Back to the band."

"Yes."

"I ... I remember last night oh so well. And Mom, this morning, told me you—that you two talked him into going back out there."

"It wasn't easy, Jamal," Ursula said.

"I know."

"Not at all, I guess. Your mother—"

"But I'm glad ... glad, Ursula, you did, Ursula. I'm going to pass those tests this morning with no sweat. It just feels like a bump on the head anyway, now. Otherwise, I'm fine," Jamal said, touching the bandage on his forehead, actually wincing, but then bravely ignoring it.

Arlene and Ursula laughed.

"Well, at least you're full of, brimming with confidence this morning, Jamal," Arlene said.

"I should say so," Ursula added.

"It's just my ankle, Mom, Ursula—and even that, why I'll be up and on my feet in no time flat."

Jamal's ankle was in a plaster cast. He'd been put in a wheelchair and taken to the testing area. Arlene and Ursula hung back in Jamal's room. He'd been out the room for a little over a minute.

"So ... my dad got off to International all right this morning?" Arlene said from across the room, breaking the silence.

Ursula looked up from her legal notepad. "Yes, just fine."

"It, how did he sleep last night?"

Ursula hesitated. "Maurice was a bit, somewhat restless—what's for him. But then settled down. His restlessness didn't last long. He was bone tired."

"The flight in. The rush to the hospital. The worry. Anxiety."

"They were all contributing factors."

"Yes."

"Where were you, may I ask, when it—oh ... that's right, Alma told me. She called you."

"Yes, I was in the house."

"Uh, yes." Pause.

"I'd just gotten in from the university. Was about to fix dinner. I drove here t-to Faraday, but I don't know how. Thomas, Alma's brother, came for her last night. Yes ... we got here, but I still don't know how. But Alma, she did help out a lot. Was of immense help to me."

"It's only when we got here, to the hospital, that I think she began losing it too, e-emotionally, that is. Jamal's just as much a son to her as Armon's to me."

"Yes, last night, she was emotionally spent."

"Yesterday's rains just hit so fast. So sudden."

"I've ... I've noticed it's typical in Walker City. The rains."

"Very, yes, very typical." Pause.

"You got my dad right away? Were in immediate contact with him?"

"Yes, Shorty Boy and Twelve Fingers—"

"You know them?"

"Yes. I do. I met them when, the time they came to Walker City. The house together. They—"

"T-to do what?"

"You don't know? Maurice, your father didn't tell you?"

"No."

"He, I … well, you see, I called them to come down. To see if Shorty Boy and Twelve Fingers—"

"Dad mentioned how you initiated it but nothing more. Their coming down to … oh, so … so that's how it worked. Shorty Boy and Twelve Fingers came to talk about Dad's career. To get it off the ground again."

"Yes."

"To get my dad back to where he belonged. Something I believed in for so long. But something I … I couldn't do, didn't think about doing. But I'm glad someone did. My father's a genius. I knew that even when I was small." Pause.

"My mother—you don't mind, do you?"

"Oh no, I'm well beyond that now," Ursula said.

"My mother said it's how she felt about my father's talent too. That Dad was a genius. So I've lived with that notion of my father since small."

"It's how I feel about your father's music too. It was clear, vividly clear from my first experience listening to it."

"There's just so much struggle with this kind of music. The blues, so little fame, attention."

"It's the personal satisfaction. Fulfillment."

"Of course. And keeping a tradition alive. And doing something that you love—and doing it well."

"Your father, I think—correct me if I'm wrong—has never lost sight of that. Not for a day of his life."

"No, and you're not wrong. This ethic's never left him. Dad's music has so much integrity. It hasn't forgotten its roots. Traded it in for something less responsible or authentic. Populist music."

Jamal was back from his tests. The nurse was wheeling him in his wheelchair and into his room.

"You can be proud of your son, Mrs. Wilkerson," Nurse Shirley Connors said. "He—"

"Told you I was going to pass those tests with flying colors. Told you no sweat!"

"Yes, that's true, that's true," Arlene said.

"That you did, Jamal!" Nurse Connors said.

"It was a breeze," Jamal said as Nurse Connors helped him out the wheelchair and into bed.

"And so we're going to move him in to another room today, Mrs. Wilkerson. Jamal will be out of the suite," she laughed. "And into ... well, it won't be a private room like this. Jamal'll be with other patients. He's already been told the bad news."

"Aww ... that's okay, Nurse Connors, I'm not going to be here long anyway. Since I'll be out in no time. Wait and see."

"I hope you're not planning a jailbreak," Arlene laughed.

"Aww ... Mom, come on ..."

"Uh, by the way," Ursula said, "let me call your grandfather, Jamal. I told him I'd call as soon as I got good news."

"Great, Ursula. Great!"

Ursula was heading for the door.

"And tell him I said hello, please, Ursula. That I love him!"

"He's doing fine, Maurice. Jamal said he was going to pass those tests, whatever Dr. Zhu threw at him, and he did."

"Yes, that's my grandson."

"And, he's already checked himself out the hospital—if you want to know everything. The whole story."

"Cocky, yes, cocky."

"He is. And, oh, before I forget, Jamal says he loves you—not that he sends his love but loves you. And I love you too, Maurice. Me and the baby," Ursula whispered into the phone. "I wanted to say that to you before hanging up. I love you."

And then Ursula sensed there was someone standing behind her, over her shoulder.

"Okay, Maurice, I—"

And Ursula, when she turned, saw it was Arlene.

"May I speak to my dad?" Arlene said.

"Maurice, hold on."

Ursula handed the phone to Arlene.

"Thanks," Arlene said. "Uh, hello, Dad. Hello ..."

CHAPTER 29

Following day.

Ursula had gotten Jamal's new room number from the desk.

Jamal was told the move would take place this morning. Ursula stayed until four o'clock yesterday and then left Faraday. Arlene was still in the hospital when she left. Today, Ursula was at Faraday the same time as yesterday.

"Hi, Ursula!" Jamal said from across the room.

"Hi, Jamal."

This room was big. Ursula greeted two other patients in the room who responded cheerfully.

"Good morning," Arlene said.

"Good morning."

"How do you like my new room, Ursula? Not bad, huh?"

The windows were larger, and today's sun made the room warm, maybe too warm, Ursula thought.

"No, not bad at all, Jamal." She kissed his forehead, avoiding the bandages. She felt comfortable doing it. She was without her yellow notepad and laptop. She'd decided not to stay as long today since Jamal's situation had changed drastically for the better.

"Two more days, Ursula," Jamal said while Ursula took her seat. "And I'm, then I'm out of here Dr. Zhu says. Not much to count, huh?"

For some odd reason Ursula looked at Arlene, who was sitting on the other side of Jamal. And she knew why, for Arlene's body had shaken slightly at Jamal's pronouncement, and Ursula wondered why but would dare not ask.

"It's not bad here, Ursula, so I'm not complaining. Everybody's been real nice to me, but there's nothing like home ... r-right, Mom?"

"R-right, Jamal."

"It's going to feel great to sleep in my own bed again. My own TV. My computer. The works."

"Simple pleasures, huh, Jamal? It's what you miss most, probably, the most when you're away from home. The small—"

"And plus, Ursula, Mom's going to have to wait on me. B-but wait a minute," Jamal said anxiously. "Mom, Mom," Jamal said looking at Arlene, "I can't believe it, Mom."

"What can't you believe?"

"I hadn't thought of it! And you either, with all that's going on. I forgot, in two days, ma'am, y-you're supposed to be going off on your lecture tour to Harvard and Princeton. That's right."

"Uh, right, Jamal."

Oh, that's why she looked uncomfortable before, Ursula thought.

"B-but today I was going to call both universities to tell them it will be, my lecture will have to be cancelled due to my son's injury."

"Dag, what rotten luck. Now I really feel bad about the accident. Just awful, ma'am."

"Don't, Jamal. Just thank God you're alive. It's—"

"W-who was going to take care of Jamal if—"

"The Brewers. But not now, under these conditions. That would be taking advantage of them. Asking far too much of them after the accident."

"Yes, the Brewers, like always, Ursula. When Mom leaves for her lectures." Jamal folded his arms out in front of him, seemingly displeased with the current state of affairs.

"Yes, of course. You've told me that be—yes, of course, the Brewers. How did I—"

"But not now, Ursula. Dag, Mom. Dag!"

"Forget."

Ursula was thinking hard and fast and then stood.

"Only, maybe I can help, help then," Ursula said assertively.

"You, Ursula?" Jamal said.

"Just how many days are involved—that you'll be gone?" Ursula said, the question directed to Arlene.

"A total of four, four days in all."

"That'll be easy. Jamal can stay with me at the house the four days you're gone."

"You?" Arlene said.

"Yeah, Mom. Ursula. With Ursula, Mom. Ursula!"

"Y-you'd do that?"

"Why not. It'll … it should work out fine. Just fine for us."

"I mean, I would—my flight that day's not until two thirty."

"Yeah, Mom. Yeah. You can drive me home, and then Ursula, Ursula can come by with the car and pick me up—"

"Slow down, Jamal. Ha. Slow down, honey," Arlene said. "Let's not jump the gun. G-get too far ahead of ourselves with this."

"Right, Ursula? Right?"

"You bet, Jamal!"

"See, Mom? See, it's been worked out for you. Harvard, Princeton—my mom is definitely on her way!"

Ursula covered her mouth to laugh before picking up the phone to talk to Teardrop.

"Hello, Maurice, guess who's coming to dinner? Or, should I say, to stay with me for four days in the house? You'll, ha, never guess. Never!"

Ursula was off the phone. She felt stimulated, fired up. Teardrop couldn't believe his ears. He was blown away. He said he loved her like crazy for jumping in the breach like she did (she felt like saying "feet first"). For "saving the day," as he'd put it.

"It was the right thing to do. Anybody in my position would've done the same."

But since she'd made the suggestion and the idea had been sealed, she'd been floating on cloud nine. Here she was carrying Teardrop's baby in her womb, and now she was to have Jamal for four days. What other luck was going to fall her way? Ursula thought.

And since Jamal had spent so many days at the house with her and Teardrop over the past year, she knew what his favorite meals were.

"It's going to be fun. With me and Jamal in the house."

Today, Arlene, before leaving Faraday Hospital, thanked her. Privately she'd thanked her. It was genuine, not warmly done, but Ursula wasn't looking for that. All that mattered was she'd done the right thing, was present in the room, was privy to information, recognized a potential problem and pitched in to help whether on good terms with Arlene or not. She held no bad vibes, negative feelings toward Arlene; she simply assessed the problem and did something about it.

"I have a surprise for Jamal though." Pause.

"I'm surprised by—that I hadn't thought of it sooner. Hmm. Jamal's going to be bowled over, just you wait and see. Like I said, it just surprises me it's the first I've thought of it. Hmm. I'm slipping. Must be. I'm usually better than that."

Then Ursula patted her stomach. "Your mother talks a lot to herself, doesn't she? It's your father's fault, Maurice. You see, he leaves your mother in this big, old house by herself. So blame it on him. Your father, if you're going to blame anyone. O-okay, Maurice?"

(Ursula had already named the unborn baby boy.)

The nurse had wheeled Jamal to the Faraday Hospital's entrance. She stopped. Jamal smiled. "Thanks for everything, ma'am."

"Yes, thanks for everything, Elizabeth," Arlene said.

Then Arlene handed Jamal his crutches.

"Thank you."

Jamal stood up on one leg, and the crutches were all his. Of course he'd practiced with them, becoming quite adept with them at this early stage of the game.

The red Impala was in wait.

"Mom"—Jamal grinned—"your car never looked better!"

Arlene smiled.

"Wow," Jamal said, drawing air into his lungs, "doesn't the air smell de-delicious!"

"It's always the little things we miss most when they're taken from us, Jamal. That count. The things we take for granted. Life's small details."

"I'll remember that," Jamal said, hopping into the car, Arlene taking his crutches so she could put them on the backseat. "Definitely, Mom."

Ursula knew Arlene said it would be all right for her to get to the house by 10:30 a.m. Eager? Ursula couldn't' help but be eager about today, almost to the point of turning this entire thing into a mass production—to start this new "adventure" with Jamal. Ursula parked the turquoise station wagon outside the house in anticipation of them.

And Ursula waited no more than a minute for the red Impala to roll toward the house.

"Mom, Ursula's already here!"

"Yes, she is."

"Can't wait, I guess. Neither can I!"

Arlene glanced at Jamal and saw how crisp his brown face looked.

"Ursula!" Jamal yelled out the car window. "Ursula!"

Ursula got our the car and waved to Jamal. "Hi, Jamal!"

"You're early, Ursula!"

"I know, Jamal!"

Each sounded as if they were shouting at the other over an airplane's engine sitting on a runway about to take off into the mist.

"Mom said ten thirty, and it's …"

"What? Ten thirteen?"

"Yes, Ursula."

The car stopped right in front of the house. Arlene was the first out the car.

"Hi," she said.

"Hi," Ursula said.

Arlene got Jamal's crutches. In two seconds flat, Jamal was standing up on them.

Yesterday, at Faraday's, Ursula saw him up on the crutches, so she knew Jamal was gaining confidence with them.

"Stay there, Ursula. Stay there."

"Okay, Jamal."

"Don't move."

Ursula didn't move an inch.

It's when Jamal walked over to her and Ursula kissed his forehead.

"These things are like cool, beyond cool—real nifty, aren't they, Ursula?" Jamal said, looking at his crutches. "I mean they are. D-definitely are."

"Definitely, definitely are, Jamal."

Jamal turned to Arlene. "Okay, ready, Mom, for I can direct you on how to pack, what I'll be taking to Ursula's. Off to the house."

Jamal's suitcase was in the station wagon's cargo area. The small suitcase was light, something even Ursula could carry in her delicate condition once she and Jamal got to the house. Jamal's underwear, socks, one pair of jeans and three pin-striped T-shirts, brush, comb, and toothbrush.

The car's door was open. Jamal was kind of lingering there by it, just holding on to Arlene.

"I'll call, honey. Don't you worry."

"Promise, Mom?"

"Oh, Jamal, don't be … oh …" Arlene hugged him. "Love you."

"Love you, Mom."

Ursula was behind the car's steering wheel.

Arlene and Jamal kissed.

When Jamal sat down on the car seat, Arlene took his crutches and opened the car's back door, laying the crutches across the floor's length.

Ursula figured it was time to go.

"G-good-bye. Have a safe trip," Ursula said to Arlene.

"Yes, good-bye," Arlene replied. Arlene held on to Jamal's hand for a good three seconds and then let go.

"Talk to you later, Mom."

"Will do, Jamal."

Ursula sensed the time was right for her to start the car.

To say Jamal was settled in by now would, indeed, be an understatement.

He was in "his" room (actually the guest room).

"How do things look, Jamal?"

"Terrific, Ursula. Yeah, terrific."

Jamal was sitting on the bed. Ursula was standing. Jamal began patting the bed. "This bed's going to beat a hospital bed any day. Any day of the week, Ursula."

"It is a good—"

"This mattress is about five, six inches thicker. I bet. M-much firmer."

"Well …"

"You didn't have to sleep on them, Ursula—I did!"

"Jamal, ha, that's true."

"Ursula …"

Ursula could feel the shift in mood.

"You really came through."

"I—"

"I mean with this whole thing. Idea of yours."

"It's what f-families do for one another when there's a problem. You should be able to turn to family. Someone should pull you through. I have that kind of family back in Jersey City."

"I would've met your family too. Them at the wedding, if it hadn't been for ..."

And Jamal went completely mum.

Ursula didn't know what to do or say as she looked at Jamal and saw more than a frown on his face—something that looked more like a struggle.

"I wanted to go to the wedding. I—"

"I know you—"

"New York. At your and ... and Granddad's wedding. I ... I wanted to be there, Ursula."

"Jamal, you—"

"I cried. A lot. I ... but I didn't let Mom see me. Let on to Mom I did. I know you and my mother don't get along. Almost from the beginning. When you first came down here for that magazine interview with Granddad. We hit it off right away but not you and Mom ..."

Ursula just stood there and listened to Jamal, for it seemed he had a lot to get off his chest, and it's what he was doing, unbundling his feelings, trusting her with them implicitly.

"And it wasn't your fault, Ursula. Not at all—none of it. You didn't do anything wrong. No, no way."

"No, I didn't," Ursula said as if to further set the record straight.

"Nothing. It's been Mom's fault all along, and I know it."

Pause.

"But have you ever loved someone, Jamal?"

"Y-yes, Ursula. I mean you and Granddad and Mom and Grandmother. Yes, Ursula."

"Sometimes you can't let go of that love. Can't bear to let go of it. You see, Jamal, your mother had an ideal family. A family who, in her eyes, was perfect. And your grandmother became, it was like she, in a way, ran the family with your grandfather out on the road so much with the band—had become, by default, the head of the household. The family.

"Jamal, are you ... do ... are you following me so far?"

"Yes, so far."

"And so then when your grandmother died, well ... your grandfather just couldn't go on with his career. Not without your grandmother. So when he moved in with your mother—"

"Mom, in a way, Ursula, in a way, became the head of the household … Ur-Ursula?"

"Right. Right. See?"

"Yes, I—right, right."

"This is what it's been about. From the start. N-nothing more. Your mother has felt the loss of two people she loves: her mother and her father. The loss of family as she once knew it, Jamal. How it'd been for her."

"Oh."

Pause.

"But, okay, right, right, Ursula. B-but you still didn't do anything wrong. Anything bad to hurt Mom, d-did you?"

And Ursula felt a burning sensation in the lining of her stomach. "No."

"Then …"

"Sometimes things in another person's heart can't be changed. Sometimes it's just something we all must live with. But it doesn't mean we stop trying. Not that. It—I don't think it should ever mean that or it should get to that point."

Jamal looked at Ursula and then down to the floor and then back up to her.

"Ursula …"

"Yes, Jamal?"

He squirmed a bit. "I'm going to be back riding my bike in no time flat!"

"You are?"

"You know me!"

"Of course I do!"

"I already told Armon."

"How's he—"

"He's over it. I wouldn't let him sulk. It wasn't his fault anyway, what happened."

"No, it wasn't, Jamal."

"In fact, I was going to call him."

"Go ahead. There're some things I have to do around the house. And then later fix your lunch. And I have—do I have a surprise for you."

"You do? A surprise?"

"Why I hadn't thought of it before, I don't know."

"Me either," Jamal said, grinning slyly as only he could.

"Oh, this is going to be a great four days—you and me together, Jamal. It's already started off with a bang."

"Ursula, uh, can I try guessing what the surprise is?"

"Of course. Go ahead, guess away, because you'll never figure out what—"

"A video game?"

"No."

"A … a movie?"

"No."

"Uh … uh … uh …"

Ursula waited while smiling wickedly to say no to Jamal again, or however many more times it took.

Ursula and Jamal ate lunch. And by now Jamal had bugged Ursula to death, to no end about "his" surprise (not even coming close to what was making Ursula laugh harder and louder with each failed attempt). Ursula told him to go to his room, and in eight minutes she'd be there with his "big, big" surprise.

No doubt, Jamal acceded to such an innocuous request. Ursula was in the kitchen. She laughed as she did her thing, at the joy and vitality Jamal brought to the house, and thought of the baby, of its potential possibilities.

"Jamal and those crutches of his."

For Ursula was getting used to the *thump* of the crutches in the house, from floor to floor, signaling when Jamal was on the move or on the prowl, as Ursula had summed it up. Later, Armon was to visit. The two of them were to play video games and catch up on things.

Ursula was ready or, better still, the surprise was ready. She was proud of herself, quite. Jamal would be thrilled to death! She thought.

"I just know it. I've outdone myself. N-now to get upstairs without falling!"

Of course Ursula knew she was just having fun at her own expense. She wouldn't fall up the stairs, no way, no shape or form, while carrying Jamal's surprise.

"Ur-Ursula, is that you?"

"Who else, Jamal? It's too early for ghosts to come out the woodwork."

"Aww ... you wouldn't scare me anyway. Even though I bet there are ghosts in Walker City, uh, just not in this house. But definitely elsewhere."

"I see your radar's working extremely well, keenly, since I'm coming with your big, big—"

"Ursula, should I shut my eyes?"

"Oh ... by all means, Jamal. Do!"

"Done. I can't see a thing, even if you put it, the surprise, that is, in front of me!"

"Are you sure, Ja—"

"Sure!"

"Because I'm about—"

"I know where you are. Like you said, Ursula, boy is my radar working. Is hot now!"

Ursula was but a foot away from the room. She steadied herself. She felt her toes tingle. "Oh no!" Pause.

"This is ..."

""Ursula ... well?"

"Voila!" Ursula said, springing into the room. "You may open your eyes, Jamal!"

"A ... wow, a *banana split*? Wow, Ursula, *wow*!"

"Yes, the Walk-In Restaurant's not the only one who can serve up a fancy banana split in Walker City. Ursula Williams can too!"

Jamal was back on his bed, his crutches laying across it, his good foot tapping the floor. "It looks delicious, Ursula, just delicious."

Ursula brought the banana split to Jamal, and he took it out her hand and then picked up the large spoon that had been at the bottom of the long, wide-shaped container it was being served in, and began eating his banana split like he was in the Walk-In Restaurant in the heart of Walker City, having had his main course, of course, with Ursula and Teardrop earlier.

The container was empty.

"It was, Ursula, it was really too good to be true." Jamal was rubbing his stomach. "To believe, Ursula. Unbelievable ..."

"Thank you, Jamal. We'll do it again before Sunday?"

"We will?"

"There's plenty left in the refrigerator."

"Ursula, you didn't fix yourself one?"

"I'm going to have enough problems, uh, weightwise, with the baby. No sense looking for trouble, Jamal. Not now."

"Yes … I see what you mean, Ursula. The baby. Ha. Yeah, the baby."

"So Armon will be by—"

"By three o'clock. On his bike."

Jamal fell back on the bed. "Too bad he missed the banana split," Jamal said sarcastically.

"Oh … there I go again, Jamal, I wasn't thinking."

"It's okay. Give Armon a can of Coke and some nachos, and he's fine. Doesn't take much to please him."

"Which we have plenty of in the house, I might add."

Jamal was holding on to his stomach. "But I'm so full though. I think I'll pass on the nachos and Coke, Ursula, when Armon gets here."

"We'll see, we'll see about that, Jamal," Ursula said warily.

It's when Jamal came off his back and looked at Ursula's stomach. "May I, Ursula?"

And Ursula knew what Jamal was referring to.

"Yes, Jamal, even though there's not much activity going on right now. But who knows, the baby might just fool us soon," Ursula laughed as Jamal's hand reached out for her stomach.

Armon had come and gone. Ursula and Jamal were down in the kitchen. Dinner was about forty-five minutes ago.

Ring.

"Let me, Ursula. Do the honors. I want to get all the practice I can on my crutches."

"Right!"

"Mom! Mom, how are you doing, Mom? Y-you did? What a day. What a day Ursula and I are having, Mom. Unbelievable! Ursula"—Jamal looked over at Ursula—"sprang this great surprise on me. A banana split, Mom! My favorite. Ursula made it. Ursula!"

The ensuing conversation between Arlene and Jamal had hit about the five-minute mark when Jamal turned to Ursula, saying, "Ursula, my mom would like to speak to you."

"Yes, oh, hello."

"Hello."

"I see you got to Harvard, Boston safely."

"It was a pleasant flight in."

"That's nice."

"Jamal told me everything."

"Yes, I know."

"The banana split—everything."

"I, yes, I heard him." Ursula smiled at Jamal. "I guess he can't keep a secret."

"Not when he's having so much fun. The way he is with you."

Long pause.

"Thank you, Ursula."

It was the first Arlene had called her Ursula without sarcasm seemingly dripping from it, and Ursula wondered what her face looked like when she had.

"Y-you're welcome, Arlene."

"W-well, I have, must go. C-can you put Jamal back on, please?"

"Oh sure, sure. Jamal, your mother."

"I'll call again."

"Of course."

The four days at the house had been on a fast track (just ask Jamal and Ursula just how fast).

"We have everything, don't we, Jamal? Everything's on board in the car?" Ursula asked, looking to the back of the station wagon.

"The suitcase, you mean, don't you, Ursula?" Jamal said, his voice flat as an iron.

"Yes, the suitcase," Ursula said, knowing what she'd said made no sense, that her anxiety got the better of her and so was quickly exposed by Jamal—but not in a deliberate way.

"I'm glad Mom's coming home and all from her trip"—Jamal appeared close to sulking—"but where did the time, four days go? Even Granddad over the phone last night said the same thing."

"The baby too, Jamal."

"Ha. But the baby can't talk, Ursula."

"But that doesn't stop me from talking to him. He'll make up for it, our one-sided conversations, one day."

Jamal looked at the front yard's grass.

"The only good thing about being on crutches," Jamal laughed, "is I don't have to cut the grass!"

"Jamal!"

"It's true, Ursula. I'm not kidding. I mean, I miss riding the bike, but as soon as I'm able to—"

"Which will be soon …"

"Yeah. Then Mom's going to have no pity on me, I guess. She's going to make me cut the grass no matter what."

"Think so?"

"Watch, you just watch and see."

Then Jamal glanced at Ursula's stomach. "I hope you give him a break. I mean, when he gets about eight or nine, around the age I started cutting the grass. Became my responsibility to do."

"I don't know, Jamal. Maybe by then, you'll be able to build a good case for him."

It was Saturday, 3:25 p.m.

If all went as planned, Arlene should be at the house. If she wasn't, Ursula and Jamal would wait in the car.

Arlene's car was parked in the driveway.

"Mom's home, Ursula!"

"That she is, Jamal!"

"Boy, Ursula, I can't wait to see her!"

Ursula gripped Jamal's hand.

Arlene had heard the car proceed up to the house. In a flash, she was out on the front porch. The sun shone in her face. Jamal couldn't wait to get out the station wagon—crutches and all.

But quickly, Arlene rushed toward the car, and Jamal and Arlene hugged and kissed. The car door closed, but the window was open. Ursula got out the car and opened the back door and handed Arlene Jamal's crutches.

"Thanks," Arlene said.

Ursula stepped back.

"Here you are, Jamal."

Jamal took his crutches. "Thanks, Mom," he said, hopping on them. "Ursula, thanks."

Ursula shut the car door.

"I'm really fantastic with these now, Mom—r-right, Ursula?"

Then Ursula opened the cargo door to get the suitcase.

"I'll take it. Thank you," Arlene said.

Jamal was still showing off with his crutches.

"'Fantastic' is the word all right, Jamal. Out of this world," Arlene said, turning her head back to him.

Ursula began following Arlene.

Then she stopped, for she realized, practically by rote, she was about to step on the house's front porch, go into Arlene's house, something she hadn't done when Jamal packed for the four-day stay at the house, preferring to stand out on the porch then, even having the time to walk the yard, waiting until everything was done, everything of Jamal's was stowed away in the station wagon. After all, the last time she was in Arlene's house was the same day she was told to never walk in it again.

Arlene took the suitcase as far as the front staircase, not beyond.

"Are ... are you coming in?" Arlene said, for Ursula was still out on the porch, standing on it in a daze, thinking yet not thinking at this point while things swirled around her.

Her stomach had a sick, queasy feeling. But Arlene opened the screen door for Jamal, and she held it open for Ursula.

Once in the house, Ursula still felt uncomfortable, almost as if she'd developed this manic phobia. She used her hands to try to hide her face.

"Ursula, are you okay? T-the baby? Can I get you a glass of water?"

"Yes ... that would be fine, fine, Jamal. Yes, yes, the baby, Jamal."

"Sit then," Arlene said, taking hold of Ursula's arm, helping her over her to the couch.

"T-thank you."

Pause.

"I ... I guess I'm faint, a little faint."

"Does this happen often?"

"No, this is—"

"The first time?"

"Yes."

"Back with the water, Ursula. And I didn't spill a drop. Told you I'm good with these crutches, Mom."

"So I see, Jamal. You weren't just bragging before."

Ursula took a sip of water from the glass and then held the glass of water steadier.

"Did you knock them dead, Mom?"

"Jamal, I'm proud to say, yes, I did. And I came up with so many new ideas during the trip. I've done a series of papers, but now I want to write a book, really stretch my ideas, find a number of hard-core themes and integrate them. Weave them into a whole. But I don't know how … how to do that. That construct."

"Then Ursula can help, Mom. Ursula knows all about that. After all, Ursula's a writer!"

Water from the glass spilled off Ursula's lips.

"Right, Ursula?"

"Oh, I'm sorry … ," Ursula said, apologizing, since water had spilled on the rug.

"Don't worry, Ursula. I'll get a napkin. I should've brought one for you in the first place. Be right back."

Thump.

"Ursula …"

So it's what she looks like when she uses my name, Ursula thought.

"You know Jamal by now. H-how impulsive he is. That side of his nature."

"Yes, v-very," Ursula stuttered.

"T-to make such a suggestion, it's out the question."

"Yes, yes, it is," Ursula said, agreeing. "I'm in the midst of writing my own book. My own book project. I—"

"Let's face it, we're both victims of Jamal's impulsiveness. He was trying to think for the two of us." Arlene frowned. "He didn't know any better, but we do. I think cooler heads will prevail," Arlene said rationally.

Jamal was able to talk Ursula into staying for dinner. She'd been in Jamal's room for some time. They'd been talking. She said she was about to leave, but Jamal said he had to go to the bathroom and asked if she would wait for him till he got out. He wanted to walk her to the car.

"Ursula, is that you out in the hallway?"

"Yes, Arlene."

"Where's Jamal?"

"He's in the bathroom. I'm about to leave."

Ursula was between Jamal's room and Arlene's study.

"Why don't you come into the study."

Of course Ursula had never been in Arlene's study. She'd passed it in the hallway but not been inside it.

When Ursula entered the room, Arlene stood. "What do you think?"

"Think? What an ideal retreat. Reminds me of my study in the house."

"Yes, I agree. On about the same physical scale, I'd say."

Pause.

"I get a lot done in here."

"So do I, my workroom."

"Exactly." Arlene smiled.

"Are you—"

"Yes. The book, Ursula. The book. Trying to put it into some kind of simple, sensible order—at least some semblance of order."

"Can … may I see what you have? Y-you've done up to now—far you've gotten?"

"Uh …" Arlene looked down at the desk. "You know what, I'd prefer for you to see what, something I've written. Completed, instead. A sampling of my writing."

"Yes, that would do—should be helpful."

Ursula sat.

Arlene pulled out old material. She handed it to Ursula. Ursula started browsing through it. Arlene stood a few feet from her. She was nervous—very.

"Mmm good, very good."

"But in writing the book, it would be better served, I feel, if the prose were better."

"Uh, yes, I see what you mean."

"You agree then?"

"I do."

"To sustain reader interest."

"Of course."

"For it not to be so … well, it is highly technical, pedagogical. Even though it is, the material is, presumably, being written for a specific, preselected, targeted audience, an academic one, I still want, would want it to read—"

"Smoothly. Enjoyably."

"Yes."

Ursula looked up at Arlene. "Maybe I can help. Help out."

"But you said—"

"I've never tried this. This kind of writing. Almost like a translation—"

"Of some hieroglyphics. Anthropological finding."

"Yes. It's a challenge for me. It'll take me into a new world, a new space. Where I've never been before. I enjoy that. Find it exciting. But, of course, you'll have to do a lot of explaining to me. Pruning. I'll be like one of your first-year economic students."

"I'll get you up to speed rather quickly, don't you worry."

Ursula handed the papers back to Arlene.

"But first ... first I'm going to have to organize my own thoughts on this, like I said, so it ... it won't be anytime soon, Ursula. Maybe two months or so down the road—if that."

Suddenly Ursula thought about Jamal but knew he was smart enough to know she and his mother were in the study talking. That Jamal had probably heard them from the bathroom.

And now Arlene was practically staring at Ursula.

"Ursula, if I may ... may be so presumptuous ..."

Ursula's eyes didn't waver from Arlene's.

"Before. Before coming into the house, it had nothing to do with the baby, did it? I mean if it did then ... then I am—"

"No, Arlene."

"No," Arlene said softly. "I thought not ... You were thinking of before, the past, going back—what happened between us, me telling you that you were not welcomed in my house."

"Yes."

"It's what produced your anxiety."

"I suppose I had a panic attack."

"Yes."

"That was an awful day for both of us."

"Both of us." Ursula stood. "Arlene ... I'd better get back, your father is to, should be calling." She glanced at her watch. "In another twenty minutes. Give or take a minute."

Arlene laughed. "That's Dad. My dad all right."

She stood and she and Ursula shook hands.

"And if it's okay with you, Ursula, I'd like to talk on and off with you about the book. Periodically. Over the phone."

"Oh, yes, Arlene, that'd be fine with me. By all means."

"See you then."

"Yes."

Ursula turned her back and began walking away; Arlene felt relieved and then returned to her desk chair.

"Jamal ..."

Thump.

"Coming, Ursula. Coming!"

She began walking toward the staircase. Jamal whizzed by the study on his crutches like black lightning.

Arlene laughed.

"Ursula, you know Granddad calls in about twenty minutes. I was hoping you wouldn't forget."

Oh, Arlene thought, hearing Jamal's remark. Jamal knows the routine too.

"No, Jamal, I count the minutes between talking to your grandfather. Why, you know that."

CHAPTER 30

Teardrop was on the plane from San Francisco to Walker City. The two-week stint was a rousing success. Teardrop basked in it but not for too long—not like Shorty Boy and Twelve Fingers. For though he and Miss Lillian had a ball every night they played, at the end of the night, with his thoughts of Ursula and the baby, he couldn't wait to get back home.

And this was the day, the hour, and Teardrop couldn't wait to see Ursula. And for a lot of reasons. One, because each day he felt more and more in love with her. Talking to her over the phone, he just wanted to kiss her through the telephone a thousand times until the phone wires melted or some other supernatural phenomenon occurred.

All Teardrop could think of these days was how good she was and how she had handled his absence, taking Jamal in, making Arlene's situation better by removing obstacles from it. And the way she did it, seemingly, with no fuss or bother. And she held no grudge nor showed any animosity, hostility, or bitterness toward Arlene.

I am a lucky man, Teardrop thought. *The luckiest man in the entire world!*

And when he saw her at the airport, he didn't know what he was going to do—tear her to pieces from limb to limb, maybe, but then again he did have to think of the baby. That must be sacrosanct, upmost in his mind—Teardrop chuckled—in his consideration. It just might save her!

"Maurice, I'm glad you thought of the baby too."

"Unless … oh, I had plans, Ursula. Big, wicked, perverse ones. But yes, I had to think of the baby. Otherwise, I think I would've squeezed you into nothingness. Air."

"I'm so glad things went so well in San Francisco for you and the band."

"Uh, by the way, lest I forget, Shorty Boy and Twelve Fingers said hi, baby. They'll be calling the house in a day or two to check up on you. My favorite wife!"

"I'd better be your only wife!"

"Ha. The only one I can think of at the moment." Pause. "And let me tell you something, Ursula. You are some wife. Some terrific wife, baby!"

They were twelve miles from the house.

"Ursula, I'm going to call Arlene and Jamal as soon as we get in the house."

"Then let me be the first to inform you, which I was, of course. Arlene and Jamal are coming by the house tomorrow evening for dinner."

"T-they are? Ar-Arlene and Jamal? I mean, Arlene, Ursula?"

"There's a lot that's been going on back here in Walker City I've been keeping from you. Under my hat."

"Why? How come?"

"I was being wary, cautious, you might even say scared. Not willing to get ahead of myself, jump the gun, I suppose."

"You … you and Arlene—"

"Our relationship—"

"But really, Ursula, in reality, there'd been none."

"I, yes, I know. We really started from nothing. Ground zero."

"And now, what? You're saying that now there's some basis for saying that there is a relationship?"

"We're building one. Arlene and I are beginning to talk on the phone now, at least."

"You are?"

"Arlene's writing a book. An economics book."

"That I didn't know."

"And she's seeking my professional advice, uh, guidance. Eventually she'd like me to help her write and edit it before it enters publication."

"You can do anything, Ursula. Anything you set your pretty mind to. You're such a gifted, fabulous writer."

"Thank you, sir. So, Maurice, tomorrow evening, the Wilkersons, Jamal and Arlene, will be at the Williamses, Ursula and Maurice."

"Sounds great."

"It does."

"Like great fun. A real special treat."

Ursula took Teardrop's hand and kissed it.

"Of course you'll cook!"

"Oh, if you didn't just deliver the coup de grâce, Mrs. Williams!"

～ォん～

"Maurice, Byron said hello."

"That was Byron on the phone?"

"Yes, he held on as long as he could, but I told him you were in the bathroom grooming. So I didn't know how long that would take."

"If anyone should understand a man's ego, it's, by far, Byron."

"But you do look gorgeous this evening."

"So do you. And how's Byron doing? Uh, I should say, behaving himself these days in New York City?"

"You know, Byron. He was just checking in, as usual."

"The baby?"

"The baby, Maurice. You'd swear he was the father. I mean, give me a break already!"

"Ha. Did you tell him about this evening?"

"Yes. Arlene. A breakthrough. He was thrilled to death to hear it. He hopes this is the end of it."

Ursula had a brush in her hand; she brushed the back of her Afro.

"You look sensational. Just sensational. Like any mother in your condition should look, Ursula."

Ursula was nervous again, and so was Teardrop. This evening was monumental. One couldn't lean on the other; there was too much at stake. What they did was hold hands when they went to the front door when the doorbell rang.

It would be the first time Arlene had been in the house she'd been raised in since she and Ursula exchanged words, when Arlene all but trashed Ursula and exalted her mother's memory even more into sainthood.

"Ar-Arlene."

"Dad."

Last night they talked on the phone, but it's the first they'd seen each other since Faraday Hospital, Jamal's bicycle accident.

"Hi, Granddad. Ursula," Jamal said.

"Hi, Jamal."

"Hi, Jamal."

"Hello, Ursula."

"Hello, Arlene."

When Arlene stepped into the house, it no longer felt like hallowed ground to her. For her, the old house felt new. It had a different kind of vibe in it, and she fell right in tune with it.

"I couldn't wait to see what you'd done to the house, Ursula. And right off, I feel the changes."

"Then come into the living room," Ursula said. "By all means."

"Oh, Ursula, you have made changes. Wonderful changes."

Teardrop and Jamal looked at one another and grinned.

"I love it. Just love it!"

"Thank you, Arlene."

"And I know there's more. There has to be. You know, Jamal, Ursula—"

"Yeah, Mom. I tried to describe it, everything, but I'm only twelve years old. My vocabulary is but so big. Expansive."

"Then lead on, Ursula. It looks like I'm in for a spectacular tour of the house."

Teardrop went over and took Arlene's hand, and off on the tour of the house the four went.

"Even though this was done on a limited budget, mind you, Arlene. Uh, being economically frugal. Something my professor daughter would, I'm sure, have some—"

"Just how limited, Dad, are we talking about?"

"Ursula, uh, would you handle, wish to handle Arlene's question for me, if you don't mind very much?"

"Dad, you haven't lost your touch. Not at all. I miss those meals of yours."

"Well, Ursula and the baby and I can drop by anytime, Arlene. In fact, how about every other Friday. How's that? I'll do the salmon special."

"What do you say, Jamal?"

Jamal tapped his cane (Jamal was graded down from crutches to cane). "Great, Granddad!"

"Dad, have you and Miss Lillian visited the woods yet today?"

"Uh, no, the whole day. I guess I've been nervous about things—this evening. I gave Miss Lillian the day off. Uh, why'd you ask?"

"Would you and Jamal mind? I want to talk to Ursula alone."

"No. Oh no. But we'll go to the edge of the woods with Miss Lillian. Spend time there. The terrain would be too much for Jamal. Too rough on his ankle. How about it, Jamal?"

Teardrop and Jamal were out the house.

"I haven't heard Miss Lillian in a long time, Granddad."

"It has been, hasn't it?" Teardrop said, his hand placed atop Jamal's shoulder. "That's right, Jamal."

They kept walking the grounds, Jamal with his cane. He was walking well for someone still on the mend.

"Mom and Ursula have a lot to talk about, don't they, Granddad?"

Teardrop stopped in his tracks. "They do, Jamal."

"Ursula, she's the best."

Arlene helped Ursula remove the dishes from the dining room to the kitchen, but Ursula knew they weren't going to talk there, that the location was not of the right character—the dishes, the mess, somehow remarkably reflecting in every sharp contour their past history.

"The living room, Ursula?"

"The living room, Arlene."

When they sat, each crossed their leg on the same brown, earth-tone three-seat sofa.

"May I begin, Ursula?" Arlene said after both appeared comfortable. "I'm sorry for the past two years. Truly sorry for what I've done to my family—and to you. Especially to you. It was un—"

"Accepted, Arlene. Apology a-accepted!" Ursula said, trembling, seemingly having waited for this moment, eager to have everything end, reconciled, everything put away to rest for things could start afresh from today, like it's all she'd craved to hear from Arlene.

"No, no, not so fast, Ursula. It mustn't be that fast. Not something like we've experienced. Have been put through."

Ursula's face expressed surprise.

"We mustn't. I don't think it serves us well to brush aside our emotional waste too fast. Cut something that's sunk so profoundly inside both of us away like it was never there. It never happened. What's brought of us to this day. As if the scars have been stitched, closed, and healed."

It's when Ursula came to her senses. "Yes, I know it's not that easy, Arlene. And it shouldn't be."

"I put the scars there, so it's now time for me to try to remove them. We must get to the bottom of what happened. For me, I must do my own soul-searching in order to heal myself. I mean, in a large part, I have, but I want you to hear me out, for you'll know just how much I've thought through this. How seriously, sincerely I've considered what I've done, and to have glossed over it would be tantamount to further insult ... o-offense. To not give it the respect it's due.

"And I don't want to do that—not that to us."

Ursula clasped her hands together.

"So where do I start ... I suppose at the beginning. How this whole ugly mess began between us."

"Were you threatened from the beginning, Arlene?"

"No, just irritated by your presence. You being a writer. Someone who was trying to resuscitate my dad, get him back on stage when he was comfortable where he was. A genius who was little known. And you and that magazine—"

"*Currents.*"

"Of course, yes, *Currents*, trying to upend this whole concept, idea of his. So I didn't dislike you in any personal way but disliked what you, as a writer, were trying to do. Came to represent."

"Then?"

"Then it escalated, didn't it? When Dad didn't want to expose to you why he really left his music career, the reason for it. That it was because of Mom. Coming off the road and Mom no longer here at the house for him," Arlene said, looking around the living room. "The loneliness of that. The fear of it. Actual morbid fear he went through. What, psychologically, it produced for him."

"Maurice has read it. The article. I wrote it anyway. Of course it wasn't published, ever published, but—"

"W-what did he—"

"He was touched by it." Pause.

"And then, of course, he couldn't live with what happened between you two. His reneging on the interview. Not finishing it. And my attitude towards you, driving you to Miss Ingram's place, telling you ... well ... you know rest of course."

"Yes."

"And then the letters. Your letters. Those letters of yours. It's when I began to despise you. Resent you. I read those letters. I had no shame, you see. None at all. Only loathing for you. You suddenly coming from out of nowhere and invading my father's world."

"I can understand that."

"And then when Dad found out what I'd done, I loathed you even more. More than before, for you'd come between us, not only causing me to do this clandestine, despicable act but causing me—I blamed it on you. All of it on you. It's how I felt: you were to blame. You were … You should never have come to Walker City." Arlene's hand was shaking. "Not here."

Ursula was beginning to feel the power of what was her own fused anger back then, the ugly, negative energy of it. Her own difficulty with Arlene, no matter how badly she tried to take the high road, try to be the daughter, put herself in Arlene's shoes, not the woman who'd already fallen in love with Maurice "Teardrop" Williams as if preordained.

"Now it was you," Arlene continued. "Now it had become personal. You were trying to destroy everything my mother and father had worked for over their thirty years of marriage. Now you were a threat. Now you were the target. The enemy. I perceived you as much. Real. Now I had to protect my father from you at all costs, and I couldn't. Couldn't. It was so frustrating. So frustrating."

Arlene was crying, beside her body shaking.

"And so needless to say, my hatred was driven even deeper. And I relished it. Loved it. It gave me power. Tremendous power, Ursula. For it was protecting me, w-wasn't it? Making it possible to become the person I'd become.

"But then Dad announced—"

"Our engagement, Arl—"

"Oh, yes. That, yes, that destroyed me. That piece of information literally destroyed me. But then … then I thought that maybe I should change my tactics." Arlene was wiping tears from her eyes, and they looked cunning.

"Change tactics. My strategy, I said. Toward … maybe I can live with this, and—"

"You didn't want to lose your father, did you?"

"Not my father. Not Dad. But then when you came down to stay those two weeks and he told me he was staying in the house, my parents' house. My mother, Ursula … my—"

"You were back protecting her memory."

"Mother's memory. Yes, exactly. You didn't belong here," Arlene said, looking around the living room again. "Not in my parents' house. This was out the question!"

"But your father forgot to tell, no, no, I'm sorry—he refused to tell you something. You'd accused him, us, of having sex in your mother's bed, but nothing was further from the truth. Maurice and I didn't have sex, not until we married. There was a perceived misrepresentation of the, there never was premarital sex. It was your father's choice, not mine. But I abided by his decision … Respected it."

"B-but it wouldn't've mattered, Ursula. No, not in the least. Why would it … should it? If you had sex or not in my mother's bed. I hated you. There was nothing you could do or say that could bring any honor, any goodwill between us.

"You didn't belong. You could never be Mrs. Williams. There was only one Mrs. Williams: Maureen Williams." Pause.

"And then the baby."

"How much more could I take … take? How much more could I hate you? Possibly loathe you until I felt I might die, actually die because of it. It was bad. It's a miracle I was able to function. That my schoolwork and my relationship with Jamal both didn't suffer. Weren't destroyed. You'd gone too far, Ursula. You and Dad, this time. A baby. Bringing a baby into this family. I'd not thought of that. Never thought of that, a baby as … as a possibility."

"Neither had your father."

"A half brother. What a concept. How inconceivable it was …"

"It is quite a—"

"I never gave you a chance. Not once. My father fell in love with you. It was so easy for him. Jamal fell in love with you. It had the same level of comfort, ease, rapture. Why? Why, I continually asked myself. But now I know why. It's no longer a secret. It's, there's no magic: you are as good and kind and trusting and loving a woman as I've known.

"You're all these qualities. It's what I feared too, of finding out the truth. Finding out it was me who put this family in jeopardy, at risk, threw it into chaos. Me, Ursula. Me!"

Arlene's arms reached out to Ursula. They clutched each other.

"Now if you can forgive me. Please forgive me, Ursula!"

"Yes, Arlene! Yes, yes, I forgive you!"

"Want to take a chance, Granddad?" Jamal's cane looked about as eager as him.

"What, Jamal, go back to the house?" Teardrop said, leaning against an oak tree, playing Miss Lillian while looking over to the house.

"Yes, sir. Between Mom and Ursula, do you think everything's okay b-by now, sir?"

Teardrop didn't reply. He simply slung Miss Lillian over his shoulders, for she could lie, like always, across his back.

"Granddad, did I ever tell you I wanted to be a bluesman like you when I was something like four or five when I used to see you carry Miss Lillian like that?"

Teardrop and Jamal kept in time while making it back to the house. "No, now I don't recall you ever mentioning it, Jamal. So what happened to the idea?"

"I don't think I hear music that well, Granddad. S-so hot. Not like you."

"That you have to be able to do: hear the music. That's a must."

"It's what I figured."

"If you can't hear it, Jamal, then how can you play it?"

"So ... uh, I did the right thing?"

"Yes, I'd say so. You made a very wise decision at a very young age."

"Nope ... guess I wasn't cut out to be a bluesman." Jamal was now looking at the house. "It still looks like it's standing, sir."

"Just the way we left it."

"Yes, Granddad. I think it'll be safe to go inside."

"So do I, Jamal. So do I."

"Besides, the sun's about to go down soon. And both of us forgot our bug spray."

Suddenly Teardrop slapped his skin.

Smack!

"Ha. See, Granddad, I told you."

"You know, Ursula, I'd reached a point where I said, 'Ursula? Why that's not even a black person's name.'"

"I know, I know," Ursula laughed. "My father got it from—"

"Don't tell me. A James Bond movie?"

"Right. *Dr. No.* Dad had a mad crush, according to him, on Ursula Andrews, the Swiss bombshell, at the time."

"No wonder!" Pause. "Your mother and father, are they ever coming down to Walker City to visit?"

"They are. They told Maurice and I once the baby's born. Their grandchild arrives."

"And I can't wait to meet them."

"You'll love them, Arlene. Just love my parents. Iris and Harry."

"May I turn serious again?"

"Yes, by all means."

"The inside of the house. To think the furniture was covered in sheets. Bedsheets. As if possessed by ghosts, not by life. Haunted. Mother would never approve of that. The dead state of the house. How things were."

"I, yes, Arlene, I think I know enough about Maureen Williams to—"

"Dad's whole again."

"Arlene—oh, Maurice and Jamal are back from their walk."

"They are. Ursula, do you mind …"

"What?"

"Occupying Jamal for a few minutes. I'd like to talk to my father."

"Oh, sure. Sure."

Ursula got up and went to the front door.

Teardrop came into the living room. Arlene stood. She and Teardrop embraced.

"I feel so much better, Dad."

"I'm so proud of you, Arlene."

"I don't know why."

"Because you're my daughter, that's why."

"Is it that simple?"

"Uh-huh. No more simple than that."

"We're a family again, aren't we? W-whole again."

"You bet we are, Arlene. We're as strong a family as we've ever been."

CHAPTER 31

Seven and a half months later.

Ursula and Arlene were like sisters now. Ursula was about two chapters short of completing her first novel: *Abiding Faith*, a slave story. She had a New York publisher and editor. So far, the editor, having read 90 percent of the book's galleys, loved it.

And Arlene's unnamed book was coming along in stages. A book more complex in research and application than Ursula's, but Ursula was adding the necessary touches of prose Arlene had desperately sought. Arlene's book would be published by her school's university press. She didn't set a timetable, but inside her head, a clock was responsibly ticking.

Jamal, needless to say, was back to his old tricks. He'd been riding a new bicycle (red again, a Schwinn, bought by Teardrop again). The accident derailed him only temporarily. And he'd suffered no psychological effects. But he'd made it immediately clear it wouldn't. And Arlene, Teardrop, and Ursula had no qualms whatsoever about his bike riding, not even in the early stages when Jamal and Armon took back to riding together on the Walker City roads; no big deal was made of it.

Teardrop was in the kitchen cooking. He was looking down into the frying pan at the browning pork chops, but he might as well have been looking deep into a reflecting pool since his mind was a trillion miles away. Ursula was upstairs in the study working.

"The baby—it'll be here any day now. That's just the plain facts of the matter."

It's as if Teardrop was spaced out but still able to get in touch with his feelings; so incredibly passionate they were. For him, he was back to square one, he thought, frying the pork chops in the virgin-oil-coated pan.

"I might as well be back to when Ursula first came into my life. This new reality."

Three months ago, he and the Tearmakers stepped back into the studio to record a new CD. The CD, *Waiting Out Time*, was to be released by Torch City Records in five weeks. According to McKinley Scofield, *Waiting Out Time* was going to make a "killing" in the blues market. Teardrop, Twelve Fingers, and Shorty Boy appreciated the advance hoopla—even if it was from their personal music manager.

But now the tough part had come, and looking down at the chops he knew it. It was his music career again.

"Again. It's happened to me again." This thing that had taken him back on the road, back to playing his music, him and Miss Lillian. He was losing it again, plain and simple. The desire for him to still do that, not with the baby due—just a few days short of being born.

"And now this dilemma I knew with Maureen has been recycled. Already I've spoken to the guys and they understand. I just haven't spoken to Ursula … yet. She's the only obstacle I have to overcome. That I must convince.

"But I want to be with Maurice. Not like I was with Arlene. I was there, yes, when she was born, but I was out on the road so much. Playing. Pinching pennies together. I don't have to do that now. I want to be here. With Ursula. With my wife and child. Maurice, my son."

The past six months had found him on the road, playing less frequently with the band. To everyone it was obvious what was evolving right before their eyes.

"Ursula has to be aware of this. She has to feel what's going on. The music no longer dominates me," Teardrop said, turning the knob off, the pork chops beautifully browned. "I want to get back to this kind of peaceful, gentle life. Being with Arlene, Jamal. Sharing time with family— not being told about things anymore. Firsthand memories, not second. I want to be in those family photographs.

"At my age, it's still something I haven't had enough of. With Maureen, I was young. But what's the excuse now?"

It was family now that had an incredible rhythm to it like music. A vibe, vocabulary, language; and Teardrop wanted to be a part of it—in on it like never before. This was to be his second family, the second go-round.

"Totally, with no compromise or ... or so-called convenient excuses."

Teardrop took the four chops and put them on top a large platter. "Now for the succulent brown gravy to follow, ha," Teardrop said, putting a low flame beneath the preheated pan.

Now that that was underway, the gravy began bubbling up.

"Maurice."

"Oh, Ursula," Teardrop said; his head swung to his right.

"I had to come down to the kitchen. I could smell the chops f-from upstairs."

Being in her eighth month, Ursula was as big as a blimp. She looked like she was carrying twins. Her doctor said, "Look out, Ursula, the baby's weight could very well top the Walker City record." In fact, when Ursula walked, she actually waddled like a duck with ten ducklings trailing her from behind.

Teardrop rushed to her.

"Sit, Ursula. Sit."

"Cut it out, Maurice, you know I could probably wrestle a steer to the ground—even in my delicate condition!"

"Probably. You know I wouldn't put it past you."

"Maurice, you know I've felt so ... so extraordinarily strong today," Ursula said, reaching out her hand, taking hold of Teardrop's.

"The gravy, Ursula. Let me finish browning it."

"Oh, yes."

"Plop the chops in the pan so I can turn off the oven."

She watched Teardrop for a while and then suddenly sighed. "I miss my husband. It was the pork chop's aroma, yes, but—"

"It's what I want to talk to you about. It's related to that."

"I sensed something was coming. I've felt it, Maurice. I have."

"If anybody would, it'd be you, baby."

"A journalist's—"

"Don't say 'nose.'"

"Yes. Ha."

"No, it's not—"

"With the baby coming—"

"It means a new life for us."

"That … I know."

Teardrop was back at the table, but he was on his knees and laid his head on Ursula's stomach protruding from the green robe as Ursula caressed his right temple with her fingertips.

"This is where my heart is now, Ursula. Right now, baby. My soul. Here. With what you're carrying inside you. Our child. You and Maurice."

"So"—she sighed—"you want to come in from the road. Off the road then."

"Yes, for now, baby. For now."

"It's ironic, isn't it …"

"Yes, I've looked at it, the irony of it. It's come full circle."

"This is what will make you happy, Maurice?"

"Happier than I've ever been in my life."

Ursula chuckled. "And Miss Lillian, have you consulted with Miss Lillian, heard her out?"

Teardrop lifted his head and looked seriously into Ursula's eyes. "You know, I'm afraid to." And then Teardrop laughed, laying his head back down on top Ursula's bulging belly.

"She, Miss Lillian's never had a child. Been a parent. So, I don't know …"

⌒If⌒

It was two o'clock in the morning. Ursula was having contractions.

"It's time, Maurice! I … I think it's time!"

It's like a bomb had gone off in the bedroom.

"Don't move, Ursula!" Teardrop said, snapping to attention. "Everything's ready. Everything!" Teardrop popped on the wall light. "I'll … I'll call Dr. Singh! Just keep breathing in and out. In and out. Don't stop, Ursula. Don't stop!"

"Woo-wooo! Woo-woooo!"

"Oh boy, Maurice," Teardrop said, picking up the phone. "If you aren't giving your mother and me fits already!"

They were in Faraday Hospital's maternity ward.

Ursula was on top a fast-moving gurney. There was a death grip on her hand being administered by Teardrop.

"I'm with you, Ursula. Don't worry. I'm with you. W-whatever good that's going to do," Teardrop said under his breath.

Teardrop had been to Lamaze classes, so he was going to be there in the delivery room through Ursula's labor. Dr. Singh's advice to him was to carry a catcher's mitt to catch the baby in. Of course, it was said in good humor, nothing more.

CHAPTER 32

Faraday Hospital was in the car's rearview mirror.

"Waaa! Waaa! Waaaa!"

"Oh, he has healthy lungs, doesn't he?" Teardrop boasted. "And is in tune."

"Uh, Granddad, do you think, uh, maybe he'll be a blues singer?"

"Could be. Someone like Howlin' Wolf."

Teardrop was driving the turquoise station wagon for a change, considering Ursula's pristine condition—of course, just being released from Faraday today. They were about a quarter mile from the house.

"Oh, he was trouble all right," Ursula said, still feeling the sensation of baby Maurice's head inside her stomach but right now was in the car's front seat holding him like he was a bundle of soft bread.

"Eleven pounds and nine ounces worth, Ursula. He made sure he was going to make a grand, auspicious splash into the world."

"No doubt, Arlene," Teardrop said. "But Maurice missed the record."

"Yes, Dr. Singh said it's thirteen pounds five ounces. I'm so relieved he did!" Ursula winced. "That it still stands!"

"Waaa! Waaa! Waaa!"

Baby Maurice's adorable, beet-red face peeked out the blue blanket.

"I don't have to call him Uncle Maurice, do I?" Jamal asked. "Not that, do I?"

"No, I think not. You can skip that formality, Jamal."

"Good. But like I said before, Granddad, as long as he knows who's boss, I don't think there'll be any problems between us."

"Home sweet home," Ursula said, looking at the house at 18 Dawkin's Road.

"It's what I said too, Ursula, when I came home from Faraday with Jamal."

"You … you did, Mom?"

"Certainly, Jamal. My exact, same words," Arlene said, looking over at him, both sitting in the car's backseat. "My same sentiments."

Miss Lillian was sitting in the backseat with them, Teardrop taking her along for the ride.

"He's wet," Ursula said. "It's why he's so cranky." Her hand felt baby Maurice's bottom through the wetted diaper.

"Well, everything's set up in the house, Ursula, for you and Maurice. Dad and I got busy on it yesterday."

"And where were you during this, Jamal, preparation, since I haven't heard your name mentioned, not once?"

"Aww, come on, Ursula, you know I was riding my bike. I don't have time for that stuff. Me and Armon."

Teardrop got out the car, ran around to the side door, opened it for Ursula, and then did the same for Arlene. He helped Ursula out the car as she held tightly to baby Maurice.

Ursula looked great, her Afro aflame.

"I think I'm finally calming down. Reality's finally setting in. F-finally relieving me of my burdens."

"Are you sure, Dad?"

"I'd like to think that, Arlene."

Ursula looked at Teardrop. She kissed his lips. "I love you, Maurice."

"I love you, Ursula."

"Waaa! Waaa! Waaa!"

"Let me take little Maurice, Ursula. Hold my baby brother," Arlene said.

"Thanks, Arlene."

"He's so heavy, aren't you, Maurice? Aren't you, honey? Coo-coo, coo-coo," Arlene said.

"Maurice …"

"Yes, Ursula, I'll bring everything in the house."

"Ha."

"I'll give you a free pass. A free ride, this time around."

Ursula joined Arlene as they walked up the porch steps. Ursula's arm encircled Arlene's waist.

"And what about you, Jamal?"

Jamal looked over at his bright new red aluminum-framed Schwinn bicycle leaning against the white railing where the blue balloons bounced about buffeted by a soft breeze.

"D-do I have to watch little Maurice get his diaper changed, Granddad?"

"Why no, you don't, come to think of it, Jamal."

Jamal sprinted off to his Schwinn, hopped on its hard-as-nails saddle seat and then took off.

"I'll see you later ... Later on!" Jamal shouted, waving back to them. "When I get back from Armon's house, Granddad!"

Ursula and Arlene were on the porch. Ursula opened the house's door for Arlene and then turned back to look at Teardrop. She smiled at him.

Teardrop, smiling back at Ursula, picked up the suitcase and looked off toward the dense woods and then toward Jamal, who had just reached the edge of Dawkin's Road, pedaling his red bike, and then back to the grand-looking white-painted house.

"Who'd ever think this would happen to me? Living again?"

He was about to take another step, when he pivoted back to the station wagon, looking down through the side window.

"How could I? I almost forgot Miss Lillian's on the backseat."

And quickly Teardrop changed what could've been a disaster from happening.

"So we might as well join the women," Teardrop said, removing Miss Lillian from the backseat. "No telling what Arlene and Ursula are up to by now, Miss Lillian.

"Do you agree?"